He was staring at me . . .

And I could see the color of his eyes as clearly as if he were right in front of me. Dark blue, a brilliant, mesmerizing shade of cobalt framed by thick lashes. They held on to me, making my stomach clench and roll like I was on a fairground tilt-a-whirl ride. And then he moved his mouth, lifting the corners in a lazy, sensual smile that almost had me stroking out. My chest became a vise, slowly expelling all the air from my lungs and forcing my heart to beat faster. I saw the brilliant gleam of his teeth as his lips parted, and as if asphyxia wasn't going to be enough to deal with, I was suddenly flooded with the oddest sense of déjà vu.

Intuitively I knew that if he widened his smile by just a few millimeters, it would reveal a dimple hidden in his left cheek. Right on cue, as if wanting to prove me right, he did just that, and . . . there it was. What could so easily be considered a flaw I thought was the sexiest come-on I'd ever seen. It was crazy, I know, but his expression seemed familiar. As if I'd seen him smile at me like that before. Which was completely impossible, of course. And then the final, totally insane thing happened.

You know who I am.

A
VAMPIRE'S
PROMISE

Carla Susan Smith

KENSINGTON BOOKS
KENSINGTON PUBLISHING CORP.
www.kensingtonbooks.com

First Electronic Edition: June 2014
eISBN-13: 978-1-60183-289-4
eISBN-10: 1-60183-289-3

First Print Edition: June 2014
ISBN-13: 978-1-60183-290-0
ISBN-10: 1-60183-290-7

Printed in the United States of America

Acknowledgments

I am indebted to the following people for helping me achieve my dream:

To my husband, Jack, for never losing faith in me, and who stopped me from pressing the delete key on more than one occasion.

To my son, Joe, for being a constant source of surprise and wonder regarding all things supernatural.

To my BFF Sharon, for daring me to write in the first place.

To Lynne Harter, for doing my first edits and for being a sounding board and friend.

To my boss, Suzanne, for letting me bring my laptop to work!

To Annette and Donna, for putting up with my craziness for longer than any sane people should!

And last, but not least, to Alicia Condon at Kensington, for taking one hell of a chance on me. Thank you.

CHAPTER 1

I was folding laundry and watching an old CSI rerun on TV when Laycee called.

"What are you doing?" she asked.

I told her.

"And where are you tonight—New York, Miami, or Vegas?"

There was only one place where the plucky female investigator would consider going dumpster diving wearing heels and white pants. "Miami," I told Laycee.

"You do realize this makes you certifiably pathetic, right?"

I wasn't sure if it was the laundry or my viewing choice that warranted the certifiable part. Tucking the phone between my ear and shoulder, I continued folding.

"I prefer to think of it as a useful way to amuse myself while I wait for Brad Pitt to call," I told her.

Laycee sighed—an exasperated, you're-beyond-all-help sound that I caught before it was swallowed up by background noise. From the hum of voices and clinking glassware I guessed she was in a bar. Confirmation came with the sound of a female voice crooning sorrowfully about men and bad choices. The tone was more jukebox quality than live band, and I felt my eyebrows pull together, wondering if the song was Laycee's choice or just bad luck. Either way, it seemed kind of prophetic. Why else would my best friend be calling me on a Friday night when she was supposed to be out on a date?

"Where are you?" I asked her.

"Out at Rosie's."

The song began to fade. I'd never heard of the place. "Where?"

Being involved with a man who is separated from his wife but not yet divorced means contending with a few "difficulties." Difficulties that become a lot more complicated when he's also the town sheriff. The need to meet in places where no one recognizes either of you is just the tip of the iceberg. And why my best friend wanted to put herself through all this drama was something I was still trying to figure out.

"Rowan, I need a ride. Can you come get me?"

There was a catch in her voice, one I was certain she didn't know was there, but I heard it as clear as a bell. Perhaps I was expecting to.

"Where's Jake?" I asked cautiously.

"Had to leave."

Her tone changed, becoming more pissed-off than poor-me, which was a relief in a way. Having witnessed both, I much preferred dealing with an angry Laycee than a tearful one.

My best friend isn't generally stupid, but like any woman, she is guilty of making foolish decisions at times. It's still too early to tell if her involvement with Jake will fall into this category. Tonight it would seem so. Having your so-called boyfriend go AWOL in the middle of a date is not only rude, it's embarrassing. But he must be doing something right because Laycee lights up like the proverbial Christmas tree whenever he's around. I guess you don't always get a say in what your heart wants, and following it doesn't always guarantee a happy ever after.

"So, you gonna come rescue me?"

Like she had to ask. "You realize this means I'm going to have to stand Brad up, right?"

She laughed, another good sign. "Yeah, well, I'm sure you can find a way to make it up to him." I grinned as she began arguing her case. "C'mon, Rowan, it's Friday night. Stop watching damn reruns and get your ass out here! Seriously—what else have you got to do?"

Absolutely nothing, and no one knew that better than Laycee.

"Okay, okay," I told her. "Stop twisting my arm!" It was pathetic how much of a fight I didn't put up.

She gave me directions and broke the connection before I could say good-bye. Or change my mind.

Rosie's was an almost thirty-minute drive across the county line, and I nearly missed the turnoff. Laycee had mentioned something about a neon sign, only I guess she forgot to mention most of the bulbs had burned out. I was just grateful no one was behind me when I slammed on the brakes.

Miraculously there was an open space beneath the lone working light in the gravel-strewn parking lot. I made sure all the doors were locked before making my way toward the brick building I'd passed on the way in. Checking the other parked vehicles gave me a pretty good indication of Rosie's clientele. I could count on one hand the number of vehicles that weren't either a truck or some sort of SUV. And that was including my car.

Climbing the three steps leading up to the porch, I pulled open one half of the double doors and was immediately greeted by a fair number of good ol' boys, all wearing the standard uniform of jeans, boots, and shirts with no sleeves. What is it about country boys and the need to expose armpit hair? I have no idea, but I think there's a certain security in having a visual reminder of passing puberty. Stepping to one side, I tried to be unobtrusive as I searched for Laycee while getting my bearings.

There was an aged, shabby look to the bar. It had probably first opened a couple of decades before I was born, and whatever profit it made wasn't being wasted on updating the décor. I suspected the obligatory deer-head trophy on the wall had witnessed the first beer ever served, and anything electrical could probably use a serious upgrade. A fresh coat of paint would do wonders, along with a good airing. There was a definite odor that lingered—a faint mix of old beer, stale cigarettes, and pine floor cleaner. On the plus side, the bar looked well-stocked and the glasses all seemed clean. Lord knows, I'd been in a lot worse places.

It didn't take much reconnoitering before I found my girl. All I had to do was look for the nearest group of guys standing about with their tongues hanging out, metaphorically speaking. In this case the group was draped over their pool cues, appreciating Laycee's rear end. I came up on the opposite side of the table and waited until she took her shot. A chorus of good-natured groans rippled around the periphery as she sank her ball. Men, I have observed, will always accept being beaten by a girl if she's pretty enough. And Laycee fit that bill.

With her hair pulled back in a high ponytail and wearing a hot pink T-shirt, jeans, and red heels that made my arches ache just looking at them, she positively screamed trailer trash. Nevertheless, I adored her for knowing exactly who she was, and not giving a shit what anyone else thought.

We were complete opposites, at least as far as looks went. Fair-haired and blue-eyed, Laycee was a doll, providing that doll was Trailer Park Barbie. I was more a reflection of Cabbage Patch Colleen with chestnut hair, green eyes, and freckles confirming my Irish heritage. Also Laycee managed to keep around a hundred pounds on her five foot five inch frame with very little effort, while I weighed . . . more. But being four inches taller has to count for something. If she wasn't my best friend and I didn't love her so much, it would be easy to hate her.

"Popular place," I commented as a waitress stopped by the booth we'd chosen to take our order. She returned almost immediately with a pitcher and two frosty glasses, and I put a mental check mark in the plus column.

For the next half hour or so Laycee and I made small talk, covering all the important things. Sex and men, sex and clothes, sex and makeup. I didn't inquire about Jake's absence and Laycee didn't offer to tell me, which was okay. I figured I'd get the scoop on the ride home.

Returning from the restroom, I noticed my BFF checking out the bar area. Not that unusual, all things considered, but the look on her face was definitely out of place. My first thought was Laycee had seen someone she recognized, so I also looked. Growing up in a town as small as ours, we knew the same people. Not seeing a familiar face, I couldn't imagine what was keeping her attention so fixed.

"What is it?" I asked. "See someone you know?"

She snapped back into focus and reached for my glass, refilling it from the pitcher and making sure it had the perfect head of foam. "*You* have an admirer."

"Oh yeah?"

Guys rarely look at me when I'm with Laycee. I mean they look at me, but not like they look at her. And not in the way she was implying.

"Yeah, you do." My skepticism caused her to raise a penciled eyebrow. "I wasn't sure at first, but I am now."

I remained doubtful. "What makes you think he's looking at me?" It wasn't an unreasonable question. Laycee turns a lot of men's heads. Women's, too, but that's for an entirely different reason.

A sly smile curled the corners of her mouth. "Because he just tracked you going to the restroom," she declared triumphantly.

This, as any woman knows, is the only universally accepted way to measure a guy's interest. If he watches you cross the room and doesn't get distracted or lose focus, then he definitely wants to get to know you better. Unfortunately, I wasn't as enthusiastic about the prospect as my best friend was.

Laycee and I had very different ideas about the opposite sex and the role we expected them to play in our lives. I also wasn't sure that, good intentions aside, she was the best person to give me romantic advice. Laycee always seemed to attract guys who came with complications of one sort or another. Like a wife. Still, I'm the last person to pass judgment on any relationship. Best friends are hard to come by, and I wasn't going to make Laycee feel bad about her choices or her morals. Besides, my limited romantic experience had shown me that while you may think you have a situation sized up, most of us don't have a clue what's really going on between two people.

"Okay, so where's the father of my unborn children?" I suspected it was one of the guys Laycee had been shooting pool with earlier, and wondered if I was being looked at as a consolation prize. If so, it was a bad idea, and one I intended to squash right away.

"The blond at the end of the bar," Laycee said pointing a surreptitious finger in the right direction. "I think he might be the bouncer. He's certainly built for it."

The idea that a bar like this would require a bouncer in the first place might seem absurd, but I've seen good ol' boys fight. When they're drunk, a difference of opinion can turn ugly real fast. And while a physical altercation every now and then is perfectly acceptable, expected even, on a regular basis it's bad for business.

Twisting around in my seat and looking over my shoulder would be a little too obvious, so I got up and parked myself next to Laycee. Casually I let my gaze wander over the bar area. He wasn't hard to miss.

Tall, blond, and very well put together—I could absolutely see how Laycee would think he was a bouncer, but she couldn't have been more wrong. I couldn't say what he was, but I knew he didn't belong in a place like this. And it wasn't just because his T-shirt had sleeves. Still, the bar was pretty crowded and the lighting not that great, two elements that could easily contribute to a mistake in judgment. And Laycee, God love her, sometimes saw things a little skewy where I was concerned.

If the guy had been looking at me before, and I'm not saying he hadn't, he certainly wasn't now. Distracted by the bartender, he seemed fascinated at how the words on her T-shirt were being stretched across her chest. *Juicy Girl* indeed!

My immediate assessment said the bartender had no idea the kind of man she was flirting with, or how to do it with any degree of success. Unable to discern the difference between real interest and being polite, Miss Juicy couldn't tell he wasn't the type to be impressed by the obvious, no matter how it came wrapped. If she expected him to respond to her, then she was going to need a more subtle approach. A wayward curl escaping from an elegant up-do, the slip of a spaghetti strap down a bare shoulder, a hint of shimmer dusted over cleavage . . .

I started, taken aback by whatever tangent my brain was trying to pursue. Why on earth would I think such things—and why assume they were applicable to him? I had no idea, but deep down I knew they were true. Kind of like the way I just knew the black jeans and T-shirt he wore hadn't come off the rack at Men's Wearhouse.

This was the type of man who was noticed the moment he stepped into a room. I could only imagine the ripple he'd caused coming into Rosie's and was sorry to have missed it. Even as far apart as we were—and there had to be at least twenty-five feet between our table and the bar—I could see the confidence he exuded. Used to having people look at him, he simply accepted it, even if it was made up of both female adoration and male jealousy. Miss Juicy leaned over the bar in his direction. I watched him pull back, subtly maintaining the distance between them. *Stupid girl!* Either she didn't notice, or else she just didn't get it. Or him.

My gaze flickered over the people around him, curious to see their reaction to his presence. From the way heads were turned and chins tucked, it seemed all the guys were doing their best to avoid any type of eye contact with him, which struck me as typical pack behavior. A show of deference in the presence of a more dominant male.

But the women had no qualms about making contact, with their eyes or other body parts. And the bartender wasn't the only one who was clueless. Every female in the place, present company excluded, seemed to be hitting the restroom with an alarming frequency. Only they were taking the scenic route to get there. I know my own single trip to the bathroom hadn't required me to make any detours.

Also aware of the apparent estrogen explosion, Laycee poked me in the side with her finger, and we both watched a Jessica Simpson look-alike make her way across the floor toward his end of the bar. Unfortunately, she was so busy trying to catch his eye that she failed to check for obstacles in her path and hit the squared-off corner of a table with her leg. Wincing, I pictured the bruise that was going to color her thigh in the morning. But from the look on Jessica's face, it was all worth it.

Stumbling had redirected his attention away from the bartender, and Jessica greedily caught hold of the steadying hand he offered. Saving herself from complete humiliation by not going base over apex, the blonde gushed at him. The invitation she offered was more than blatant. It glowed like a neon sign. And it was one he declined.

"Ooooh—her tip jar's gonna be short," Laycee observed, glancing at the bartender. Annoyed by the interruption, Miss Juicy glared at her competition.

"He's got to be waiting for someone," I murmured. It was the only plausible explanation for his being in Rosie's to begin with, as well as his lukewarm response to the women around him. Either that or he was gay, which I couldn't count out, but doubted. If he was looking to get lucky with another guy, why send out vibes that had them all backing off? No, whoever he was waiting for, I'd bet my next pay-check they were of the female persuasion. Probably more than one someone. Now how depressing was that?

I was about to share this insight with Laycee when he chose that exact moment to turn his head and look right at me. His gaze lit me up, held me fast, and dared me to be the first to look away.

I didn't.

I couldn't.

The world as I knew it came to a screeching halt and tumbled off its axis. And I knew, no matter whatever else happened to me in the rest of my life, something had just changed. It was one of those pivotal moments that happen once in a lifetime. One that said nothing was ever going to be the same.

CHAPTER 2

He hadn't moved, except to carefully peel Jessica's fingers from his hand before resuming his place at the bar. But it felt as if he knew that I'd been looking at him, and now he was saying *Okay... my turn.*

He was staring at me, and I could see the color of his eyes as clearly as if he were right in front of me. Dark blue, a brilliant mesmerizing shade of cobalt framed by thick lashes. They held on to me, making my stomach clench and roll like I was on a fairground tilt-a-whirl ride. And then he moved his mouth, lifting the corners in a lazy, sensual smile that almost had me stroking out. My chest became a vise, slowly expelling all the air from my lungs and forcing my heart to beat faster. I saw the brilliant gleam of his teeth as his lips parted, and as if asphyxia wasn't going to be enough to deal with, I was suddenly flooded with the oddest sense of déjà vu.

Intuitively I knew that if he widened his smile by just a few millimeters, it would reveal a dimple hidden in his left cheek. Right on cue, as if wanting to prove me right, he did just that, and... there it was. What could so easily be considered a flaw I thought was the sexiest come-on I'd ever seen. It was crazy, I know, but his expression seemed familiar. As if I'd seen him smile at me like that before.

Which was completely impossible, of course. And then the final, totally insane thing happened.

You know who I am.

The words jolted inside my head, whispered in a silken voice I didn't recognize—and they were completely untrue! If I'd seen this guy before, trust me, I would have locked him away in the old memory bank. He had a face no woman would ever forget. Lightly touching my hand, Laycee jerked me back to reality. I sucked in a greedy lungful of air as my heart found its rhythm.

"Rowan, are you okay?" She looked at me, concern marring her carefully made-up face.

"Yeah, of course. Why d'you ask?" For some reason my voice sounded perfectly normal, which was strange, considering I hadn't been able to catch my breath a moment before.

"No reason, except your mouth's hanging open and you look sort of . . . *hungry.*" A wicked smile replaced the concerned look. "Don't worry, it suits you."

Self-conscious, I closed my mouth, pretending I had no idea what she was talking about as she turned her head and looked back toward the bar.

"Smile," she hissed suddenly. "He's looking at you!"

Tell me something I don't know.

I was in the process of trying to get my head unscrambled when the look of dismay on Laycee's face told me it was no longer necessary. He wasn't looking at me anymore. But I knew that too. The clenching in my stomach ceased and my ribs no longer felt as if they were on fire.

Turning my head, I saw my now not-so-ardent admirer had picked up where he'd left off. He'd returned his attention to Miss Juicy, who, utterly enthralled, kept flicking her dark hair over her shoulder so nothing would interfere with his view of her assets. The gesture irritated the crap out of me, and woke up my inner bitch.

How about we just go slap the shit out of her?

I declined the offer, even though an inexplicable jealousy was swirling through me. After having the humdrum predictability of my world so thoroughly shaken, I was more than a little annoyed at being passed over without so much as a second glance.

Miss Juicy laughed. Her cackle ricocheted across the bar with enough of a screech factor to set my teeth on edge. I thought it sounded forced, which just went to show how much that odd little episode had unnerved me. Why was I mad at her? As much as I hated to admit it, it wasn't her fault I didn't have the goods to hold his interest.

I drowned my unreasonable attitude in a long swallow of beer. The interaction at the bar had not escaped Laycee's notice. How could it with that laugh that sounded like a jackass braying?

You sure you don't want to go slap her? My inner bitch snorted.

Shaking my head, I put down my glass. Laycee stared at me. "Don't worry," I assured her with a nonchalance I didn't feel. "Nothing would have come of it anyway. He's really not my type."

"You're such a liar." The words were said affectionately, but the look in her eyes had me thinking she knew exactly how his gaze had affected me. "What would you do if he was to come over here right now and ask you out?"

I honestly didn't know. I told myself the reason for my tilt-a-whirl experience was because it had been a while since a guy had looked at me with any real interest. I was out of practice and had gotten flustered. That was all. No big deal. Except it really was a big deal. No man had ever looked at me before and made me feel excited and terrified all at the same time. I wasn't sure if I liked it, and I certainly didn't know how to handle it.

It's not that I don't want a boyfriend; I've plunged headfirst into the dating pool several times. It's just that, on an intellectual level, I've waded back out again seriously disillusioned. Is it too much to want a guy whose choice of reading material goes beyond *Popular Mechanics, Field and Stream,* or something that comes in a plain brown wrapper?

Actually I might not have a problem with pornography if it meant I had a sex life, but the guys I've been dating must only be looking at the pictures because I'm still technically a virgin. Efforts to change my status so far have resulted in two broken zippers, a bad case of muscle cramps, and a real empathy for the embarrassment that comes with premature ejaculation. Same guy, three times. But it hasn't been a complete waste of time. On the plus side I have learned a lot about foreplay.

Tapping the surface of the table with a long, red fingernail, Laycee tilted her head. "I think you're all wrong about him waiting for someone," she murmured in a low voice. "I think he's just found what he's been looking for."

I looked up, astonished to see Miss Juicy herself heading toward us with a tray balanced on the upturned palm of one hand. I knew the exaggerated sway of her hips was definitely not for my benefit. Stopping at our table, she popped out her hip before placing her free hand on it. My inner bitch was straining at the leash.

"From the guy at the end of the bar," she said, taking the lone glass off her tray and placing it in front of me.

My first instinct was to tell her she'd made a mistake, only the look on her face said she already thought that. How I had managed to hook such a catch was beyond her comprehension. It took all I had to keep the shit-eating grin off my face. Guess I'd rated that second look after all.

Next to me, Laycee was almost quivering with excitement. This was something straight out of one of her trashy romance novels. The only thing that could have made it even better was if I'd gotten champagne. Somehow I doubted there was a bottle of Dom Perignon hidden behind the bar.

I'm not a complete idiot. Men have bought me drinks before, but usually I'm on a date with them. This was the first time I'd been singled out in such a way, and while I was pleased it got Miss Juicy's panties all wadded up, on another level I wasn't comfortable with the attention. I felt out of my depth, mainly because I didn't know what kind of expectations came with the drink, and there would be some, there always were. But I was certain of one thing. He was a man who was very sure of himself and, I suspected, used to getting what he wanted.

The decision made, I picked up the tumbler, catching the familiar whiff of bourbon, and placed the glass back on the tray. "Tell him thanks . . . but no thanks."

Laycee spluttered and almost sprayed beer over the table, while

Miss Juicy opened her eyes wide. Confusion was replaced by stunned surprise. Perhaps I didn't realize *who* had sent the drink? I could almost see the conflict inside her as she tried to decide whether to do a brisk about-face before I changed my mind or give me the chance to rectify my mistake. She earned my grudging admiration for the choice she made.

"Are you sure?" she asked, "It's the big blond guy." Nodding her head in the direction of the bar, she added, "The one all in black."

"Yeah, I know who you mean," I said slowly. "The guy who looks like a Viking."

Any admiration I felt vanished when I saw her face light up with barely contained glee at my apparent stupidity. After landing something so mouth-wateringly delicious, I was throwing it back? How dumb was I? Still, my turning down all that testosterone meant she could have another crack at him. I almost told her to go for it, but I'm not that nice.

"Whatever," she said, blowing out an exaggerated breath that matched the lift of her shoulders. I watched her walk away, wondering how she would rephrase my refusal.

"Are you like, seriously, out of your fucking mind?" Laycee hissed.

"Laycee, I'm not about to accept a drink from some guy who's just passing through."

"You don't know that."

"Aw, come on!" I rolled my eyes. "Take a good look at him."

"I have been," she snapped irritably. "Problem is, he hasn't been looking back!"

I opened my mouth, but nothing came out. This was a big admission on her part. The only guy I ever knew not to look at Laycee had had the world's only justifiable reason. He was blind. But as his seeing-eye dog did try to sniff her crotch, it still counted as looking in my book. To hear her say that my Viking—*when had I become possessive?*—hadn't as much as glanced her way was astonishing.

"Not once?" I queried slowly.

"Not. One. Single. Time." The end of her ponytail swooshed across her shoulder as if helping to emphasize her point. "Trust me,

Rowan, every time his head's been turned in this direction, his focus has been fixed on you, girlfriend, and only on you."

Any comment I was about to make was drowned by the burble of her cell phone. She answered and immediately began glowing. I didn't need to be a psychic to know who was on the other end.

"Guess you're not gonna need me to give you a ride home after all, huh?" I said when she was done grinning and murmuring. I poured the last of the beer into her glass, but I lacked her deft touch and the foam spilled over the rim and ran down the side of the glass.

"Sorry, Ro, guess not." Grabbing a handful of napkins, she helped me blot up the mess I'd made.

I glanced over at the bar and saw Miss Juicy grab her own napkin, only she was using it as notepaper. After scribbling something down, she slid it across the bar to the Viking. I figured it was probably directions to the nearest motel, along with her phone number. She looked like the type of girl who always sat in the front car of a roller-coaster ride and kept the safety bar in the upright position.

"I think she'll be a much better fit for him, in more ways than one," I said, knowing Laycee had also witnessed the exchange. A stab of jealousy rolled through me, but I told myself it was only hurt pride. Something that a good night's sleep would cure.

"Yeah, well, you gotta admit he *is* a looker." Laycee sounded wistful, and now that the rest of his evening was apparently decided, I could agree. He *was* incredibly good-looking.

"Guess I'll just have to put him in the *One That Got Away* column," I said glibly.

"One of these days you're gonna learn to take a chance," my best friend said earnestly. "Quit playing it safe, because all that will guarantee is that one side of your bed is going to be empty. And don't tell me you're okay with that because being alone sucks, big-time." Her eyes flickered over to the bar before returning to me. "You're one of the smartest people I know, Rowan Marie Harper, but if you're saving yourself for Mr. Right, take it from me, honey; he doesn't exist anywhere but here." She tapped her temple with her finger.

"No one is gonna hand happiness to you. You've gotta grab it for yourself, no matter how it comes packaged, because if you don't, there's always going to be some other girl willing to take what you turn down." She paused. "And once it's gone, you can't ever get it back.

"Every guy's a jerk in one way or another, it's in their DNA, but sometimes you get lucky and meet a guy who isn't a complete ass-hole. The trick is recognizing him when he comes knocking on your door. You have to make sure there's enough good in him to let you overlook his faults." Chuckling, she shook her head. "And trust me, he'll have a shit-load of 'em!" The smile she gave me was warm and genuine. "You just haven't met the right guy yet," she ended prophet-ically.

I hoped she was right. I'd hate to think he might have already come and gone. And, God forbid, been my premature ejaculator. "Maybe that's the problem," I said with a grin. "I really should be looking for a *girl*friend."

"Puhleeze—you are so not gay!"

"How do you know?" I was curious to hear her answer.

"Honey, I fix hair for a living. Trust me, I know gay and you're not it."

I couldn't argue with her logic. Laycee was about to say some-thing else when I tapped her on the arm. "Jake's here."

"Hey, Rowan, how are you?" he asked, taking the seat I'd vacated so he could sit next to his girlfriend.

I was always surprised by his voice. It was soft and low, and not something most people would expect from a member of law enforce-ment, no matter how small the jurisdiction. But the smile he gave me was genuine, and I could tell he was thankful he didn't have to hide his relationship with Laycee from me.

"I'm good, Jake, thanks for asking," I replied, "and I'm glad you're here, because I gotta go."

"Girl, you're going to make me think I'm scaring you away," he protested jokingly.

"No danger of that, but I've got work in the morning."

Grabbing my jacket and purse, I said my good-byes, waving off their half-hearted protests at my leaving. Nothing more useless than a fifth wheel.

My eyes strayed over to the bar. I'd told myself I wasn't going to look because I couldn't care less, but I'm a lousy liar. It's not every day I find a guy who can rock my world with a single look. Crushing disappointment left an unexpected hole in my gut. The Viking was gone. So was Miss Juicy.

CHAPTER 3

Reaching the double entry doors, I turned back around. Catching Laycee's attention, I put one hand to the side of my head and made the universal gesture that said *call me*. She waved in acknowledgment, so I pushed the door open with my butt and continued on out.

If I'd been looking where I was going I would have seen him, but I was busy rummaging in my purse for my keys and never stood a chance. Crashing into a wall of solid muscle knocked the breath out of me, and I began to fall backward. The only thing that saved me from landing on my ass was a pair of strong hands grabbing my upper arms and holding me as my knees buckled.

"Shit! I'm so sorry!" I blurted, automatically taking the blame for the collision as my feet scrambled for purchase. As my uncoordinated dance played out, my purse hit the deck and spilled its contents. The hold on my arms loosened, and we both bent to retrieve my belongings.

I never realized how much junk I carried until I saw it spread out at my feet for the entire world to see. They say you can tell a lot about a woman from the contents of her purse. I hate to think what mine says about me. Disorganized, messy, and juvenile. The last a direct reference to the Spongebob Squarepants Band Aids I carry. Just in case. Slightly embarrassed, I began shoveling everything back inside the leather tote. It was no easy task. Even with help.

"You forgot one."

I looked up to see long, slender fingers wrapped around a tube of Pearly Pink lip gloss.

"Thanks," I said, grateful it hadn't been the emergency tampon I also carried.

Getting up off my knees, I looked at him. And wished I hadn't. Across a busy room, he'd been incredibly good-looking; this close, he was drop-dead gorgeous.

The night air was heavy, and the humidity hadn't let up one lick. I could feel the sweat starting to bead at my hairline. A few more minutes and I'd feel like I'd just taken a shower. Only I'd be hard-pressed to say with any certainty if the cause was atmospheric pressure or the way he was looking at me. I took a step back

"I'm sorry. Did I hurt you?" he asked as his brow furrowed with concern.

For a moment I thought he was talking to someone else, and I actually glanced over my shoulder, expecting to see Miss Juicy, but the bartender was nowhere in sight. We were the only two people standing on this side of the door. I turned back and gave him my full attention.

The porch suddenly seemed to have shrunk in size, becoming far too small for the two of us, and I became acutely aware of his presence filling every inch of available space. Something else I hadn't taken into account was how the distance between us inside the bar might have altered his physical proportions. Obviously, I'd been able to tell he was tall and broad through the shoulders, just not how tall or how broad. And I really hadn't allowed myself to take more than a superficial look at his features, a mistake I decided to correct.

The light streaming through the window behind me highlighted the bone structure of his face, revealing planes and hollows that caught my interest. He was definitely magazine cover material and then some, but this was no pretty boy hoping he'd look more adult if he skipped shaving. I avoided his eyes, already aware of their effect. His nose was long and straight, dividing the symmetry of his face perfectly, and his mouth . . . yeah, that was a place I didn't need to spend too much time examining either. Wide enough to balance his features, the full bottom lip was a suggestive promise all by itself.

If he thought any woman needed a reminder of his masculinity, I could have told him the five o'clock shadow was unnecessary. The determined line of his jaw, with a chin that hinted at stubbornness, was proof enough. Even the long blond hair did not detract from his maleness. His face matched his body. Strong, hard, and definitely alpha male. I stared back at him, and my own body unexpectedly zinged. Something it hadn't done for quite a while.

"I'm fine," I managed to get out, still able to feel his fingers wrapped around my arms. "I didn't hurt you, did I?" Amusement flickered across his face at my concern.

"No, at least not this time." His voice was smooth, like melting honey, and it sent weird little thrills running through me.

"Excuse me?" I forced myself to get a grip and focus on his mouth, which wasn't the smartest move on my part.

"You did quite a number on my ego earlier, and a man's ego, as I'm sure you know, is a fragile thing."

I managed not to snort, which would have been rude. That particular statement might be true about any other man on the planet, but not him. "Oh yeah?" I raised an eyebrow. "How so?"

"You sent back my drink." The dimple appeared and winked at me. "May I ask why?"

"I don't accept drinks from guys I don't know."

Good Lord! Could I sound any more sanctimonious? But I noticed he paused, as if considering the validity of my answer.

"Any chance I could ask you to reconsider?"

Oh, shit! I blinked at him. I couldn't possibly have heard right. And then the sensation that we'd met before prickled again, making the hair at the nape of my neck stand up.

"Sorry, am I being pushy?" he asked.

His words slid up and down my spine, and the smile he gave me said he wasn't sorry at all. An alpha male, he was simply following the rules of an age-old game. A game that I was being invited to play. And suddenly I knew this was about so much more than a drink.

"Pushy?" I mumbled.

"Yeah." The smile became flirtatious. "It means forceful, insistent, and . . . you're staring at me."

"Oh Christ! I'm sorry." I apologized again and dropped my eyes, which meant I was now looking at his belt buckle, or rather the area just below it. His jeans were a snug fit. Shit! I looked back up at his face, perturbed at the unaccustomed warmth burning my cheeks. This guy was rattling my cage in ways I'd never thought possible. "Look, I know this is going to sound ridiculous, but . . . have we met before?"

He didn't laugh at me, even though I'm sure he was tempted, nor did he regard me with some sort of patronizing sneer. Instead he became surprisingly serious. "Why, do you think we have?"

I was the one who laughed. Too loud, and too shrill. One of those Oh-God-I'm-such-a-moron laughs. No doubt the reason he seemed familiar was because he was a model and I *had* seen him before. Only it was in a magazine and, let's be honest, who really gives more than a cursory glance at pictures of men selling aftershave or deodorant? But that still didn't explain why he would be in a dive like this in the first place. Unless—

"Oh God—you weren't stood up, were you?" The words tumbled out of me before I could stop them.

His smile was very superior. A man like him, with his face and body, didn't get stood up. Ever. Not only was I behaving like an idiot, I was behaving like a rude one. My question was way out of line, and I felt awful, apologizing for the third time in as many minutes. What the hell was wrong with me?

"I'm sorry, it's just that you don't seem like the normal type of . . ." What? Supermodel? Fantasy calendar poster boy? Exotic male dancer? None of which I had any experience with, but I would bet my last dime they wouldn't be caught dead in a place like this out of choice. *Way to go, Rowan! Let's get a backhoe in here because I really think you need to dig that hole a little deeper.*

I wanted to bite my tongue just to shut it up. He said nothing. Instead he folded his arms across his chest and leaned back against the railing, watching me squirm. And he was enjoying it far too much, if the gleam in his eye was any indication. All I could do was gawk at his perfect toothpaste-commercial-white grin.

"Look, I'm sorry, please forget I said anything."

"Only if you'll let me buy you that drink."

I didn't get him. After what I'd just said, any other man would have been running in the opposite direction. Fast. It suddenly struck me that perhaps he was one of those guys who can't accept it when a woman says no. Their egos tell them that anything with ovaries is instantly smitten in their presence. With this new train of thought running through my head, I narrowed my eyes and stared at him, seeing him in a different context.

I tried to imagine what Laycee would tell me to do. It wasn't much of a stretch. I could almost hear her whispering in my ear to check if he'd had a tonsillectomy—with my tongue. Her words about playing it safe and my empty bed rolled around inside my head.

My very own pinup uncrossed his arms and slipped his hands into the front pockets of his jeans, waiting for me to give him an answer. The easy grin had vanished; his face was serious as he waited for me to speak. I looked up and caught the unnatural shade of blue of his eyes. No one had eyes that color, which meant he was wearing contacts and, strangely, that made me feel better. He wasn't so perfect after all.

And there was something else. He still might turn out to be a jerk—I didn't have enough evidence one way or the other to be sure—but for whatever reason, he really did seem to be interested in me. At least he was giving off all the right vibes. If he'd actually come over himself instead of sending Miss Juicy, I might have had some first-impression nerves, worried that I had lipstick smeared on my teeth or something, but I would have invited him to sit down and join us. Yeah, life is full of moments labeled woulda, shoulda, coulda.

I sighed and looked at him, feeling my stomach do a lazy, really good kind of roll. Apparently my body had some very definite ideas what my answer should be, and that in itself disturbed me. My physical reaction to him was unnerving. He was unnerving.

"Why?" I finally managed to blurt out.

"Well, not only did you refuse my drink, you're also the only woman who made a point of avoiding me when you went to the bathroom."

I laughed again. Not quite the moronic sound I'd made before but still steeped in anxiety.

"Sorry, maybe another time," I told him.

CHAPTER 4

Okay, so I wasn't expecting him to be crushed by this second rejection of mine, but he could have faked being disappointed. It would have been the polite thing to do. He didn't. Instead he tilted his head slightly as if he hadn't been expecting me to say anything else. And then it was his turn to look at me, narrowing his eyes as if, on a purely academic level, he was mentally listing my reasons for saying no. I imagine it didn't happen very often.

"Then may I walk you to your car?" The look he gave me this time didn't make me think we had met before. It made my thigh muscles jump. My body was more than happy to accept a consolation prize.

None of this made any sense. If I wasn't going to let him buy me a drink, why would I allow him to potentially trap me between parked cars in a poorly lit parking lot? What did he think I was? Desperate, easy, or stupid? Turning his head, he looked out over the sea of vehicles.

We were standing close enough that anyone passing would know we were talking, but far enough apart that we weren't *together,* if you know what I mean. I stared at his hands. They were large, the fingers long and well-manicured, and it didn't look as if he made his living with them. Unless he was a surgeon or something. And then I thought about Laycee's current beau, and checked for a wedding band or a telltale tan line. I saw neither.

"I'm sorry?" I said, suddenly aware he'd been talking and I hadn't heard a word.

As he turned back toward me, his hair fell over his shoulder like a white waterfall. It reached the middle of his chest, and with his pale blond features, he really did remind me of a Viking from a storybook. All that was missing was the horned helmet and sword, although I remember reading somewhere that horned helmets were usually saved for religious ceremonies, not for battle.

"A parking lot isn't always the safest place," he said, "especially when the lighting isn't good."

He was right about that. The lighting here was nonexistent. I had parked beneath the only functioning pole in the entire lot, but the illumination it put forth was about as strong as the night-light in my bathroom. And just as effective.

Then, as if to illustrate his point, one of the good ol' boys stumbled out of the bar. How he made it down the three steps off the porch without falling over was a miracle in itself. Having reached the bottom, the drunk turned and leered at me. At least I think that's what he was doing, but he could just as easily have been trying to work out why he was now outside the bar. Still, I could tell from the way he screwed up his face that he wanted to say something. Probably proclaim himself the best thing that was ever going to happen to me. Thankfully, the effort of getting his brain and mouth in sync took more skill than he currently possessed. The Viking took a step forward and the drunk swiveled his head dramatically. He hadn't realized I wasn't alone. With a baleful glare at my porch companion, he belched, thought better of trying to hit on me, and took off. I watched him weave his way unsteadily through the parked cars.

"I hope he's not planning on driving," I mumbled under my breath.

"He isn't." The reassurance came from behind my shoulder, making me jump. I hadn't realized the Viking had moved that close to me. "He's just going to climb in the back of his truck and sleep it off."

"Friend of yours?" I mean, how else would he know that?

The mane of blond hair moved across his shoulders. "No, but I saw him give his keys to the young lady behind the bar earlier."

My inner bitch perked up. *With her assets, I'm surprised you even noticed!*

He gave me a strange look, almost as if he, too, had heard the voice in my head. I flexed my fingers, making my own set of keys jingle noisily.

"May I?"

My would-be protector smiled as he stepped past me and stretched out his hand toward the open lot. A stranger was offering to walk me to my car, and I couldn't help but hear the warning bells that went off in my head. He might be a deranged serial killer! Yeah, but he did have a nice smile. Of course, so did most serial killers. I think it's some sort of prerequisite. It was on the tip of my tongue to refuse his offer, but I could definitely feel something zinging. Somehow, I didn't think he was dangerous. Well, not in a homicidal maniac way.

"Thank you, I would appreciate that." I used my best you-better-not-fuck-with-me voice as I stepped off the porch, determined to prove a point to myself, if no one else.

We headed for the far end of the parking lot, maintaining the same distance between us. I don't know if he had still been conversing with Miss Juicy when Jake had arrived, but part of me hoped so because then he would know I was on a first-name basis with a member of law enforcement. You can always recognize a cop, even when they're dressed like the rest of us.

My car, which I affectionately refer to as the POS, came off the General Motors assembly line sometime in the mid-seventies. It still ran fairly well, with help from the guys down at the local garage, and it got me pretty much wherever I wanted to go. I don't think, however, the folks in Detroit actually have a name for the paint job it had been given by a previous owner. I know I didn't, but Pimping-It-Purple came close.

The good thing was, no one was ever going to steal it.

The bad thing was, no one was ever going to steal it.

"Well, here I am," I said, in my best cheerleader imitation.

Whatever his first impression of the POS, he did a magnificent job keeping it to himself. He walked slowly around my car, doing whatever it is guys do when they walk slowly around cars. Checking to see how much duct tape was holding it together? When he reached the front of the car, he paused, standing beneath the pathetic arc of light, and I realized he was more than gorgeous. He was . . . beautiful. How could I not have noticed?

The T-shirt he was wearing fit like a second skin, almost shrink-wrapping his upper body, and he didn't require a visual reminder of passing puberty. Permitting myself a glance south, I saw the rear of his jeans was just as great as the front, and I was appalled at being so easily swayed by his physical appearance. Realizing I was on the verge of stepping into something I had no idea how to handle, I put my key in the lock in the driver's-side door, relieved to hear the soft thunk as it released.

"Your friend was right about one thing." The honeyed voice stopped me in my tracks.

"Yeah? And what was that?" I turned back around, knowing I was probably about to be fed a line of absolute BS, but wanting to hear it anyway. This is what happens when you have no love life to speak of.

A grin lifted the corners of his mouth, which looked very kiss-able. "I *was* looking at you."

The flame exploded somewhere just below my solar plexus and rushed up my chest and neck before slapping me in the face. I was grateful the light wasn't any better. What the hell was I supposed to say now? For the first time in—well, never—a guy was actually telling me that he'd been staring at me. On purpose. And not just any guy. *This guy.* Only I still couldn't figure out why.

At this point my brain went into some sort of shutdown, like a computer that freezes up and needs rebooting. My body was lighting up for him like it was the Fourth of July, and I stopped questioning his motives. Any vestige of good sense completely evaporated as the vain hope that he might want to separate me from my underwear filled my head.

With absolutely no idea what had gotten into me, I was filled with the urge to peel off his T-shirt, cover him with whipped cream, and lick it off . . . *slowly.* I have never, and I mean *never,* had this type of reaction to a guy. Frantically I tried to remember if Laycee's well-intentioned lecture applied to sudden, all-consuming lust. I didn't much care.

Nervously I waited for the potential father of my children to say something else, but he remained quiet. Moving from the front of the POS, he stopped barely an arm's length away from me and folded his arms across his chest. I watched, fascinated, as his biceps bunched and flexed. Some girls like a tight ass, others a well-defined six-pack, but me? I'm an arm girl. Nicely toned forearms, a great pair of biceps, topped by a terrific set of shoulders. I am so there.

"Wh-why would you b-be looking at me?" I stuttered, sounding like Minnie Mouse on crack. Ogling him was affecting my voice.

"Why wouldn't I want to look at you?" He seemed genuinely puzzled, and not at all distracted by my speech impediment. "Why wouldn't any man?"

He didn't move, but I suddenly felt as if he was surrounding me, using his body to push me back against the side of my car. And then, just as quickly, the odd, claustrophobic feeling vanished.

"Are you sure you won't reconsider?" he asked. "About the drink, that is?"

Oh my God, was he for real? Shit! Shit! Shit!

"Yes." The word rushed out of me before I lost my nerve.

"If you'd rather, we could just have coffee—"

What was wrong with him? Hadn't he heard me?

"Yes!" This time I shrieked.

He looked startled and then relieved, almost as if he had been expecting me to turn him down again. *Three strikes and you're out!* The dimple appeared in his cheek. God, it was sexy.

"Great. Is tomorrow night okay?"

My brain unfroze itself, rebooted, and rescued me by closing down my tongue. Apparently it couldn't be trusted to function properly. All appropriate responses were going to be reconfigured as head movements. I nodded at him.

"Shall we meet here, around eight?"

I nodded more vigorously, which I think he took as a sign of encouragement because he closed the distance between us, giving me the insane idea he was going to kiss me. Of course, he didn't. Instead, he reached behind me and opened the car door. I got inside.

Keeping one hand on the roof, he leaned down, and the scent of something flooded the space between us. I didn't know if it was his cologne or shampoo or soap, but it made my senses purr.

"I like your car," he said with a grin. "It's a classic."

No one had ever called the POS that before.

"Th-thanks. It's old." I managed to squeak. Not quite Minnie now, but still a close relative.

"Don't worry"—he flashed the dimple at me again—"wait until you see mine. It's even older."

He closed the door, and I hurriedly rolled down the window, my hand cranking the lever for all it was worth, in case he had more he wanted to say to me. He did.

"Drive carefully. See you tomorrow."

I barely noticed the ride home. The POS managed to negotiate the twisting county road with no guidance from me whatsoever. Or at least that's how it seemed. Perhaps she, too, had been charmed in the parking lot.

It had been an eventful night. I had a date. In the grand scheme of things a single woman going on a date was nothing to get excited about, except I hadn't been on one for, geez—had it really been that long? I was stunned at how simple a process it had been. He'd asked and I'd said yes. Okay, so I hadn't actually managed to articulate the word, but I had nodded like a demented bobble-head doll. Suddenly I jerked the wheel and nearly ran the car off the road.

Shit! I had a date, all right—with a guy whose name I didn't even know!

CHAPTER 5

The alarm clock yanked me awake with a rude, annoying buzz as it always did, only this morning I wanted to throw it across the room. Knowing I would have to buy a replacement was the only thing that stopped me from putting thought into action. And then the reason for my sour mood hit me like a sledgehammer.

I had a date.

I lay back down and groaned. Putting an arm over my eyes, I prayed the previous night's events would turn out to be nothing more than wishful thinking projected into my dreams. After all, in dreams you can do anything. Even agree to go on a date with a total stranger. A gorgeous, how-soon-can-I-see-you-stripped-down-to-your-boxers stranger, but a stranger nonetheless. How could I have not gotten his name? Had I told him mine? I couldn't be sure, but I didn't think so. And it wasn't a dream. I had a date.

In the cold light of morning, all of Laycee's words about grabbing happiness where I could find it became the most idiotic claptrap I'd ever heard. I really didn't give a shit about watching TV reruns or microwave dinners. And who cared if half my bed was empty? At least I wouldn't have to worry about someone hogging the blankets. My lack of a boyfriend was my problem, not hers. And besides, I didn't really think it was a problem. Not yet anyway.

So why had I agreed to go out with the Viking? Because of a physical attraction that was off the charts? Puhleeze! That type of thing only happens in romance novels ... doesn't it? I wanted to lay the blame for my impetuous decision on either alcohol or drugs, but as I hadn't had enough of the former and didn't do the latter, I was left with only one viable excuse. I'd had a brain seizure. One that allowed me to appear as a normal, functioning adult, when in reality I had been anything but. Yeah, the old gray matter misfiring on all levels. I groaned, and the Viking's face suddenly popped up front and center behind my eyelids, making my thigh muscles jump.

You know who I am.

I sat bolt upright. What the fuck? I had no idea where this particular voice was coming from, but it was no manifestation of mine. I had even less of a clue what it meant. I didn't know who the Viking was. I'd never seen him before last night. Hell—I'd never even fantasized about someone like him! But there was no denying the bizarre sense of déjà vu I'd felt when he'd smiled at me. Had we met before? He hadn't actually denied it when I'd asked him. Hadn't confirmed it either. So where did that leave me? Oh yeah. I had a date.

Throwing back the covers, I got out of bed and padded across the hall to the bathroom. Beneath the needle spray of a hot shower, my inner bitch woke up and offered me a solution. *Who says you have to show up?* Who indeed? I'd never been to Rosie's before, so even if the Viking went looking for me, which I very much doubted, he'd be out of luck. No one there could tell him who I was. Last night didn't need to be a disaster after all.

Stepping out of the shower, I dried off and tried to ignore my sudden pangs of guilt about intentionally standing someone up, something I'd never done before. I consoled myself with the thought that, wherever he was right now, the Viking was most likely waking up in the same frame of mind as I. Feeling a little better, I brushed my teeth and got ready for work.

It was supposed to be my day off, but I had agreed to cover for my co-worker Angela that morning. Greenley Heights is a fair-sized city and a good thirty-minute drive for me, a little longer if the Department of Transportation is out repaving potholes, a seemingly never-ending project. Nowhere near the size of Chicago or Los Angeles, it's still big enough to boast a couple of decent malls, a modern hospital, and a ten-screen multiplex movie theater. And the bookstore where Angela and I work.

I like my job because it affords me the opportunity to interact with my fellow human beings, and I get first dibs on new publications. I'm an avid reader, hence my dismay at the literary habits of guys I've dated in the past. Unfortunately the rumor mill says the folks at one of the big chains, Barnes and Noble or Books-A-Million, are looking in our direction. I'm not sure what will happen if they decide to open up a store nearby. I'm doubtful we could offer much in the way of competition. But that was the least of my worries as I got in the POS and pulled out of my driveway.

Angela brought me a berry smoothie topped with loads of whipped cream when she came in at noon. I listened sympathetically as she ranted about what an ass her ex was, an all-too-familiar subject these days. I considered getting her take on my almost date, but decided at the last minute not to. She was in full all-men-are-scum mode, and any advice she might give was hardly going to be fair and impartial. Besides, as I'd already decided not to go, it seemed redundant even to ask.

I changed my mind on the drive home.

Most people have a conscience that looks out for them. I have my inner bitch, who has an opinion about *everything*. Only sometimes it's difficult to know if she's on my side or not. I'd just cleared the city limits when she piped up, totally uninvited, and began giving me her two cents' worth about my recent behavior.

You actually agreed to go out with some guy you met in the parking lot of a seedy bar?

Yeah, I did.

I know you've been in a drought lately, man-wise, but don't you think that's kind of dumb . . . especially for you?

My inner bitch was right. It ranked as foolish behavior, and I didn't do foolish, but then she stepped over the line and pricked my vanity by asking the sixty-four-thousand-dollar question.

Why would he want to go out with you in the first place?

No idea whatsoever. God knows it wasn't due to my razor-sharp wit or scintillating conversation. I countered by saying the why didn't matter because I wasn't going out with him anyway. But wouldn't you know, she just had to get in one last dig.

Just as well, because guys who look like him don't go out with girls like you.

Like I said, sometimes I can't tell whose side she's on, and unfortunately I let her snotty, supercilious tone get under my skin.

Just because I didn't have impossibly gorgeous men asking me out on a regular basis was no reason to suppose it *couldn't* happen, right? I might not be a head-turner the way Laycee is, but I'm no wallflower either. I've received enough attention from the opposite sex to know that guys find me attractive, and besides, I hadn't done the asking. He had. It wasn't like I tricked him into it or anything.

What does it matter? You've decided not to go . . . haven't you?

Of course I had. Except, well, maybe it would be kind of shitty of me to just not show up. The decent thing to do would be to meet him, admit we'd made a mistake, apologize, and go our separate ways. No doubt he would be as relieved as I was, if he actually showed up. I couldn't be held responsible for his behavior, but if he *was* a no-show, then it would prove I was right about not going out with him after all. Which kinda sorta made sense in a weird way if you thought about it.

I washed my hair and took a soak in the tub, staying in the water long enough for my fingers to prune. Back in my bedroom, I stared good and hard at my reflection in the mirrored closet door. I'm sensible enough to see myself for what I am, which means I'm not that bad to look at. A C-cup may be a little on the generous side, and I wish my legs weren't quite so long, but thankfully, I've never relied on my looks to keep a guy interested. That's the job of my brain and my sarcastic tongue.

But now, for some reason, my brief interaction with the Viking had me fixated on my appearance. I reminded myself there wasn't a female on the planet who, if you stripped her down, was satisfied with the way she looked. Unless she'd paid a lot of money for it, and even that was no guarantee.

Turning away from the mirror, I told myself I wasn't going on a date, but breaking one, so it really didn't matter what I looked like. I very nearly ditched the jeans and red blouse I'd picked out in favor of baggy, gray sweats. But then good sense intervened. Personal pride dictated I look my best. Or as close as I could come to it.

CHAPTER 6

He was waiting for me. Leaning against what, at first glance, I took to be a small boat. And he was smiling. Confidently. Yeah, this guy didn't get stood up. Ever. I slid the POS between two trucks, both equipped with tires so big, it made me think their owners had serious compensation issues. My door was being opened before the sound of the engine died.

"I'm glad you came," the Viking said, holding out his hand to me.

Flustered by the gesture, I hesitated. The last adult male who had helped me out of a car had been my dad on the night of my senior prom. I'd been so drunk I could barely stand up, let alone walk. This was so not the same thing.

"Thank you." I gave him my hand, noticing how cool and smooth his palm was. Strong fingers closed around mine. Exiting the POS, I was grateful I'd chosen jeans over a skirt. I've yet to master the art of sliding out of a vehicle gracefully when wearing something that doesn't cover my knees, which means the probability of flashing my panties to an unsuspecting bystander remains distressingly high.

"I thought you might have changed your mind," he said.

"Changed my mind?" *Who me?* I could feel the burn in my cheeks. The innocence in my voice could have got me nominated for an Academy Award.

"Yeah," he shrugged his big shoulders, "you know . . . maybe stand me up."

I know I looked guilty, I had to, and I gave him a weak smile. Crap! Now what was I supposed to do? "Um, no . . . that never crossed my mind," I lied.

"Good, glad to hear it." His smile grew wider. It really was nice to look at and, I decided, not at all like that of a serial killer. "So, are you ready?"

This was my last chance to back out and tell him it had been a mistake. That I was turning him down in favor of a microwave dinner and a TV rerun. Only I realized a fundamental truth about myself. Sometimes I *am* a nice person even if I don't always think so. Damn it! He could have been the biggest jerk in the world, but I still would have shown up and gone out with him because I'd said I would.

Telling myself I could manage one drink, just to be polite, I heard myself mumble, "Uh yeah, sure," and began walking toward the bar.

An old Brooks and Dunn hit escaped as the doors opened, the melody carried out on the warm night air. I hoped Miss Juicy wasn't working tonight. As much as I'd like to stick it to her, it wasn't going to be much fun having her eyes boring holes in my skull all night long. She'd probably spit in my drink, too.

I'd covered half the distance before I realized I was walking by myself. Stopping, I looked back over my shoulder. The Viking had resumed his position against the boat.

"What?" I immediately went on the defensive, wondering why he had stopped. Perhaps he'd changed his mind after all.

His chuckle was a low deep rumble, and I felt my face flush with embarrassment, even though he didn't sound mean or unkind. Hitching my purse farther up my shoulder, I waited, hiding behind my confusion to take a look at him as he walked slowly toward me. Take a really good look at him.

He appeared much as he had last night, except the long blond hair was neatly tied back and the body-hugging T-shirt had been replaced by a black dress shirt. Judging from the sheen, I thought it might be silk. The sleeves were rolled up to his elbows, and he'd left the collar open, giving me an excellent view of his throat. In my opinion, most men who wear a silk shirt and jeans look pretentious, but on him the clothes looked stylish and very *GQ*. Even with the boots he was wearing. They were biker boots, the kind worn by real bikers, not those pseudo wannabes dealing with a mid-life crisis by trying to re-capture what they never had going on to begin with.

I checked—again—for a wedding ring, but the only jewelry I could see was a very large watch. I was willing to bet a paycheck it was a Rolex. My Viking was definitely not a good ol' boy. But also not the same guy who had walked me to my car last night. Well, he was, sort of, only now he just seemed *more so*.

I looked up as he reached me and saw his contacts doing their thing. The amazing shade of deep blue made me feel a little better, re-minding me he wasn't so perfect. He was now close enough to reach out and touch me if he wanted, but instead he made sure he didn't crowd me. Any physical contact was going to be down to me.

"I had thought we might do something else." I could hear the humor in his voice. "But if you'd prefer," he waved a hand at the building over my shoulder, "we can stay here."

"Ah, what did you have in mind?" I asked, retracing my steps and jumping at the chance to avoid Miss Juicy.

"A movie maybe?"

His suggestion came couched with caution, making me think he wasn't as sure of this whole date thing as he made out. I smiled. A movie was good. A movie I could handle. If nothing else, I wouldn't have to make small talk for a couple of hours, and the theater would be air-conditioned.

"Sure," I said, "a movie sounds great."

"So, what do you think?" he asked, with a wave of his hand.

What is it about guys and their cars? I swear there's a genetic link between mechanized horsepower and male DNA. Nevertheless, auto-moron that I am, even I could appreciate something this lovely to look at. "She's beautiful," I told him sincerely.

I didn't need to be an enthusiast to appreciate the care and time taken to restore and maintain such a vehicle. It almost qualified as a work of art. I had no idea the year or the specific make and model, but I did know enough to recognize that "she" was from a time when Detroit was synonymous with muscle cars. She was powder blue with a cream interior, and her chrome work sparkled like a beauty pageant queen all dressed up for a night on the town. She was even wearing classic whitewalls. It was almost criminal to make her sit next to vehicles better suited to a mud rally.

"What is she?" I asked.

His face lit up like a little kid, eager to show off a new toy "A Ford Fairlane."

"What year?" I asked, only because I know that's what you're supposed to do.

"Fifty-seven."

Wow. He hadn't been kidding when he'd said his car was older than the POS. But despite the generosity of his comment last night, I think the Fairlane rolled off the assembly line already a classic.

"Does she have a name?" I asked, half-jokingly.

"Francine."

Of course. What else would you call a Ford Fairlane? And I have absolutely no idea where the wave of jealousy came from, but it rolled through me with a vengeance. This was a car, for God's sake! Talk about being ridiculous. But it was nice to know the Viking had a "she" in his life that weighed a hell of a lot more than I did.

He looked at me and hesitated a fraction of a second before saying, "If you'd rather drive your own car I won't be offended."

Now it was my turn to hesitate. Common sense said that was exactly what I should do, thereby guaranteeing I had a ride home if, for some reason, the evening went belly-up. Only the flip side of that coin was that I'd be sending the message that I was expecting the evening to be a disaster.

While it was true I had come here with every intention of telling him this was a mistake, the words hadn't made it out of my mouth. And since I'd already concluded he wasn't a serial killer, it seemed churlish to refuse to go with him. Moreover, how often was I going to get a chance to ride in such a vehicle?

He tilted his head and gave me a look that created a pocket of warmth inside me. "I promise I won't let anything happen to you."

And he wouldn't. Don't ask me how I could be so certain; I couldn't have explained it if I'd tried, but I knew it was true. He would protect me with everything he had. I nodded, and he opened the passenger-side door for me. Francine's bench seat made me feel like I was sitting on a plush couch rather than in a car. The Viking got in the other side and then turned and looked at me.

"What kind of movies do you like?"

"Pretty much everything," I said with a laugh, pleased that it wasn't nervous sounding. "But I'm not a great fan of musicals, I think anything with subtitles is pretentious, and slasher flicks are, for the most part, insulting."

The silence told me I probably should have stopped after "pretty much everything."

"Slasher flicks?"

Was he serious? The look on his face said apparently so.

"You know," I explained, "lots of gratuitous blood and gore, with stupid D-cup bimbos running around half naked in the middle of the night chased by an axe-wielding homicidal maniac."

Another silence, then, "D-cup?" I lifted an eyebrow. If I had to explain that, we had a serious problem. "Ah, I understand."

He caught on quick. I like that in a man. As he turned the key in the ignition, I felt, as well as heard, Francine's engine come to life with a loud, throaty purr.

"What do you think of Quentin Tarantino?" he asked.

"Certified genius." I grinned, unable to believe my luck. Was it possible that I wasn't the only person in a three-county radius who thought *Reservoir Dogs* was a classic masterpiece?

"Great, then let's go."

He was about to throw the column shift into drive when I leaned over and put my hand on his arm. In all honesty, I did it without thinking, and I almost snatched my hand away at the electric thrill that jolted through me from the contact. He turned with a questioning look in his eyes.

"Don't you think, before we go anywhere, we should introduce ourselves?" I felt a little silly saying it, but I needed to know what to call him. "Gorgeous," while completely apropos, was far too intimate for me to use out loud, and I couldn't go around calling him "Viking."

"I'm Gabriel," he murmured.

Hearing his name made my stomach flutter. "Like the angel?"

"Yeah . . . like the angel." He spoke the words as if they were the punch line to an inside joke. One he wasn't going to share. Bummer.

"Pleased to meet you, Gabriel. I'm Rowan," I paused, and my brain went into overtime trying to come up with something witty. Sadly all I could manage was, "Um . . . like the tree."

"Yes," he said, gifting me with a show of his incredibly sexy dimple. "I know."

I didn't know that the multiplex in Greenley Heights dedicated one screen every Saturday night to a specific director and showed a notable feature. That's what you get for having no social life to speak of. Tonight it was Quentin's turn to be in the spotlight, only it wasn't *Reservoir Dogs* but *Pulp Fiction* that was being shown. Excellent second choice.

There were only a handful of patrons filling the seats, which didn't surprise me, and I didn't even think twice when I fished my glasses out of my purse once the house lights dimmed and the movie started.

"You look very studious," Gabriel whispered, leaning toward me, "like a schoolteacher."

I laughed self-consciously and hoped he didn't find them a turnoff. I guess he didn't because about a third of the way into the movie I felt him take my hand. And it wasn't one of those I'm-just-reaching-for-my-soda-and-your-hand-was-there-too type of moments. No, he wanted to hold my hand, and he made sure I fully understood that while also giving me the chance to slip my fingers free if I chose to. Holding my breath, I kept my hand right where it was, not exhaling until I felt those long, elegant fingers close around mine. It seemed the most natural thing in the world, and he didn't let go until the credits rolled.

"Would you like to get some coffee?" he asked as we stood in the main lobby.

Feeling wonderfully confused by his attention, I nodded. I had just been sitting in the dark holding hands with undoubtedly the most gorgeous-looking man on the planet—what girl in her right mind wouldn't want to go for coffee? At this point, I was up for almost anything if it would mean being in his company a little while longer. He grinned and reached for my hand again as we left the movie theater.

Heading toward the parking lot, I got a sudden attack of nerves, so I began running off at the mouth about other movies I liked. Grinning easily, Gabriel seemed content to let my bout of verbal diarrhea run its course, until I felt his fingers unexpectedly tighten around my hand as we came to a stop. He pulled me a little behind him, as if wanting to shield me. I stopped in mid-sentence and looked up at his face before following his gaze. It seemed Francine had gained some admirers.

CHAPTER 7

There were three of them. Two guys and a girl, and they turned their heads almost in unison to look at us. The first thing that struck me was how impossibly beautiful they all were. Like Gabriel, they seemed to have stepped out of the pages of a high-fashion magazine. And my second thought was I knew, without having to be told, that somehow he belonged with them. Straightening up, they positioned themselves next to Francine's rear bumper.

Gabriel loosened his fingers slightly and then squeezed again. It felt like he was offering me reassurance that everything was going to be all right. What did he think would be wrong?

The taller of the two guys broke away and came toward us. His footfalls struck the asphalt with authority, and if he wasn't ex-military, then he was doing a damn fine imitation. He had the look down pat, but it was more than just the army greatcoat he was wearing. Something about the way he carried himself yelled "soldier" at me. I had no doubt he was ex-military. His hair was a dark buzz cut, and he was big, although it was difficult to tell how much was him and how much was coat. I was surprised he wasn't sweating inside the heavy wool fabric, but he seemed comfortable enough.

His face was almost comic-book square, and beneath dark brows his eyes were piercing. They latched onto me, and I shuddered involuntarily, but in all fairness, that might have been because, now that he was closer, I got a good look at the scar on his face—a vicious line running from temple to jaw that made him look dangerous. Whoever had stitched him up had cared little about aesthetics, but I had to admit, even with the scar, he was still a head-turner. He stopped in front of us and gave a single nod of his head.

"Gabriel." His voice was a deep, agitated rumble.

"Aleksei."

By comparison Gabriel's voice was calm, but I thought I detected a trace of irritation. I didn't know if the reason was seeing the soldier or having the soldier see me.

"See, I told you it was his car," he flung over his shoulder at his companions. "No one else drives a blue Fairlane."

Now I could hear his accent. If asked, I would have said he sounded Russian, even if I wasn't sure exactly where that was anymore. Civil unrest, global upheaval, and shifting borders had changed the landscape in that part of the world. His companions exchanged glances, but neither of them spoke. I had the feeling they weren't expected to.

Standing this close to Gabriel, the soldier Aleksei almost matched him for height, which meant he was well over six feet. Neither of the other two seemed to be as tall, but both had me beat. With the heels the girl wore it was difficult to judge her true height.

The other guy was probably closer to my age and matched Aleksei in the impact of his wardrobe, but his fashion statement was a leather bomber jacket with a sheepskin collar, something I've seen World War Two pilots wearing in history books. It had a worn look about it, so I guessed he'd probably picked it up in an army surplus store. Also, his hair was longer. Light brown, it curled against his collar and flopped across his forehead. He had a wholesome look, one of those flawless all-American faces that people like Ralph Lauren love to use to sell overpriced clothes.

The girl was another matter altogether.

Her hair fell in a straight curtain to her hips and was so black it shimmered blue. She was wearing a scarlet jacket that seemed to be more zippers than material, and a skirt so short I wondered why she bothered wearing one at all. But then I figured she needed something to break up the space between the bottom of her zipper jacket and the top of the thigh-high killer boots she had on. Looking at her made me feel awkward, gauche, and horribly insecure—and yanked my inner bitch wide awake. This was no inept barmaid I could reasonably hold my own with.

And it didn't help that she returned my gaze with a disdainful stare, dismissing me with a look that told me in no uncertain terms I was way out of my league. As if I wasn't beginning to figure that out for myself. I clenched the muscles in my jaw, several uncomplimentary thoughts running through my mind as I scanned her face, searching for flaws. I couldn't find a single one. The exotic slope of her eyes, her pert nose, and her impossibly red mouth were all *perfect*.

Dismayed, I tore my eyes away and looked back at Gabriel . . . who was watching Aleksei . . . who was watching me.

"Aren't you going to introduce us, Gabriel?" he asked.

"Of course, my apologies."

Gabriel moved so he was now standing behind me with his hands lightly on my shoulders. His long fingers circled below my throat like a necklace . . . or a collar. It was a gesture that smacked of pure possessiveness, a statement of ownership almost, saying I belonged to him. I should have been pissed. Such an assumption was way out of line, but for some reason Gabriel didn't make it feel at all proprietary. With him it felt nice, it felt safe. Just like holding his hand had been.

"Rowan," I felt him lean down and his lips brush the top of my ear, "allow me to introduce you to Aleksei."

Most people would have followed that up with additional information. Something like *he's an old college buddy,* or *we grew up in the same town,* or *we work together,* something like that. Instead what I heard in Gabriel's voice made me think that their relationship was something more than co-workers, but less than tight friends, and couldn't be defined. And it felt weird.

One hand moved slightly. A finger stroked my neck. The possessiveness became a little more intense. "Aleksei . . . this is Rowan."

The soldier stepped forward and took my hand. Lifting it in an old-fashioned gesture, he kissed the back. It startled me, but I figured it was the custom in Russia or wherever he was from.

"So, this is Rowan."

He made it sound as if he had been waiting to meet me, but as that was completely ridiculous, I put it down to English not being his first language. The wrong inflection can unintentionally alter what is meant. Raising a finger to the livid scar on his face, he winked at me.

"Please don't let my good looks sweep you off your feet."

I couldn't stop myself from smiling back at him. He was ferocious and charming, all rolled into one. "It'll be hard," I said, matching the playfulness of his tone, "but I'll do my best to resist your obvious charms."

The rumble in his chest exploded as a laugh that made me jump.

"If you don't mind?" With a gentle tug I persuaded him to release my hand.

"She's charming, Gabriel," he said, looking over my head, "simply charming."

This had to be another European peculiarity because he should have been addressing me.

"So, why have you come looking for me, Aleksei?" Gabriel asked, his voice still courteous, but now with an edge.

In that moment I knew that even though he shared something in common with the three of them—and what that might be I had absolutely no idea—he was also somehow different from them.

"Permit me a moment of your time?" Aleksei's manner returned to its earlier unease, and the finger stroking my neck paused as something passed between the two of them. "It's important," the soldier added.

Dropping his head, Gabriel spoke. "Forgive me, Rowan, this will take only a moment."

Inordinately pleased that he felt it necessary to apologize to me, I smiled up at him. "Of course, take as long as you need."

There was another silky stroke along my neck before he strode away, followed by Aleksei. They went far enough that their conversation could not be overheard, but curiosity made me observe their body language.

Aleksei was definitely tense. The playful manner he'd used to put me at ease had vanished. There was a noticeable stiffness to his posture that carried through in the thrust of his comic-book chin, and the sharp, edgy way he used his hands to emphasize whatever he was saying. I could tell it was important, and serious.

Gabriel, on the other hand, appeared relaxed and unfazed. Though his arms were folded across his chest, there was no tension in his stance. He seemed to be listening with an air of unruffled calm. And it was obvious who was in charge. Even though Aleksei gave off a menacing air—due to his military training, no doubt—it was Gabriel who seemed the more dangerous of the two men. I had no idea why such a thought should occur to me, but it did, sending a shiver down my spine as I thought it. Not wanting Gabriel to think I was trying to eavesdrop, I turned around—and about jumped out of my skin.

The exotically beautiful girl was now standing right next to me. She'd managed to walk across the asphalt in her fabulous spiked heels without making a sound.

"It seems that both Gabriel and Aleksei have forgotten their manners," she said with a theatrical sigh. Like her companion, she, too, spoke in accented English, although with enough of a difference to tell me she and the big guy were not from the same place. "I am Katja."

Another first-name-only deal, but she said it with a certain amount of expectation. Like it meant something. It crossed my mind that perhaps she really was a model or, failing that, some tabloid personality. I hoped she wouldn't be disappointed by my lack of fawning recognition.

"I'm Rowan," I said, sticking out my hand and deciding I could play the single name game as well.

She dropped her chin slightly, looking down at my outstretched hand as if she didn't know what to do with it. The expression on her face made me do a double take just to make sure I didn't have something icky smeared on my palm. It took all I had not to wipe it on the leg of my jeans. And then, almost as if something in her brain was kicked into life, she clasped the offending part of my anatomy in her own. I'd been expecting her to barely grasp my fingertips and make a somewhat half-assed, limp-wristed effort, but her grip was surprisingly strong, although the movement was stiff and jerky, as if shaking hands wasn't something that came naturally to her. But that was the least of my worries. My inner bitch was gnashing her teeth. Loudly.

Up close, Katja was even more dazzling and perfect, and I found myself staring at her. Probably being horribly rude about it, too, but I couldn't help it. Only she didn't seem to mind. I suspected that, like Gabriel, she was used to having people stare at her. How could she not be?

Her face was oval with skin so pale it looked unnaturally white. I wondered if that was because she was European. It seems to me they don't get as much sun over there. Her eyes, smudged with kohl and far too big for her small face, were the color of violets. But it was her mouth that caught my attention. Her lips were flawless in both size and fullness, and were colored the most amazing shade of dark red. I wanted to ask her what brand of lipstick she was wearing, only I wasn't a hundred percent sure it was lipstick. I couldn't see any telltale line edging her mouth. Had to be lip stain, I told myself. Really good, very expensive lip stain, the kind movie stars and models wore. *Well, duh!*

As I watched, she parted her lips and smiled at me. Her teeth were very white, gleaming behind the pout of crushed cranberry, and curling the tip of her pale pink tongue, she ran it across her lower lip. I was gripped with the sudden, insane need to touch her. The urge to run my fingers across her satin-smooth skin, to taste the sweetness of those cranberry lips was intense, overwhelming—and completely irrational. I've never wanted to do the girl-on-girl thing, not even as an experiment.

"Katja!"

Her name was a whip crack that snapped inside my head. Strong hands gripped me from behind as I realized, with a start, that I was leaning toward her. Leaning so far forward I was about to fall over. It was Gabriel who had called her name, but the hands that saved me from kissing the ground weren't his. They belonged to the guy wearing the bomber pilot's jacket. I'd been so focused on Katja, I'd all but forgotten he was there.

"It's okay, ma'am, you're safe with me."

I almost laughed aloud with relief at the comforting midwestern twang, an accent I easily recognized. I shook my head before looking back at Katja. Her hand had been almost wrapped about my waist, and she now slid it off and raised it to my face. Softly she stroked my cheek, a perfect imitation of what I had wanted to do to her. It was shockingly intimate, making me jerk my head back and bounce it against the hard chest of Kansas Boy.

"Never mind, Little One, perhaps next time," she cooed huskily.

There was something horribly condescending in her tone, and it pissed me off. "I don't think so," I said, turning my head away.

Her hand gripped my chin, twisting my head so I was forced to look at her. She appeared to be of barely legal age, yet I knew I shouldn't be fooled by her youth. She was older than I thought. Pouting her lips, she gave me an air kiss before releasing my chin and walking away. I shuddered with relief as I watched her go.

"Thank you." I murmured, tilting my head up and looking over my shoulder at the Ralph Lauren model, grateful his quick action had saved me from complete humiliation.

"You're welcome." I could almost hear the summer breeze rippling through fields of wheat as he loosened his grip and stroked my upper arms lightly with his hands. "If there's ever anything I can do—" He broke off suddenly, his face flushing unexpectedly before he turned on his heel and went to stand next to Katja.

Gabriel and Aleksei reached me, and I let Gabriel enclose my hand once more in his, although I was puzzled by Kansas Boy's reaction. To my mind it was completely uncalled for. It was as if he had crossed an unseen line by speaking to me. I glanced over at Aleksei, who was staring at Katja. His eyebrows were knitted together, making him look quite fierce. He reminded me of a bear. A big Russian grizzly bear.

Smoothing out his expression, he turned to me. "Don't mind Katja," he said quietly, "she's all bite and no bark."

"You mean all bark and no bite," I corrected.

"If you say so." He chuckled before nodding once at Gabriel and then addressing his companions. "Come, my business is done."

They headed across the parking lot, rounded the movie theater, and disappeared out of sight. For a few moments there was nothing but silence, and I savored just sharing the space Gabriel occupied. Raising the hand he held, he brushed his lips across my knuckles.

"Do you still want to go for coffee?" he asked me.

In the space of five minutes my hand had seen more action than the rest of my body had in quite a while. I nodded. After that little episode with Katja—and I wasn't sure what had happened exactly— I desperately needed a big jolt of caffeine.

CHAPTER 8

We went to an all-night diner that I didn't know was still in business. It was situated in what had once been Greenley Heights's only shopping district, and I remembered my dad would always make sure we stopped there for lunch whenever we had to come to town. It was the only place you could get a milkshake made by hand. But then great tracts of land had been sold to become shopping centers; malls had been built, and folks stopped going downtown. I couldn't say which surprised me more: that the diner was still in business, that Gabriel knew it was, or that he had chosen to take me there.

Glancing through the large plate-glass window, I could see it was empty of customers, save for a couple of burly construction-type guys sitting at the counter. But it still looked the way I remembered: clean and well-lit, with high-backed booths that offered privacy. Still feeling a little unsettled, I excused myself and headed for the restroom. My reflection in the mirror was pale, and I knew it wasn't all due to the bathroom lighting. Running some cold water, I splashed it on my face. It seemed to help, and I felt better seeing the color returning to my cheeks.

The diner's lone waitress, a tired-looking thirtysomething with a bad bleach job, was flirting with Gabriel. She gave me a poisonous look as I slid into the seat across from him. I really couldn't blame her. He was easy on the eye at any time, and probably even more so at this hour of the night. Two oversized coffee cups had been put in front of him, and he now pushed one across the table to me. An amused smile twitched the corners of his mouth. The mocha-colored liquid gave off an amazing, tantalizing aroma. I took a sip. It was heavenly, hot but heavenly. The mix of hazelnut and caramel was just what I needed, but it surprised me because I know I hadn't told Gabriel what to order for me.

"Lucky guess," he said before pointing to his upper lip and then at me. Sheepishly I pulled a napkin from the tabletop dispenser and blotted the foam away.

"Do you come here often?" I asked, curiously.

He shrugged. "Occasionally."

I looked around and wondered if my dad had ever come here as a teenager looking to pick up girls. "I didn't even know this place was still open," I murmured.

Gabriel made no comment, so I sipped my coffee as we fell into an awkward silence. At least I thought it was awkward. I had no idea what was going through Gabriel's mind, but he suddenly seemed distant, enough so to make me think I'd better drink up so we could leave. I really didn't want the waitress watching as I got the big kiss-off. I'd had more than enough experience with that scenario.

I had a really nice time tonight . . . but . . .

Leaning forward, Gabriel fixed me with his dark blue eyes. "Are you all right?"

"Of course." If I was about to get dumped, then I was determined to handle it graciously, like the adult I was supposed to be. "Why would you think otherwise?"

"When you first meet him, Aleksei can sometimes be a little overwhelming, and Katja . . . well, she can be . . ."

"Extreme?" I offered helpfully.

"Yes," Gabriel said, leaning back in the booth, "I suppose you could say that."

Yes, you could. But it came nowhere close to describing what she was. I was as much at a loss as he to find the proper adjective to describe the glossy, dark-haired girl with the supermodel looks. And I was still disturbed by my reaction to her. At least I could find words for the episode. *Disconcerting ... alarming ... unnerving.*

"Are they friends of yours?" I wrapped my hands around the cup, feeling the warmth seep through.

"Friends?" Gabriel looked thoughtful, as if he was reflecting on the full meaning of the word to see if it was applicable. "Aleksei yes, but not the other two, I think, at least not in the way you mean. Acquaintances would be a better word." A worried frown creased his smooth brow. "I apologize if Aleksei was intimidating."

I thought about that. Had the big guy been intimidating? I didn't think so, not intentionally, but there are some people who can appear menacing without even trying. It's just a part of their makeup. I couldn't say for sure this was the case with the Russian, but he had scared the crap out of me at first. Of course I wasn't about to say so now that I knew Gabriel regarded him as a friend.

"He wasn't intimidating exactly," I said, brazenly lying, "but he was a little, um ... intense." The look on Gabriel's face said he knew I was being diplomatic, and the reason why, but he wasn't going to press me on it. "But you can't really blame me, not with that whole Special Forces persona he has."

"Special Forces? Ah, you think he is in the military?"

I stopped with my coffee cup halfway to my mouth to see if he was joking. He wasn't. "Well, yeah, I mean the clothes are a dead giveaway, along with the GI Joe buzz cut, but it's also the way he carries himself." I hesitated, hoping I wasn't about to put my foot in it. "I half expected him to whip out a grenade launcher from inside his coat," I finished with a nervous laugh.

Gabriel looked puzzled. "I think he just wears what he feels comfortable in."

Whoa. He really didn't see it. Perhaps the guy had been dressing that way for so long no one noticed it anymore. Not altogether unheard of, but still a little strange.

"So he's not a soldier then?" I asked.

"No, he's not."

"Is he Russian?"

His head nod was accompanied by a slight smile. "Yes, he is."

"From Moscow?" It was the only place in Russia I could think of on the spur of the moment.

"No, he's from a small town that doesn't exist anymore."

I wasn't sure what to make of that. A casualty of civil unrest and shifting borders perhaps? "Oh, well that's a really nasty scar on his face. Do you know how he got it?"

Gabriel picked up his spoon and began to stir his coffee. "Why all the questions about Aleksei?"

I felt mildly embarrassed, and picked up my own spoon. "Well, he's not the sort of guy you're going to forget anytime soon."

"Really?"

I shrugged. "Yeah, really." Glancing across the table, I saw Gabriel pull his eyebrows together ever so slightly and wondered if he was mistaking my general curiosity for interest of a different kind. *And I imagine he'd be quite devastating without the scar.*

I didn't realize I'd spoken that part out loud until the look on Gabriel's face told me so. It really wasn't a smart thing to talk about one guy while you were out with another, especially not on a date and without your own car.

"Sorry," I apologized. "That was rude of me."

"I'm sure if you were to ask him, Aleksei would tell you how it happened."

I couldn't tell if Gabriel was expecting me to meet up with the big guy again, or if he was offering to set me up. Neither was something I wanted to happen. Silence ensued once more, the air between us becoming thick and heavy, making me positive I had just blown whatever chance might have existed of seeing Gabriel again.

Way to go, Rowan. No wonder you're sleeping alone.

I could just imagine what Laycee was going to do with this scenario when I told her. The thought prompted me to take a wild stab at damage control. What did I have to lose?

"I'm not interested in him, you know . . . at least not like *that.*"

"Like what?"

Gabriel's expression became one of extreme politeness. Putting his hands on the table, he bracketed his coffee cup with his long fingers. I remembered how they had felt resting around my neck. He knew exactly what I meant about Aleksei, but I was being punished.

A reprimand to make me feel uncomfortable because it *was* rude of me to talk so much about another man. Okay, I was woman enough to accept I'd made a mistake.

"I'm not looking at him as potential boyfriend material," I said with as much detachment as I could. "I was just curious. I've never met anyone like him before."

Gabriel deliberated over my words. "And are you looking at me as potential boyfriend material?" he asked finally.

I shouldn't have been surprised by the question. I'd kind of opened myself up for it, but even so, I was surprised that he'd actually articulated it. Was I looking at him like that? Actually, no, I wasn't. The inferno he'd ignited in my pelvis made it hard to think about anything beyond getting naked with him, but a relationship that was exclusively physical wasn't a good blueprint for a boyfriend.

"Your coffee's getting cold," Gabriel said, settling back against the booth and giving me a smile that told me he really hadn't been expecting me to answer. The look in his eye, however, confirmed my suspicion that he knew my interest in Aleksei wasn't sexual, and my interest in him was.

Raising my cup, I decided it would be a good idea to keep my mouth shut before I really did put my foot in it. I could feel his eyes roaming over me. Not staring exactly, more like he was examining me. Mentally checking me out. I wondered if I'd be found wanting, and an image of the bartender from Rosie's flashed into my head. For some reason I felt incredibly sorry for her.

Wanting or not, I didn't much care for Gabriel's scrutiny. By now he probably knew the exact number of freckles scattered across my nose, the length of the scar above my right eye, and the distance between each piercing in my left earlobe.

My gut said he was waiting for me to bring up the incident with Katja, but I felt horribly self-conscious even thinking about it. It must have looked as if I was about to kiss her. God knows, I'd leaned in close enough to do just that. Did Gabriel think I swung both ways? I could still feel her hand as she stroked my cheek, her fingers wonderfully smooth and cool. It felt very bizarre in a strange, surreal way, and I could feel the heat rising to stain my cheeks. I cleared my throat and, for the first time this evening, wished I had my own way to get home.

I was grateful when Gabriel suggested we talk about something else, and for the next hour he charmed me and made me laugh, and I relaxed as the earlier tension washed away. We covered a number of inconsequential topics that, by themselves, were mundane and harmless but, strung together, revealed an awful lot about a person.

I confessed that, as a child, I'd had a goldfish who I thought lived for a really long time until I found out my dad had been secretly replacing each one as it died. In a three-year time span I cared for five fish named Brian.

"Don't ask," I muttered in response to Gabriel's raised eyebrow over the un-aquatic-sounding name.

I had also been the proud owner, for a very short time, of a terrapin (named not Brian, but Lancelot) who managed to escape captivity. To this day, I like to think that he enjoyed a good life somewhere in our backyard before going to reptile heaven, although I suspect he didn't get farther than the linen closet. I vaguely recollect smelling an odd, unaccountable odor not too long after his disappearance. We touched briefly on sports; Gabriel was a hockey fan, but he shook his head in mock despair at my ongoing love affair with professional football.

"I'd better make sure you don't ever meet Sebastian," he said with a wicked grin.

"Why? Does he hate football too?"

"No, just the opposite. Put you two together and you'll forget I'm even in the same room."

I didn't know who Sebastian was, but I doubted very much Gabriel would allow himself to be forgotten. Sensing potential friction, I steered the conversation back to shared interests such as movies and books; we agreed that we didn't know each other well enough to discuss politics or religion.

"At least not yet," Gabriel responded with an odd look.

I suppose it was a typical first date. Although, not having had many of them in recent memory, I was a little rusty. Still, I like to think we were behaving the way people do who are trying to get to know one another, to see if they make enough of a connection to warrant a second date. But I wasn't stupid or unobservant. For all the talking I was doing—and it seemed Gabriel was able to pull information from me as easily as any Internet search engine—he said very little about himself. The few details he did reveal—originally from Norway (I've heard stronger accents from people born in Minnesota), no living family, and an occupation that involved doing *this and that*—he offered cautiously. Instinctively I knew not to push him, telling myself he needed to get more comfortable with me before revealing personal details. It was better than thinking he didn't want to waste time sharing information with someone he had no intention of seeing again.

If there was one unsettling aspect to the evening, it was the physical attraction—mainly because I had no control over it and had no idea if he felt anything remotely similar for me. If Katja was a sample of the kind of woman he was used to being around, then I was completely screwed. And not in the way I was hoping for. I couldn't even console myself with the fact that he'd held my hand during the movie. Since getting into the car after leaving the movie theater, he hadn't tried to touch me in any way.

Finishing my second—or was it third?—cup of coffee, I glanced at my watch. "Oh geez, is that the time? I really need to get home."

"Why?"

His question caught me off guard, and I looked up, certain I'd misheard him. There was no actual reason, but I thought I'd be graceful and give him a way out. Surely he'd had enough of my inane blathering by now? He tilted his head, and I stared into his eyes just as the overhead light caught his contacts, making them shine with an eerie glow. No matter how much I wanted to, I couldn't look away. The deep cobalt blue intensified, deepened even more, if that was possible, making me think I could see *something* moving in the depths. The circle of color began to shimmer and then started to bleed out into the surrounding sclera. It reminded me of spilling old-fashioned ink onto a piece of white paper, and I felt him catch hold of my hand and pull me into his arms.

The rational part of my brain said this couldn't be happening because for Gabriel to do such a thing would require passing my physical body through the table. A table that was bolted to the floor, thank you very much. My irrational side, however, simply told me to shut-the-fuck-up. The booth, the table, the sad waitress who continued to stare longingly at Gabriel like he was the special at an all-you-can-eat buffet, everything would be gone if I would only open my eyes and look. So I did. And it was.

Gabriel was holding me in his arms, and as in any worthwhile fantasy, we were both naked. I could feel the warmth of his skin pressed against me, the smooth firmness of his chest against my more than ample one, the muscles that rippled and flexed beneath my touch. His thigh was wedged inside my open stance, with his erection pressed against my belly.

I gasped at the feel of him, too intimidated to actually lower my eyes, and he kept one hand pressed firmly against my lower back so I wouldn't be tempted to move away. I looked up at him. His mane of white hair appeared to be longer than before. Caught on a breeze I could not feel, it drifted around us like a sensual blanket. I stared in wonder, and then amazement, as I watched his eyes change.

The cobalt had now totally bled out, obliterating the white completely, and his pupils began to transform themselves. They were no longer black, but a brilliant gold. If I was supposed to be afraid, then I was going to seriously disappoint someone, because I wasn't. Intuitively I knew Gabriel would never harm me. Instead I felt this was exactly where I was supposed to be, and the sense that we had met before returned. Only it was much stronger this time.

You know who I am.

The words came at me again, the voice filling my head, trying to shake free a memory that lay buried inside. Only I didn't know who the memory belonged to, or what it might do to me once it was recovered. So I tossed the voice out of my head, smiling a little at the sense of frustration that it left behind. *Yeah, you and me both, buddy.*

Turning my attention back to Gabriel, I concentrated on the strength I could feel pulsing through him, a strength woven with a desire that shattered any doubts I had about reciprocal physical attraction. Whatever was flowing through Gabriel went beyond the uninhibited need to possess me bodily. Stronger than anything I had ever known, it was something deeper. The breath caught in my throat, and my legs trembled, the wetness between them a release of my desire, my need for him. Shamelessly I rubbed myself against him, letting him catch the scent of my arousal, feeling him respond with a thrust of his hips.

If I thought my need of him was intense, it was nothing compared to how he wanted me. Every thick, gloriously hard inch of him throbbed impatiently, demanding to get inside me and show how any hunger I had would be satisfied. I gasped, sucking in a great mouthful of air, wanting nothing more than to feel his lips against mine, wanting his tongue inside my mouth, taking everything I had to give him before he—

"Rowan, are you all right?"

The sound of his voice, along with the stroke of his fingers across the back of my hand, jerked me back from the edge of the sexual mirage I had stepped into. Snatching my hand away, I sent my empty coffee cup spinning wildly across the table while I blinked frantically and looked around me. My mouth was open, I was practically panting, and I could feel perspiration on my upper lip. My breasts felt achy, my nipples hard, and a wave of longing throbbed at my core. What the hell had just happened?

A wild glance showed everything was just as it had been before. The table between us remained bolted to the floor with the plastic menus neatly stacked behind the sugar and ketchup bottle. Reaching for my spinning cup, Gabriel set it back on the saucer in front of me. My mouth felt dry and I licked my lips. Noticing, he signaled to the waitress to bring me a glass of water.

"What happened?" I asked, staring intently across the table. *Were his pupils ringed with gold?* I shook my head and blinked. The gold disappeared, and I realized I was still caught up in my fantasy.

"I think you zoned out on me for a moment," he said gently, knowingly.

"Really?" I pulled at my lower lip with my teeth, not realizing his focus had shifted until I heard an unrecognizable noise coming from him. Whatever it was, it was highly sexual. "That's never happened to me before," I said quickly, wanting to shift his focus away from my mouth.

"Me either."

He sounded normal, so I told myself my ears had been playing tricks, fueled, I was certain, by my wanton imagination.

"Where did you go?"

"I have absolutely no idea," I told him truthfully.

"What do you remember?"

"Nothing. I must have blacked out or something—can you do that sitting up?"

I was babbling and convinced Gabriel knew I wasn't being a hundred percent truthful. But how could I admit I was so attracted to him that my brain had sent me off into fantasy sex land? He gave me an odd look, one that said I didn't need to explain. He knew exactly where I'd been.

"Are you sure you're okay?"

"Yes." I gave him what I hoped was my most reassuring smile. "Probably just too much caffeine."

The waitress brought over my water, and I gulped down half the glass before stopping to take a breath. Gabriel raised an eyebrow and gave me a thoughtful stare, and then signaled for the check. The flirty waitress looked positively heartsick that we were leaving together.

CHAPTER 9

"Are you sure you're okay?" Gabriel asked me again when we were in the car.

I nodded and smiled at him. "Yeah, I'm sure. I think I'm just over-tired. It's been a long day."

"Of course, I'm sorry. It was selfish of me to keep you out so late after you've been working. Sometimes I forget."

"Forget what?" I chose not to correct him about my working habits. At this point, I'd rather have him think I was a lightweight who couldn't keep her eyes open past two in the morning than have him ask me any more questions about my strange little brain seizure.

"Not everybody's a night owl."

"Is that what you are, a night owl?"

He nodded. "You could say that."

"Out of choice or necessity?" I asked.

His hair shimmered in the glow of Francine's dashboard lights. It looked silky and heavy, and I wondered how it would feel in my hand . . . or brushing across my skin.

"Necessity, to begin with." He glanced over at me. "But now I don't think I could function during the day."

"Is this because of your job?"

"Partly."

He was being vague—in the nicest possible way, of course—but I wasn't so out of it that I couldn't tell when a door was being closed on me. This was a man with secrets. Of course, everyone has secrets; it's just that some are similar to keeping a tiger in a cage. You never know how dangerous it is until you rattle the bars. I decided not so much to rattle as to give a little shake.

"What is it you do again?" I asked, with as much innocence as I could muster.

"Oh, this and that."

Same thing he'd told me earlier. I looked over at him. His face was turned away as he concentrated on merging Francine into traffic. There were more cars on the road at this time of night than I would have guessed.

"Are you in the import-export business?"

I watched his eyebrows pull together in bewilderment. "Why would you think that?"

Movies involving drug dealers—successful ones, that is—always show them working in the import-export business. I figured it was based on something factual because *this and that* was not an occupation. It was a way of telling me not to poke my nose into something that didn't concern me. If he had a legitimate occupation, he would tell me, so all I could do was speculate that he was involved in something that was possibly illegal.

Just because he doesn't want to tell what he does doesn't automatically mean he's a criminal. There are plenty of occupations that, out of necessity, are performed at night.

For some strange reason my inner bitch was taking Gabriel's side. Pursing my lips, I shut her down, even though I admitted the truth of her statement. Maybe I was watching too much TV.

"I have absolutely no idea why I said that," I said with a smile, leaning my head back against the seat and closing my eyes. "I don't make much sense when I'm tired."

The rest of the ride back to Rosie's was uneventful, and silent as far as conversation went. I kept my eyes closed because I had a feeling that, given the opportunity, Gabriel might start questioning me again about my blackout. I couldn't say he would, but there was something in his face that made me think he wasn't buying my version of the event.

Through half-closed lids, I saw his long fingers turning the dial on the radio as he searched for a station. His car was a classic, and I thought his sound system might need an upgrade. I changed my mind when the sound of something classical and surprisingly soothing spilled out of the dashboard.

"Too loud?" He took his eyes from the road long enough to glance over at me.

"No, it's lovely." I graced him with a real smile before turning my head so I could stare out the window, watching the dark night rush past us.

There had been no respite with my eyes closed. Instead, I had been able to reassemble the image of Gabriel holding me in his arms much too clearly. It felt so real I could taste the sweat beading on his chest, hear the steady rhythm of his heart beating, see the fascinating way his eyes changed from normal to . . . I don't know what. The physical hold he had on me leapfrogged to a scale I had never known before. My pelvis suddenly flared with a raw ache, as if reminding me. How was he able to do this to me?

I searched for some sort of rational answer. Was this what people meant when they said they were instantly attracted to someone? Picking up on pheromones that caused a chain reaction directly linked to their libido? Or was I just hallucinating without the help of hormones? I had absolutely no idea. The only certain thing I was able to hold on to was the fact that I have never felt such an overwhelming urge to get inside a guy's pants as I did right now. And I really needed to put some distance between the two of us before I did, or said, something stupid.

Upset at being disregarded, my inner bitch chimed back in, dispensing one last piece of advice. *Men like him don't go out with girls like you . . . and they don't sleep with them either.*

The neon sign for Rosie's had been turned off, although there were a few lights still shining through the windows. Some last-call drinkers and the bar staff cleaning up would be my guess. I wondered if Miss Juicy was one of them. Saturday was probably a good tip night. I hoped Gabriel didn't want to find out.

Francine slid over the gravel toward the POS, which looked positively forlorn. The monster wheel guardians were long gone, leaving her all alone. Pulling alongside, Gabriel killed the engine and got out. Coming around, he opened my door for me, and even though he'd done it earlier, I was still flattered by the gesture. Most guys these days wouldn't have bothered. I gave him my hand as I got out, moving forward as he shut the door behind me. He gently muscled me back until I was pinned against the car. Tipping his head, he looked down at me, frowning just a little.

"What did I do wrong?"

His question took me by surprise, and I drew in a sharp breath. He was close enough that my breath also caught the scent of him, which made my head spin and my stomach roll in a really good way. I immediately became flustered. "You didn't do anything wrong."

"Then why are you angry with me?"

I stared back up at him, feeling my own forehead furrow in puzzlement. "I'm not angry with you."

"Could've fooled me."

Where the hell was this coming from? He stepped back, and my head began to clear, letting me see the expression on his face clearly. It told me that, as far as he was concerned, there was a problem, one that was escalating. He wasn't going to be satisfied until it had been resolved one way or the other. Trouble was, I had no idea what was going on.

"Why did you shut me down in the car?" He took a step toward me. "And don't give me that bullshit about being tired. I thought we were having a good time."

"We were—I was!" I protested.

"So why the change in attitude?"

I dropped my eyes, afraid that he would read the truth in them. What was I supposed to say? Looking at you makes me want to see how big the back seat of your car is, especially from a horizontal position? Somehow, I didn't see that going over too well. The only vibe I'd gotten that he was physically attracted to me had come via my lit-

tle sex fantasy. Sure, he'd held my hand in the movie theater and be-
haved possessively in front of his Russian pal, but that was a far cry
from saying I want to jump your bones. Taking a deep breath, I
forced myself to look at him. Aw, shit—no fair! He'd folded his arms
across his chest.

"Trust me, Gabriel," I began, "you didn't do anything wrong. The
problem is with me—"

The angry, impatient breath he blew out cut me off. Okaaaay. Apparently he didn't much like where I was going with that one. I decided to try a different approach. Honesty. Shit.

"Look, it's been a while since I last went on a date, and to be honest, I never was much good at them to begin with." I saw his shoulders relax. "When I arrived here tonight I *was* going to tell you the
whole date thing was a mistake and we should just forget about it."

"Then why didn't you?"

"I don't know . . . I honestly didn't think I would have to . . ." He
looked puzzled. "I thought you'd be a no-show."

He looked insulted that I considered him capable of such a thing.
"I wouldn't do that," he said stiffly.

"Yeah, well . . ." I scuffed the toe of my boot in the gravel, kicking
up a gray cloud of dust that dulled the polish. Keeping my eyes
downcast, I continued. "Anyway, when I got here tonight you didn't
really give me a chance to speak, and you still seemed to want to go
out with me, so I thought what the hell, let's give it a whirl and see
what happens, and . . ."

"And?"

I raised my head. "And I had a good time." I could see a glint of
frustration in his eyes. I didn't blame him. As excuses went, this was
pretty lame. I plowed on before he had a chance to stop me. "So
much so, it made me nervous. I was opening up to you in ways I've
never done before, certainly not on a first date, and I think being so
comfortable with you . . . well . . . I'm just not used to it." He stared at
me with a look I couldn't read. "Believe me, Gabriel, you did absolutely nothing wrong." I shoved my hands in the front pockets of
my jeans and hunched my shoulders up to my ears, feeling like I was
twelve.

"Are you sure?"

I nodded miserably. "Yeah . . . I'm sure."

There was a long pause before he said, "Do you promise to tell me if I do?"

My heart skipped a beat, and an unexpected warmth bloomed in my chest. Not the fiery burn-a-warehouse-down-to-the-ground inferno that I had felt before, but more of a nice roasting-marshmallows-over-a-campfire heat. Gabriel had phrased his question in the present tense.

"You can trust me on that one," I said with a shaky laugh.

Completely at ease, he came forward, his wide shoulders blocking the sight of my car and reminding me just how big he was. "I really had a nice time tonight as well."

He softened his tone, changing it to a husky whisper that was ten times worse than the liquid silk. I could feel my spine start to liquefy, and I pressed myself back against the Fairlane so I wouldn't fall down. The image I'd seen before in my brain seizure suddenly flashed in my head. I closed my eyes and saw him as he was then, all muscle and golden skin. And very, very naked. I swallowed. He noticed.

"Rowan?" Mild concern sounded just as good delivered in the same husky voice.

"I'm fine, really, I'm fine." This whole reassuring thing was becoming exhausting.

"Would it be okay if I called you?"

It took me the space of two heartbeats to realize that the planets and stars were in perfect alignment, and the gods were smiling down on me. This really was my lucky night. I didn't know if I was glowing; I felt as if I should be, but I was certain that if not for the couple of tons of steel propping me up, I definitely would have fallen down. My legs were that unsteady.

Gabriel leaned back, watching my face. I couldn't begin to imagine what it was he saw, but I tried to be cool and behave as if stunning men who dripped massive amounts of sex appeal asked to call me all the time. I know I failed miserably.

"Um, that would be nice," I said, hearing my phone number fall out of my mouth before I could change my mind.

He repeated the string of seven digits once, committing them to memory, and then leaned back toward me. Placing his hands very deliberately on Francine's powder blue roof, he caged me with his body. I reached up and put a palm tentatively on his chest. He was solid, all muscle, and suddenly the idea of seeing him stripped down became nerve-wracking, especially when I thought of how soft my own body was. I made a mental note: first thing Monday morning I was going to join a gym and tone up. Leaning his head a little farther forward, Gabriel brought his mouth to my ear. I found myself hypnotized by the hollow at the base of his throat.

"May I?" he whispered.

I raised my chin so I could look in his eyes. Big mistake. They were huge and luminous, framed by thick, dark blond lashes; I could see shades of green hidden in their depths. I wanted to jump off the edge and drown in them. "May you what?" I must have missed something.

"Kiss you."

I didn't say anything, I couldn't say anything, but I didn't need to. Gabriel took my silence as implied consent and leaned forward, his mouth on mine. And he knew how to kiss.

I suffered a pang of disappointment when he pulled away, wishing the moment had lasted longer, but when I opened my eyes I saw the look on his face change. It became hungry and wanting. He pulled me into his arms, and I molded myself against him, my arms going up around his shoulders, hard muscles flexing beneath my hands as the powerful strength of his torso pushed back against me.

And this time he really kissed me. It wasn't his eyes I should have been worrying about, it was his tongue. Velvet soft, it teased the corners of my mouth before gliding smoothly inside. Probing gently, he filled me with the promise of things I didn't even know I wanted. Keeping one hand cupped behind my head so I couldn't pull away, he dropped the other to my breast, caressing the fullness as he ran his thumb over my nipple. Even through the shirt and lacey cup of my bra, it burst into life, becoming erect under his guidance, begging for more. His hips surged forward, his spine clenched and his erection pressed itself into me. I felt, rather than heard, him groan in frustration at the barrier of clothing that stood between us.

"*Rowan!*" he murmured urgently against the corner of my mouth.

I didn't know my name could sound so erotic, and it felt good to know I wasn't the only one who wanted to get horizontal. And then the reality of what was happening, what I was hoping for, gave me a wake-up call. Images of my past failures in attempting sex rushed into my brain. Every muscle in my body froze, making Gabriel immediately pull back and stare down at me.

"Goddammit!" He ran it all together like one word. "I'm sorry, I should have known better. Too much, too soon, right?"

"No, you're just fine," I reassured him, my voice breathy.

While I was thrilled to know he felt the same attraction I did, I was also scared to death that this would turn into another dismal failure. And I couldn't bear to have that happen. Not with him.

Before this moment, sex had never been a subject that I spent a lot of time obsessing over. I'm pretty sure my prior unsuccessful attempts were the reason for my disinclination to review the matter. The prospect of sex leading me into foolish or reckless behavior had always been laughable, until now. It had been a while since I'd had anything more than a lukewarm interest in a guy, but what was running through me now was a ravenous force that threatened to overwhelm me. An oxyacetylene torch had fired up, and my body was responding to Gabriel with a need I didn't know I was capable of feeling.

Unfortunately, this newfound lust, no matter how compelling, also brought with it a major obstacle. My relative lack of experience with sex. Of course I know all the mechanics. I was probably one of the few kids who actually paid attention in sex ed class, and I have a more than passing knowledge of foreplay, but I've never actually closed the deal. As far as sex goes, I've only got my learner's permit.

My brain suddenly balked at the idea of telling this walking aphrodisiac the full extent of my inexperience. Even if gut instinct said he would have no problem finishing what he started. Broken zipper? Hah! He'd just rip the offending article of clothing off with his bare hands. Muscle cramps? Plow right through them! Premature ejaculation? Never gonna happen!

With Gabriel I had the feeling there would be no frustrated, unfulfilled promises. This was a man who could realize every sexual fantasy I had, and then give me some I hadn't even thought of. So would it be too terrible to let him figure out for himself that I was still technically a virgin? Provided of course we actually made it to the naked-in-bed scenario.

Abruptly he let go of me and stepped away. The expression on his face was searching. Without thinking, I looked at his erection pushing hard against the denim of his jeans, my brain as scrambled as my libido.

"I need to go home," I muttered awkwardly.

My body protested, screaming for more up-close and personal contact with his. Perhaps Gabriel was right. It was too much, too soon, and tempting as the back seat of his car might be, I didn't want to do something I would later regret. If I was going to lose my virginity, then it would happen in the proper surroundings. And preferably in a bed.

Gabriel stared at me, and I saw something in his face I hadn't noticed before. A sudden vulnerability. In a flash of intuition I realized that in spite of his good looks, or perhaps because of them, I wasn't the only one holding something back. Being beautiful can open up a lot of doors, but that doesn't necessarily mean they all should be opened. Some are best kept closed. And tightly locked.

Yeah sure, Gabriel was drop-dead gorgeous, a feast for the eyes in more ways than one, but there was more to him than that. There had to be. How often had anyone ever bothered to look beneath the surface to see what was behind the window dressing? What dreams did he have? What hopes? What fears? I wasn't the only one who needed some reassurance.

"You're gonna call me, right?"

Lifting his head, he gave me a look that was so sensual it almost took my breath away. "Yeah, I'm gonna call."

I nodded, not trusting my voice to speak. Another look like that and to hell with regrets, I'd let him take me across the hood of the Fairlane any way he wanted. I turned with my hand on the door of the POS. "Can I ask you something?"

He inclined his head. "Of course." He was, if nothing else, unfailingly polite.

"What *were* you doing out here last night?" I nodded toward the building at the other end of the lot, noticing it was completely dark now. "Really."

A slight hesitation, barely an intake of breath, but I noticed it. "I don't understand what you mean."

"Oh c'mon, let's not play games." This had been bugging me ever since I first saw him leaning against the bar. "You don't belong in a place like this, no matter how much you try to dress down, and I don't think any woman in her right mind would stand you up."

"Why not? You thought about doing it."

Ouch. "Yeah, but I didn't follow through, did I?"

He smiled at me, a heartbreaking lift of his lips. I had to stop myself from reaching up and putting my fingers against his mouth.

"I never said I was stood up." No, he hadn't. "I only said I was waiting for someone." He looked thoughtful. "So tell me, Rowan, where do I look like I belong?"

I could feel my cheeks heating up as I shrugged. "Oh, I don't know, some swanky nightclub in either L.A. or New York." And with someone who looks like Katja on your arm, I added silently.

"What is it you really want to ask me?"

It sounded as if I was questioning his motives, and he'd given me no reason to be mistrustful. "Just what I said. What were you doing out here last night?"

"I already told you . . . I was waiting for someone."

Are you sure you really want to know?

Yeah, I did. "For who?" I asked, my voice barely registering.

He smoothed the hair away from either side of my face with his palms, and then caught the curls at the nape of my neck and leaned into me. I thought he was going to kiss me as a way of avoiding the question, but he didn't. Instead, he tilted his head and began to nuzzle the side of my neck, caressing my skin with his tongue, and nipping lightly with his teeth. It was the most incredible turn-on, and the muscles in my legs trembled.

"For you, Rowan," he whispered, catching my earlobe between his teeth and tugging gently. "I've spent an eternity waiting for you."

If any other guy had said such a thing to me I would have laughed, but here's the thing. I never once doubted the sincerity of his words. And this time my heart did stop. I swear it actually missed a beat, stumbling before playing catch-up with the rhythm. Gabriel started to lift his head, but my hand pressing against the back of his neck stopped him, surprising both of us. In his eyes I could see a glimmer of hesitation. He was no more certain than I about what we were doing.

You know who I am.

The words echoed gently in my head. Did I? I wasn't a hundred percent sure, but I was more than willing to explore the possibilities.

I pulled his face closer. "Then what took you so long to find me?" I said, brushing my lips gently over his.

CHAPTER 10

I was dreaming. I knew this because, like most dreams, there were clues that told me I wasn't in my own reality. The bed was definitely one of them. A huge four-poster affair big enough to accommodate six people, with room to spare. Plus the sheets were a dead giveaway. One day I am going to buy a set of red satin sheets for no other reason than I can. But that day hasn't arrived. Yet.

Then, there was my clothing. Depending on the season, I sleep in either a T-shirt and shorts or a T-shirt and long flannel pants. None of which has a single strip of lace or romantic ruffle anywhere. In my dream, I was wrapped in a white lacy sheath, ruffled at the edges and held closed by a satin bow strategically tied between my breasts. And no panties. I can only assume the color choice was my subconscious's way of proclaiming my virginal state.

However, the biggest clue of all, the one that said without a doubt I was in fantasy la-la land, was the snow. Flakes the size of my hand were falling all around the California king-size bed. Not actually on the bed itself, you understand, but just beyond the perimeter. Oh, and I wasn't cold. I am sure some therapist who analyzes dreams would tell me the snow was another reference to you-know-what, but he'd be wrong. I think my mind conjured it up for no reason other than I like it. After all, I was born in winter, it is my favorite season, and I always regret living too far south for snow.

"Does it please you?"

The sound of Gabriel's voice was warm and melodic. I wasn't surprised he was in my dream. Why else would I be going to all this trouble if not for him? Or was it because of him? I was a little fuzzy on that point. Turning my head, I saw him standing just beyond the foot of the bed, and watched the snow as it fell on his head and shoulders. Holding out his arms, he gestured to a sky that I couldn't see, and I thought about his question, wondering whose dream this really was.

"How did you know?" I asked.

"How could I not? Your dreams, your hopes, your desires, you have shared them all with me. You don't remember . . . but you will."

His answer didn't surprise me, and it didn't alarm me either. In dreams, everything is perfectly reasonable, plausible, and acceptable. He lowered his arms and smiled at me, and any uncertainty on my part vanished.

Somewhere in the pit of my stomach, I could feel the heat evolving as it flared to life. Gabriel began unbuttoning his shirt, the same black silk he'd worn on our date. I felt my breath catch as each button that slipped free revealed more skin. He moved slowly, more slowly than I would have done, teasing me with glimpses of his body, and then slipped the shirt off his shoulders, at which point it dropped out of sight.

He was so indescribably beautiful.

The ambient light played with the sculpted musculature of his body, creating hollows and planes that teased my senses. I watched his abdomen tighten, the muscles rippling as he unbuckled his belt, unzipped his jeans, and let them join the shirt. His legs were strong, heavy thighs straining against the edge of black boxers. And that wasn't all that was straining. I decided to see if this really was my dream. If so, then Gabriel would follow my lead. I wanted the boxers to stay. For now. He smiled, hooking a thumb inside the waistband . . . and hesitated.

I could only imagine what my face looked like. It must have been flushed fire engine red, but I didn't care. Putting a knee on the bed and wearing a sinfully erotic smile, Gabriel came toward me. He moved with the grace of a predator, prowling across a red satin landscape. I thought of a leopard, all golden pelt and powerful rolling shoulders as he came closer. Leaning back on my elbows, I watched him stalk me, forgetting how to breathe.

Thump! Thump! Thump!

My heart was going ape shit inside my rib cage. Gabriel had one hand planted next to my hip, and with the other he reached forward and tugged on the satin bow between my breasts. The filmy sheath I was wearing dissolved, falling away from my body and turning me into my own image of carnal decadence. Naked, breathless, and lying on red satin sheets. Holding me fast with his eyes, Gabriel stroked his hand over my skin. Long elegant fingers sweeping across my flesh, raising goose bumps that had nothing to do with the falling snow. Moving back a little, he dipped his head, and I shivered with delight at the silky feel of his hair whispering over my thighs. It was exactly as I had imagined. And then his hand caught the curve of my waist, sliding around me, encouraging me to raise my hips.

Thump! Thump! Thump!

He brought himself closer, long white hair sliding across my stomach, up my rib cage, and over my breasts. With my palms against his chest, I felt movement as he inhaled, his breath ragged and deep while he struggled to maintain control. Nudging my legs apart with his knee, he settled himself against me, letting me feel him through the thin material of his boxers, and I gasped. God, he was big!

Anxiety took hold as the thought struck me that I might not be able to take him, my body unable to stretch far enough to sheath him, but then I realized I was worrying needlessly. My body wanted him, had wanted him from the first time I'd seen him, and it would not refuse him. I was on fire, and he was all I wanted.

He made a sound that came from deep in his throat as he slipped both arms around me and moved his mouth close to my ear.

"Rowan . . ."

Thump! Thump! Thump!

"Rowan . . ." Lips grazing over my jaw, pulling on my earlobe, trailing a sensuous path down my neck. "I don't think they're going away."

"Going . . . what?" My hair spilled over my face as I pushed him off me and sat up.

Thump! Thump! Thump!

It wasn't my heart doing a rhumba in my chest after all. Someone was knocking—no, make that pounding—on the frickin' door! But this was my dream and there wasn't a door. I hadn't asked for a door. Only a spectacular bed, Gabriel, and snow. Oodles and oodles of snow. And then I saw it. The white curtain of ice crystal flakes lifted just enough for me to see the outline of a door beyond the foot of the bed. The sight raised enough doubt to make me think this might not be my dream after all. Right on cue, the thumping sound came again. Louder and more insistent. I sighed. My lover was right; whoever it was did not intend to go away. I had no choice but to go answer the damn door.

Reaching for me, Gabriel pressed his lips against the curve of my neck, the tip of his tongue tracing small circles on my skin.

"Will you still be here when I return?" I asked, sliding free of his embrace.

"You think there is somewhere else I would wish to be?"

For some reason his answer did not reassure me, and sensing my uncertainty, Gabriel took my face in his hands and kissed me. It was soft and gentle and very thorough. And all the reassurance I needed.

Thump! Thump! Thump!

I went to answer the door.

Rolling over, I opened one eye and saw the clock on my night-stand. The red digital numbers glowed 2:27, and the position of the red dot told me it was afternoon and not the early hours of the morning. I opened the other eye and confirmed I was back in my own bed. Queen size, blue cotton sheets with a white daisy pattern, and no precipitation of any kind inside my bedroom. I pushed down the covers, relieved to find myself wearing shorts and an Indianapolis Colts T-shirt.

Thump! Thump! Thump!

Shit! Whoever was at my door had better be bringing me news of an impending global catastrophe or wanting to tell me I'd won the lottery. I wasn't about to forgive anything else.

Thump! Thump! Thump!

"All right, all right—I'm coming!"

Making my way downstairs, I figured it had to be Laycee. Who else would it be on a Sunday afternoon? And I decided that yanking me out of a fantastically hot erotic dream had earned her a verbal beat-down at the very least. Twisting the dead bolt, I yanked the door open, and my mouth formed a near perfect O of shocked surprise. I sure wasn't expecting this type of company.

The woman standing on my doorstep was a petite brunette wearing a pale lemon skirt and jacket ensemble trimmed with white piping. The swatch of lace modestly covering her cleavage told me these were Sunday church clothes. I found myself inexplicably drawn to the large sunflower earrings she wore, wondering if they hurt her ears. Her dark hair was pulled back in a low ponytail and tied off with a matching pale yellow scarf. She carried no purse, but the heels she was wearing were more suited to a strip joint than a house of worship. Definite CFMPs. Talk about sending mixed messages, but maybe I was reading too much into it. Yeah, the hooker heels were probably just because she was vertically challenged. She'd also been crying— a lot. It was hard not to notice. What had once been a carefully made-up face was now a train wreck of smudged mascara and eyeliner.

I stared at Suellen DuPree.

I'm not sure what she was expecting when I opened the door, but the tight, disapproving line that was her mouth said it wasn't me in my pajamas at two-thirty in the afternoon with a bad case of bed hair. I came fully awake in an instant.

"Fuck me."

The words accidentally fell from my lips and were loud enough for my visitor to hear as one thought ran screaming through my head. *She knows about Laycee and Jake.*

It was just a matter of time. In most small towns, secrets are community property, and ours was no exception. Someone had obviously decided it was time to check their own superior moral compass by bringing the sheriff's wife up to speed. And now Suellen was on my doorstep wanting me to confirm that what she'd been told about my best friend was true. Of course I intended to lie my ass off.

She stood there staring at me. It didn't take a genius to see her crying jag had been put on the back burner for the time being, and now she was madder than hell.

"Well, I think that just about covers it, Rowan Harper," she said in response to my slip of the tongue.

Her voice was amazingly calm, and for a moment I was fooled into thinking I was mistaken. That she was here for some other, completely innocuous reason and her husband's infidelity was still a secret. Regrettably her face hollered "fat chance."

It crossed my mind that I was being impolite by keeping her on the doorstep, and I was actually making a motion to invite her inside when my face exploded. Bells that would put Notre Dame Cathedral to shame went off inside my head, and I got a multicolored light show courtesy of the fist that connected with my right cheekbone. I had no idea the mother of two, a woman barely over five foot three—okay, five foot six in the hooker heels—could pack a punch that hard. My face hurt like hell.

"Did you think I wouldn't find out, you whoring bitch?" she exploded. The calm demeanor had been replaced by a shrillness that would have made any fishwife proud. "Did you think I'm so stupid you could flaunt it in my face and get away with it? Fucking my husband in your house in the middle of the day!"

My hand flew to my face, and my vision blurred as hot tears threatened to spill. Damn it! I sure as hell didn't want to give Suellen DuPree the satisfaction of knowing she'd made me cry. I took a step back into my hallway, horrified when it looked as if she was going to follow me. Alarmed, I held out a hand to stop her, but not before I got a glimpse of the bewilderment filling her own eyes. Guess hitting me hadn't been part of her original idea. It was a safe bet that she was more surprised than I at the result.

Taking advantage of her hesitation, I slammed the front door shut, which only enraged her further. She began pounding on the wood with her fist and screeching like a banshee. Thanks to my throbbing face, I only caught every third or fourth word, but judging from the workout she gave *slut, bitch,* and *whore,* I guessed her husband's affair was no longer a secret. And confirmed Suellen had a limited vocabulary.

In all fairness, I was partly to blame for her putting two and two together and coming up with five. Allowing Laycee and Jake to use my house for clandestine lunches might not have been such a good idea after all. I wouldn't put it past Suellen to have had Jake followed, but whoever was spying for her had done a half-assed job. Seeing Jake, or more likely his cruiser, parked in my driveway, they had assumed I was the "other woman," convincing Suellen her husband was sleeping with me. If my face didn't hurt so much, I would have laughed myself silly.

The sound of squealing tires told me my visitor had left. I sighed with relief and let the tears fall. My cheek was throbbing and my vision was going blurry, which meant my eye was starting to swell. Dropping my hand, I saw a smear of blood in my palm, which scared the crap out of me. I ran to the bathroom.

Suellen loved costume jewelry, especially big clunky cocktail rings, and she had been wearing one on the hand she'd punched me with. It had caught me in just the right spot, opening the skin below my eye. Thankfully, the cut didn't look too bad, and the bleeding had stopped by the time I got the first aid kit out from under the sink. My reflection in the bathroom mirror said a Band-Aid was only going to make me look worse. Some things Spongebob just wasn't meant for.

I rinsed a washcloth in some cold water and held it to my face. My eye hurt and the skin was already beginning to discolor, but the cool water felt good. Carefully I wiped the rest of my face. It seemed there was destined to be more than one train wreck in town this afternoon. I was going to have one hell of a shiner.

Coming back down to the kitchen, I got a package of corn from the freezer, and held it to my face while I rummaged in my purse for my cell phone. I needed to give Laycee a heads-up about her boyfriend's wife. She picked up right before it went to voice mail.

"Yeah?" From the way she mumbled, I hadn't been the only one still abed past noon.

"Did I wake you?"

"Yeah, but s'okay." She yawned and I heard the rustle of bed sheets. "Wassup, Ro?"

"You at home?"

"Nah."

"You alone?"

"Nope." She giggled.

I don't know why I ask questions I already know the answers to. If Laycee was at home she wouldn't still be in bed, and the fact that she was meant she wasn't alone. Confirmation came with the sound of a low murmur in the background, which for some reason really pissed me off. How dare she be getting her itch scratched when all I was guilty of was dreaming about the possibility, and then being thumped for my trouble. Would Suellen have hit me if it hadn't have been so obvious I'd just woken up? Taking a deep breath, I reined in my temper. This was not the time to go off the deep end.

"Laycee, when you and Jake meet at my house, where do you park your car?"

I could almost picture the perfectly penciled eyebrows being drawn together.

"Round the back, of course, why are you asking?"

"Uh-huh." I ignored her question. "And does Jake park out front?"

"Sometimes . . . why?"

"And I'm guessing he's usually in his police cruiser, right?"

"Yeah . . ." She drew the word out slowly, and I could hear the cogs starting to turn in her head. "But no one would see it from the road."

Ordinarily that would be true. My house sits far back from the road, so I've never had to be concerned about nosy neighbors, and the turnoff from the main road bends, obscuring the driveway for the casual observer. But follow the road a few more yards farther up, and you've got a clear view of my property. And if someone had a reason to be looking . . .

"Rowan, what's going on?" Laycee's voice was anxious, and I could tell she was fully awake now.

"You need to let Jake know the shit just hit the fan."

"Why? What happened?"

"Suellen knows he's been visiting my house in the middle of the day, only she thinks he's been coming to see me."

"But you're at work," Laycee pointed out, confused. Apparently she wasn't quite as awake as I'd thought.

"Gee, guess that must have slipped her mind." I didn't mean to sound sarcastic, but being smacked in the face will put a buzzkill on the best of moods.

"Wait a minute." The cogs in Laycee's head were turning a little faster now. "How do you know she thinks that?"

"Because she just paid me a visit and told me so."

The decibel-shattering screech on the other end of the phone was proof of how mortified Laycee was, and not for herself, but for me.

"Fuck! Fuck! Fuck!" she shrieked. "What the fuck happened?"

"I already told you. Suellen knows her husband's been fooling around, but she's under the impression that I'm the other woman." The corn was beginning to thaw and soften, and I moved the pack around to find a frozen spot. My face was starting to throb again, painfully.

"Oh crap—what did she say?"

The background murmuring was getting louder, and Laycee paused long enough to instruct Jake to "shut-the-hell-up-and-go-put-your-pants-on!" I had to love her for that.

"The details don't really matter," I said, getting her full attention again, "but she cursed up a storm right after she hit me."

"SHE DID WHAT!" I held the phone out in the hope of saving my eardrum.

Laycee was beyond upset now. She was absolutely livid. "What did she hit you with?"

"What d'you mean *what did she hit me with?* With her fist, of course." Did Laycee think the woman had come at me with a baseball bat?

"Don't you go anywhere, Rowan. I'll be there as soon as I can."

"Trust me, I don't plan on it."

The frozen corn squished in my hand, so I dropped it in the trash can. A Ziploc baggie filled with ice was a much better substitute, which was a good thing because I didn't have a whole lot in the way of frozen vegetables. I popped a couple of Tylenol and went to lie down on the living room sofa, holding the makeshift ice pack to my face. Even as upset as I was, I decided to cut Laycee some slack for ruining my dream. She had way bigger problems to deal with.

CHAPTER 11

I was dozing on the couch when she came barreling through the front door like a small platinum-blond tornado. I had considered trying to find my way back to my earlier scene of sensual bliss, but concluded it was probably better if I didn't. For one thing, you normally can't reenter the same dream without the aid of psychotropic drugs, and for another, I wasn't sure if my black eye would come with me. It could put a serious damper on any erotic rendezvous I was hoping to have with Gabriel.

The cushion shifted as she sat down, and I felt her fingers gently smoothing the hair from my forehead. I opened my eyes—well, my one good eye at least—and gave her a crooked smile.

"Hi." My voice sounded raspy.

"Hey there."

Whatever anger she'd been feeling, it had been purged from her system on the ride over, and I knew Jake would have taken the fallout. I wondered if he'd ever seen Laycee lose her temper before. I doubted it, since they were still in the honeymoon phase of their relationship. It was quite an experience, and I didn't feel in the least bit sorry for him.

"Let me see." She picked up the half-melted bag of ice. "Ouch! That looks like it hurts."

"You should feel it from my side," I muttered, trying to be funny.

Despite the calmness of her voice, I could tell she was upset—almost on the verge of tears upset, and Laycee hardly ever cried. She turned her head toward the open doorway.

"You better get your ass in here and come see this for yourself."

It had never crossed my mind that Jake would be with her, and I was appalled to see him standing in the open doorway. "You brought him with you?" I hissed, unable to disguise how pissed off I was. "What the hell for?"

"Because he's got more experience with black eyes than I do," Laycee said in an effort to calm me. "And for all I know, you need to go to the hospital and have a doctor look at it."

"Oh." I hadn't thought of that.

"Hey, Rowan."

Shuffling his feet in embarrassment, Jake fiddled with the set of keys he was holding, jangling them noisily. I've never seen a more hangdog expression on any man.

"Hey . . . Jake."

"I can't tell you how sorry I am you've been dragged into the middle of this."

Looking me in the eye, he sounded sincere, and I had no choice but to believe he truly was sorry.

"Could you do me a favor?" I asked, scooting up into a sitting position, acutely aware I was braless and my sleeping shorts were more than a little threadbare.

"Anything you want, Rowan."

"Could you just be Sheriff DuPree while we talk about this, and not Laycee's boyfriend?"

"Sure thing."

He gave me a hesitant smile, revealing his crooked front tooth and reminding me again why my best friend had fallen for him. For a man with such big hands, his touch was surprisingly gentle. I only winced once as he examined the delicate tissue around my eye and upper cheek.

"Well, nothing's broken from what I can tell, but you're gonna have one hell of a bruise. It might not be a bad idea to let a doc check it out." His expression turned decidedly guilty. "Just to be sure your vision's not impaired or anything."

"Did you know she would do this?" I said, unable to stop myself from asking. "I mean, when she found out?"

Jake looked at me, horrified. "I swear to God, Rowan, I had no idea Suellen was even capable of something like this." Glancing toward the open doorway, he searched for Laycee. The sound of the kitchen faucet running told me she was making coffee. "Do you want to press charges? It would be within your rights."

The question hadn't occurred to me, and I thought about it for a few moments. Weighing the pros and cons, I came to the conclusion it would be akin to throwing gasoline on a fire. When the truth of the matter came out, and I knew in a very short while it would, Jake's wife was going to have to face the fact she'd made a huge mistake.

The failure of their marriage was none of my business, but I'm smart enough to know it's never all one person's fault. There's usually blame on both sides. But the deciding factor for me was Suellen and Jake's kids. They were going to have enough to deal with, and I didn't want to add to the drama.

"No, Jake, I'm not going to press charges," I told him, getting up from the couch. "C'mon, you look like you need a cup of coffee more than I do."

A short while and one terse phone call later, Jake left to go and deal with his wife. It was unfortunate that what should have been kept a private matter was now going to become a public one. Gossip in a small town tends to take on a life of its own, and anyone still in the dark about the state of the sheriff's marriage was about to become enlightened. Maintaining any type of façade was impossible now. Laycee told him he needed to come clean about who he was sleeping with, and Jake agreed.

They both wanted to salvage my reputation, which was very decent of them, but as far as I could see the damage was already done. No matter the truth, there would always be those individuals who would go to their graves believing Jake had been sleeping with me. Hearing about Laycee would just make them think he'd been sleeping with both of us, probably at the same time. Woo-hoo, lucky guy! I had my doubts that telling Suellen she had made a mistake was the smartest thing to do right now.

"Give her a couple of days to get over the shock and humiliation of everyone knowing," I told Jake. "She's embarrassed and hurting, and if she thinks I'm to blame, then she won't be going after Laycee. Right now she's still so angry, if you push her she may do something really stupid."

I knew that neither Laycee nor Jake had ever anticipated this happening, and neither had I, or I would have urged them to be more careful using my house for their lunchtime trysts. Still, looking at the two of them as they sat holding hands, I couldn't help smiling, as much as I was able to. They looked so right together.

"I think one person getting punched out is more than enough entertainment for a Sunday afternoon, and besides"—I wasn't about to let Jake off that easily—"it has forced everything out into the open."

"I'm real sorry you got dragged into this, Rowan," he repeated.

"Yeah, well, what's done is done." I looked down at my faded T-shirt with its frayed hem. "At least your wife can't accuse you of buying me sexy lingerie."

On that note, and having been reassured that I was going to be okay, Jake had Laycee walk him to my front door. Low murmurs filled the hallway as they said good-bye, but she couldn't hide the deep line creasing her forehead as she came back into the kitchen.

"Are you two going to be all right?" I asked. "This isn't going to be a problem, is it?"

"Going to be?" She shook her head and gave me a rueful smile. "It already is." Sitting across from me at the table, she took my hand. "My best friend got punched out by my boyfriend's wife. It sounds like some god-awful talk show."

She was right, it did. "But it wasn't your fault, or Jake's, not really. No one could've guessed Suellen would do this."

"Yeah, who would've thunk it?" The worry line on Laycee's forehead deepened. "And it is my fault. I knew the risks that came with seeing Jake. You even told me yourself; it's just that, I swear, Rowan, never in a million years did I think anyone else would get hurt. And certainly not like this!"

Pulling her to her feet, I hugged her. She was beating herself up far more effectively than I ever could. "Laycee, do you think you love him?"

She nodded without any hesitation, and her face took on a glow that I'd never seen before. "I know it sounds like a cliché, but I've never felt this way about anyone."

I smiled and rubbed her arms. "Well, that's good to know because I'd be real pissed to think I got this for nothing more than just casual sex."

"Oh, Ro! I do love you, and you know I'd do anything for you."

"Yeah, I know, but topping this is gonna take something pretty big." I pretended to think. "I'll let you know if I ever need a kidney or something."

She tried grinning at me, but the most her mouth would give up was a sorry, half-assed watery smile that told me she was more upset about the incident than I realized. Still, I had the feeling she was worrying herself over things that hadn't happened. Yet.

"Don't worry about Jake," I told her gently as we both sat back down. "He's a big boy and can take care of himself, and he knows how to handle his wife."

The look she gave me was doubtful, and with no idea how long Jake would be gone, clock watching was only going to make things worse. Laycee needed a distraction, something else to focus her attention on, and I had just the thing.

"Wanna know where I was last night?" I asked nonchalantly.

Sniffing, she got up and yanked a piece of paper towel off the wall dispenser. She blew into it, noisily. "Sure."

"I had a date, thanks to you."

You would have thought I'd just announced I'd had sex on the counter at McDonald's. She was struck dumb for almost sixty seconds.

"You went on a *date*?"

God, it must have been longer than I'd thought. I nodded. "Uh-huh."

Her eyes narrowed as she slipped into the role of inquisitor. "With who? And I'm responsible how?"

I could almost hear the squeal of brakes on Laycee's mental highway as she made a U-turn. One minute I was looking at a weepy-eyed girl about to drown herself in a vat of remorse, and the next she was ready to gnaw her arm off with curiosity. The sudden shift in her attention was amazing, and not necessarily a bad thing under the circumstances.

"Well, you already know who," I teased. "After all, you set us up."

"I did?" Her eyes narrowed a little further, and I could tell she was taking a mental inventory of every guy we both knew. Unfortunately, she needed to focus on the ones we didn't know. I saw the lightbulb go on. "You don't mean the blond out at Rosie's?" She sounded dazed. And thrilled.

"None other."

"Oh. My. God. Rowan Marie Harper—I need details!"

"And I need to take a shower, so come talk to me in the bathroom."

I let her take full credit for my date with Gabriel, believing her "grab happiness" line had done the trick. Despite her announcement, Laycee didn't press me for the kind of details I feared she might. I put this down to her guilt about me getting popped. On the other hand, I've never been the gossipy type, but I was glad the shower curtain was between us. Laycee can always tell when I'm holding something back. I wasn't ready to tell her just how *into* Gabriel I wanted to be, given half the chance. Making my evening sound like it was no big deal was a lot easier with a closed shower curtain between us.

"Do you think Suellen was having Jake followed?" I asked a short while later as Laycee and I sat on the back porch swing drinking iced tea.

"'Yeah, I think so," she answered in a resigned voice.

"Well, if it's any consolation, they didn't know what they were doing."

"What makes you say that?"

Looking puzzled, Laycee took her spoon and began mashing her slice of lemon in the bottom of the glass. I stared at her. She's a sweet girl, heart of gold, but sometimes the obvious eludes her.

"Well, don't you think they would have got it right if they did? About who Jake's been sleeping with, I mean."

She flashed me a guilty look. "Oh yeah, I guess so."

Putting my arm around her shoulder, I gave her a squeeze. "It's okay, Laycee; everything will work out for the best."

I felt her relax. "You know, I'm kind of glad it's out in the open now," she said, "and I think Jake is, too. We both hated all the sneaking around. You wouldn't believe how exhausting it is having to be careful what you say and who you say it to."

"I can only imagine," I murmured, thinking this was another item for my checklist entitled "Reasons not to Date a Married Man."

"I mean, if we ran into each other in a public place I have to be 'Oh hi, Sheriff DuPree' and pretend that we just knew each other casually, when in reality I'd had his cock in my mouth the night before."

"Jeez, Laycee!" The visual image that popped into my head was one I could have done without. Especially as it had Jake in uniform.

"Sorry." She looked anything but.

I sipped my tea, hearing the ice cubes clinking pleasantly in the glass. I hate that most restaurants nowadays serve their cold beverages in acrylic glasses, even though I understand the reason for it. Ice cubes just don't sound the same.

"Why hadn't Jake told Suellen about you?" I wasn't meaning to criticize Jake's character, but I did hold him partially to blame for his wife's meltdown on my doorstep. "I mean they're already separated, so why not just admit he was seeing you?"

"I think he was just waiting for the right time."

I shifted closer so we were hip to hip and put my head on her shoulder. There really wasn't much else to say, except, "You wanna call for pizza?"

Emotional trauma affects people in one of two ways. It either kills the appetite stone dead or makes you feel like you could eat half a cow. Laycee and I both fell into the cow-eating category. My face was beginning to throb again, so while she called our order in, I headed for the bathroom and another round of Tylenol. I had just put two white caplets in my mouth when the familiar ring tone of my cell phone sounded.

"Want me to get that?" Laycee called out, her voice floating up from the bottom of the staircase.

The thought flashed through my mind that it was Suellen wanting to yell at me some more. Maybe this time she'd be yelling because I *hadn't* slept with her husband and wanted to know why not. Of course I wasn't exactly thinking straight; I mean, how would she have my number in the first place?

"Yeah, if you could," I called down.

I heard the ring tone stop, Laycee's voice, and then the sound of feet pounding on the staircase, which set off alarm bells. My Barbie doll look-alike friend doesn't run anywhere.

She was grinning from ear to ear. Okaaay, not Suellen then.

"Who?" I mouthed silently as I finished drying my hands.

She jabbed the phone at me, and I watched her grin get even wider, if that was possible. She could have given lessons to the Cheshire cat.

"Hello?" I said, cautiously.

"Rowan? Is everything all right?"

Liquid silk sounded just as good over my cell as it did in person. "Gabriel, I uh, yeah, um, sure, everything's fine." I shooed Laycee out of the bathroom.

"Have I called at a bad time?"

"Of course not." I padded across the hallway into my bedroom and checked the clock on my bedside table. Surely that wasn't right? It was past seven? "Why would you think it was a bad time?" I asked.

"Someone else answered your phone."

"Oh, that was just Laycee." I didn't mean to be dismissive, and I was grateful to know that if she'd heard me, Laycee wouldn't take offense. I sat down on the edge of my bed.

"Laycee? Your girlfriend from the bar?" The voice in my ear was all curiosity. "The blonde?"

"Yeah, that's right." He'd noticed her and I felt dismayed. Guys noticed Laycee all the time, only this time it bothered me. Really bothered me.

"Then I will apologize for disturbing you while you have company." His voice dropped to the low huskiness that made my toes curl and started a chain reaction up my legs. "Should I call back later?"

I don't know whether it was because I was looking at my bed and trying to imagine how much of it he would take up, or because the throb in my cheek spiked wickedly, having one last hurrah before the Tylenol kicked in, but I said the first thing that popped into my head. "I'd rather see you." And the next thing I knew all I had in my ear was dead air. "Hello? Gabriel, hello?"

Like a moron, I stared at the phone in my hand. The red and black oblong casing that housed the wonder of modern technology lay silently in my palm. Had my battery died? Nope, the icon said the charge was still strong. It took another second or two of confused thinking before it hit me that Gabriel was the one who had broken the connection, not me.

Great. Way to go Rowan. You don't need that backhoe after all.

Despite what had been said last night, I was the one coming on too strong. When he'd suggested that he call back, I was too dense to catch on. Instead, I went right ahead and put my foot in my mouth. It would be the icing on the cake if I'd managed to scare Gabriel off. When I screw up, I go all out.

Filled with a sudden desperate need to justify my pathetic, insecure behavior, I was tempted to call him back, to see if I couldn't repair the damage. But calling him back would probably make me seem anxious and needy.

A sudden wetness pricked behind my eyes. Great! Just what I needed, another crying jag. That would be twice today already. Taking a deep breath, I told myself to get a grip. If Laycee saw me all red-eyed and runny-nosed, it would only lead to more questions, something I really wasn't up to handling right now. Returning to the bathroom, I splashed cold water on my face. There was nothing I could do to fix things.

Back in the kitchen, I headed to the freezer for more ice, determined to avoid Laycee until I was sure my leaky eye issue had been resolved. I have never been so glad to have a black eye. I could use it as a cover for my misery, although I needn't have worried. Sitting at the kitchen table, Laycee had her phone pressed to her ear. From the way she was clutching a paper towel in her hand, she had leaky issues of her own to deal with. Her expression was worried, and her eyes shone just a little too brightly with the wrong kind of sparkle.

"Well, I guess that's it, then," she said, snapping her phone shut a few minutes later.

"What happened?" I got a bottle of water out the fridge, filled with a terrible sense of dread.

"Jake told his kids. No more pretending for appearance's sake."

She burst into tears, but I could tell they were tears of relief and happiness. It didn't last long, and, as she wiped away what was left of her makeup, she slumped down in the chair as if not quite able to believe it all.

"So?" I asked. "What happened?"

"Can you believe Suellen was burning the clothes he'd left behind in the backyard barbecue pit? The fire department got there the same time Jake did."

"Jesus Christ!" It was a day of revelations all around. "That woman is full of surprises."

"Isn't she just?" Laycee agreed with a nod. "Thankfully she hadn't gotten to his work clothes."

"D'you think she was going to burn them as well?"

"Oh yeah. Not a doubt in my mind."

I sipped my water. "So, what's Jake going to do now?"

"Pack up the rest of his stuff, then come get me so we can hit Walmart and replace whatever he needs." She reached for my hand and went all boa constrictor on it. "Is it really bad of me to say that even though I'm so sorry about your face, I'm also eternally grateful?"

I knew exactly what she meant. "No, it's not bad of you, it's fucking despicable, and I want you to know I will never, ever sacrifice my reputation for you again—I don't care how much you beg me to!"

I had her for a moment. She blinked owlishly at me in total shock before exploding in spontaneous laughter. I grinned, ridiculously pleased that everything was now out in the open. It hadn't happened the way I would have planned it, but now there was no going back, and Jake apparently intended to stay with Laycee. God knows, one of us deserved to be happy, and Laycee certainly was that one right now. Perhaps I needed to rethink my preconceptions about dating married men.

"What's wrong?" I asked, seeing the look on her face suddenly wavering between joy and misery.

It took a couple of swallows before she was able to get the words out. "It's a little overwhelming, that's all."

"Kinda makes it all real now, doesn't it?"

"Yeah. Guess I'd better get used to it." She nodded and blinked a couple of times, and wiped her nose with the paper towel she held in her hand. Her platinum ponytail bobbed as she got up and took our coffee mugs to the sink. "So," she said, turning around and giving me a bright smile. "Was that *him*?"

"Yeah," I mumbled, repositioning my bag of ice and hoping she would assume my face was the reason for not returning her smile.

"Well? What did he say?"

"He's gonna call me back later," I lied. I didn't really have it in me to say the potential love of my life had already bolted. Now was not the time.

CHAPTER 12

The pizza arrived in record time, delivered by Bobby Wilkins.

"My luck just keeps getting better by the minute," I muttered under my breath as I watched him come up the front porch steps.

The lanky, acne-riddled teenager didn't say a word, but stared at my face with the type of rude fascination only a seventeen-year-old boy can get away with. I guess he was trying to picture how a little thing like Suellen DuPree had been able to pop me this good. I was tempted to ask if he'd volunteered to do the delivery so he could give his mama a full report of my injuries. Roberta Wilkins was Suellen's closest friend, after all. The situation went from mildly annoying to downright hysterical a few moments later when Jake's cruiser came up the long driveway to my house. I didn't know whether to laugh or cry at the horrified expression on Bobby's face when he saw Jake walking up to my front door, carrying a case of beer.

"You get that taillight fixed yet, Bobby?" Jake asked conversationally as the teenager brushed past him on the steps.

"N-no sir, Sheriff, sir, I was planning to get it taken care of to-morrow." Like most boys his age, he seemed guilty of something.

"Well, make sure you do, son." Jake told him genially, as he watched him almost trip over his own feet in his haste to get back to his vehicle.

Holding up the beer, Jake said, "Figured if you were springing for dinner, I could at least provide liquid refreshment."

It's a well-known fact that, when faced with an unexpected and momentous upheaval in your life, pizza and beer is the best way to deal with it. And surrounding yourself with people who care. Jake DuPree handled his decisive, life-changing moment with grace, and a good dose of humor. I had the feeling Laycee was going to be a very welcome change for him.

"You have to look on the bright side," he said, helping himself to the last slice of pizza after Laycee and I both refused it. "I'll never have to wear another shirt with some pansy-assed logo on the pocket again." He shuddered dramatically. "She really did me a favor by pitching them in the barbecue pit."

"What sort of clothes do you like?" I asked, probing his fashion sense.

"Shorts and Hawaiian print shirts," Laycee interjected. "The louder the better!"

I cracked up, trying to picture Jake in a hot neon shirt with parrots printed on it. On a more serious note, he told me that his wife was aware of her mistake in confronting me.

"I didn't much care about her cussing and carrying on about me in front of the fire department, but when she started on you..." He pursed his lips and shook his head. "Well, it just wasn't right."

I resisted the temptation to ask if Suellen had gotten more creative now she'd had time to calm down a little. "Dragging Laycee's name through the mud isn't right either," I pointed out.

"Trust me, Rowan, I can handle it." Laycee kissed Jake on the cheek.

I was still worried. "You don't think she'll try giving Laycee some of this, do you?" I pointed at my eye.

"No, I told her I hadn't been able to convince you not to press charges—yet." He didn't look all that ashamed at the fib, and I felt a little better.

I began stacking our dirty plates in the sink. It's an odd quirk of mine, but I can't stand paper plates, even for pizza. Laycee helped me with the dishes, making some dumb comment that had me laughing aloud. I was telling her to stop it because it hurt my face to laugh when a knock came at the front door.

"Want me to get it?" Jake offered, noticing my hesitation. I didn't think his wife would be paying me another visit tonight, but who could tell? Hell hath no fury like a woman scorned and all that crap.

"Thanks, Jake, if you wouldn't mind." He went to the door and returned a few minutes later. Alone. "Who was it?" I asked, stacking the last plate to drain.

"Some guy with a bitchin' sweet ride."

The expression on his face was pure envy, laced with a good dose of unabashed adoration. Laycee frowned and I could tell she was wondering if her boyfriend had completely lost his mind.

"What kind of sweet ride?" she asked, drying her hands off on the dish towel and handing it to me.

"A Fairlane," Jake answered reverently. "A goddamn fifty-seven Ford Fairlane."

"Oh shit!" I threw the dish towel at him before running down the hall.

"Oh yeah, and he says he's your boyfriend!" Jake's voice called after me, the word "boyfriend" coinciding with my wrenching the door open.

Gabriel stood on the porch, tall and gorgeous, his long blond hair falling straight back like a white cape draped over his shoulders. I felt breathless and giddy just looking at him, and that oxyacetylene torch immediately burst into life. If this was going to happen every time I saw him, then flammable gas and I were going to have to come to some sort of an understanding.

"You're here!" I blurted out.

He looked slightly confused. "I'm sorry, I thought you—" I saw two deep grooves appear between his eyebrows. "What the hell happened to your face?"

His expression twisted into something fierce as he grabbed my hands and pulled me over the threshold so he could get a better look beneath the porch light. Taking hold of my chin, he gently turned my head, first one way and then the other, examining the bruising.

"Ah, yeah well, it was actually a big misunderstanding," I said, licking my lips, unnerved by the anger I could feel simmering just below the surface. "And you'll probably think it's really funny when I tell you."

"That's a black eye, Rowan, not a misunderstanding." He stared down at me, his blue eyes hard. "And I'd say it looks painful, not funny."

He stroked his fingers down the side of my face. It felt wonderfully soothing, but did little to disperse his anger. I guess he didn't like seeing women smacked around, which was a good thing. I just hadn't been prepared for the depth of his feeling. Lowering his head, he put his lips close to my ear.

"Is that why the sheriff is here?"

I shook my head. "Not exactly."

Straightening up, he flicked his eyes at Jake's cruiser before coming back to me. "So, who hit you? And don't try telling me you walked into a door." The vertical lines between his eyes had almost completely disappeared, but his mouth remained a grim line.

"Why? Can you tell the difference?"

He nodded, "Of course." The sound of Jake's deep, beefy laugh floated down the hall. Gabriel's eyes narrowed. "And if the sheriff isn't here in an official capacity, then why is he here?"

"Because it was his wife who hit me." I sighed. Better to get it out now.

"His wife?" Gabriel was incredulous, as if the idea of one woman belting another had never occurred to him. "Why would she—"

"She thinks I've been having an affair with her husband." I figured I might as well get the rest of it out as well.

His eyes opened a little wider, and I saw him look briefly over my shoulder as Laycee's girlish laugh now joined in with Jake's deep rumble.

"She got the wrong girl," he said quietly. Emphatically.

"Yeah." I nodded, thrilled at the absolute certainty in his voice. "I told you it was all a misunderstanding."

He cupped my chin with his fingers and leaned down, briefly touching my lips with his. A slight pressure, a whisper of warmth, and I felt wonderfully giddy.

"I'm sorry you were hurt." His long fingers gave one final stroke down the length of my jaw before he released his hold on my face.

"I feel better now you're here."

He must have heard something in my tone that I hadn't intended because he gave me a look I couldn't read. "Didn't you want me to come?"

"Of course," I said quickly, "but I wasn't sure you would. You hung up on me."

"Ah, that." Now he looked decidedly sheepish. "I didn't want you to change your mind."

"Oh . . . I see."

"Have you?"

"What?"

"Changed your mind?"

"No." My heart was pounding so hard in my chest, I almost forgot how to breathe. "Of course not."

"Good, I'm glad." He grinned, his perfect mouth lifting in a way that made me want to suck the life out of his lip. Either one would do; both would be better.

Turning, I stepped back into my house and was halfway down the hall when I realized he wasn't following. I looked back. He was still standing outside, his hands braced on either side of the doorframe. "What's wrong?"

"You haven't invited me in."

I thought for a moment he was kidding, but his face looked serious enough. Wasn't the fact that I hadn't closed the door in his face enough of an invitation? I suddenly thought of Aleksei, the big Russian, and figured that maybe this was similar to kissing the back of my hand. Some type of old-fashioned manners. It might even be a Norwegian custom. I shrugged and shook my head in amusement. "Okay, would you like to come in?"

"Yes, thank you. I would like that very much."

After he stepped over the threshold and I closed the door behind him, I couldn't help thinking the smile Gabriel wore was one of relief.

* * *

I have never known Laycee to be stunned into silence by a guy. It was quite a revelation to see her sitting next to Jake, holding on to his arm for dear life, completely tongue-tied. I made the introductions, handing Gabriel a beer along with my apologies that there was no pizza left.

"It's okay," he said, grinning. "I can eat later."

He looked at me as if there was only one item on the menu. Me. I turned away, hoping the flush I could feel stealing into my face wouldn't be noticeable. I picked up my glass of beer. Another weird quirk of mine. I hate drinking out of aluminum cans. As I raised the glass to my lips, a bell suddenly began clanging loudly in my head. One that had nothing to do with my injury. Narrowing my eyes a little, I looked at Gabriel and asked, "How did you know where I live?"

"When you dropped your purse, your driver's license fell out, and I glanced at it. I have a good memory. GPS did the rest."

"Uh-huh." I'll give him credit; he looked me right in the eye and didn't flinch. Had my license fallen out? I couldn't remember. Perhaps it had.

"You're lucky; not many people find the turnoff." Jake's voice sounded all cop. And a hundred percent suspicious.

"Well, I did miss it the first time," Gabriel admitted, not at all put out by Jake's tone. Carefully, he put his beer can down on the counter behind him and folded his arms across his chest. His biceps flexed, and I watched, fascinated, as his sleeves stretched with the movement. "So, which one of you is going to tell me how Rowan got a black eye?"

The question was addressed directly to Jake and only to Jake. I saw a look pass between them, some mysterious posturing having to do with one alpha male acknowledging the presence of another, and agreeing not to piss on already claimed territory. Yeah right, whatever.

Ten minutes later the incident was told, only it wasn't as funny as I had thought it might be. Both Jake and I did the telling, me for the actual confrontation, and Jake for what happened with his wife afterward. Gabriel seemed pleased that the sheriff had "manned up" and told his wife about her mistake, and his reasons for doing so. But I still voiced my opinion that he could have waited. Taking hold of my hands, Gabriel pulled me to my feet, dropping one hand to my waist as he pulled me closer. Since he had told Jake he was my boyfriend, it was nice to see he didn't have a problem with open displays of affection.

"I know your concern is for Laycee," he said, staring down at me, "but what would people think if they saw me coming out of your house, and believed the sheriff was your paramour?"

Paramour? He actually used the word *paramour*. Good job I read romance novels or else I wouldn't have a clue what he was talking about.

"Well, I think it's unlikely anyone would see—"

"Someone saw the sheriff at your house," Gabriel said, effectively squashing my protest.

Yeah, except the more I thought about it, the more I wondered just how much discretion Jake had used for his daytime trysts at my house with Laycee. It was safe to assume he hadn't been off duty for all of them, and a police cruiser is hardly inconspicuous. Perhaps he didn't care if anyone saw him turning into my driveway.

"Besides, Rowan, you don't need your reputation to be trashed more than it already is," Laycee said, finding her voice.

Gee, thanks.

Placing a finger beneath my chin, Gabriel tilted my head up, frowning as he glanced at my face in the glow from the overhead ceiling light. "Do you have a better light?"

Why? Was he going to interrogate me?

"The bathroom upstairs."

It was the most unflattering light in the house, which made it perfectly unforgiving when I was putting on makeup.

"Show me."

Gabriel held out his hand. I gave him mine, feeling his strong fingers clasp my palm against his.

"Excuse us," I said. He might have forgotten the other two people sitting at my kitchen table, but I hadn't. Leading the way, I stifled a chuckle at the dumbfounded look on Laycee's face.

Upstairs, Gabriel was all business as he examined the contents of my first aid kit. I leaned back against the sink while he gently dabbed a wet cotton ball against my face. His mouth became a serious line as he assessed the swelling beneath the harsh glare of the bathroom light. I placed a hand on his hip.

"I like it better like this," he murmured, taking both my hands and wrapping my arms firmly around his waist, moving himself closer to me.

The heat of his body pulsed through his T-shirt, and this close, he smelled good. Really good. His cologne or soap or whatever was a subtle fragrance of spicy undertones and a splash of something that I couldn't quite put my finger on but seemed annoyingly familiar. I stopped trying to guess what it was. It would come to me eventually.

Dropping the cotton ball in the trash can, he examined my face with his fingers. His touch was much lighter than Jake's had been, barely whispering across my skin as his fingers probed the area around my eye. I don't know why, but it didn't surprise me that, like Jake, he also had some experience with black eyes. Finally he let out a small, satisfied grunt.

"Your cheekbone isn't broken, and your eye will be okay once the swelling has gone down, most likely in a day or two. I don't think you need a doctor, but you should probably rest tomorrow and not go to work."

"Okay."

His physical proximity made it hard to disagree. I looked up, my good eye involuntarily squinting. Turning, Gabriel reached out and flipped the switch on the wall, plunging us into darkness. His hands grazed my hips as he grasped the edge of the sink, imprisoning me inside his arms.

"Is there anything you want? Anything I can do for you?"

He brushed his lips against my ear, and the sweet warmth of his breath fanned my neck. His voice was a sensuous caress that sent shivers down my spine, and the image I'd had of him earlier, the one where he was taking up so much space on my bed, suddenly jumped into the forefront of my mind. Talk about lousy timing. This so wasn't the right moment to explore that option. I made myself push it away.

"You don't happen to have a pint of rum raisin ice cream in your pocket, do you?" Humor is a great deflective tactic, I have learned, and it seemed the best approach in such a small space in the dark when I wasn't sure if I should accept what was being offered.

"Regretfully, no." He laughed softly, moving his head so his lips could brush mine a little more firmly than they had before. "And I think your friends are about to leave." He stepped back, releasing me from his embrace. "I can leave also, if you wish it," he said as Laycee's voice called out my name.

Catching my hand, Gabriel lightly entwined his fingers with mine. I suddenly felt like a teenager with her first big crush. I shook my head. "No, I'd like you to stay," I told him, seeing his teeth gleam brightly in the dark as he brushed his lips over my knuckles.

"I'd like that," he whispered huskily.

When we reached the bottom of the stairs, Laycee let me know by her expression that my face was as red as I imagined. Her eyes flickered over my shoulder as the reason for my blush silently followed me.

"Jake and I are gonna head out," she said with a grin.

"Okay, well, you take care," I said, giving her a big hug.

"You gonna be okay?" She didn't need to look at Gabriel; I knew what she meant.

"Everything's fine," I assured her.

Together we watched Jake and Gabriel do the guy head-nod thing. That weird communication gesture that is only understood by those born with a cock. I have no idea why guys do that instead of actually verbalizing, but it seems to work for them. I put it down to one of those men-are-from-Mars things. Out of the corner of my eye, I saw Gabriel go into the living room as I steered Laycee toward the front door. We hugged again, and I was surprised when Jake also put his arms around me as he said good-bye, taking care not to make contact with my face.

"I'm gonna call you first thing in the morning," Laycee yelled, standing next to her car. "And I'll drop by as soon as I get off work— you're not going in, are you?"

I shook my head. "No, I think I'll spend the day on the couch, watching soaps and eating ice cream," I called back. "But thanks for reminding me. I need to call Angela and let her know."

"Okay, well, 'bye." Batting her eyes, she beat the flat of her hand dramatically on her chest. It was her seal of approval regarding Gabriel. I hoped he wasn't watching out the window.

CHAPTER 13

Once my father realized my love affair with literature was serious, he turned one entire wall in our living room into a floor-to-ceiling bookcase. It was one of the best presents he ever gave me. Leaning against the open doorway, I watched Gabriel slowly perusing my library. His long fingers danced over the spines, his mouth critiquing my taste with either a smile or a grimace. One title in particular seemed to warrant further inspection, and he pulled it from the shelf, turning it over to read the jacket cover before wrinkling his nose in apparent distaste. I made a mental note to check it out later.

"Want another beer?" I asked.

"Please." I felt a warm glow, watching his hair sweep over his shoulder as he turned toward me. Women would kill for hair like that. I would kill for hair like that. "Do you mind?" He gestured to the books.

I shook my head. "Not at all, help yourself." I paused. "I need to make a phone call." I jerked my thumb over my shoulder. "About missing work tomorrow."

"Good."

I scuttled back into the kitchen, taking a few minutes to rehearse what I was going to say to Angela before dialing her number. Thankfully I didn't have to provide a detailed explanation, but she did sound a little dubious when I said I'd run into a door. I could tell she didn't quite believe me, but she finished up by telling me to take care and let her know if things got worse.

I went back into the living room carrying a glass of beer in each hand, and suddenly feeling nervous about being alone with a man. It was stupid because I'd not only invited Gabriel in the first place but told him he could stay when Jake and Laycee left. Still, the last time I'd been alone with a man in my house, it had been the state trooper who came to tell me my father had been in a head-on collision with a drunk driver. The drunk had walked away, my dad hadn't been as lucky. I hadn't been alone with another guy since. Not even any of my dating disasters had warranted an invite, which should have told me something right there.

I wasn't nervous in a bad way. It felt scary-good watching Gabriel move about the room, touching my things. Only now that it was just the two of us, I realized I didn't know very much about him. I had no intention of revisiting the whole deranged serial killer routine again, because I'd put that one firmly to bed. I mean, if he wanted to hurt me, he'd had plenty of chances to do so already. No, my anxiety came from being worried that I would say or do something brainless, and I really didn't want to screw this up.

"Did you find anything you like?" I asked, handing him his glass and taking a seat on the couch as he made his way down to the far end of the bookcase.

"You have a lot of books."

Talk about stating the obvious. Maybe I wasn't the only one who was nervous.

"Well, it's silly not to take advantage of my employee discount."

"I suppose." His fingers tiptoed across the shelves, flirting lightly with the occupants. "You seem to like romance," he said, and I could hear the smile in his voice even with his back to me.

"One of the perils of being single. Besides, don't you know the men in those books are always so much better than reality, even when they're bad?"

"As long as you remember they're only fiction."

"Of course." It seemed an odd remark to make.

"Who is your favorite romantic hero?" He raised a quizzical eyebrow as he turned to look at me.

That was too easy. "I have two actually, Mr. Darcy and Mr. Rochester."

"Ah, Miss Austen and Miss Brontë. Why doesn't that surprise me?"

I opened my mouth to comment, but he turned his back and continued to study the shelf in front of him. "I am, however, surprised you would like this." Retracing his steps, he pulled out the volume that had made him wrinkle his nose, holding it up for me to see. I looked at the familiar cover of pale hands cupping a red apple.

"Well, it is still hugely popular, and I do have a wicked soft spot for vampires."

"Really?" The eyebrow arched again, in surprise this time. Glancing down at the book in his hand, he shook his head and looked back at me. "Even so, I just don't see you reading this."

"Okay, I confess. It was given to me as a gift." I laughed a little self-consciously. "And I must admit I had to constantly remind myself the heroine was only seventeen."

"Why was that?"

"Because I kept wanting to slap her."

Gabriel grinned as he replaced the book in the open slot on the shelf. He looked thoughtful for a minute and then leaned down and pulled out another book. "What about this one?"

I tilted my head to check out the novel in his hand, although I really didn't need to. I pretty much knew what was on each section of shelving, and I knew by heart the titles of everything housed on that particular shelf.

"Ah, well, if I was ever going to be tempted into immortality, then those are definitely my type of vampires."

"Tempted into immortality, eh?" A sly look glinted in his eyes. "So you like vampires with questionable ethics and near-insatiable appetites?"

I'd never quite thought of it like that, and the look in his eye said I could please myself about which appetites were insatiable. I wondered how he knew what the book was about. My job has given me some pretty accurate insight about the type of fiction a person reads. Just a few questions and I can tell if you're a secret Regency romancer or a murder and mayhem addict. I definitely wouldn't have guessed Gabriel to be a J. R. Ward fan.

"If you're gonna put it like that, then yeah, I guess so," I answered, "but there's really no comparison. It's two completely different takes on the same subject."

He was staring at me, the sly look replaced by something unfathomable that made me feel uncomfortably warm, though I had no idea why, because my personal blowtorch was behaving itself. I tipped the glass to my mouth and took a long swallow as Gabriel slid the book back into its open slot. He walked over to the entertainment center, looking at the framed photographs clustered on top.

"Your father?" he asked, picking one of them up.

I put down my glass and joined him, taking the frame out of his hand. Out of all the frozen moments captured on film, he'd picked my favorite. Dressed in summer clothes, we were sitting on the back porch steps holding hands and laughing at each other. It was one of those wonderful, unscripted moments when we were both caught totally off guard. I have no idea who took the picture, but it was a real Kodak moment.

"Yes." I put the frame back, standing it among the others.

"How old were you when that was taken?"

"Oh, I don't know for sure. Probably eight or nine."

"I don't see any pictures of your mother," Gabriel observed, scanning the collection a second time.

"That's because there aren't any."

I resumed my seat on the couch, sitting cross-legged and clasping my ankles with one hand. I tilted the glass to my mouth, letting the cold beer slide effortlessly down my throat. Gabriel joined me, sitting at the other end and taking up a lot of room. I didn't mind.

"I'm sorry," he apologized. "Did she die?"

Our conversation in the diner had touched briefly on the lack of family we shared, but not in any detail, so his question wasn't unreasonable or unexpected. I rested my glass on the inside of my knee. The icy bottom made me flinch a little, but it felt good. I don't normally talk about my mother, not even to Laycee, but for some reason I wasn't at all hesitant discussing her now.

"I don't know if she's dead or not. She went to Louisiana to visit family when I was three years old . . . and never came back."

"Perhaps she couldn't," Gabriel said quietly.

"She was my mother." I could hear the reproach in my voice, criticizing her even now, after all these years. Some things you just don't get over. "I would never abandon my child like that, not without a single word."

"Maybe she had an accident, or lost her memory."

I shook my head. "She didn't. After my dad was killed, I found a box where he kept letters that she'd written. She wrote one a month for the first two years after she left us, and then she just stopped."

"Did she say why she left you?" he asked.

I swigged my beer. This was really personal stuff, and I had no idea why I felt compelled to open up and talk about it right now. I'd never told anyone about finding the letters, or the pain that twisted inside me because my dad had kept them from me. I had questions, questions only he could answer. Like any parent, I'm sure he had a good reason for his secrecy, but that didn't make it any easier to deal with.

"No, she didn't," I replied. "All she did was ask our forgiveness and say she had to leave." I glanced at him. "I thought we were her family, but I guess I was mistaken."

The bitterness souring my words said I'd been carrying this particular piece of baggage around with me for some time, and I couldn't believe I was bringing it up now. Maybe it was time. After all, sometimes it's easier to unburden yourself to a stranger than to a friend.

"Anyway," I continued, "I sent a letter to the return address on the last letter she'd sent, telling her about Dad's passing. I never got a reply." I shrugged and forced myself to smile, not wanting my mood to taint the atmosphere any more than it already had. "It's all ancient history now."

"And your father never remarried?" Gabriel queried softly.

"Difficult to do when you're still technically someone's husband."

"But after a certain amount of time he could have divorced her, couldn't he? Her abandonment would have given him grounds."

I nodded, tucking a stray curl behind my ear. I had no idea why he was so curious. I just accepted that, for some inexplicable reason, he was. "Yes, he could've, but I don't think he ever loved anybody else quite as much. Not even me."

"I'm sorry, forgive me. Having no family of my own, I tend to pry. It's a bad habit, and sometimes I forget how rude I can be."

"It's okay." I gave him a forgiving smile. "Like I said, it happened a long time ago, and I really don't remember much about it."

"And how long has it been since your father passed?"

"Almost six years now."

I felt the unexpected hot sting of tears behind my eyes. It happened sometimes when I thought of my dad, especially if I hadn't prepared myself. This was turning into a real sob Sunday for me.

"Excuse me." I got up from the couch and headed for the kitchen.

I was getting all mopey and weepy, and the timing couldn't have been worse. Standing at the sink, I forced myself to breathe, trying to cap the emotional wellspring that threatened to erupt. As if it had happened only yesterday, it all came back to me.

I'd been sitting at the table, flipping through a magazine and enjoying leftover peach cobbler when the knock on the door came. Opening it, I found myself staring at a state trooper. His gray uniform, looking crisp and very sharp, was bisected at the waist by the heavy black utility belt he wore. I remember seeing the holster on his hip and thinking his gun didn't look real. He asked to come in and followed me to the kitchen, where he told me my dad was never coming home again. The fluorescent ceiling light caught his shoes. They were black and very shiny, the kind that just needed to be wiped clean with a soft cloth, which was a good thing because his words made me vomit chunks of undigested peach all over his feet.

God bless him, he never said a word, and I've never eaten peach cobbler since.

"Rowan?"

I didn't realize Gabriel had followed me until I felt his hands on my shoulders. It seemed the most natural thing in the world to lean into him and let go. "I'm sorry," I apologized when my crying fit was over. "I have no idea where that came from."

"Don't ever apologize for what you feel, not to me."

Pushing my hair back, he put his hand in his pocket and pulled out a handkerchief.

A real, honest-to-goodness linen handkerchief, which shouldn't have surprised me. So many things about him were different from regular guys. I took it reluctantly. It seemed too nice to use. Sighing, he pulled it from my fingers, opened it up, and dabbed gently at the moisture that had managed to leak from between my swollen lids.

"Better?" he asked after a few moments of silence. I nodded. "Good." He sounded satisfied.

I tried to smile, but the throbbing in my cheek suddenly kicked in, and I winced.

"You look like you need some more ice on that."

Refilling my Ziploc bag with fresh ice cubes, I held it to my face as Gabriel moved in front of me.

"It's okay, I've got you," he said, and in one smooth movement he was holding me in his arms. I thought he meant to carry me back to the living room, but instead he climbed the stairs.

Nudging my bedroom door open with his hip, he put me down on the bed. I could feel the blowtorch cranking up, and despite the huge sexual attraction, this was not what I hoped the first time would be like. Not with him, not with anybody. After being punched in the face, then the embarrassing weepy episode, I was so not ready to tell Gabriel that he was dealing with a virgin who desperately wanted to jump his bones. Anxiety formed a huge knot in my chest, making me sit up.

"No, stay where you are," Gabriel said sternly.

I lay back down, watching nervously as he slipped off his boots before walking around the foot of my bed. My anxiety level cranked up several notches.

"Lie on your side," he said gently.

I turned over so I was facing him.

"Your *other* side," he chuckled softly.

I rolled over and felt the mattress dip as he lay down next to me, answering my earlier question. He took up a lot of bed. I found the arm he tucked around me a comfortable weight. He pulled me back until I was flush against his chest with my butt nestled in his groin. I almost jumped at the feel of his erection, which was impressive, but he gave no outward sign of wanting to do anything about it. Apparently, it was enough for me to know he was aroused. Talk about making a girl feel special when she wasn't feeling so good.

Propping himself up on one elbow, Gabriel carefully held the bag of ice to my face. The knot in my chest started to expand, and part of me hoped it might crowd out my lungs and stop me from breathing. If I suffocated, I wouldn't have to tell him anything.

"It's okay, Rowan," he whispered, the warmth of his breath fanning my neck and cheek. "Nothing is going to happen between us tonight, no matter how much we both desire it. I'll stay only until you fall asleep."

The knot loosened and started to unravel as the anxiety and tension flowed out of me. He would never know how grateful I was to hear he had no expectations, grateful that he was content to hold me, grateful that I might still get a chance to wear my Victoria's Secret underwear for him.

He lifted the bag of ice. "Your bruising is quite nasty," he said, running a feather-light finger across my cheek. "May I give you something to help with the swelling?"

"Sure," I mumbled, as exhaustion began to steal over me. At this point, I would have agreed to let him perform open-heart surgery with a Swiss army knife if he had asked. The mattress shifted slightly, and the scent of something coppery filled my nose, making it wrinkle in distaste. It lasted only a moment, and was replaced by the most glorious scent of pine and juniper berries, both of which reminded me of . . . "Christmas," I sighed.

His fingers smoothed across my bruised cheek and over my eyelid, wiping the wonderfully scented cool salve across the skin. His hair tickled my neck as he bent close.

"What?" he whispered in my ear.

"Smells nice . . . like Christmas . . . ," I murmured.

I didn't need to see his face to know he was smiling.

"I dreamed about you, Rowan."

"Me too." My voice was barely more than a sigh, and I was fighting a losing battle with sleep.

"Do you know how beautiful you look on red satin sheets?"

I felt the warm pressure of his mouth on mine, his tongue tasting my lips, before I slid headfirst into la-la land.

CHAPTER 14

It wasn't my alarm clock that woke me up the next morning, nor the sun streaming in through the open drapes. I couldn't even blame it on the raucous cawing of the crows that were holding an avian board meeting in the tree outside my window. No, what pulled me up from the depths of dreamless sleep to wakefulness was a fragrance. Light and sweet, the perfume drifted across me, teasing me awake as I drew in one sleepy breath after another. The scent was both familiar and maddeningly elusive. Something I already knew but was unable to place. Wanting more of it, I opened my eyes.

I was alone.

It would have been too good to be true to wake up still wrapped in Gabriel's arms, but I had hoped that was exactly what would happen, even though he had told me he would only stay until I fell asleep.

Trying to reconcile hurt feelings is easier said than done. Relationships are complicated, and I had no idea if what had happened between Gabriel and me could even be construed as the beginnings of one. He was a man who overwhelmed me on so many levels, but lying in his arms last night I had felt something hidden beneath the sexual attraction. A different type of desire, one with a flavor all its own. And it was something I wanted to taste. Sadly, my pool of experience regarding men and dating was a puddle in the Sahara.

The wonderful perfume teased my nose again, making me roll over. I quickly discovered the source. On the pillow next to me, resting in the indentation made by his head, was a single, heady spray of golden-yellow freesias.

I don't need a boyfriend to know that most men are pretty clueless when making romantic gestures with flowers. Most of them, if they can actually connect with their inner Romeo, will opt for either red or pink roses as their flower of choice—a safe bet even if they have no idea that each color has its own, significant meaning. But I've never been a rose girl. Instead I adore freesias, finding the vibrant colors and rich fragrance intoxicating.

Picking up the spray, I marveled at the deep yellow blossoms attached to the spring-green stem, wondering at the coincidence of finding this particular flower on my pillow. I must have let something slip when I was running off at the mouth over coffee, or perhaps I had told him in my sleep. As a little girl, I talked in my sleep, or so my dad had always said. Maybe I still did.

I pushed back the covers and got out of bed, holding the delicate stem in my fingers. For a few moments I simply stood and looked at the messed-up bed, picturing Gabriel repositioning himself as I moved in my sleep. I'd never slept with a man before. Okay, I still hadn't if we're going to get all technical, but this was as close as I had come as an adult. I have always held the belief that sleeping with someone, the actual act of resting in an unconscious state, is a far more intimate experience than sex.

Asleep, you are completely defenseless, and it is an act of supreme trust to put yourself in the care of another when you are that vulnerable. That being the case, I figured I'd just had the most intimate night of my life, and it didn't matter if Gabriel left a few minutes after I fell asleep . . . or before I woke up. I had felt safe with him.

After discovering that I didn't own anything that could pass for a vase, I filled an iced-tea glass with water and put the blossoms on my bedside table. Then I went to check my face in the bathroom mirror. The bruising was worse. Deep indigo and eggplant now stained my eye in a glorious rampage of color, but the swelling was significantly reduced, and I was surprised to find I could open my eyelid without too much difficulty.

The white of my eye was bloodshot, which was to be expected, and I began tearing up beneath the light, so I resolved not to overuse it. Running the tips of my fingers gently over my cheek, I was surprised to find it was barely sore, and the throbbing ache was gone. A faint line was all that showed where Suellen's eighteen-wheeler of a cocktail ring had split my skin. It wouldn't even scar. Whatever ointment Gabriel had used had done the trick.

True to her word, Laycee called me a little while later. Like me, she had also taken the day off, but she was using her free time to go apartment hunting. At some point while they were buying socks and undershirts, she and Jake had decided to move in together. I wasn't terribly surprised and invited the happy couple to supper.

Despite my promise, I didn't lie on the couch watching soaps or eating ice cream. Guilt over missing work was doing a number on me, and as reading was out of the question, I decided to punish myself by cleaning. I vacuumed, wiped down my bathroom, mopped the kitchen floor, and then vigorously swept both front and back porches outside. By the time I started to make dinner, I felt tired, but it was a good kind of tired.

Except it didn't stop me from wondering why Gabriel hadn't called. Or stop me from checking my phone every fifteen minutes to see if I'd missed a call. I told myself that he was probably sleeping. He did mention being a night owl due to his somewhat ambiguous "this and that" occupation. I scolded myself for being needy.

Laycee showed up, alone, a little after six. Jake was still at work so wouldn't be able to make it, but she sniffed appreciatively as I took garlic bread out of the oven. Over spaghetti we discussed the strange turns of events both our lives had taken in the past forty-eight hours. Jake's indiscretion was now all over town, although there was still some confusion about the identity of the "other woman." I'd already accepted that some folks would never believe it hadn't been me, no matter how much Jake and Laycee denied it.

"How's he doing today?" I asked, curious to know if there was any fallout at the Sheriff's Department.

"Good," Laycee answered. "I don't know what Suellen was expecting, but it's not like he's going to quit being sheriff or anything. Thank God he got reelected last year." She stacked our plates in the sink. "He's good at his job and being with me doesn't automatically mean scandal and ruin. I doubt anyone is going to demand his resignation because his marriage is over. We're not in the Middle Ages anymore."

"And thank God for that, or else you'd probably have been put in the pillory so Bobby Wilkins and his mother could throw rotten fruit at you—or something worse!"

"Well, the overall impression I get is most people are being very understanding and wonder why he didn't leave Suellen years ago." She filled the sink with hot water. "Of course, the kids are the ones who will be hurt the most."

"Do you think she'll try to turn them against him?" I knew from television and the media how vindictive some wives could be in a divorce, especially if it turned ugly.

Laycee shrugged her shoulders. "Who knows? But Jake has already set up a separate account for their support."

"He's a good man, Laycee."

She segued right into it. "So, speaking of good men, tell me about Eye Candy." She gave the bottle of dish detergent a generous squirt before sudsing up the water.

I hesitated. "What do you want to know?"

"Is he just as gorgeous without his clothes on?"

"Laycee!" I pretended to be shocked.

"Okay, I know, I know—you're not the slut I am!" She rinsed a plate and set it in the drainer. "But tell me there's a possibility you might be able to answer that question in the not too distant future?"

"I don't know," I said, watching her pout. "But I hope so!"

She shrieked with delight. "So what time did he leave last night?"

"I have no idea." I told her about Gabriel staying until I fell asleep, but omitted my crying episode. Laycee would want to know why, and I didn't want to hurt her feelings by admitting I had opened up to Gabriel about my mom.

"Wow, that's some serious shit," she commented when I was done. Her face took on a thoughtful expression. "He must be really into you, Ro."

"I hope so, I just . . ."

"What?" She pounced on my trailing sentence.

"I don't know. I get the oddest feeling that we've met before, even though I know it can't possibly be true."

"Weird," she agreed. "I mean, you would remember someone who looked like that, right?"

I nodded my head. "Totally."

"Maybe it was in a different lifetime." She began humming the theme to the old *Twilight Zone* series while rinsing the last plate. After removing the stopper from the sink, and laughing as the water drained away with a loud gurgle, Laycee dried her hands and checked her phone. "Oops, sorry to eat and run, but I better hustle if I want to get Jake out to those apartments tonight."

She kissed me on my good cheek before picking up the Tupperware containing leftover spaghetti. I walked her out to her car.

"Are you going to work tomorrow?"

I nodded. "Yeah, I think I'll be fine."

"I'll pick you up in the morning."

I snorted in exasperation. "I said I'd be fine."

"Yeah, but I don't think you're up to driving yet." The finality in her voice said it was a waste of time arguing. "By the way"—she rolled down her window—"whether you've met him before or not, he's still very easy on the eye."

"Holy shit, girl, just lookit your face!" Angela's screech was an almost comical mix of horror and concern. "Walked into a door, my ass!"

This was the second person telling me any excuse about a run-in with a door would not be believed. How did other women get away with it? Maybe that was the point, they didn't. More than forty-eight hours later, the deep purple bruising around my eye had lightened considerably, and I could see faint tinges of avocado in the mix. I couldn't wait until the whole sorry mess turned a vivid chartreuse green.

"I'm okay, Angela, really. It looks worse than it is."

She shook her head and gently grasped my chin, making loud tutting noises as she inspected my face. "Seriously, Rowan, you give me the bastard's name and I'll bitch-slap him into the middle of next week for you!"

I stared at her, more than a little shocked at her willingness to inflict physical harm on my behalf. Judging from the degree of her vehemence, I figured she must have had a run-in with her ex, and the outcome had not been good.

"Are you fighting with Ronnie again?" I asked.

"Bastard!" The hissing noise she made confirmed my suspicion. "He's parading a new girlfriend around."

Figuring she needed it more than I did, I gave her a sympathetic hug. I have long suspected that Angela remains hopelessly in love with her ex; unfortunately it's not mutual.

"Well, if you must know, it wasn't a man that hit me," I said, releasing her from my embrace. "It was a woman."

"Oh," she paused, and I saw a flicker of dismay in her eyes. "Want me to kick her ass instead?" What happened to getting bitched-slapped into next week?

"No, Angela, it's just fine, really. If there's any ass-kicking to be done, then I'm more than capable of doing it myself."

"Really?" She dubiously raised an eyebrow. "So what happened?"

In the three years we have worked together, I have learned practically every detail of Angela's life. From the crush she had on her math teacher in ninth grade to the racy little number she wore on her wedding night. But she knows next to nothing about me. Of course, until now there hasn't been much to tell her, only she doesn't know that. She takes it for granted that I'm a private person.

"Sorry," she said quickly, "I understand if you don't want to talk about it."

"No, it's okay." I squeezed her hand, touched by her concern. "It was a case of mistaken identity. Someone thought I was sleeping with her husband."

I didn't know whether to be relieved or insulted by the smile she was trying her hardest to suppress.

"*You?*" Angela snorted, getting a major kick out of imagining me sleeping with someone else's husband. "This was a stranger, right? Someone you've never met before."

I shook my head, remembering how Suellen looked when she was crowned homecoming queen. "No, she's kind of known me all my life."

"No, girlfriend, she most certainly does not know you." Waving a forefinger in my face, Angela continued. "If she did, she would know that you sleeping with her husband—with any woman's husband—is off-the-wall ludicrous."

It was quite a shock to realize my co-worker thought I was such a paragon of virtue, and a little annoying, too.

"Do you think I'll scare off customers?" I asked, wanting to steer her concern in another direction. Tilting her head to one side and peering at me over the top of her glasses, Angela considered my question thoughtfully. "I have an eye patch," I told her.

Pulling it out of my purse, I put it on. The guffaw escaped before Angela had a chance to cover it with her hand. The patch had originally been part of a sexy pirate outfit, and I couldn't be sure, but I don't think the red sequins did me any favors.

"I think that will scare people more than your shiner," Angela said, struggling to keep a straight face. She took a deep breath and regained her composure somewhat. "We got our shipment of new romance novels yesterday. How about you set up the window display instead?"

I accepted gratefully, relieved that my interaction with the general public would be kept to a minimum. As I walked away I could hear the sound of Angela trying to smother more laughter.

I spent all morning arranging and rearranging copies of a dozen or so new titles until, perfectionist that I am, I was finally satisfied with the way our window display looked. After lunch I turned my hand to the children's section and was on my knees between *The Very Hungry Caterpillar* and *Where the Wild Things Are* when Angela yelled my name. I figured she'd messed up the cash register—not an uncommon occurrence when she was angry with Ronnie. I gasped when I saw the floral display on the front counter. The vase was huge, holding long-stemmed red roses that were complemented by an impressive amount of baby's breath.

"Rowan Harper?" The delivery guy held out a clipboard while he gawked openly at my face. "Um, sign on line fifteen, please."

I signed where he pointed, feeling slightly irritated by the open-mouthed gawking; his sympathetic smile told me he'd drawn the wrong conclusion. Obviously he thought the flowers were an apology. A really big apology.

Angela stared at the bouquet for a long moment before turning her head toward me. "How big of a mistake did you say it was?"

I felt myself squirming. Not much gets past Angela, and even I didn't think Suellen would send me flowers as an apology, certainly not red roses. Angela busied herself looking over the flowers.

"Ah, here you go," she said, handing me a small white envelope. I opened it, pulled out the card and read *No freesias. Hope you will forgive the substitution. G*

Happiness exploded inside me like a cork from a champagne bottle.

Angela arched an eyebrow waiting for me to reveal the identity of my admirer, and good-naturedly resumed her fussing when she realized I wanted to keep it a secret. "Well, you need to tell whoever it was they got ripped off," she declared.

How did a florist rip you off unless you specifically asked for, say, roses and they sent daisies instead? I didn't see how that could apply here.

"Aren't long-stemmed roses sold by the dozen?" Angela asked, giving me a look.

Never having received them before, long-stemmed or otherwise, I had no idea. But in all the novels I've read, when the hero sent something other than a single bloom, it was usually a dozen. Or a roomful. "Um, yes, I think so."

"Aha!" she yelled triumphantly. "Well, there's only eleven in here." Her hand reached for the phone. "Want me to call the florist and have that cheeky kid come back? I wouldn't be surprised if he didn't lift one to give to his girlfriend. Bet he thought you'd never notice."

I hadn't, and truth be told, I didn't really care. "It's okay," I said, smiling at Angela, "Perhaps his girlfriend needs it more than I do."

As beautiful as my flowers were, they took up far too much space at the front counter, but they would be the perfect finishing touch to my window display. An hour later my cell phone jingled. It was Gabriel.

"Thank you so much for the flowers," I gushed, before he had a chance to say anything.

"You're very welcome." He seemed surprised by my enthusiasm. "So, may I take you to dinner tonight?"

I hesitated. In such a public setting, people would no doubt stare at my eye and, like the flower guy, assume I was in an abusive relationship. They might also think Gabriel was my abuser, and I certainly didn't want that.

Picking up on my indecisiveness, he jumped in. "I want to take you somewhere very quiet, very discreet, where the food is excellent."

I melted. "Okay then, but just so you know, I do have an eye patch I can wear."

Unlike Angela, his laugh was one I wanted to hear. Rich and warm, it rumbled in my ear. "I can't wait to see it. I'll pick you up at closing time."

You know who I am.

The words jolted through me as I snapped my cell phone closed. I was beginning to get annoyed at this nagging little declaration that seemed to pop into my head every time I was around Gabriel. If this was some sort of puzzle that I needed to solve, then goddammit, I needed more clues.

CHAPTER 15

Angela was fit to be tied. A phone call from a frantic teenaged babysitter meant she was going to have to leave before giving Gabriel the once-over. Sadly, he couldn't compete with a puking six-year old who'd also had gum cut out of his hair by an older brother. It was difficult to tell which incident was the more upsetting.

I'd just finished balancing the cash drawer when the sound of tapping on the door made me look up. The sun had already dipped below the horizon, and it was that beautiful time of day when it's no longer daylight, but still not quite night. Gabriel cast a huge shadow standing in the doorway. I unlocked the door and let him in.

"I just need to get my purse," I said, relocking the door behind him.

He caught my arm and pulled me close, leaning down so he could kiss me. His mouth felt wonderful on mine, and I relished the feel of his tongue as it sweetly invaded my mouth. My internal flame ignited. Naturally.

"I need to ... go get ..." I was dangerously close to babbling when he finally let me go.

He was wearing a smug smile and looking way too pleased with himself, and I felt his eyes following me as I made my way to the far end of the store. I slipped the day's receipts into the night safe in my boss's office and retrieved my purse from the small cubbyhole that Angela and I jokingly refer to as the Employees' Lounge.

Coming back to the front of the store, I noticed he was taking in my morning's effort in the front window. The flowers he had sent were prominently displayed.

"Please don't be cross," I said hurriedly, "I'm sure it was just a mistake by the florist." I didn't know if my order being short a flower would matter or not, but I really didn't want the delivery guy getting in trouble.

Gabriel looked at me as if I was speaking in Swahili. "What was a mistake?"

"The roses. I know I'm missing one."

He looked back at the deep red blooms. Thanks to the heat from the window lights they would be completely open by morning, making the display even more impressive. Gabriel shook his head, the curtain of white hair a moving invitation to run my fingers through it.

"No, you're not," he assured me.

"But aren't there . . . ? Shouldn't there be twelve?" I suddenly felt ridiculous questioning him.

"Yes, but I told the florist to take one out."

"Oh." *Why would he do that?* "Why would you do that?"

He reached for my hand, entwining our fingers before gently brushing the fingers of his other hand across my bruised cheek.

"Don't you know?" he asked in a seductive whisper that made my legs feel weak. I shook my head. "You're the twelfth rose, Rowan."

Oh boy, wait till Angela heard that.

I looked for Francine but didn't see her anywhere. Instead, parked right out front, in the no parking zone, was a bright red sports job that sat very low to the ground. It looked foreign—and fast. With his hand at the small of my back, Gabriel guided me toward it.

"I thought this might be a little cozier," he said with a grin. "Now I won't have to reach so far to hold your hand."

I snorted. With the length of his arms, he'd be able to reach right out the passenger-side window without too much difficulty.

"What is it?" I only asked so I could slot the information away to use as pizza conversation with Jake. I recalled how covetous he'd been of the Fairlane.

"A Ferrari." His grin expanded as if he knew I was just as clueless about this car as I had been about his other one. "Want me to write it down for you?" he teased.

"No, I think I can remember that." Even I'd heard of Ferrari. I walked around the car as if I was in a showroom and interested in buying it. I nearly kicked the tires but thought better of it. Each one probably cost more than my monthly paycheck. "And what do you call this one?"

"Francesca."

Why did I even bother to ask?

"Well, she's very flashy and looks fast," I commented.

"Oh, she is."

He was grinning so wide it was a wonder his face didn't split in two. He opened the door for me, and I almost fell into the seat, slightly unnerved by the realization of how close my ass was going to be to the road. That thought, however, was put on hold as I waited to see how Gabriel was going to pretzel himself into the driver's side. He pulled it off with ease and grace—damn him! Heading out of the parking lot, he turned right, and for a minute I thought we were going to the same all-night diner as before. I could just imagine the look on the waitress's face if she saw my black eye. But we passed the diner, turning down a series of small side streets before stopping in front of a restaurant.

Gabriel quickly came around and helped me out, which was a good thing because, left to my own devices, I would have resorted to crawling on my hands and knees before trying to stand up. As it was, I almost tripped over my feet trying to get my legs out.

"I have no idea how they do it," I muttered, tightening my grip around his steadying hand.

"How who does what?"

"How any woman gets out of something like this without falling flat on her face!"

"It just takes practice."

I made a rude noise that drew a laugh. It was nice knowing I could do that. The building before us reminded me of a Swiss chalet with its leaded windowpanes and window boxes overflowing with colorful summer flowers. And the interior looked just as I imagined it should. Thick black beams broke up a whitewashed ceiling and walls, while heavy, rustic furniture completed the picture. I could hear soft music playing, something with a lot of violins. If asked for my first impression, words such as *discreet* and *intimate* would have figured prominently in my description.

However, minor anxiety came in the form of a stunning blonde with an elegant up-do, wearing a black, figure-hugging sheath that she had to have been poured into. And the smile on her face was more than the usual hostess greeting. Clearly she knew Gabriel, and jealousy flared in my chest as she took his hands in hers and kissed him on each cheek. Good Lord, what was wrong with me? First I'd felt resentful when Gabriel had noticed Laycee, and now I was getting all green-eyed over the hostess.

I pulled myself together as introductions were made, and immediately felt ashamed of my insecurity. Like everyone else I seemed destined to meet these days, the hostess had an accent and only one name, Anasztaizia, but the greeting bestowed on me was warm and filled with genuine friendliness. Yanking the leash on my jealousy, I made it go sit in the corner. Anasztaizia seated us in an alcove off the main dining area, and I was grateful for the privacy.

"I'm going to ask you to forgive me," Gabriel said, reaching across the snowy white tablecloth for my hand, "but I'm going to talk with Anasztaizia in her own language for a few moments."

This was the second time he'd apologized for having a conversation that didn't include me. Idly, I wondered if his talk with the soldier had been in Russian. Any further speculation on my part was disrupted by an unfamiliar, but still lovely, cadence that now flowed around me. Unable to understand what was being said, I occupied myself with my napkin. Unfolding and smoothing the heavy square of linen, I laid it across my lap while surreptitiously checking our hostess's body language as she exchanged words with Gabriel.

Not understanding a language isn't necessarily a hindrance when emotions and gestures can speak volumes by themselves. I might not have known what was being asked, but I could tell when Gabriel was posing a question. And every response from Anasztaizia was accentuated by a lift of her shoulders, a hand gesture, or a display of emotion on her lovely, expressive face.

The sudden change in her tone, however, caught my attention. Whatever Gabriel was saying seemed to annoy her, and she was doing her best not to be rude. I think she decided to redirect their conversation because I suddenly felt the weight of their eyes on me. I stared back at both of them as I heard Gabriel's voice soften. He was apologizing to the stunning blonde for something. Tilting her head, Anasztaizia gave him the kind of smile that said all was forgiven.

"What was that all about?" I whispered across the table at Gabriel as soon as we were alone. "The last part I mean."

"Anasztaizia said she was would kick my ass if I didn't take better care of you."

Regardless of the amused twinkle in his eyes, this was exactly what I'd been fearful of. People jumping to the wrong conclusion. "Didn't you tell her it wasn't your fault? That you weren't involved?"

"It won't make any difference." He shrugged and made a dismissive gesture with his hand. "Anasztaizia is Magyar."

"Magyar? What's that?"

"The Magyars are the true people of Hungary."

The significance was lost on me, and I was about to ask him what he meant when our waiter appeared with the menus. He was a short, barrel-chested man with a shiny bald head and the most amazing moustache obscuring the lower part of his face. Handing each of us a menu, he gave a stiff little bow and left. I'd never seen such a thing before and was momentarily stunned.

I looked across the table at Gabriel, but he had opened his menu and seemed to be studying the bill of fare intently. With a sigh I opened my own menu and was filled with dismay. Not only did it seem I'd been given a small book to read, but I didn't understand half of what was written, and most of the choices were completely unfamiliar.

"Have you ever tried Hungarian food?" Lowering his menu, Gabriel looked at me from beneath his thick lashes. He was flirting. I shook my head, not wanting to admit the most adventurous I'd ever gotten was Taco Bell. "Then may I order for you?"

"Thank you, yes," I answered, relieved.

Our waiter returned with a bottle of red wine and, after uncorking it, poured a small amount into Gabriel's glass. I watched in fascination as Gabriel swirled, sniffed, and then tasted the wine. Raising an eyebrow, he nodded in approval, much to the waiter's delight. It was just like something out of the movies. My own glass was generously filled. I'm not a big wine drinker, so my first sip was a cautious one, taken only to be polite. I changed my mind in a hurry. The wine, whatever it was, was fabulous.

"It tastes the way velvet feels," I murmured, and the look that came back across the table to me made my internal flame jump up and lick my breastbone.

I have no idea what we ate, although I did recognize the word goulash. Our waiter, delighted to discover Gabriel spoke not only Hungarian but his own particular dialect, insisted on speaking it for the rest of the meal. Gabriel tried to apologize for this perceived rudeness, but I didn't mind. I was too busy allowing myself to be seduced by the rhythm of our server's words, We finished our meal with some sort of pastry torte crowned with a big dollop of heavy cream, and a dark, aromatic coffee that I knew would not be on any Starbuck's menu.

Pleasantly full, I leaned back in my seat, enjoying the light buzz I had going. The wine was absolutely delicious, and I'd had more than a token glass. I think. It was difficult to tell just how much I'd actually drunk as my glass was never allowed to empty. Gabriel did not seem at all affected, and I know his glass was replenished as often as mine had been. It suddenly occurred to me that perhaps we ought to call a cab.

"It's all right," he said, reading my mind or, more likely, the expression on my face. "I'm perfectly okay to drive." He tapped the wine glass with his fingernail, making a wonderful ringing sound. "Alcohol doesn't affect me in quite the same way as you, and besides, I've been drinking this stuff for a very long time."

"It's wonderful. Can I buy a bottle?"

He shook his head, making a long strand of blond hair shimmer against the dark silk of his shirt. "It's a house wine that Anasztaizia's family makes themselves. Sadly, they don't market it."

I was disappointed. "Oh, pity."

He leaned forward. "You know, I'm still waiting to see your eye patch."

I giggled. I had completely forgotten all about it because my eye had felt so good, but now I pulled the sequined patch out of my purse with a flourish. "It's the least I can do after such a magnificent meal," I told him before slipping it over my head and covering my eye. "So, what do you think?"

Putting both elbows on the table, Gabriel rested his chin on the back of his hands and stared at me. His face became a study in solemn contemplation that began to worry me, until I saw the slight twitch at the corners of his mouth.

"Yeah, that's what I thought," I said, slipping the patch off and returning it to my purse. It wasn't designed for any practical purpose, and truth be told, I felt better without it.

"Perhaps if I saw it in relation to the rest of the costume," Gabriel said, "I'd get a better perspective."

"Unfortunately it was donated to Goodwill a long time ago."

"Pity," he murmured, "I think you would be a most charming pirate."

He grinned, I laughed, and we finished our coffee. As we were leaving, the lovely Anasztaizia surprised me with a bottle of the wonderful house wine.

"Make sure you bring her back many times," she ordered Gabriel. I didn't feel at all jealous when she kissed him this time.

"I've never been given a bottle of wine to take home," Gabriel said once we were outside. He sounded slightly petulant.

"Well, be nice to me, and I might be persuaded to share," I told him as he helped me fall into his Ferrari.

On the ride home, I got a taste of just how fast Gabriel's sporty foreign car could go. It was the most exhilarating, white-knuckle rush, and I held on for dear life as trees and fields blurred past us. I should have been terrified, but I wasn't, although I was pretty sure I managed to leave the imprint of my fingers in the soft leather of Francesca's passenger seat. And I was grateful not to see any cops, but how they would have caught us in order to issue the appropriate citation was beyond me.

My fingers were shaking as I fumbled the key in the front door. I wanted to believe it was because the adrenaline was still pumping from the ride home or the effect of the wine buzzing through me. But either would have been a lie. I was responding to Gabriel, who was standing close enough that I could feel his breath on the nape of my neck.

The door key fell out of my hand as he spun me around, covering my mouth with his. This was what I wanted, what I'd been waiting for. His tongue swept over my lips, and I greedily encouraged him to tease and taste me. I had never been kissed like this before, and I surrendered myself to him without hesitation.

As I fisted my hands in his hair, the silky heaviness slipped through my fingers, making me giddy as I imagined how it would feel sliding across my naked skin. Moving his mouth, Gabriel trailed kisses along my jaw and up to my temple before latching onto my earlobe. Applying just enough pressure with his teeth, he made it sting. It was surprisingly erotic, and I couldn't get enough of him.

My hands, moving of their own accord, dropped to his waist and began tugging at his shirt, pulling it out of his pants. Slipping beneath the material, I stroked his velvet skin and was rewarded with a low, sexy rumble that seemed to catch in the back of his throat.

"Rowan . . ."

My name became a pulsating sexual vibration, and reclaiming my mouth, he swept me into the middle of a storm, a raging tempest that demanded my complete surrender. As if I had any other choice.

Gabriel was hot and hungry. Pressing myself against him, I felt the hard length of him pushing back, and hoped he would let me come up for air before I passed out. But I didn't really care if he didn't.

He pulled his face away, his breath a ragged gasp, and there was a strange, almost iridescent glow in his eyes. I told myself it was nothing more than the moonlight reflecting off his contacts.

"Are you all right?" I asked, my own voice a barely recognizable breathy whisper.

He kissed me again, slowly this time, allowing me to savor the taste and feel of his tongue as it gently caressed mine. He nudged my legs apart with his knee, and I willingly opened myself to him. Settling himself inside the space I offered, he pushed his hips against me, and I gasped.

Gabriel pulled my blouse free with a lot more skill and grace than I had used on his shirt. The small pearl buttons slipped loose seemingly of their own volition, eager to welcome his hands inside the opening. I shuddered at the feel of his fingers brushing over my skin.

One hand moved to the small of my back, while the other remained at the opening of my blouse. Leaning into me, he pressed his mouth against my throat, the tip of his tongue tracing little circles along my collarbone as his clever fingers opened the front clasp of my bra. Pushing aside the satin cup, he caressed my breast, making me moan and glide toward the edge of something potentially explosive. He rolled my nipple between his thumb and forefinger, and I jerked my hips forward.

Pulling his head back, Gabriel moved his hand away, making me groan in frustration as he released my breast. Running the pad of his thumb over my bottom lip, he swiped the moist fullness. I looked up at him. His eyes were incredible, framed by lashes so thick and long, they almost touched his cheek. I could feel myself drowning as he stared at me, my body irresistibly drawn to him, knowing he was everything I could ever want in a lover.

All the heavy petting I had indulged in prior to this moment was suddenly reduced to a series of crude fumblings perpetrated by man-boys unable to give me the ultimate satisfaction. I had always made them carry the blame for their inability to take my virginity, but now I knew that wasn't fair. Or true. I carried more than my share of blame. Some instinct, hidden deep within me, had always risen just long enough to ensure any serious attempt at sex would fail. Somehow I'd known that the man I was destined for was holding me in his arms right now. Gabriel was every sex act I had ever imagined, rolled up with others I was more than wanting to try.

With trembling fingers, I undid the buttons of his shirt. Pushing aside the fabric, I placed my hands on his chest, able to feel strength and power moving beneath my hands. I devoured him with my eyes, taking in everything from his thick neck to his flawless pecs to the tight ridge of his abdominal muscles. Shamelessly I flicked out my tongue and traced a path up his sternum, tasting the maleness of him as it exploded on my tongue and relishing the growl of pleasure he uttered at my touch.

Grabbing a handful of curls, he pulled my head back. I could see the hunger in his face, a hunger so intense and raw I'd be lying if I said it didn't scare me. A lot. But, scared or not, every muscle in my body was ready to propel me forward into uncharted territory. I was fully prepared to drag him up the stairs to my bedroom, even though I had serious doubts my legs would make it that far. I might just have to lose my virginity in the hallway or on the kitchen floor if I could make it that far. Either would have been a good second choice.

Burying his face in the curve of my neck, Gabriel growled again, and I felt him drag in a great rush of air as he inhaled the scent of my skin. My own personal blowtorch kicked into forest fire range. I reached for him, my hands ravenous to feel his smooth flesh against my own.

And then, with an abruptness that shocked me . . . he let me go.

Suddenly Gabriel was staring at me from the other side of the porch. The look on his face was pure agony, almost as if he thought he was doing something wrong, only he didn't want to stop. If he was concerned about our being spied on by neighbors, I wanted to reassure him that there were none close enough to see my house, much less what happened on my doorstep. But before I could say anything, he raised his hand to his mouth, his long fingers shuddering against his lips.

Bewildered and confused, I had no idea what was happening. He wanted me. I knew it. I could feel it. And it wasn't just his cock. Every fiber in his body, every muscle, every sinew was screaming for me. I could hear it.

You know who I am.

Well, if I didn't, I certainly wanted to! God knows, I was more than willing and had no intention of refusing him. So what had just happened? What had I done wrong? The only thing I could think was that somehow Gabriel had guessed the meager extent of my sexual experience. In my eagerness I'd revealed exactly where it stopped, disappointing him. A wave of despair unfurled itself, threatening to wash through me at the unfairness of it all.

"No." Gabriel's voice cut through my mental ranting like a knife. "That's not it." He ran his hands through his hair before his eyes latched onto mine, glowing weirdly. "I know you haven't given yourself to a man. That only makes me want you more . . . not less."

I gave a little gasp as one hand clutched the edges of my blouse and the other flew to my mouth. I *knew* I hadn't voiced that particular concern aloud, but perhaps I shouldn't have been surprised that he could tell what I'd been thinking. He was able to read me far too easily, especially when I didn't take enough care in guarding my emotions. I took a few breaths and regained part of my equilibrium.

"At least now I don't have to worry about how I'm going to tell you," I said, feeling an unexpected lift.

Gabriel flashed me a startled look. "You were worried about telling me you were pure?"

My mouth went suddenly dry, forcing me to nod my head as the heat of embarrassment burned my cheeks. I didn't think *pure* was an accurate description of my current state. To my mind it implied someone who'd never been touched in any way, and that wasn't me. But at least now Gabriel knew.

Yeah, he knew all right, and that made him want me *more*? How could that be when he was backing away from me? It didn't make any sense. Something had changed in the past ten seconds. I just didn't know what.

"If I were to ask, would you give yourself to me? Asking no questions, demanding no promises?" He sounded weirdly disconnected. His voice held none of the passion he'd just shown me. I wasn't sure if he was expecting an actual answer, but I gave him one anyway. The "yes" that managed to slip out of me was thick with need and desire, and I saw the blue of his eyes deepen, becoming almost black, making his gaze unfathomable. "I have to leave you."

His words hung in the air. The abruptness of them punched their way past my rib cage and squeezed my heart with an icy grip. I heard quite clearly what he'd said, as well as what he hadn't. Gabriel hadn't said "I have to leave" as in it's time for me to go. He'd said "I have to leave *you*." Huge difference. Significant, life-altering difference.

No matter how much you tell yourself you know it's coming, you're never actually prepared for the pain of being rejected. There's a moment right after the words have been spoken, before realization hits you, when everything seems to stand still. A crystal-clear hiccup in time when you tell yourself denial is still possible. The words *can* be yanked back, you *can* pretend you never heard them. Only that moment is a lie. No matter how it's phrased, or how carefully it's wrapped, the words can never be taken back.

"Why?" I blurted, hating myself for my weakness in needing to ask. What possible difference could it make?

"Because this is all wrong." Turning his head, Gabriel looked away.

"What is?" I asked, as the horrible sinking feeling churning in my stomach began to grow.

"I can't ask this of you . . . not now."

I had absolutely no idea what he was talking about, but I recognized the desperate, almost angry tone in his voice. He sounded as if he were fighting a battle, one that he was losing, and could do nothing to even the odds. I might be inexperienced in a lot of ways, but I knew where this was heading, and I didn't want to give up without my own fight.

"Tell me you don't want me."

"Ah, Rowan, please . . . don't."

"Tell me." I clenched my fists at my sides. "Say the words, and then you can walk away. I won't try to stop you."

"Rowan, you don't understand—"

"—then make me understand!"

Tears pricked the backs of my eyes. He was talking nonsense and I could feel him slipping away. Turning my back, I quickly rebuttoned my blouse before leaning my hands against the doorframe, in need of some sort of support.

"If you knew the truth about me, you would not want me, not like this." The resolve in his voice was firm, telling me his mind was already set on its course. This was it, the big kiss-off. I could feel my insides ripping apart. How was it possible to hurt so much when I had known him only a few days? Was I already in love with him? Was it even possible? "Rowan, look at me."

"You'd better go. I don't want to keep you from anything."

For a moment I thought someone else was speaking because I didn't recognize the colorless monotone of my own voice. But I understood the reason for it. Self-preservation had kicked in. No way in hell was I going to let him see me distraught, hiccupping words, heartsore, and barely coherent.

"Rowan, please—it mustn't be like this, not between us."

Like what? Gabriel's voice had changed also. It was charged with frustration, and he sounded even angrier than before. I was shocked. How dare he?! What gave him the right to be angry with *me*? Suddenly my vision blurred and I blinked my eyes. Shit! This was not the time to start crying. I felt a wet trickle along the side of my nose and I needed to sniffle—badly—but I didn't dare because then he would know for sure I was losing it. I heard him sigh. It was a weary sound, filled with despair.

"Rowan . . . turn around and look at me."

The familiar liquid silk wrapped itself seductively around me, settling in my belly and producing a heat I desperately wanted to extinguish.

"Rowan . . . please?"

Stubbornly I shook my head. If I looked at him, he would see how pathetic I really was. Bending down, I picked up my keys from where they had fallen. All I had to do was insert the correct one in the lock and give a turn. Move the mechanism forty-five degrees to the right and push. I would be inside. I could shut the door on him. But Gabriel, sensing my intention, closed the distance between us before I had a chance to blink back the next wave of tears.

Turning me around, he pulled me into his arms, kissing me so hard I could already feel the bruises he was leaving on my lips. And then, as the tip of his tongue tasted the salty wetness at the corner of my mouth, I heard a noise. It was indescribable. Something I'd never heard before, but I recognized the volatile mix of rage and despair. It was primordial and made my eyes fly open. The sound was emanating from Gabriel. Rushing up his throat and out between his lips, it coiled itself around me.

Before I could take a breath, he was back on the far side of the porch, his head lowered, his face obscured by his long hair. I was stunned and now even more confused.

What had just happened?

"Gabriel . . . ?"

Torment looked back at me from brilliant, dark blue eyes. It was an agony that pierced me to the core. This was suffering, a pain whose origins I couldn't begin to fathom, but I could see the anguish ripping through him. Taking a step forward, I reached for him, but he moved first. How could he move that quickly? Catching hold of my wrists, he pressed his lips fiercely against the inside of each one.

And then he was gone.

CHAPTER 16

Unsure of what to do, I waited until the following day before calling. My call went straight to voice mail, as did the next one and the one after that. In all I left five messages, each more wretched and pitiful than the last.

Gabriel didn't call back.

I decided to give him forty-eight hours with no contact from me. Surely that would be long enough to work through whatever it was he needed to deal with?

He still didn't call back.

When I tried calling again, it didn't go to voice mail. Instead a disembodied voice said the number I had dialed was no longer in service, but if I thought the message was in error to try again. There was no error. I continued making excuses for him until the end of the week. It took me a little longer to stop making excuses for myself.

I'd been dumped. Discarded. Cast off. Forsaken.

Staring at my tear-stained reflection in the bathroom mirror, I recalled every conversation we'd ever had, starting with running into him outside Rosie's and ending with the last time I whispered his name on my front porch in the moonlight. Like a scientist with a microscope and a boxful of slides, I examined and reexamined every sentence that had dropped from my lips, every nuance and inflection in each word uttered, looking for a sign to explain his complete and utter abandonment of me. Had I been too eager or too hesitant? Was it my hair, my clothes, the stubborn ten pounds I couldn't seem to lose?

My mind kept taking me back to the beautiful Katja, showing me how painfully unsophisticated I was by comparison. But if Gabriel wanted someone like Katja, why had he been at Rosie's that night? Slumming? Wanting to see how the not-so-gorgeous people lived? And why would he say he was waiting for me? It wasn't as if I'd backed him against a wall and twisted his arm.

Wallowing in self-pity wasn't a pretty sight. The way we had parted, the intensity of the emotions flowing from both of us, had given me false hope. I told myself that, once he had thought things through, Gabriel would regret his decision. I had not pushed him away. He had left of his own accord, and with words that still made no sense. Knowing I was a virgin made him want me more? For God's sake, what did that mean?

And still he kept his silence.

Heartsick and despondent, I eventually reached the only conclusion left to me. The one Gabriel had triggered by implying that if I knew the truth about him, I would not want him. The truth about what? His life? The *this and that* he didn't want to talk about? Whatever the truth was, he believed I couldn't handle it. And that hurt worst of all. Not giving me the chance to decide for myself.

I told myself I'd been a fool. A complete idiot. He'd been playing me. Except I didn't believe it for one second, and deep down I knew it wasn't true. There was no question about the physical desire Gabriel felt for me. His body made all the right responses, responses you couldn't fake, but was that all there had been? There had to have been more, or else why not just sleep with me? Unable to speak for Gabriel, I could only speak for myself. All I knew, with any certainty, was he made me feel things no other man had ever come close to eliciting. He had unlocked my very own Pandora's box, except for me it was worse. At least Pandora had been left with hope. My box was empty.

The pendulum controlling my emotional arc swung perilously from one extreme to the other. I was either crying in my coffee or snapping and snarling at anyone who came near me. Apologies fell from my mouth with such regularity, they quickly became meaningless. Laycee and Angela, the only friends I had, stoically bore the brunt of my mood swings. Guiltily, I knew they deserved far better than I was giving them. It wasn't their fault I dealt with rejection so badly.

You know who I am.

That nagging little voice kept up its litany, rolling the words around in my head until I felt like screaming. I *didn't* know who he was. We had *never* met before. Believe me, I *would* have remembered. But as the words kept repeating themselves inside my head, I heard something else. A whisper that told me not to jump to any rash conclusions. Things weren't always as they seemed, and maybe there was a good reason for Gabriel's leaving me as he had. Yeah, and maybe Santa Claus and the Tooth Fairy were kissing cousins.

After a month of complete Gabriel-silence, I finally decided to deal with the problem the only way I knew how. Calling in to work, I didn't even pretend to be sick. Angela sounded profoundly relieved when I asked her to cover for me. I couldn't blame her. I'd been particularly bitchy lately. With my pendulum stuck at the *incensed fury* end of my mood swings, I'd managed to supplant her all-men-are-scum theory with one of my own. Men, especially tall, fantastically built blonds who looked like Vikings, weren't only scum, they didn't deserve to breathe the same air as women. Fortunately, Angela recognized I'd never been through this before, so she cut me some major slack.

"It's about time, Rowan," she said brusquely on the other end of the phone. "I don't care what you do. Get drunk, cry your eyes out, make an effigy and stick pins in it, but don't let me see you again until you've got this man out of your system!"

Weighing my options, I decided getting shit-faced was the way to go. Crying was exhausting and made my eyes puffy, and I didn't possess the necessary skills to make an effigy. Not that I wouldn't enjoy sticking pins in it. And ripping the head off.

As there didn't seem much point in saving it anymore, I started with the bottle of Hungarian wine. I was on my third glass when Laycee showed up.

"What are you doing here?" I asked in surprise as she swept past me into the kitchen. It was Saturday afternoon, her busiest time in the salon.

"Having my period and cramping." Dropping her purse on the counter, she got a glass out of the cupboard and then took the wine bottle out of my hand.

"Do you want some Midol?" I asked solicitously.

Laycee shot me a look of exasperation before snorting, "I'm not really having my period, you idiot. That was just the excuse I used to get off work. Angela called and thought you shouldn't be alone, especially if you plan on getting wasted."

Her eyes fell on the counter, where small pieces of cork lay scattered next to a knife with a serrated edge, and a screwdriver and hammer.

"Don't have a corkscrew," I mumbled. I'd tried to dig the cork out, which explained the knife and shredded pieces next to the sink, only it was taking too long. So I figured it was just as easy to push the damn thing in as it was to get it out. Which explained the screwdriver and hammer. Pleased with my problem-solving skills, I watched as Laycee eyed the butchered cork bobbing gently in the wine. "Doesn't affect the taste," I assured her.

"Looks like I've got some catching up to do." She poured a generous amount into a glass, took a healthy swallow, and raised her eyebrows in surprise. "Wow, this stuff is pretty good."

"Yeah . . . I know."

I wasn't sure whether I should be grateful or pissed she was here, but I did know I owed her big-time. I had been particularly brutal when she'd called a day after Gabriel did his vanishing act.

"Are you going to get drunk?"

"That's the plan," I said, as if getting wasted at one-thirty on a Saturday afternoon was akin to finding the cure for cancer. It was a cure all right; at least I hoped it would be.

"So, it's really over then?" Pulling out one of the chairs, she sat across from me at the kitchen table.

"Looks that way."

"Wanna talk about it?"

I shook my head. "Not really."

"Yeah you do." Her mouth twisted in a quirky smile. "It's time, Rowan."

I flashed what I hoped was a menacing look, warning her not to go down this path, but she blew me off. What did I know? This was my first breakup that had teeth. It made no difference how long the relationship had lasted. The hurt was real enough.

"Have you tried calling him?"

"You can leave if you're going to ask stupid questions."

Ignoring me, Laycee repeated herself. At times she was like a dog with a bone, and the only way to get her to shut up was to just go along.

"No longer in service," I muttered sourly.

In all my misery I'd never actually told either Laycee or Angela what had happened with Gabriel, at least not in any meaningful detail. All they knew was that Gabriel had taken me to dinner, brought me home, and . . . dumped me for reasons unknown. And it was bad.

I tried telling myself that the reason I had remained so closed-mouthed, especially with Laycee, was because I didn't want to put a crimp in her happiness by wailing about yet another romantic failure on my part. Yeah right, like she was going to believe that.

Nevertheless, she was right about me wanting to spill my guts. I was halfway through my last glass of wine before I began to pour out my sad, sorry tale. Spilling everything, down to the last detail. I think she was more disappointed than I was, though for completely different reasons, about my not getting Gabriel horizontal between my sheets.

"D'you think he was gay?" she asked with a sympathetic twinge.

"Absolutely not!" I exclaimed, tilting my wine glass in her direction. "Trust me, I can tell when a guy is interested, and he was plenty interested." I recalled with perfect clarity just how interested he'd been with my hand pressed against his fly. "There are some things the human body, excuse me the *male* human body, can't fake."

"Then do you think he was married?"

I opened my mouth, ready to issue another denial, but snapped it shut. It was a legitimate question, and I was glad Laycee had been the one to raise it. The possibility had crossed my mind more than once when I'd been crying into my pillow, but other than looking for a wedding ring, I had no way of knowing. The only cheating married man I knew was Jake, and he wasn't much of an example. In hindsight I should have hit Laycee up for tips, but that's the thing about hindsight. It's always twenty-twenty.

"Bastard," Laycee muttered.

"Bastard," I agreed with a shrug, staring at the glass I didn't remember emptying. I went in search of something else to drink. If all else failed, I had some cooking sherry in the pantry. Thankfully, lurking in the back of the fridge were the beers Jake had brought. Two cans later and I was well and truly in the "poor me" groove. I told Laycee about Francesca.

"I thought you said his car was called Francine?"

I told her about the Ferrari.

"What a fucking whore!" Waving her arms, Laycee decorated the floor with a generous splash of beer.

"I thought only women were whores," I said, thinking she had overtaken me on the inebriation highway.

"Not in this day and age!" Five minutes later my knowledge of whores was greatly expanded. "Hey, let's see if we can Google the bastard."

I shook my head morosely. "Already tried."

"Oh . . . and?"

"Don't have a last name," I said with a sigh. "You have any idea how many results you get just with Gabriel?"

"Fuck it!" She was genuinely put out by my admission because now she couldn't ask Jake to utilize the resources of the Sheriff's Department on my behalf.

"Good idea, though," I said in an effort to cheer her up.

I don't remember very much about the rest of the day, except when the beers were gone I found a bottle of Jack Daniels I'd forgotten about in the back of a cupboard. It was at least three-quarters full when we started, and between us we emptied it. At some point I can remember being undecided whether I should bawl my eyes out or smash every piece of crockery I owned. As if destroying all my dinner plates and cereal bowls would punish Gabriel for leaving me.

Laycee persuaded me crying would be more cathartic. She didn't want to have to sweep up broken dishes.

I can safely say that crying while drunk as a skunk is even more exhausting than crying while sober. When my eyelids became unnaturally heavy, I knew I had to lie down before I fell down, but managing the stairs wasn't going to happen. I'd have an easier time climbing Mount Everest in high heels. Laycee helped me to stumble into the living room, where I fell, face first, on the couch. She left me muttering drunkenly about what pigs men were and making snorty, grunting sounds. Or so she told me later.

I vaguely recollect Jake coming to get his girlfriend and saying something pithy about the dangers of women drinking without proper supervision. He was, however, thoughtful enough to bring me a bucket from the utility room and set it next to the couch in case I needed to upchuck. The last good guy on the planet, even if he was already taken. I managed a sloppy "thank you" before passing out completely.

I returned to the land of the living around noon the next day, convinced any sudden movement would make my head explode. I promised myself I was never going to drink like that again. However, I'm not sure making such a pledge while kneeling in front of the toilet holds much weight. Nevertheless, the binge had the desired effect. Having to deal with my hangover made me realize what an unbearable misery I had been to everyone around me. It wasn't their fault that my latest foray into the world of romance had ended in disaster—again. I think the screw-up fairy must have heard the only way to make me truly happy was to totally fuck up my life. Not wanting to disappoint, she determined this to be the pattern of my days.

But the reality of my situation was very simple. No matter what I felt, no matter what had been said, Gabriel was history. It was time to move on. I owed it to my friends. I owed it to myself. And despite Laycee's protests to the contrary, I was glad I hadn't had sex with Gabriel.

Even though my feverish imagination assured me it would have been the most mind-blowing experience possible between two consenting adults, I would be feeling worse than I already was. I told myself

I was grateful Gabriel had left me when he did. If I kept repeating it enough times, I might actually come to believe it.

If I had slept with him, would he still have dumped me? Probably. Maybe. Who knows? But I grudgingly gave him a brownie point for doing it before jumping my bones. Still, I had to agree with Laycee about one thing. It would have been worth it just to see him naked.

It took time, but eventually I resumed my life as a normal functioning member of the human race. Even my internal flamethrower got with the program and stopped roaring into life every time I thought about long blond hair, great biceps, or Vikings. It was hard, but what's that old saying? Time heals all wounds? Well, maybe not heal, not completely, but at least it let me cover the hole with a big enough Spongebob Band-Aid so it didn't leak as much. I would be okay as long as I didn't try to take it off.

And so . . . life went on.

CHAPTER 17

I envy people who live up north, and not just because winter is my favorite time of year. I'm especially envious of the folks who live in Vermont and get to experience a true fall. Having your senses dazzled by nature's spectacular kaleidoscope of changing leaves must really be something. One day I'm going to experience firsthand those weeks that mark the end of summer.

Where I live, the trees are mostly pines, but you can always find a handful of deciduous ones growing among them, like gate-crashers at a party. I've always felt they don't truly belong. And they know it. In their greenery they can blend in, pretending to be some sort of evergreen hybrid, but the minute the season changes, the game's up. It seems to me the swiftness with which they shed their leaves is almost indecent. On the drive to work Monday, they're still mostly green but curling slightly at the edges. Come Tuesday and Wednesday they've turned an all-over sickly yellowish-brown. On Thursday they start to shed, really getting into the swing of it by Friday, so when the weekend arrives, all you're left with is a naked tree trying not to be noticed. Not exactly what I would consider a positive herald for the onset of cooler temperatures.

Halloween fell on a Saturday, and I optimistically prepared for some trick-or-treaters to call. I live too far off the beaten track for little kids to come to my house, but I can usually count on at least one group of teenagers to hit me up. So I get the good candy. No suckers or bubblegum and not a single gummy anything. Strictly chocolate at my house because whatever is left, I'm going to eat.

What none of us had counted on was the rain. It began late in the morning and continued on through the afternoon and evening, showing no sign of letting up. It was the wettest Halloween since, well, I couldn't remember, but at least since I was old enough to get dressed up and go trick-or-treating.

Those parents who prefer that their kids not go door-to-door have the option of attending the Fall Festival, an annual event put together by local churches of all denominations and held in the volunteer fire hall. The kids still get to dress up and are encouraged to indulge in a free-for-all sugar high. There are the usual games, raffles, and bake sales, as well as contests for most original, most frightening, and funniest costume. Anyone under ten gets a prize, no matter how they're dressed. Personally, I think they should just give each kid a handful of sugar cubes and a big glass of Kool-Aid as they come through the door.

The Sheriff's Department has always been heavily involved with the festival, and for the past couple of years it was Suellen DuPree's task to organize the event. This year she declined, which was no huge surprise to anyone, but even Laycee agreed that asking her had been the right thing to do. After all, it wasn't as if she and Jake were actually divorced yet.

However, with Suellen's refusal, everyone looked to Laycee to step up and take charge. The fact that she was the sheriff's girlfriend was conveniently overlooked, as long as she was willing to pitch in. Surprisingly, everything went off very smoothly. Everyone else involved—deputies' spouses, significant others, and various church members—appreciated Laycee not trying to take over and run things single-handed. She was more than willing to accept help wherever she could find it, and I don't think Suellen was missed at all. Except maybe by Bobby Wilkins's mother.

Of course I attended the Fall Festival in order to show moral support for my best friend. Despite popular opinion, the witch costume I wore had not come from the Frederick's of Hollywood catalog. Laycee helped me pick it out at a store in the mall after deciding it was time for me to live up to the expectations of those folk who, despite the fact that Jake and Laycee were now living together, still believed Jake had slept with me at least once. Fishnet stockings, high heels, and a push-up bra certainly helped reinforce such beliefs. Still, my outfit was greatly appreciated by most of the men in attendance. Their wives and/or girlfriends, not so much. Go figure.

It was past eleven and still raining hard when I got back home. I made a mad dash from the POS to the front door, grateful not to twist an ankle. If witches wore stilettos like the ones I had on, then it wasn't surprising they also rode brooms. Leaning against the kitchen counter, I eased off one of the torturous shoes so I could rub some life back into my foot. I didn't think anyone, even teenagers, would be dumb enough to be out in this weather, but the loud knock at the door proved me wrong.

"Just a minute!" I yelled, stuffing my aching foot back into the high heel and grabbing the dish of candy off the counter. Anyone braving this downpour deserved the full effect of my saucy witch outfit. And that included stiletto heels.

I swung the door open wide, and felt my smile turn into an O of complete blow-me-away surprise. I stared, transfixed, waiting for the figure before me to vaporize into thin air or something. But it didn't, and I was stuck with my deer-in-the-headlights imitation.

He was soaked through. The denim of his jeans was rain-black, and his T-shirt clung like a second skin, emphasizing the build of his chest and shoulders.

Had he been working out or was he always that big?

Although wet, his hair was still a glorious waterfall of white, and as I gazed at him in total shock, I realized he was still the most gorgeous man on the planet.

This was the moment I should have shut the door on him. A gentle push would suffice, something with enough force to secure the latch, keeping him on one side and me on the other. Except I didn't do that. My hand and arm were inexplicably paralyzed.

"G-Gabriel?" Unfortunately, his name wasn't the only thing I stumbled over.

As I took a step back, the narrow heel of my shoe got caught in the fringe of the rug, throwing me off balance. As though it was a cinematic dream-sequence shot in slow motion, I saw the dish of candy fall from my hands and roll between Gabriel's legs, disgorging more of its contents with each revolution. It struck me, as I fell backward with my hands clutching at thin air, that soggy Snickers were the least of my troubles.

At least that's what I thought happened.

In reality, the dish never made it to the ground. Seeing the bowl slip from my grasp, Gabriel caught it with one hand. His outstretched palm balanced my trick-or-treat dish with barely a jostle, while his other arm snaked around my waist, saving me from an undignified sprawl on the floor.

I couldn't take my eyes off of him.

Leaning forward, he buried his face in my neck, inhaling deeply as if reminding himself what my skin smelled like. The warm exhalation of his breath raised gooseflesh on my skin and triggered an explosion in my solar plexus—an emotional storm that couldn't decide if its course should be a deluge of joy at finding myself in his arms once more or a torrent of fury at his desertion. Apparently, I hadn't let go of him as completely as I'd thought.

"Gabriel."

This time I delivered his name smoothly, although my vocal cords had been convinced they would never utter it again. He pulled his head back and gazed down at me. The same cobalt-blue eyes looked at me, glowing with the promise of something I was too wary to acknowledge.

"Hello, Rowan."

The deep, rich timbre reverberated inside my head, exactly as I remembered it, although I thought I heard a hint of uncertainty in the tone. It occurred to me that perhaps he was thinking he'd made a mistake—that showing up uninvited wasn't such a great idea after all. My inner bitch offered her own warped sense of reassurance.

Puh-leeze! This man doesn't make mistakes. Uncertainty is strictly your domain.

So . . . invite him in or send him away?

My brain was having enough difficulty processing the fact that he was here in the flesh and not a figment of my imagination. My body, however, was having no such problem.

Behind my ribs my heart was pounding like a jackhammer, creating all sorts of complications for my lungs as they tried to inflate. And I could feel my blood, hot and sizzling, racing through my veins. Like Old Faithful, my very own personal blowtorch roared into life, persuading everything south of my navel to wake up and hold a parade.

How could he do this to me?

And the voice I hadn't heard in quite a while, the one I was certain had taken up residence in someone else's skull, suddenly came roaring through the barren landscape of my mind.

You know who I am.

My temper flared, making me snap back on the same mental wavelength.

Oh yeah? Keep telling yourself that if it makes you a happy camper, but I don't think so. Here's an idea, why don't you get over yourself, and just tell me who the fuck you are?

Nothing but silence.

Yeah, that's what I thought.

Acutely aware of Gabriel's arm around my waist, long fingers splayed against my hip bone, I was even more disturbed by the path my own hands had taken. Flattened against his chest, my palms covered his nipples, feeling them through the wet cloth of his T-shirt. The sensation was very arousing . . . and unsettling.

"You're wet," I commented, demonstrating my flawless command of the obvious.

The corners of his mouth twitched and his eyes crinkled with humor. "So it would seem."

"Let me get you a towel."

He placed the candy dish on the floor and helped me stand. My heel was still caught in the rug. Dropping to one knee, Gabriel took hold of my calf with one hand and the shoe with the other. Standing on one leg, I automatically put my hand on his wide shoulder, balancing myself as he eased the twisted fringe off the stiletto heel.

"Nice shoes," he murmured, letting his hand drift toward my ankle.

"Thank you." My eyes flickered beyond the open door. The POS was the only vehicle in the driveway. "Where's your car?" I asked.

"I parked farther back," Gabriel said slowly.

"That so?" The only way he'd be so wet was if farther back was in the next county. I put enough disbelief in my words to make it clear I knew he was lying. I just didn't know why. A thousand questions were falling over themselves inside my head, but I was determined not to reveal how his presence was affecting me. Taking a firm grip on the roller-coaster ride my emotions were enjoying, I adopted what I hoped was an air of indifference. "Let me get you that towel."

His eyes followed me as I walked down the hallway and into the kitchen. I would have given anything to be wearing something other than black fishnets and a skirt that barely covered my ass. Shapeless, baggy sweats would be a good choice.

Gabriel had closed the door behind him when I returned, and the candy dish was now sitting on the hall table.

"Aren't I supposed to invite you in?" My tone was slightly accusatory as I held the towel out to him.

"Only the first time."

A warning bell clanged loudly inside my head. There was another, hidden meaning in his words. Something I already knew but couldn't recall at this precise moment. And then I forgot all about warnings as his fingers, reaching for the towel, brushed the back of my hand. A bottle rocket exploded inside my chest. In what alternate reality had I convinced myself I was over him?

As he stood dripping in the hallway I could sense him studying me, trying to assess my reaction to his presence. At least that's what I assumed his look meant. It's what I would do. But I don't think he found me as easy to read as before because he shifted his attention and began to focus deliberately on everything from my neck down. Locking my backbone in place, I did my best to ignore the feel of his eyes sweeping over me, concentrating instead on the puddle of water forming at his feet. Was he going to punish the rug by drowning it?

"You know that works a lot better if you actually use it," I said, pointing to the towel hanging idly from his fingers, "and it'll save my rug from getting waterlogged."

He gave me a rueful look and unfolded the oversized bath sheet.

My thigh muscles jumped as I watched him wipe his arms. How could he make such a simple, mundane task so blatantly erotic?

"Coffee?"

I'm not sure which of us was more startled by my offer. What was wrong with me? I ought to be kicking his ass out the door, not playing Patti the Perfect Hostess. I told myself it would be a test, a way to prove to myself that my initial reaction to him was all due to shock. Something that would right itself in a more normal setting.

Yeah right, of course it would.

Besides, I was curious to know why he was here.

"I don't want to put you to any trouble," Gabriel said, pausing in mid-wipe. His voice was quiet, nothing overtly sexual, yet it still managed to wrap itself sweetly around my spine.

"Trust me, you won't." I looked down at the spreading water stain. "You'd better come into the kitchen. It'll be easier to mop up the floor than dry out the rug."

I managed to pull all the requirements together to make coffee even as the rational part of my brain wanted to know if I had gone completely insane.

Aren't you keeping track? the irrational part snapped back.

Allowing Gabriel inside my front door wasn't an automatic invitation back into my life, no matter what my pelvis thought. I consulted my mental checklist, just to remind myself why such an idea was monumentally bad.

He *had* left me with no explanation, hurting me in a way I'd never thought possible.

I *had* spent more nights crying over him than I would ever admit to.

He *was* absolutely one hundred percent wrong for me.

My mouth fashioned itself in a tight smile. My reasoning was sound. There was absolutely no way I was going to let him get close to me again.

Fool me once, shame on you; fool me twice, shame on me. Or something like that.

The coffeepot, announcing the end of its brew cycle by sputtering loudly, seemed to agree with me. "You can sit down if you want," I told Gabriel as I reached into the cupboard for mugs. I was inordinately pleased at how well I was handling things.

"I think I'd better not."

Glancing over my shoulder, I saw him eyeing the padded seat of my kitchen chair as he blotted his hair with the towel. I shrugged and fixed his coffee, black with one sugar—funny the things you remember. Only I forgot how fast he could move. After putting his mug on the table, he caught my arm and pulled me to him, his mouth covering mine.

I responded instinctively, parting my lips so I could feel his warm breath and taste his spicy sweetness. Loosening his hold on my arm, Gabriel swept his hand down my back. Long fingers danced over my spine, moved along my waist, and caressed my hip. I was floating in a warm rush of desire as he pulled his mouth away and looked down at me.

The way my body had been cranking up since opening the door, it was stupid to think a kiss wasn't going to send it into overdrive. But I was damned if I was going to let him think he could just pick right up where he'd left off. As if the past couple of months of abject misery had never happened. God knows I have some pride.

Resting my hand lightly on his arm, I felt his bicep flex invitingly beneath my fingers. His mouth became a satisfied curl that reinforced the confident gleam in his eyes and shattered the tenuous grip I didn't realize I was using to restrain myself. I let my temper get the upper hand, reacting as any normal female with sufficient backbone would by slapping him across the face. Hard. So much for indifference.

My reward was seeing the self-assurance change to disbelief, punctuated with a flash of hot anger. I think it was safe to assume Gabriel didn't get slapped much. Slipping out of his embrace with my own satisfied smile, I watched him raise a hand to his cheek.

"Guess I deserved that," he muttered a little sourly.

"Yeah, I guess you did."

Leaning back against the kitchen sink, I kept my hands lodged firmly behind me so Gabriel wouldn't see how badly they were shaking. I know my slap had surprised him, but surely he should have expected it? You don't run from someone the way he had and not expect repercussions. Every experience we have leaves an imprint that affects us. Good or bad, it's just a matter of degree.

Taking a deep breath, I pushed my surface temper down. Unchecked, it was liable to make me do, or say, something regrettable. "Why are you here, Gabriel?" I asked.

The minute hand on the wall clock made a click before he answered, "I've come to apologize."

"Bit late for that, don't you think?" It might have been unnecessary, but the sarcasm felt good.

He stared as if seeing me in a totally different light. The girl he'd left standing on the porch, breathless and teetering on the edge of explosive sex, had been replaced by someone he wasn't quite sure of. I didn't think I'd changed that much, but then I wasn't seeing me through his eyes.

"Perhaps an explanation then?"

"Sure." I folded my arms across my chest. "Knock yourself out."

Picking the towel up off the floor, he carefully folded it and then laid it down on the seat of the chair. He was relaxed, sure of himself, and I hated him for it. Where was the anguish, the torment? I wanted—no, I needed—to see that.

The silence between us grew, becoming heavier with each passing minute. Surely he'd had time to come up with *something* since that night. If he didn't speak soon, I was going to jump right in and rip him a new one for what he'd put me through. I wouldn't be able to stop myself.

Taking a steadying breath, I let my eyes reacquaint themselves with the width of his shoulders, the broad expanse of his chest, his tapered waist and hips. Like I really needed to do that? I hadn't forgotten how he looked, and my body tingled.

Running his fingers through his hair, he looked unexpectedly frustrated. "I'm not sure you're going to believe me," he admitted.

"That bad, huh?"

His eyes narrowed. He thought I was still being sarcastic, but I wasn't. Okay, that was a lie, I was. Only now his admission had piqued my curiosity and I really did want to hear what he had to say.

"I had to make a decision, Rowan, an important one."

"Thank God for that. I would hate to think you dumped me for something trivial."

I waited for him to continue. Almost began a toe-tapping routine with my pointy stilettos before I realized he was done. That was it? After nearly three months, this was the best he could come up with? *He had to make a decision.* Talk about disappointed. I'd been hoping for something with a little more imagination. Puffing up my cheeks, I blew out a breath, seeing his eyes narrow a little further. Good. At least I didn't have to tell him just how much bullshit I thought his answer was. He could read that on my face clearly enough.

"So, what was it about, this important decision of yours?" I couldn't have cared less, but I wanted to see how far he would stretch his feeble excuse.

Gabriel rolled his shoulders, loosening tense muscles. "Whether or not I wanted the return of something, something that I was forced to give up a long time ago."

The disappointment became crushing, although I'm not sure what I'd been expecting. An elaborate fairy tale about a disinheritance coupled with a declaration of everlasting love? In truth, I had expected whatever he said to involve me in some way, and my feelings were hurt as I learned I wasn't the reason for his absence. But I was also relieved in an odd sort of way. It would have been too easy to lie.

"Is it valuable?" I asked slowly.

He nodded. "Yes, but not in any monetary sense."

"But it would mean a lot to you, to have it back?"

"It would change my existence."

"Seems like an easy enough decision then." And definitely not one that would have taken me three months to make.

Gabriel settled his mouth in a grim line. "There's a . . . complication."

Ah, isn't there always? For the first time I noticed dark shadows under his eyes and realized he looked tired. "What sort of complication?" I asked.

He hesitated, and I could tell he was trying to decide what to tell me. He didn't have to tell me anything. It wasn't any of my business.

"The return requires that certain reparations be made," he said reluctantly.

"By whom?"

He scrubbed a hand over his face before saying, "The current possessor of the . . . item."

"And you don't think they'd be willing to do this?"

"*I* don't want them to do this."

"Why not?" The question popped out of me before I could stop it.

"Because it will cost them everything they have."

"Perhaps you could come to a different arrangement?"

Giving me an odd look, Gabriel took a deep breath that made his nostrils flare. "No. The terms were set a long time ago and cannot be altered. Besides, it's a moot point. I've decided I don't want the item back."

"But if it's valuable, and means that much to you—"

"—I won't have that sacrifice on my conscience!"

I stared at him in bewilderment. "And it took you almost three months to figure this out?"

Tilting his chin, Gabriel stared at me, his face devoid of all expression. It was as if he needed to keep his emotions under the tightest of control. "Yes, Rowan, it did. All decisions have consequences, and I needed certain assurances before making this one."

I wished I'd never asked because I had no idea what he was talking about. Still, something in his eyes said it hadn't been easy.

"Then I'm sorry you found it so difficult," I told him. And I meant it.

"Something worth doing is never easy."

"No, it isn't," I agreed, but it still didn't explain why he'd felt it necessary to cut off all contact with me.

In my experience, most people make decisions fairly quickly; no one takes three months weighing the pros and cons of a course of action. And it didn't explain anything Gabriel had said when he'd left me that night.

His silence had been deliberate. He knew how upset I was, and he could have reached out to me if he'd wanted to. A voice or text message would have been okay if he didn't want to speak with me directly, but disconnecting his service so I couldn't contact him had been especially cruel. If I wasn't important to him then, I certainly wasn't now.

And knowing that crushed me.

CHAPTER 18

"You're wrong," I said quietly, "I do believe you. No one in his right mind would make up such a pathetic story." I made my voice as cold and cutting as I could. "And now that I've heard it, I'd like you to leave."

Gabriel stared at me, dumbfounded. "You want me . . . *to go*?"

Oh God, what did he think I would want? Not that, apparently. I watched him clench his jaw, working the muscle. It had been eighty-seven days since I'd last seen him, but who was counting? Surely he didn't actually think he could pick right back up where we'd left off? From his stunned expression it seemed he did.

My temper began to rise at such presumption. "Did you really think you could just walk right back in here and pretend that nothing had happened? Act as if you'd never been gone?" I leaned forward, hands on my hips, forgetting just how much cleavage my skimpy costume showed. "I don't care if it was the fucking Hope Diamond you were getting back. Do you honestly expect me to believe you couldn't call me? Not one single time?"

"I couldn't."

"Why not? Where the hell were you? Bora Bora?"

I had absolutely no idea what reception was like in that particular island paradise, but it was the only really remote place I could think of on the spur of the moment. The look on Gabriel's face changed. He thought I was being unreasonable. Fuck him! I didn't have to be reasonable.

"I knew, that night, that you weren't coming back." He opened his mouth to protest, but I cut him off with an impatient wave of my hand. This had been stewing for a while, and I really needed to get it out. "Only you really should have had the balls to tell me what *leaving* actually meant." I emphasized the word, giving it the weight it warranted.

"If you were too cowardly to tell me to my face, then you could have found some other way of letting me know. God knows, you had enough options. But you just left me hanging, never knowing for sure, without a word from you. I almost went out of my mind wondering what had happened to you!" I paused and took a breath before continuing, "You wanna hear something funny? And I don't mean funny ha-ha." The question was rhetorical, and I stabbed the air with a black painted fingernail aimed at the middle of his chest.

"I was so scared about the way you drove out of here in your shiny red car that I called all the hospitals in a three-county radius to make sure you hadn't had an accident. Hadn't gone and wrapped your fancy Ferrari around a tree, or something equally stupid." His eyes opened wide, but whether it was due to my confession or the fact that I remembered what type of car he drove, I couldn't be sure. "Only everyone I spoke to figured I was totally wasted on something because I couldn't give them your last name, and at least one nurse thought my physical description of you sounded like something out of a fucking romance novel!"

I stopped and took a breath. And then another, a deeper one. And then I got a wake-up call that yanked hold of my temper and smacked it down, hard. Yelling at Gabriel wasn't going to make me feel any better. Did he really think I cared about some stupid decision he'd had to make, one that didn't even concern me? Couldn't he see how much effort it was taking to stop myself from grabbing him, latching onto his mouth, and sucking the life out of his lower lip? Exhaustion took hold of me, and I was suddenly too tired to fight, or argue, or anything. My feet hurt, and I needed to get out of my scratchy costume.

"I had no idea I put you through that," he said quietly. "I am sorry."

"Yeah, well, it doesn't matter now. It's all water under the bridge, a valuable learning experience." Placing a hand over my eyes, I took a moment before looking back at him. In all likelihood it was for the last time. "Thank you for coming to explain what happened," I said wearily, "I'm glad to know you're all right, but it's late and I really want to call it a night."

"Ask me why I'm here, Rowan."

"You already told me. You came to apologize." The flaring resurgence of my internal flame was becoming harder to ignore.

"That's not the real reason." He took a step toward me and dropped his voice, "Ask me why I'm here."

My hand went to my throat as I whispered, "Why are you here, Gabriel?"

"Because I cannot stay away from you any longer."

I must have missed something.

I was tired, my brain was scrambled, and he was playing with me. I'd never doubted Gabriel felt something for me. It just didn't equate to the all-consuming inferno going on inside me. And now he was saying he couldn't stay away from me? What type of bull was that? I was not about to be led down that particular path again, certainly not by him.

I shook my head, hoping my own incredulous expression would reinforce the lie. "I'm sorry to burst your bubble, Gabriel, but whatever you think there was between us is long gone. At least it is on my part."

In the blink of an eye he closed the distance between us. One minute he was by the door, and the next I was trapped between his body and the edge of the sink pushing against the small of my back. It was unnerving how quickly he moved. Almost as unnerving as the heat I could feel coming off him.

He spoke in a low, menacing snarl that had my heart doing cartwheels. "You can lie to yourself if you choose to, Rowan, but never lie to me."

I swallowed and licked my lips nervously—a mistake I realized the moment I saw his eyes tracking the tip of my tongue.

"I'm not lying," I lied.

"Then why are you trembling?"

"Because you're scaring me," I told him. And he was, albeit in a good, sexy way that I was never going to admit to.

Ignoring my words, Gabriel leaned forward and traced a path with his tongue down the side of my neck and along my collarbone. "That's not fear I taste," he growled softly as he pulled back and fixed me with his eyes. "It's desire. Tell me you don't want me."

I steeled myself as the memory came flooding back. Actually it had never been that far away, but I was angry that he would use my own words from that night against me.

"You bastard!" I spat out between clenched teeth. "You were the one who ran away! Leaving me with nothing but nonsense about things that were wrong and how I wouldn't want you if I knew the truth. I didn't understand any of it then and I still don't, but it really doesn't matter because you just took off and left me. Well, I've had plenty of time to think since then, and you know what?" I brought my hands up and pushed hard against his chest as a way of underlining my lie. "I don't want you."

And then, with the nearness of him compounding my precarious emotional state, I felt the wetness exploding between my thighs and saw the shift in his expression.

"I told you not to lie to me," Gabriel murmured, delivering the words with a sensual, predatory smile.

My temper spiraled, offering me one last stab at saving my self-respect before it was completely shredded. "Why do you care?" I snarled at him. "You want me to admit you turn me on? Okay, I'll admit it. I'm so hot for you right now that I'd let you take me right here on the kitchen floor. Only know this, Gabriel, I'd hate you for it afterward—just not as much as I'd hate myself!"

I was scorching, and completely unaware I had the front of his damp T-shirt in my hand until I saw the dark material clutched in my fingers. I pulled, and he let me take his mouth, offering no resistance. Hot and angry, I sated my fury. Kissing him with a barely controlled violence I didn't know I was capable of. My tongue thrust inside him and I could feel myself shaking as uncontrollable need swept through me. I was about to sink my teeth into his lower lip, wanting to taste blood, when I pulled back, horrified.

This wasn't me.

I don't behave like this.

I tried turning my head, but Gabriel was having none of it. His fingers snagged themselves in my hair, twisting until I had no choice but to look at him.

"My turn," he growled.

Before I could protest, he slanted his mouth over mine. I braced myself, expecting his kiss to be brutal and vicious, but instead he destroyed me with a tenderness that I wasn't prepared for and didn't deserve. When he let me go, his tongue making a final sweep over my lips, I was dizzy and breathless. Untangling his fingers from my hair, Gabriel moved away, his eyes never leaving my face.

"I-I don't understand you," I said in a trembling voice. "Why are you doing this to me?"

"Rowan, do you think what I feel for you is only a shallow, base lust?" His eyes flooded with uncertainty, and this time I really did see doubt.

Intuitively I knew if I pushed him away, he would leave and I would never see him again. Instead of telling myself that's what I wanted, I felt hollow, as if I was on the verge of discarding something whose value was beyond my comprehension. I put a hand to my throat and said nothing, because I thought he was able to read my face again.

"I don't blame you for supposing such a thing," he said quietly, his expression changing to one of resigned acceptance. "And I understand why you would believe me insincere, but I swear to you, it was never my intention to hurt you."

"Then why are you here?"

"I already told you . . . I cannot stay away from you."

He rubbed the back of his neck, and I was struck again by how tired he looked. Only I didn't think it was a physical weariness. He'd been battling some inner demon, and in the depths of his eyes I saw a shadow move, revealing something I hadn't seen before. Loneliness that was on the verge of consuming him.

"But . . . why me?" I asked. I had given my insecurities free rein, and they were now running at full bore. "You could have any beautiful woman." I thought of the exotic Katja. "I'm no one."

Gabriel snarled, but it wasn't a mean, threatening sound. It sounded more like frustrated desperation. Dropping his hand from his neck, he fixed me with a look before saying, "You are all I want, all I need. With you my life is . . . possible."

It was that simple. Eloquently put, his words punched inside me, reaching an emotional chord that went far deeper than any physical appetite.

"But you said I wouldn't want you . . . not if I knew the truth."

"I know."

"Do you still think that?"

"The world I live in is very different from anything you have ever known, Rowan. My only thought at the time I spoke those words was for your protection. I thought, if I distanced myself from you, it would keep you safe. I never took into account the strength of the connection I have with you." His voice dropped to a whisper. "I tried to stay away, Rowan; believe me, I tried, but I found it impossible." He scrubbed a hand over his face, and I watched the movement of his chest as he took a deep breath, steadying himself. "I have no right to ask anything of you, and if you want me to leave, then you must say so. Tell me to go and I give you my word you will never see me again."

My rib cage compressed and my stomach twisted. It was my turn to make a decision, and I didn't need three months to do it. My heart had made it the moment I saw him at my door. It had just taken my head a little longer to catch up. Whatever the truth was about Gabriel, whatever existed in his world that he thought I needed protecting from, I would accept and deal with it. He wasn't the only one who had been hurting.

"I don't want you to leave," I told him, my voice a barely audible, husky whisper.

The shadow in his eyes vanished, replaced by something else. Whether it was relief or hope, I couldn't say.

"Are you sure?" he murmured, taking a step toward me. "I need you to be certain that this—that I—am what you want."

I had the sense that he was asking me something that went deeper, was more meaningful, but my brain had been through enough for one night. My ability to search for hidden meanings was temporarily lost, and it was more than ready to hitch a ride to Clueless Land. I wasn't sure about anything, but I trusted my instincts. And they told me this was right. I belonged with Gabriel.

"The only things you can be certain about are death and taxes," I said, giving him a wry grin, "but if you're asking me to take a chance, then yes, I will—only," I paused, "why would you think I wouldn't want you?" He might not be able to pick up on every emotion I was throwing his way, but surely he could still read how I felt about him?

"Because I wonder," he said, taking my hand, "if you went back to the very beginning, would you have come searching for me again?"

The silence between us was deafening, and the feeling of déjà vu returned. Only it didn't feel so strange this time. Whatever Gabriel was referring to was hidden somewhere inside that feeling.

"I wish I knew what you were talking about," I told him, "because I think it's important, but I have to tell you that right now you're making absolutely no sense." Clueless Land was rapidly expanding into the continent of the Completely Lost in the Dark.

"You need to know the truth about me, Rowan, what I am—"

"No, I don't, not right now." I held up my hand and stopped him. I was balanced on a razor-thin wire, and it took all I had not to fall off. "There's only one issue that's important right now, and I need you to be truthful with me."

"Of course, ask me anything."

"Wife, girlfriend, or significant other?"

The sudden, utter confusion on his face made me want to laugh aloud.

"I don't understand."

"Do you have one?"

Gabriel shook his head of glorious, white hair. "No, of course not."

"Positive?"

He looked hurt that I was questioning his integrity. "Rowan, I've not wanted another woman since the first time I saw you. I never have."

"That's good to know," I whispered.

He let go of my hand and clutched his forehead as though he'd just been afflicted with a brain freeze. Pursing his lips, he blew out a breath. For all intents and purposes, he looked like a man who desperately wanted to speak but was afraid his words would be the wrong ones.

Welcome to the club.

I didn't want to waste any more time in pointless conversation. It would be an exercise in futility that accomplished nothing. What was about to happen between us right here, right now, was not going to be achieved with words. Unless they were all single syllables used for instructional purposes along with some heavy-duty physical contact. My hands literally itched to get beneath his wet clothing and touch his body.

Something in my life, my luckless romantic aspirations, my failure to successfully seduce a man, had all been pushing me toward this moment. Gabriel was to be my first, perhaps my only lover. I don't know how I knew this or what turn of fate's cosmic wheel had made it so, but it was true. I had known it eighty-seven nights ago on my front porch, and the conviction was even stronger now. I made it to the staircase before Gabriel's voice stopped me.

"Give yourself to me, Rowan, and you will take no other."

I don't know if other girls have experienced such a declaration, but it didn't surprise me coming from him. I was almost expecting it, even if I wasn't completely sure I understood all the implications. Gabriel was telling me exactly what was going to happen. What his intentions were, just in case I hadn't been paying attention.

I heard myself reply, saying the words that would change my life forever. I just had no idea to what extent.

"Then make me want no other."

CHAPTER 19

I unpinned my hair, letting it tumble around my shoulders, before unzipping my risqué witch costume and sliding it down over my hips. The fishnets, amazing push-up bra, and panties quickly followed. I pulled back the covers and got into bed, lying on my side facing away from the door. I didn't hear Gabriel come up the stairs, but I knew the moment he entered the room, even though he crossed the hardwood floor without a sound. I knew because the muscles in my belly clenched.

The splat of his sodden T-shirt hitting the floor was unnaturally loud, and the metallic clink of his belt buckle made the breath catch in my throat. There was a soft scrape of wet denim down skin, and then I felt a whisper of cold air as he lifted the covers and slid beneath them. I reached to turn off the bedside lamp, but he stayed my arm.

"Please don't. I want to look at you."

I closed my eyes and swallowed, pulling my hand back and sliding it under the pillow. For what seemed the longest time there was nothing but the sound of our breathing. A steady, rhythmic inhale-exhale as I accustomed myself to Gabriel's presence in my bed. I felt his fingers stroking my shoulder, caressing the skin lightly as he explored the contours of my body. Sweeping his hand down my arm, he let his fingers jump off at my elbow and fall into the dip of my waist before traveling up over my hip. I couldn't stop trembling, and I prayed he could tell the difference between fear and anticipation.

Pushing aside my hair, Gabriel pressed his lips against my skin, covering the back of my shoulder with light, warm kisses. His hand grasped me lightly, rolling me toward him. His eyes swept over me, glowing in the soft light with the same iridescent shimmer I'd seen when he stood beneath my porch light.

"You are more beautiful than I ever imagined," he whispered, moving so that he was now above me.

Bearing his weight on his forearms, he leaned down and kissed me in a sweet, unhurried explosion of need. It felt like he was kissing me for the first time.

"Dear God . . . ," I murmured, my voice a hoarse rasp when he finally released my lips.

Clutching his upper arms, I unconsciously arched my back, pushing myself up against him. I felt the flush of heat spread throughout my body as his forefinger stroked my cheek.

"I want you so much," he told me, his mouth against my temple, "and I've been waiting so long to be here."

I had become a virgin in every sense of the word, feeling as if I had never been with a man before, had no awareness of what the male body looked like nude, had never felt muscle and bone flexing and moving beneath my hands. And I suppose with Gabriel it was all true. I'd certainly never been with a man like him before.

The width of his shoulders threatened to dwarf me, while the muscles of his chest and abdomen created their own shadows as the light played over his body. Captivated by the velvet smoothness of his skin and the glossy silkiness of his hair, I drank in every inch of him that I could see and allowed my imagination to paint me a picture of what I could only feel. All the pitiful fumbling and wretched attempts at coupling that were the sum of my experience had been wiped away with a single kiss.

"I'm not sure what to do," I whispered, as a string of panic began to twist and knot inside me.

Gabriel smiled down at me, his hair falling like snow. "Let me take you where you want to go," he murmured in his silky, melting voice.

"But I don't know where that is." Anxiety made me sound fretful.

"Don't worry"—he kissed the corner of my mouth—"I do."

Bunching his shoulders, he held himself up on powerful arms. His biceps flexed, and his eyes reflected something I recognized, something I had seen in them before. A longing that had been waiting a lifetime to be fulfilled.

"I'm going to apologize now because I may forget to do so in the heat of the moment." A crease appeared on his smooth brow. "But this first time will be painful for you."

I returned his gaze and nodded, unable to say anything. I wasn't sure if being forewarned was helpful or not. In any case, it wasn't something either of us could prevent happening. And despite my own efforts to lock it down, anxiety returned and began spiraling through me. No matter how much I told myself I wanted this, wanted Gabriel to be the first to ever take me, my muscles trembled and my heart pounded, making the blood rush through me. I was terrified I'd disappoint him.

"You won't," he whispered in my ear.

His hair swept erotically over my skin as his tongue traced a path from my throat to my navel, and back up again. Cupping a breast in one hand, Gabriel rubbed his thumb lightly over my nipple. I almost jumped off the bed as it stiffened under his touch. I have pleasured my own body, stroked myself with my hands and fingers, but it was never like this. I almost climaxed when he took me in his mouth, scraping my nipple lightly with his teeth, before suckling me. I dropped my hands to his sides, wanting to touch him as well, return some of the same pleasure, but he would not allow it.

"Not this time," he told me with a wolfish grin, "this time the pleasure is for you . . . and it is all mine to give."

Dropping his head, he continued to feast on me. I was drenched in an overload of sensation, every inch of my body becoming a slavish receptor for his touch. The warmth of his breath made my flesh dance; the sweep of his tongue teased me to heights I'd never scaled before. Moving a hand down over my hip, he applied a slight pressure at the juncture of my thighs and slipped his finger between the folds of skin, persuading me to open for him.

My own slick heat eased his finger inside me, and I shuddered with uncontrollable pleasure as he began sliding in and out. A second finger followed, increasing the heat and my own wetness, encouraging my body to open wider for him. I groaned, scraping my teeth over my lower lip as I shuddered, my own fingers digging into his upper arm with enough force to make him pause, concern written all over his face.

"Am I hurting you?"

I stared at him, my eyes no doubt wild, and shook my head frantically. I was so close to coming I didn't know whether to beg him to push me over the edge or let me ride out the exquisite torture for as long as I was able to. Feeling the surge of my body beneath his, Gabriel smiled. It was a sensuous lift of his lips that created its own set of tremors running through me, and he moved his hand again, his thumb finding my sweet spot. Unable to stop myself, I gasped, bunching the sheet in my hand as every muscle in my body tensed and he took me over the edge with just a few strokes.

I tried twisting away from him as the intensity of my orgasm ripped through me, but there was no escape. My body was one huge path of carnal sensitivity, and Gabriel's touch sent every nerve ending on a roller-coaster ride of erotic pleasure.

I had no idea I could feel so good.

He kissed me, deep and hungry, and I responded with my own hunger. Wrapping my arms tightly about his neck, I drew his tongue inside my mouth, nipping playfully at his lower lip as I did so. He groaned and settled himself between my thighs, making me open my legs wider to accommodate his hips. His cock was throbbing hot and hard against my belly, but I could feel his hesitation.

"It's all right," I told him, wishing my voice didn't sound quite so strained. "I want this . . . and I want it to be you."

Pushing himself up on his arms, his eyes never leaving mine as he locked his elbows, he lifted his hips and thrust into me with one smooth stroke.

Oh . . . sweet Jesus Christ!

Punching through my virginal membrane, Gabriel muscled his way inside me. The pain washing through me had a flavor uniquely its own, unlike anything I had ever felt before and never would again. Flesh and muscle stretched to accommodate him, pushed to the point that I was certain something would tear.

He was too big . . . I couldn't take him . . . this was destined to be another failure.

Moving above me, Gabriel carefully unlocked his elbows and lowered his upper torso until his weight rested on his forearms.

"Rowan, look at me." I did as he instructed, unaware I'd closed my eyes. "Good, now . . . breathe."

"What?"

"Breathe, nice and slow. Take a breath." I did as he asked. "Now . . . can you feel me?"

Feel him? Was he crazy? He was the only thing I *could* feel. My eyes must have telegraphed my thoughts because he smiled and repeated himself.

"Can you feel *all* of me?"

I gave a gasp of surprise as I grasped the distinction. He was flush against me, skin to skin; I had taken all of him inside my body. As he rocked his hips gently, I felt his balls brush against my ass. My body had adjusted to him; now it was up to my mind to follow suit. "Yeah . . . I can feel you."

"Are you sure?" He moved deep inside me.

"Oh yeah, I'm sure."

Slowly Gabriel pulled back, leaving a slippery burn as he withdrew. As he slid forward again, I could feel the slickness that coated him, a slickness produced by me, and suddenly his presence wasn't so invasive. It was as if I'd been waiting for him, and now that he'd taken possession, I yielded readily, greedily wrapping myself around him. My ears filled with the sound of a low, sexy purr that erupted from the back of my throat as a rippling heat coursed through me.

Gabriel answered with a rumble of his own. "Lift your legs higher, put them around my waist."

I gasped sharply as another wave of pain stung me, but it was forgotten almost immediately when I felt him go deeper. And deeper was better. There was a pounding I could feel, coming in waves, and bringing with it the most incredible sensation. I needed him to keep moving.

Sensing my heat rising, Gabriel increased the driving rhythm of his hips. His skin became slippery, not just inside me but outside as well, and my hands kept sliding down his arms. For the first time in my life I was grateful for the gene pool that enabled me to lock my ankles together as I wrapped my long legs around him. With my heels pressing into the small of his back, I concentrated on the pulse drumming wildly at the base of his throat.

"Hold onto me," he instructed in a husky whisper.

I put my arms around his neck and lifted myself up. Pillowing my breasts against his chest, I buried my face in his massive shoulder. Any sense of control I may have had, or thought I had, vanished. My body gave itself over to him, responding to every erotically whispered directive with an eagerness that stunned me.

Stretched to the limit, my flesh wrapped itself around his thick cock, wanting to make up for lost time. Gripping him with muscles hungry to be used, I pulled him further inside me, delighting in the friction as he pulled back before thrusting forward again. I could feel a mild burn along the inside of my thighs as they held him, but I paid it no attention, too focused on the unknown force building within me. A tidal wave was forming, one that danced the fine line between pleasure and pain so exquisitely I couldn't tell which was which.

"I'm sorry," Gabriel apologized, his voice hoarse and ragged. "I can't stop . . ."

He had one arm around my waist, the other bracing himself against the mattress as he drove into me.

"It's all right," I gasped back at him. "Just don't let me go!"

His arm tightened as he threw back his head, the cords in his neck straining, his body becoming as tight as a drum before exploding in a hot rush that took me with him. At the point of our release, as pain and pleasure washed through me in a golden torrent that expanded every muscle along my pelvis, hips, and thighs, I dug my nails into the back of his neck, bared my teeth and—God help me—I bit him.

His blood flowed over my tongue, flooding my mouth with a hot sweetness that quickly changed to an exotic sizzle beneath the thick, syrupy coating. And as it hit the back of my throat, there came an explosion of peppery heat, a kick that told me—*I had tasted this before.* Then my nose was flooded with the scent of pine trees and snow.

It was the most amazing thing I have ever done.

And it felt so right.

CHAPTER 20

Sanity hit me up the side of the head with a figurative sledgehammer.

What the hell are you doing?

The inside of my mouth was on fire, but the sensation wasn't in the least bit unpleasant. It felt how I imagined a sip of the world's best bourbon would taste—smooth as silk, with one hell of a kick. But I don't imagine it would be imbibed in quite the same way.

Closing my eyes, I swallowed, trying to wash down the taste in my mouth with saliva. Through a tangle of lashes I saw the circle of marks my teeth had left just below Gabriel's collarbone. I turned my head into the pillow, too ashamed to look him in the eye and totally humiliated by my bizarre behavior.

He was throbbing inside me, his presence an erotic violation on a scale that couldn't be measured. The ferocity of our passion had lessened, reducing itself to an aching soreness that was made acute by the position of our bodies. Embracing him between my legs, balancing his weight on my hips and lower back was a strange and slightly claustrophobic sensation. Releasing his hold around my waist, Gabriel propped himself up on both arms, his shoulders rolling as he moved.

"I'm so sorry," I mumbled, trying desperately to hide in the pillow. "I don't know what came over me."

Catching my chin with his fingers, Gabriel turned my head back to face him, waiting until I had no choice but to look up at him.

"You have nothing to apologize for," he said solemnly, as a fierce light shone from his eyes. "I am yours to do with as you will."

I knew, as sure as my middle name is Marie, that I had heard him say those words to me before. I just couldn't remember when or where. His lips brushed mine lightly before he swept the hair back from my face. My legs more or less fell of their own accord from around his hips, making me wince as the pressure inside me shifted.

"Hold still," he said in a low voice.

I groaned as he pulled out of me. The sudden lift of his body created an unexpected shock that made me want to lock my knees together and curl into a ball until the ache went away. I was also filled with the strange urge to throttle every writer of romantic fiction who failed to mention that losing your virginity involved pain. However, in all fairness, the fault may have been more Gabriel's than mine. He was definitely bigger than any other man I'd ever seen with his pants off.

"Stay where you are," he ordered gruffly, throwing back the covers.

Where did he think I was going to go? Down to the One-Stop Mart at the gas station to buy a quart of milk? A giggle unexpectedly bubbled at the thought, and then the scent of something delicious tickled my nose. I put my hand out, making Gabriel turn back to me. As he leaned down to kiss me, I inhaled the fragrance coming from his body. My immediate thought was cologne or aftershave, perhaps body wash, but a second, deeper inhalation, told me I was wrong. This wasn't something that lay on the surface of his skin; this came from within. And I knew exactly what it was.

"Your blood...," I said with what I knew had to be a look of amazement on my face.

Gabriel's expression changed to one of wariness. Had I just committed some massive blunder, the kind of thing that might have started a war a couple of hundred years ago?

"What about my blood?" he asked guardedly.

"That's what I smell."

"You can smell my blood?" He raised his eyebrows and looked ... amazed.

I nodded and grinned. "I'm no expert, but I always thought all blood had the same smell, sort of coppery and salty like an old penny." My nostrils flared again. "Yours doesn't smell like that; it smells fantastic. It reminds me of winter, like I'm in the middle of a pine forest, but so much better. And there's something else," I gushed, "something I feel I should know, only I can't remember." I felt myself blushing. Just how unhinged did I want him to think I actually was?

"Imagine that," he said, bending down and kissing me gently on the mouth, all signs of his earlier unease gone. I swear he was glowing.

With my fingers I traced the outline of the bite mark on his skin. I still had no idea what had provoked me into doing such a thing. "I hope it doesn't leave a scar," I told him.

Taking my hand, Gabriel pressed it against his chest, against his heart, and said solemnly, "I hope it does."

I watched as he got up and went out of the room, enjoying the spectacular view of his ass, which, like the rest of him, was stunningly perfect.

Lying back, I could feel a warm stickiness on my thighs. Gingerly I wiped my skin, smearing my fingers with a bloody, milky fluid. Semen mixed with the proof of my virginity. I didn't want to see just how much was down there. It felt like a quart at the very least.

I closed my eyes and heard the soothing sound of running water coming from the bathroom. Drifting, I was headed for some post-coital land of bliss when I felt Gabriel touch me. His wet hair, along with the fragrance of my body wash clinging to his damp skin, told me what he'd been doing. Before I could utter a syllable in protest, he scooped me up in his arms and carried me to the bathroom, where the shower was still running. Setting me carefully on my feet inside the tub, he got in behind me, pulling my shower curtain closed. It was going to have to be replaced, I decided. Yellow ducks seemed completely inappropriate for post-sex showers.

"Can you stand?" Gabriel asked, his voice in my ear.

"Yeah, I'm fine." I braced my hands against the fiberglass wall in front of me. As long as my knees were locked, I was good to go. I let the water do its job, sluicing the excess fluid off my thighs before I carefully turned around and looked at him. He took up a whole lot more of my shower than my bed.

I couldn't help noticing the questioning look on Gabriel's face as he reached around me for the bottle of body wash. He seemed determined to treat me as if I was made of fine crystal, and I decided to enjoy the attention while it lasted. I splayed my hands against the smooth hardness of his chest and leaned against him.

Not bothering with a sponge, Gabriel tipped the pomegranate-mango-scented liquid into his palm, working it up into a rich lather. Caressing my skin, he soaped me up and down, tenderly wiping away whatever evidence still remained of our lovemaking and, with it, the last remnants of the girl I had once been. He took the most exquisite care with me.

Kissing me lightly, he turned me back around so he could finish his task. I felt him pause when his fingers brushed lightly over the marking in the small of my back.

"You have a tattoo." He sounded surprised, as if completely taken aback by the inking. It was obviously something he hadn't expected to see.

I tilted my head, wondering if it was going to be a problem. "A lot of girls have them," I muttered defensively. "They're no longer the exclusive right of bikers and gangbangers, you know."

"I wasn't being critical." His soapy hand slid up between my thighs and across my buttocks. "And I don't have a problem with it."

"But you don't like it?" I probed.

"No, you're wrong. I like it very much. It was just . . . unexpected."

And to prove his point he leaned forward and latched onto the curve of my neck, sucking the skin until it stung erotically.

With his hands on my shoulders, he turned me back around and stared down at me. His hair hung straight back, and I watched the water bead on his shoulders, running down his chest in little rivulets before dispersing across his pretty fantastic six-pack.

"What does it mean?" he asked curiously.

I lifted my shoulders. "I don't think it actually has a meaning."

"Well, it's an unusual design. How did you come up with it?"

I hesitated.

"What?" Gabriel put his hands on my upper arms and shook me a little. His eyes dropped, and he licked his lips as I jiggled.

"You'll laugh at me," I told him.

"No, I promise I won't."

His voice was serious, but my C-cup fillers were a definite distraction, which wasn't surprising considering I was wet and naked. I took a deep breath, deliberately grazing his chest with my breasts as I did so, and waited for his attention to refocus above my neckline.

Finding my eyes again, Gabriel grinned sheepishly. "Sorry, you were saying?"

"I dreamed about it."

I have never told anyone where the idea for my tattoo came from. It's an odd grouping of seven characters, and the best way I can describe them is by saying they look like a marriage of Greek letters and the symbols on a computer display of unusual fonts. Not quite one or the other, and not really a blend of the two, but close. A language all its own, except I had no idea what language it could possibly be. I peered up at Gabriel from beneath my lashes, convinced I would see a smirk on his face, but his mouth remained a straight line, and there was no hidden laughter in his eyes.

"How old were you?" he asked seriously.

"I don't really remember . . . about ten or eleven I think."

"And your father allowed you to get tattooed so young?"

I laughed. "Of course not, he would have had a fit! I had to wait until I was eighteen before I could get inked. I was ten or eleven when I had the dream." He looked at me oddly, and I felt as if he was hiding something. "It means something, doesn't it?"

"I'm sure it does, but not anything that I know."

Chuckling, Gabriel put his arms around me, his hand gently sweeping over the design before cupping my ass. I knew in my heart he was keeping something back, only I couldn't imagine what or why. It was just a tattoo, after all, even if it was an odd one.

"Do you want to hear something really strange?" I asked.

"About your tattoo?"

He was back to being cautious, and I nodded.

"Okay, but wet your hair for me." Now he reached for the bottle of shampoo.

I tipped my head back under the spray and let the weight of the water magically straighten out my curls.

"About a week after I had it done, Laycee decided she wanted one. Not the same thing, of course, she wanted one of those tribal designs." I saw him nod as his fingers began working through the suds I now wore as a crown. The scent of tangerines complemented the pomegranate-mango body wash. "Anyway, she liked the way mine looked," I continued, "and as I'd had hardly any bleeding, she wanted the same guy who inked me to do her."

"Uh-huh." Gabriel encouraged me to continue as he massaged my scalp.

"Mmmmm, oh yeah, that feels good." For a few moments I luxuriated in the feel of his fingers in my hair. Now I was the one getting distracted. "Okay, where was I? Oh yeah, well, the guy didn't remember doing it. He remembered me, but not actually doing the tattoo. Not even after I showed it to him. He drew a complete blank. Is that weird or what?"

"Not if he wasn't meant to remember," Gabriel said. At least I think that's what he said, but my ears were full of soap. Rinsing them out I heard him ask, "So, did Laycee get a tattoo?"

"Nah." I shook my head, and a big glob of suds landed on Gabriel's chest. "She figured the guy was high on something, so she didn't want him anywhere near her with an instrument that had multiple needles."

"Very wise of her."

Gabriel rinsed the shampoo out of my hair, and then his fingers began kneading my shoulders and I forgot everything else. When I was washed to his satisfaction, he reached around me and shut the water off. I couldn't help smiling. He really did take up an awful lot of room. Pushing back the shower curtain, he grabbed a towel and wrapped me in it, letting his forefinger wander a little as he tucked the end between my breasts. He handed me another for my hair and then secured one around his own waist before lifting me over the edge of the tub. I frowned, wondering where the multitude of towels had come from. And then I recognized them as the same ones I had washed that morning and had left folded on top of the dryer. I guessed he must have run down in his birthday suit to get them. Good job I lived alone.

"Sheets?" he asked.

"What?"

"Where do you keep your clean sheets?"

"Linen closet in the hall." I pointed out the bathroom door.

"Good, wait here."

Again with the staying where I was. What was this obsession that I might run off somewhere either totally or half naked? Shaking my head, I wiped the condensation off the mirror above the sink and stared at my reflection. I looked the same, and yet I didn't. My skin was flushed, my lips were swollen, and something in my eyes said I knew what it was like to hold a man in the palm of my hand. And not just figuratively.

"You are now an official member of the Women's Club," I murmured to my reflection. About time, too . . . and well worth the wait.

Gabriel stepped back into the bathroom. "I put your sheets downstairs on the floor by the washer. Was that okay?"

I paused, a handful of wet curls in one hand and a wide-toothed comb in the other, surprised by his thoughtfulness in changing them in the first place. I figured most guys would have just mopped up the mess with a towel and left it at that. I opened my mouth to thank him and then closed it again. On both occasions, the towels and now the sheets, I hadn't heard him going up or down the stairs. "Sure, that's fine."

Combing out the last of my tangles, I separated my hair into three sections so I could braid it. It would still be wet in the morning, but I didn't care. At least it would be easier to comb out again.

"Here, let me do that," Gabriel offered.

It was on my lips to automatically refuse, but then I stopped. His fingers moved deftly as he wove the wet strands into one.

"A man of hidden talents," I murmured, handing him a band to secure the end.

In bed once more, in the comfort of clean sheets, Gabriel tucked me back against him so we lay together like spoons. Except I was a teaspoon and he was more of a ladle, a really big soup ladle. My butt nestled comfortably against his groin, and I felt him, semi-hard, flirting with the round curve of my ass. It would take very little effort on my part to get him all the way erect.

I felt wonderfully content, satisfied in a way I had never known before. True, I was still a little sore and achy, but in a very good way. I was also exhausted and tried unsuccessfully to stifle a yawn.

"Sleep," Gabriel whispered to me, kissing my cheek and shifting position so I could roll over into his arms.

I snuggled next to him, my hand tucked in the curve of his waist, with my head resting on his massive chest. I was just on the edge of sleep when I felt him kiss my forehead.

"I promise, I will have no other but you," he whispered softly in the darkness.

You know who I am.

CHAPTER 21

I didn't need to reach behind me to feel the cold sheet, or turn my head and see the empty pillow to know I was alone. Flinging an arm over my eyes, I fought back the hot prick of tears and told myself to stop being stupid. I had known since the moment I'd invited Gabriel into my bed there was a possibility he wouldn't stay. I just wish he hadn't felt the need to prove me right.

Rolling onto my side, I curled up into a ball and pressed my hands between my knees. It helped a little. I was still sore, but I needed to find out if the ache was going to incapacitate me in any way. I made myself stretch out slowly, feeling the burn along my thighs and a dull pain in my pelvic area. Holy crap! How come no one ever mentioned the morning after could make you feel like you'd been hit by a semi?

Throwing back the covers, I put my feet on the floor and dared my legs to give way. Deciding this would not be the morning to piss me off, they obeyed my command and propelled me to the bathroom. Everything seemed to be throbbing, from the end of my braid to my toes, but I couldn't deny it was a perfectly acceptable condition when I recalled how I'd come by it. And just in case I was struck by the ridiculous notion that it had all been a really hot fantasy, I was sporting a pretty sizable love bite in the curve of my neck.

Turning sideways, I carefully passed my hands down over my abdomen, wincing just a little when I got to my pubic bone. I had no idea if it was the fact that I was older than most girls when I lost my virginity, or that Gabriel was so big, or a combination of the two, but there was no denying I was feeling some physical aftereffects. It wasn't one of those you-can't-get-out-of-bed feelings, but more of a what-happened-was-really-good-and-you-want-to-remember-it feeling. My inner thigh muscles protested as I pressed my fingers against the skin, but amazingly there were no bruises that I could see.

Brushing my palm lightly over my nipple, I caught my lower lip in my teeth as it flared to life, sending a little pulsating arc of pleasure through me, like an aftershock from an earthquake. Unexpected warmth flared in my groin, and I hoped it wouldn't take long for me to get through this "morning after" because I really wanted to have sex again. Problem was, waking up alone had shaken my confidence, and despite all that Gabriel had said, I didn't know if he intended to return, and I certainly wasn't about to invite anyone else to share my bed.

"Well, at least you can't die a virgin now," I told my reflection smugly.

Thumbing through a magazine, with an abandoned cup of coffee at my elbow, I stared at the article I was trying to read. After my third attempt at the opening paragraph I decided to give it up. Besides, I really didn't care what hemlines were doing on Italian runways this year. My dad would have accused me of "woolgathering," and he would have been right. I was trying really hard not to think about Gabriel, which was pretty much impossible. I wanted to hear the sound of his voice so I could reassure myself. Of what, I wasn't sure, but I think I needed to know last night had not been a mistake. Although there wasn't a whole hell of a lot I could do if he thought it was.

I was tempted to call him. His number was still programmed in my phone because I'd never gotten around to deleting it for some unfathomable reason, but then I reminded myself he'd had his service disconnected and reactivated since then. No doubt his carrier had provided him with a new number. Still . . . I resisted the urge to see if it had been changed, telling myself I was acting way too needy, and besides, I wasn't the one who had gotten up and left in the middle of the night.

As if on cue, my cell phone began burbling. The inane ringtone programmed by the teenage salesman made me jump. Ordinarily the bouncy pop tune didn't bother me, even made me smile on occasion, but right now it bugged the crap out of me.

"This better be good," I snapped irritably, not bothering to check caller ID.

"Whoa, what bit you on the ass?" Laycee's voice inquired sweetly.

A big hunk of Gabriel . . . and my ass was one of the few places where he didn't put his mouth.

"Sorry," I mumbled contritely. It wasn't her fault I was in a crappy mood. "Just woke up on the wrong side of the bed, I guess." *And alone.*

"Uh-huh."

"So, what's up?" I forced myself to smile. You can always "hear" someone smiling on the phone.

"Well, I'm calling for two reasons." Her tone forgave me for being snappish. "First, I want to thank you for coming to the Fall Festival last night—"

"You're welcome, and I'm sure I can find a suitable payback," I interrupted, more like myself.

"—and the second is, Mom wants dibs on the turkey platter for Thanksgiving dinner."

"As she's the only person who ever uses it, I think I should just give it to her as a gift."

"You know she won't take it," Laycee said with a laugh. "How else is she gonna make sure you're sitting at our table on turkey day?"

I laughed with her. "I know, I know. Tell her I'll run it over later in the week."

"Great." She paused, and I heard a hitch in her breath. "Are you okay, Ro?"

I felt myself frowning. Laycee may look like trailer trash, but she's smart and very intuitive, and she knows me too well to miss when something is "off." Still, she couldn't possibly *know*. I mean not over the phone, could she? "Sure, why do you ask?"

"I dunno, you sound a little weird—not bad or anything," she quickly clarified, "just odd." There followed another pause. "You got home all right last night, didn't you. I mean, nothing happened, did it?"

Not a thing. Unless you count the most spectacular, earth-shattering sexual act that ever took place between two people.

"Of course I got home all right," I told her, bypassing the second part of her question. "Guess I'm tired, that's all—and my feet still hurt from wearing those damn heels!"

She erupted into throaty laughter and accepted my explanation. We exchanged a couple more pleasantries and then hung up. I don't know why I didn't tell Laycee what had happened; I mean, it is the sort of thing best friends share, but for some reason I wanted to keep it to myself for as long as possible. In the back of my mind I guess I figured I'd get a lecture, especially if she knew who I'd slept with. And she had every right to bawl me out, considering what I'd put her through when Gabriel left me. But I wasn't in the right frame of mind to deal with disapproval this morning, whether it was deserved or not. I could only hope to be forgiven when I finally did confess.

The phone burbled again in my hand, and this time I didn't need to force the smile. It had taken Laycee about a minute to recall the other item her mom borrowed from me every Thanksgiving.

"Just remembered about the deviled egg dish, didn't you?"

There was a slight hesitation before Gabriel asked in a mystified voice, "Did I? What am I supposed to do with it?"

Oh, shit! I was instantly flustered. "Sorry, I thought you were Laycee calling back."

"Ah, that explains it."

"Explains what?"

"Why you haven't called me yet."

I could hear the gentle reprimand in his voice, and despite the thrill of knowing he wanted me to call, the rebuke needled me.

"The last time I tried your number, you'd canceled your service," I reminded him, needing to keep whatever was happening between us real.

There was a pause, a long one, and I was getting ready to say his name, just to make sure he was still on the other end, when he spoke, "Yeah, I'm sorry. I really screwed that one up, didn't I?"

"Uh-huh. You really did." I listened as he took in a deep breath, exhaled slowly. I decided I wouldn't bring up the phone thing again.

"Can we start over?" he asked.

"Isn't that sort of what we did last night?"

"I'd like to think so."

"Me too." My heart soared, and it felt wonderful.

"I was calling to apologize for not being there when you woke up. How are you feeling?" His voice might have been only in my ear, but it covered me like a blanket. A blanket that made more than my stomach roll. I was experiencing definite muscle spasms in my pelvis.

"Fine," I fibbed, "although I missed you in the bathtub."

He chuckled, "I'm not sure how that would have worked out, given the size of your bathtub. Still"—his voice turned into a throat-swabbing throb—"I guess I could always make it up to you."

Promises, promises. "What are you doing?" I asked.

"Ask me where I am."

"Okay, where are you?"

"In bed."

"Oh really?"

"Yeah . . . really."

The sound of rustling material made me think of satin sheets, red satin sheets. I wanted to ask him what time he had left, but that seemed a little possessive. For now I was content that he had called me.

"Where are you?" Gabriel asked, turning the tables and neatly derailing my train of thought.

"Sitting at the kitchen table, drinking coffee and reading a magazine."

A seductive whisper filled my ear. "Well, I want you to take your phone and go back to bed."

"Why? You won't be with me." He wasn't the only one who could be playful.

"Trust me, I will be." There came a low growl. "You ever had phone sex?"

"No," I admitted with a little gasp, getting up the stairs as fast as I could and no longer caring if my body hurt.

"Then this will be something we're both going to enjoy."

CHAPTER 22

Mother Nature decided to play seasonal catch-up by grabbing hold of a wicked Canadian chill and one-arming it down the eastern seaboard in a straight shot. It was as if she realized the extended balm of summer had been a mistake brought on by forgetfulness and was mortified we might think she had a mild case of Alzheimer's. Determined to put things right, and cover her ass, she needed to remind us that even this far south the seasons really did change. Oh and, by the way, in case you haven't noticed, it *is* November. Overnight, the temperature plummeted.

I loved it. Which was why I was now sitting on the back porch swing, wrapped in an old comforter, drinking hot chocolate, and thinking of Gabriel.

Gabriel.

Just the sound of his name falling off my tongue was enough to send tremors spiking through me. Closing my eyes, I pictured him in my mind. Now that I was able to replace my earlier fantasies with a more accurate depiction, I was stunned at how superior the reality was to my make-believe. Especially when it came to him being naked.

The set of his shoulders, his well-muscled thighs, and everything in between made him a living, breathing billboard for sex. No wonder the women at Rosie's had been falling over themselves trying to get him to notice them. Gabriel had triggered an instinctive biological drive to mate with the strongest male and so ensure survival of the species.

And nothing was more desirable than confidence, especially when it came in such a seductive package. If God had put Gabriel in the Garden of Eden instead of Adam, trust me, Eve wouldn't have known there was a snake, much less been tempted by one.

And to think he wanted me.

My life had officially changed from what it had once been, and I don't just mean because Gabriel had taken my virginity, although on a personal level, that was an event of almost biblical proportions. I felt different now, and not just physically. Twenty-four hours before, I knew exactly who I was and had a good idea where my life was going. Now all bets were off. With Gabriel my life took on a different perspective. Like Alice, I had just fallen down the rabbit hole and had no idea where I was going to end up.

A sudden fluttering in the pit of my stomach told me I was no longer alone. I turned my head to see the object of my musings outlined in the back door. Backlit by the kitchen light, his hair shimmered like a halo. I had no idea how long he'd been standing there.

"I knocked," he said, jerking his thumb over his shoulder as he came toward me, "but I guess you didn't hear me."

I shrugged, feeling my toes curl with delight. "Guess not."

Before I'd fallen asleep for the second time, Gabriel had asked if he could come by. I'd told him an invitation wasn't necessary. Ever. My heart began back-flipping in my chest as he took the mug from my hand so he could lean down and kiss me. I guess he liked the taste of the hot chocolate on my lips because after his tongue was done telling me how much he'd missed me, he tipped the mug to his own mouth.

"Mmmm . . . that's good."

"Yeah, I know," I said, checking out the empty mug he handed back.

Scooting me forward, he tucked himself behind me on the swing seat, wrapping his arms around me as I leaned back and resumed star gazing. Stroking my arm lightly, Gabriel pointed out a few of the constellations, telling me their names. The only one I could recognize was the Big Dipper, although Gabriel called it Ursa Major, the Great Bear. To me the rest were simply dots of light in the night sky, some bunched together and some spread out, some stars that were still alive and some that had already died.

From somewhere in the dark there came a muffled whooshing sound, followed by soft scrabbling and a single, high-pitched squeal.

"An owl," Gabriel whispered in my ear, his breath tickling my neck.

"How do you know?" I whispered back.

"Just do."

He spoke with a surety that begged me to challenge him, but I didn't. Instead, I shrugged and shook my head as he chuckled softly and pulled me a little closer. I felt safe, as if this was where I was meant to be and he was exactly the person I was supposed to be with. I could tell him my darkest secrets, reveal my deepest fears, and he would not ridicule me for having them. No wonder all the other men I'd ever dated had come up short. I'd been waiting for Gabriel. I just never knew it.

"Rowan, I want you to know I meant what I said last night." There was no flirty, sexual banter in his voice.

"About what?"

"About having no other but you."

I didn't know I'd been holding my breath until I let it out. "That's good to know." My tone was as solemn as his. "You don't strike me as the kind of man who would say such a thing and not mean it."

He pressed his lips against the curve of my neck, over his handiwork, and I tilted my head to one side, giving him better access.

"How are you feeling?" His lips continued their exploration, and he pushed aside my hair so he could nibble on the back of my neck.

"Mmmmm, good . . . nice," I murmured, tilting my head forward.

His lips stopped. "No, I mean how are you *feeling?*"

Oh . . . that.

"Good . . . really." I raised my head and shifted so he could see my face. "Okay, so I'm a little sore still," I admitted, "but nothing that I can't deal with given the right incentive."

"And just what kind of incentive would you need?"

I could feel myself blushing and couldn't believe how ridiculous I was being. I've never been embarrassed talking about sex, and now I was behaving like a teenager who had just discovered her parents' "special toy" in the bedside dresser drawer.

"Maybe a demonstration would be better," Gabriel suggested as his voice turned to liquid silk and filled the spaces between my vertebrae.

He moved again, settling himself more squarely on the seat, before straddling me across his lap. His erection rose to meet me. Leaning forward, I kissed him, my lips tentative at first and then quickly becoming more urgent.

"Ask me if I'm hungry," I whispered, pulling my mouth away.

I could almost hear the cogs whirling inside his head as he tried to follow my thought process before he finally gave up and asked, "Are you hungry?"

"Very much so. Now ask me what I'm hungry for."

The sensuous lift of his lips awoke a delicious fluttering that settled itself at the juncture of my thighs. "I don't need to ask," he said with a purr, "I know exactly what you want."

Pushing his hips up, Gabriel reached for my mouth and kissed me with an equal measure of hunger and desire. Long, cool fingers slid beneath my sweatshirt, a growl of delight rumbling up from somewhere in his chest at finding I wasn't wearing a bra. A thumb rubbed lightly over my nipple, which thanked him by exploding into a stiff peak, and I felt the fluttering in my stomach change into something more demanding.

"Do you want to go inside?" he asked as his hand now attended to my other breast.

"No, out here is just fine," I gasped as his thumb and forefinger found my nipple. "There's no one who can see us, except for the owl."

Pushing his shoulders back, I put some space between us so I could lift the sweatshirt up over my head.

"Perfect." As he stroked along my spine, his mouth divided its attention between my breasts.

The chilly air whispering on my skin, his hot wetness suckling me, and the hard throb between my legs all combined to make one hell of an erotic dance. I nearly fell off the damn swing, but Gabriel's hand on my waist kept me firmly anchored against him. I could feel him straining against the fly of his jeans as his tongue began lapping little circles over my skin. A hand slid up my back and settled itself between my shoulder blades. It pushed me closer so he could lick the side of my neck, the hollow of my throat, across my collarbone.

My fingers found the first closed button of his shirt. Managing to fumble it open, I continued down until I was able to pull the black silk open and slide it off him. He was magnificent. The only blemish on his skin was the bite mark I had given him, and I guiltily ran my fingers over the bruise, feeling him shudder at my touch. I guess the look on my face concerned him, because he caught my hand and pushed it down between my legs, pressing my palm against his fly.

Feeling him move beneath me, I pressed back, seeing his eyes close as he drew in a ragged breath. Gabriel thrust upward with his hips, pulsing through the heavy denim. I clutched his shoulders, teasing him with some hip action of my own, grinding down on him and pushing my breasts against his chest. He groaned, and his hand tightened around my waist. I really didn't feel that sore anymore.

"Jesus Christ, Rowan . . . you've no idea how good that feels."

I slid off his lap, and he jerked up, eyes open wide.

"It's okay, big guy," I said, my hand possessively cupping his crotch. "I know how to make it feel even better." I brushed my lips lightly over his and pushed him back. "Last night you did something wonderful for me. Now let me return the favor."

The temperature had dropped a few more degrees, but despite being half-naked, I don't think either one of us felt cold. One of the advantages of having an internal thermostat constantly hovering on feverish, I guess. My fingers got busy unbuckling his belt and popping the button at his waistband. I was a little irked to discover he was wearing button-fly jeans. A zipper would have gotten me to what I wanted a lot faster, but then I appreciated how this would work in my favor. By the time I reached the last one, a fine sheen of sweat had broken out on Gabriel's torso, making him glisten in the moonlight. I peeled back his jeans and the sight of his cock made me suck in my breath. I felt, rather than saw, the smile on his face.

"Do you normally go commando?" I asked him, more out of curiosity than anything else.

"I think I will from now on."

I wasn't about to complain, thinking perhaps it was a good job I hadn't had a zipper to deal with after all. I could have done some serious damage in my eagerness to get his pants off. I tugged playfully at the waistband of his jeans. I really needed them off.

"Give me a minute."

His eyes had a semi-glazed look as he placed the sole of one foot against the heel of the other and kicked off his boots. Licking his lips, he lifted his hips for me, and his jeans sailed unceremoniously across the porch. When I nudged the side of his leg with my knee, Gabriel obediently opened for me. I grabbed a cushion and dropped it on the deck before kneeling between his legs.

Whatever his experience, and I knew for sure there had only been one virgin in my bed last night, his comprehension of what was about to happen suddenly hit home. He looked down at me with eyes that said he didn't quite believe what I was going to do. I hesitated, not knowing whether his surprise was with me or the act itself. What if he didn't like it? What if he'd had a bad experience?

"Is this okay?" I asked hesitantly.

"Oh . . . yeah . . ." The expression on his face said this was very much okay. "But you don't have to—" I silenced him by pressing my fingers against his mouth, and whatever he saw on my face banished any doubts he might have had about my participation.

He was hard and thick, impressive in both length and girth, and I swallowed, pretty amazed with myself that I had been able to take all of him the night before. There was no way I could repeat that with my mouth, but I knew I could do enough to achieve what we both wanted. Sliding my palms slowly up and down the length of him, I watched in fascination as he abandoned himself to the sensation.

Throwing back his head, Gabriel stretched his arms along the top of the swing seat, his fingers gripping the frame hard enough to whiten his knuckles. With every stroke of my hands, his muscles clenched. Chest expanding, abdomen rippling, his body moved with the rhythm I created. Leaning forward, I flicked a nipple with my tongue before scraping the hard nub lightly with my teeth. A rumble of pleasure came from deep inside his chest.

I ran the pad of my thumb lightly over the tip of his cock, feeling a tremor shudder through him. He wasn't going to last much longer. It was time something other than my hands got busy.

For a moment I thought he was having a full body spasm because when I wrapped my lips over the head of his cock, sliding him into my mouth, it felt as if every muscle in his body stretched itself to the absolute limit but forgot how to relax again. Gently I stroked a hand across his lower belly as the other continued to move up and down his shaft.

He freed one of his own from the death grip it had on the swing seat and buried it in my hair, relaxing his body so he could enjoy what was happening. My mouth couldn't get enough of him, my tongue stroking itself around his rigid flesh, lapping along the ridge of his foreskin, dipping inside the dimple at the tip. Increasing the pressure of my hand at the base of his shaft, I let my tongue take a back seat, allowing Gabriel to dictate the pace as he moved in and out of my mouth.

I cupped his balls. Heavy and full, they overflowed my palm, but I massaged them gently and was rewarded by the sharp intake of breath that came from above my head. Gabriel's chest heaved as he tried to draw in more air. His thighs trembled against my rib cage, his calves tightened as they jammed into place behind my legs, and then his hips began to pump in earnest. I glanced up at him from beneath my lashes. His eyes were hooded neon slits that stared down at me while he danced the tip of his tongue across his full bottom lip.

He was close to coming. I could see it in the striated bicep of the arm that still gripped the swing. I could *feel* it. Maximizing the pressure of my lips around him, I stretched my fingers, encircling as much of his cock as I could while moving my hand faster. Unexpectedly, Gabriel threw back his head and yelled, startling our voyeuristic owl from his perch. Arching his back, he thrust forward with his hips, and I automatically relaxed my throat and swallowed, taking him down in a warm salty rush, while gently milking him with both hands. When I felt his body ease, his fingers releasing their grip on my hair, I gently slipped him out of my mouth, taking a last satisfied sweep over his tip with my tongue.

Sitting back on my heels, I let my hands fall in the space between his legs while I waited for him to come back to earth. The scent of sex was thick and heavy in the air, and for a while all I could hear was the sound of his breath rushing in, rushing out, keeping pace with the pounding beat of his heart.

"Come here." His voice, throaty and raw, took me by surprise.

Placing my hand in his outstretched palm, he pulled me up off my knees. His forehead leaned against my midriff as he encircled me with his arms, pulling me closer, so his tongue could make a slow lazy sweep across my stomach. Gooseflesh that had nothing to do with the night air rose on my belly.

"Cold?" he queried, pulling his head back from my dimpled skin.

I shook my head. What he was doing was getting me hot, not cold.

Hooking his fingers in the waistband of my sweats, he pulled them down over my hips and legs, making sure he took my panties at the same time. I steadied myself, a hand on his shoulder, and kicked them off. Gabriel brushed his fingers lightly up the back of my calves and thighs on the return journey. I saw his nostrils flare as he caught the scent of my arousal. I couldn't help it. I was already wet from going down on him, and now anticipation kept me primed.

He buried his face in the juncture at the top of my thighs, and I felt his tongue, hot and demanding, slide between my swollen flesh as he tasted me. Grabbing a fistful of his hair, I tried my best not to grind myself against his mouth, because what he was doing was the most incredible thing I'd ever felt.

"Open for me," he murmured in a voice so ripe with desire, I thought it quite possible I could orgasm if he simply told me to.

Looking up at me, I saw his lips were glossy with my slickness, and he deliberately ran his tongue over his mouth, sucking me inside. I almost came right then, but he wasn't about to let that happen. Pulling my face down so he could kiss me, Gabriel made certain I tasted myself on his lips. With his tongue now otherwise occupied, his fingers took over between my thighs, slipping in and out of me, making me even wetter. My legs felt weak and my knees unexpectedly buckled.

He moved so quickly I didn't realize we had switched places until I felt the hard planking of the swing seat under my butt. Taking his turn to kneel on the deck, he pulled me forward until my ass was just resting on the edge of the seat.

"Stay right there," he said as my fingers curled around the front curve of the seat in an effort to scoot back. Ducking down, he raised himself back up with my legs over his shoulders, his hands on my hips. I watched his tongue sweep up the inside of each thigh before flattening out and lapping up the center of me.

I must have wet my finger and stuck it in a light socket. My knees locked and my toes pointed, and Gabriel had to put a hand on my belly to stop me from bucking off the swing. And all the while his tongue continued to lap at me, until he took that cluster of nerve endings between his lips and sucked hard, sending me completely over the edge.

I think I passed out. If I didn't, I came pretty damn close to it.

The next night we didn't even make it up the stairs. I will never be able to look at my kitchen table again without seeing my hands gripping the edge as Gabriel bent me over it. Oh. My. God. It seemed a very natural progression, going from sex on the kitchen table to sex in the hall to sex in the living room. I'm ashamed to say it wasn't until we were done giving the couch springs a thorough workout that the question of responsibility reared its head.

Filled with post-sex euphoria, I was tracing circles on Gabriel's smooth chest with my forefinger when the irresponsibility of our actions sledge-hammered me in the back of the head. I was embarrassed about having to raise the topic, but one of us had to be the adult. We were having unprotected sex, lots of unprotected sex.

"Gabriel?"

"Hmmmm?" His eyes were closed and his voice lazy-sleepy with contentment.

"Can I talk to you about something?"

"Anything at all . . ."

"Okay . . . I think we ought to talk about protection."

The hand that had been languidly stroking my back stopped, and he opened his eyes, staring at me in mild alarm. The dark blue color was startlingly bright.

"From whom do you need me to protect you?" he asked. "Has something happened?"

"No, of course not." I gave him a shaky laugh.

His question made me stumble a little because he assumed I was referring to an outside threat. It was a reminder of all the things about him I still didn't know. I stopped tracing circles and put my hands on his chest, resting my chin on them.

"That's not the type of protection I'm talking about."

"Oh." Closing his eyes, I felt his hand resume its glide up my back. "What other kind is there?"

Puh-leeze! Now he was being deliberately dense. He knew exactly what I was talking about; he just wanted to make me spell it out.

"The type that requires using a condom," I said in my best *can we please be grown-up about this* voice.

The corners of his mouth twitched. "Are you sure you'd be able to wait long enough for me to put one on?" My cheeks burst into flame. It was true that since I'd found out what I'd been missing, I gave all the appearance of wanting to make up for lost time and was, well, sometimes a little over-eager. "But if you think it will make sex better, then of course I'll wear one—although size may be something of a problem." He gave a conceited snort, and I lifted my chin so I could slap him lightly on the arm. He flexed his bicep in response.

"That's not the only reason to wear one," I remarked with an exasperated sigh. All joking aside, I wanted him to take me seriously. "Don't you think it would be more responsible?"

He shrugged. "Not really."

I pushed myself up, tucking my hair behind an ear, and looked down at him. "Why not?"

"Because I can't get you pregnant."

It never occurred to me that he might be sterile. Not someone as blatantly masculine as he was. I hadn't consciously been thinking about having a baby, but now that I knew Gabriel couldn't procreate, I felt a wave of melancholy wash through me. He would have fathered beautiful children. Curiosity reared its head, but it felt all wrong asking him to tell me the reason why.

"But what about . . . other reasons?" It sounded like I was accusing him of something improper. "I mean, there was only one virgin in this relationship, right?" Great. That sounded even worse.

He reached up and took my face in his hands, the blue of his eyes intensifying. "Of course, and you have every right to be concerned. Will you believe me if I tell you that I have no diseases, carry no infections or anything else that would harm you?"

If any other girl told me her boyfriend had said this to her, I would have laughed at her gullibility and told her to dump his ass and go get herself tested. But I knew Gabriel was being truthful, so I nodded.

"Yes, I believe you."

"Good." He pulled my face down so he could sweep his tongue across my lips. "And as long as you welcome my attentions, you know I will take no other."

"Ah, but how do you know I'm being faithful to you?" I teased.

"Because I would be able to smell another man on you."

This was a statement that I listened to from my very favorite place, Clueless Land, and as usual, I had no idea what he meant by it. Surely he wasn't being literal? I mean, was such a thing even remotely possible? I wanted to ask him, but Gabriel decided the time for questions was over and focused my attention elsewhere.

Taking my hand, he wrapped it around his thick cock, encouraging me to slide my palm up and down the length of him as his tongue mimicked a similar action inside my mouth. When he was fully erect, I straddled him, locking my knees against his sides and replacing my hand with my body.

Guiding my hips, he moved me slowly up and down the length of him, coating himself with my slick heat, until he exploded inside me in a great roaring rush that triggered my own climax. I collapsed on his chest, panting wildly with my face buried in his neck.

I could feel his pulse thrumming against my cheek, and for a moment I was certain I could smell his blood again. The crisp scent of pine and what I thought were undercurrents of juniper teased my olfactory senses. But I knew I hadn't bitten him this time.

I ran my fingers down the side of his neck, feeling the flow of blood as it raced through his veins. It almost begged to wash over my tongue and slide down my throat, and I wondered if Gabriel had ever wanted to taste my blood.

CHAPTER 23

Laycee called midweek, inviting me to dinner at her parents' house Friday night so I could bring over the turkey platter and the deviled-egg dish that she never remembered. I was immediately wracked with guilt because I still hadn't told her I was back with Gabriel.

For the first time in my life I was unsure about my best friend. I usually had a pretty good idea what her reaction would be to any set of circumstances, and if I didn't, it wasn't something I lost any sleep over. But this time I wasn't as confident I knew how Laycee would react once she learned I had welcomed, naked, on my back and panting, the same guy who'd put me through the emotional wringer only a few months before.

She had enough lectures in her arsenal without the addition of one that dealt with the hazards of returning to the arms of a potentially fickle boyfriend. But I knew what she'd say: If he'd left me cold once before, then he would do so again. It was going to take a whole lot of convincing to make Laycee believe Gabriel would not dump me a second time—convincing that I just didn't have the energy to expend right now.

"Looking forward to it!" I told her when she called, hoping she wouldn't see through my false perkiness. It crossed my mind, for a total of about ten seconds, to make up some excuse and beg off her dinner invitation, but that would only send up warning flags.

By the time Friday rolled around I was a wreck because I hadn't heard from Gabriel. Apparently he and I have a different understanding of what *you don't have to call* means. I could kick myself for being so blasé. It wasn't that I had doubts or still needed reassurance (well, not much), but I would have thought he might want to just touch base with me, hear my voice or something. God knows I wanted to hear his.

Now it was almost a week since I'd last seen him. I thought about calling but was afraid it might seem as if I was checking up on him. In my book that was a guaranteed first-place finish in the Insecure Female Stakes, which was never a good thing. I was just going to have to trust that I would hear from him soon.

In the meantime . . . self-doubt was a total bitch.

Before leaving for Laycee's parents' house, I wrote a note for Gabriel, telling him where I'd gone and that the spare key was under the mat. I had no idea if he was going to come by or not, but at least he'd know I was thinking of him. Dinner was a blast, and for a few hours I was able to occupy my mind with something other than my absent boyfriend. Laycee's parents were warm and loving, and it had been too long since I'd last enjoyed their company. I was glad I hadn't bailed.

The first thing I noticed when I got home was that the note was missing from my front door. Not wanting to take any chances with an errant breeze, I had secured it firmly with enough duct tape that I knew its AWOL status was deliberate. Hesitantly I lifted the corner of the front doormat, only to be disappointed by the sight of my spare key glinting in the porch light. Apparently my offer to Gabriel to make himself at home had been turned down.

I gave in to a brief moment of despondency as I retrieved the key and let myself in. Then I told myself to stop behaving like some lovesick teenager with ridiculous expectations. Gabriel had taken my note and read it, but having no idea how long I would be, he'd decided not to hang around waiting for my return. I hung up my coat and kicked off my shoes, feeling a little better. At least he'd come by to see me.

As she had done every year since I could remember, Laycee's mom had given me a list of items she needed me to bring to make certain Thanksgiving dinner went off without a hitch. This was in addition to the turkey platter and deviled egg dish. The list wasn't always about food, although I could guarantee a request for my dad's cranberry-apple relish. That was only because I refused to give up the recipe. This year she needed a few extra plates, a pitcher, and a couple of CDs. Hinder with Thanksgiving dinner wouldn't have been my first choice, but I'm all for expanding anyone's musical taste.

I had a cupboard open, craning my neck to see how many matching dinner plates I actually possessed, when I heard the sound of a throat clearing behind me. Snapping my head around, I saw Gabriel leaning against the doorjamb.

"Your door was unlocked," he said with mock sternness. "Anyone could have come in."

I shrieked and flung myself at him, my arms around his neck, my legs around his waist, kissing him anywhere my lips could reach. He tucked his hands beneath my butt and returned my affection with a great deal of enthusiasm. After pulling his T-shirt up and over his head, I had my own blouse unbuttoned and off by the time we got to the stairs.

Now that I had a lot more confidence, sex was definitely better. Sometime around one in the morning it went beyond better. Gabriel woke me up and showed me some of the other things he could do with his tongue. My orgasm was close to cataclysmic.

Unfortunately, there was an elephant in bed with us. Actually, that's kind of misleading. He wasn't *in* bed with us, but he was standing in the corner of my bedroom. Big ears, big tusks, wrinkled knees, and a long trunk. Gabriel wasn't as anxious about the elephant as I was, but that wasn't so surprising. It was his pachyderm, after all.

As I lay tucked against his side, my mind was going a mile a minute. With my arm across his chest, my leg flung over his thigh, I was enjoying the long lazy caresses his hand was making as it moved across my skin. Well, trying to. Difficult when you're not completely alone. And I didn't want to be the one who mentioned it first.

No matter how much I told myself it didn't matter what Gabriel did when he wasn't with me, it was a lie. It *did* matter. In my world no legitimate occupation is ever referred to as *this and that.* I sensed that if I were to ask, he would tell me exactly what he did for a living, and how he made his money.

The question was . . . did I really want to know?

There was a certain comfort in having a measure of plausible deniability. But what did that mean for this fledgling relationship we had embarked on? A lie was never a promising start, and even though Gabriel had told me no lies as far as I knew, withholding the truth was sometimes worse. Wasn't it? Guess it all came down to perspective. But that wasn't the only piece of baggage the elephant brought with him.

"What are you thinking about?" Gabriel asked, his voice a soft murmur in the dark.

I sighed, "Nothing."

"Liar." He spoke the word playfully and stayed his hand on a downward stroke. Gently moving me off of him, Gabriel propped himself on his side and looked down at me. His eyes were sleepy, lazy, and incredibly sexy.

"You have every right to be wary of me and my intentions; your trust is something I will have to earn again. And I know it will take time."

"Why do you think I don't trust you?"

Catching a lock of my hair, he twisted it gently through his fingers. "I left you before. It is only natural to wonder if I will do so again."

Bingo. A loud trumpeting sound in my head said the elephant was glad to be partially acknowledged.

"And will you?" I held my breath waiting for his answer, and not feeling the slightest guilt at putting him on the spot.

Dropping my curl, Gabriel put his hand beneath my chin and stroked the pad of his thumb across my bottom lip. His eyes were deep, bottomless pools, and I was drowning inside them. It would be a beautiful, endless death.

"Only if you tell me to go," he said solemnly. "I hated the way I left you before, but there were reasons for it, Rowan."

The anguish in his voice was all I needed to hear, and it changed everything. Whatever the reasons, they were Gabriel's, and I was not about to demand he share them. It was enough that we had both been miserable. He kissed me—one of those spine-tingling numbers that could make me forget my own name—and I wanted nothing more than to make sure he kept on kissing me like this . . . forever.

"Rowan, there are things about me you need to know—"

"Gabriel, hush!" I had to stop him before the elephant blew his trunk off. This wasn't the time to hear any confessions. Not when I had the feeling they could be life-changing for me.

Placing my hands on his fabulous pecs, I pushed him down onto his back and straddled him. He opened his mouth to speak, but I pressed my fingers against his lips, smiling as he pressed back against them.

"I know you're not like other men," I said, smiling down at him. "You don't have a nine-to-five job, and there's an aura about you that spells trouble with a capital T, and every sensible, sane bone in my body is telling me to stay away from you." I leaned forward just enough to tease him by brushing my breasts against his chest. "I. Don't. Care. If I wanted a regular boyfriend, I wouldn't be lying on top of you right now."

And it was true. Saying the words out loud dispelled any lingering doubts about my commitment. Consciously or not, I'd made the decision that I wanted to be with Gabriel, no matter what his past or his present. And it wasn't just for the sex. I wasn't that foolish that I'd offered up some brain cells along with my virginity.

Maybe I was just tired of the whole dating scene. The constant cattle market that always had me coming home alone. It hadn't been such a big deal a few years ago, but once I hit twenty-five, that old saying about time moving faster as you got older was definitely ringing true. It wasn't doing a Roadrunner on me, but I could feel it starting to move up a little. And maybe seeing Laycee and Jake together, knowing my BFF was shifting into a different phase of her life, was also affecting me. I knew Laycee and I would always be friends, but the fabric of our friendship had changed now that Jake was in her life. Already she didn't need me as much as she had before. And I was okay with that. It was how it was supposed to be.

I stared down at the man who lay beneath me, saying nothing, giving me the time I needed to gather my thoughts, and waiting patiently for me to speak. He was a mystery, all right, and a part of me still didn't understand why he wanted to be with me, but then that odd little voice blew through my head, and there was a feeling of *rightness* when Gabriel held me in his arms. A certainty that reaffirmed being with him was exactly where *I* was meant to be.

My hips moved with just enough pressure to make him groan and flare his nostrils. I felt the steel hardness of him pushing up against me, but despite his desire, I also saw the shadow I had seen before flicker deep in his eyes. The specter of loneliness could not be diminished that easily. Gently I stroked my fingers along the stubble that darkened his jaw, feeling the slight tension in his hand as it moved down my thigh.

Framing his face with my hands, I stared into his eyes, suddenly picturing the cobalt blue bleeding out and his pupils turning gold. It was an odd image to bring to mind, but I remembered it vividly from that night in the diner. And I knew it was a connection to the secrets he was keeping. I wanted to tell him it didn't matter. I hadn't been frightened then, and I wasn't now.

"I'm not going to deny that I'm curious. I'm female; it's in our DNA." Smiling, Gabriel tucked a stray curl behind my ear. "Of course I want to know everything about you," I continued, "about what you do when you're not with me, but I'm not ready to hear it just yet, any more than you are to tell me." He opened his mouth, no doubt to issue a denial, but I shook my head. "Let me finish this. I don't need details, but there are some things I do need to know, okay?"

Grasping my hand in his, Gabriel pressed his lips against my palm and traced a small circle with the tip of his tongue. "Ask me anything."

I took a deep breath. "What you do for a living, *this and that* . . . is it illegal?"

He didn't hesitate for a second. "Some would consider it so." His voice was serious, and even though his reply wasn't the definitive answer I'd been hoping for, it was honest. Any uncertainty or faltering would have sent up a red flag.

"Is it immoral?"

"That depends on your view of morality."

My eyebrows shot up. That was a discussion we needed to have, and sometime soon.

"Okay." I paused, unsure of how to phrase my next question, and then I just decided there was no good way, so I spit it out. "Does it involve children in any way?"

His eyes became hard. "Absolutely not. I would never do anything that would harm an innocent!"

It was my first taste of his anger, and while the vehemence of his denial scared me a little, it also sent a warmth rushing through me. Children and animals—there was no place in my life for a man who would deliberately hurt either. I brushed the hard line that his mouth had become with my lips, apologizing for my questions. His tongue in my mouth forgave me.

I raised my head. "Will I be in danger if I know any of your secrets?"

Gabriel moved so quickly I didn't realize he had flipped me onto my back until I found myself surrounded by a white curtain of hair.

"No harm will come to you, Rowan," he declared, "from either your world or mine. I swear it."

His expression was so fierce, it pushed open a door in the back of my mind. Unfortunately it wasn't wide enough to offer any real insight, keeping whatever memory lay behind it just out of reach.

"I don't doubt that," I whispered.

Relaxing his stern scowl, he pressed his lips to my forehead. "I have taken certain steps to make sure you are safe, even when I cannot be with you."

I wanted to ask him what I needed to be kept safe from, but an unexpected stab of fear pierced me, and the look in his eye said there were some things it was better not to know. Fuck! This was something I hadn't accounted for. Truly serious shit.

And it didn't change a damn thing.

At least now I knew the air of danger that surrounded him was more than just my imagination. I pulled his face down to mine and kissed him. Just as deep, just as long, the way he had kissed me. And, although I don't think I had quite the skill to make him forget his name, there was no denying the passion I awakened. When I finally let go of his mouth, my breath was ragged, my hands fisted in his hair. "Promise me that, when the time is right, you will tell me everything that I don't know."

"When the time is right," he answered in a low growl, "I will have no choice."

An ominous chill ran through me. "You think my feelings will change when I know?"

"It would be impossible for them not to," he said, his mouth settling into a sad smile, "but in what direction I cannot say."

"Hey, c'mon," I chided, "have some faith."

He was so serious about this, whatever it was, that I wanted to reassure him. Tell him he was wrong. But Gabriel decided that the time for talking was over and my mouth could be put to better use.

When I went downstairs the next morning, the blouse and bra I'd been wearing the night before, clothes that I'd eagerly stripped off, were now folded in a neat pile on the table. I imagined Gabriel's fingers stroking the satin cups of my bra, and I felt a thrill of pleasure rush through me at the thought of him touching my underwear. Whether I was in it or not.

I made coffee and went to get the Sunday paper from the end of the driveway. It was the only day I had the newspaper delivered, and as I twisted the lever to unlock the dead bolt, my breath caught.

As wonderful as my relationship with Gabriel was, it still rankled that he never stayed the night. No matter how late the hour, he always got dressed and left. I never asked where it was he had to go, and he did not offer to tell me. This was the part of his life that I wasn't ready to hear about. In reality I suspected my ignorance could fill an area the size of Alaska, and I knew if I asked, Gabriel would willingly fill in the blanks, but not until I asked him to. So he always left me with a lingering good-bye at my front door, and I playfully flashed him some skin before returning to snuggle in the warmth he left behind.

But last night that hadn't happened. I'd fallen asleep, and Gabriel had obviously decided not to wake me to tell me he was leaving.

So how come the dead bolt was still locked?

The only way to operate the mechanism was by hand from the inside or with a key from the outside. My purse was sitting on the hall table, and my set of keys clearly visible. I went back to the kitchen and opened the pantry. The spare key was hanging on the hook where I had put it after retrieving it from under the mat.

A frown furrowed my brow as I returned to the front door and stared at the dead bolt.

Snapping my fingers, I told myself I was a total idiot as the answer came to me. Of course! Even though there was no one to witness him coming and going—unless you count wildlife, and there was no way of knowing how many of them would gladly trash my reputation—Gabriel must have left by the back door.

However, a tug confirmed it, too, was locked. Shit! How the hell had he gotten out without unlocking either door? Surely not through a window? A quick check put that theory to rest. All my ground floor windows were secure.

This was going to bug the crap out of me all day, and there was no way I could hold off asking about it until I saw him again. At times I am cursed with the most awful "wait" problem. I got my cell phone and lit up his number.

"Rowan? Is everything okay?"

I was glad I'd caught him while he was still awake. "Yes, everything's fine although . . . I need to ask you a question."

"Okay, ask away."

"How did you relock the door after you left this morning?"

Payback is a bitch. It's not often I can stump Gabriel, but this was one of those times. I listened with my own smirk, picturing his face as his brain went into spasms trying to come up with something plausible.

"Look, you might as well tell me," I said quietly, before hearing him exhale in a long sigh. This was not a good sign, and suddenly I understood the reason for his silence. "Oh shit!" I exclaimed. "This is in Alaska, isn't it?" Gabriel found my descriptive euphemism for the part of his life I knew nothing about highly amusing.

"Yeah, it is," he confirmed softly.

"Aww, fuck, I'm sorry. I shouldn't have asked." My apology made him chuckle.

"No, it's okay. It was bound to come up sooner or later."

I hesitated for all of three seconds before jumping in. "So am I right in thinking you can get in and out of places without needing a key?"

He hesitated a moment more. "Yes, I can."

"Anywhere?" Even though it was wrong, I was intrigued.

"Pretty much, as long as I've first been invited."

I wasn't sure what he meant by that, but put it down to my general ignorance of breaking and entering. "Could you get into the White House?"

He laughed. "No, I've never received an invitation to the White House."

"Oh." I was disappointed.

"Would Buckingham Palace make up for it?"

I almost dropped my phone. "You've been invited to Buckingham Palace?"

"Not officially."

I was busy trying to sort through the ramifications of his answer when Gabriel slid the subject away from majestic homes. "By the way, you look gorgeous when you're asleep," he murmured, totally disrupting my thought pattern, "and I'm sorry I didn't wake you. I won't do it again if it displeases you."

I sighed. There wasn't anything he could do that would displease me. "Oh, that's okay," I told him, "at least now I won't have to bother getting an extra key made for you."

"You have the most unique way of seeing things, Rowan."

The chuckle that filled my ear this time was flavored with something more than humor, something very sexual. I decided to let him get some rest.

"Good night, Gabriel, sleep well."

CHAPTER 24

I drank my coffee and considered all the ramifications of the explanation I'd just been given. It didn't matter how I looked at it, every angle brought me back to the same conclusion and confirmed my initial speculations about my boyfriend.

Gabriel was a criminal.

I think deep down I'd known it would come to this, but a part of me was reluctant to let go of the unrealistic hope that he was a wealthy recluse, the black sheep of a very snobby European aristocratic family whose members rubbed elbows with royalty. Especially after that comment about Buckingham Palace.

You really didn't believe that, did you?

Maybe . . . maybe not. But now I was left with only one reason Gabriel would possess the skill to get through a locked door without a key. It explained a lot and told me nothing at all. And while I might not be ready to openly discuss what else was hidden in that Alaska-sized area of his life, it didn't mean I wasn't above taking little side trips on my own looking for answers.

"My boyfriend is a criminal."

Saying the words out loud, sharing them with the kitchen appliances, filled me with an odd sense of relief. And it explained a lot. Gabriel's cars, his killer, all-black wardrobe, and the $50,000-plus

Rolex he wore. Yeah, I looked that one up online. It also supported Gabriel's reluctance to tell me what he *actually* did for a living, not to mention his odd statement about keeping me safe. Safe from what? He hadn't been specific, but the fact he'd even mentioned my safety in the first place was warning enough.

And, sadly, I also understood why he expected the truth to make a difference in my feelings. Considering all the risks involved, even the possibility of prison, how could it not? The more I thought about it, the more confident I became in my assumptions. And Gabriel didn't work alone. The odd behavior of the good-looking trio we met after the movies that night was a red flag waving. They were all probably part of a sophisticated crime syndicate because, whatever else, they definitely didn't look like your typical neighborhood gangbangers.

I'll admit the only thing I knew about gangs is what I'd seen on TV and read in the papers. Obviously Gabriel wasn't in with some East L.A. posse, but I couldn't say the same about a European connection. I don't know if they have gangs in Norway, but I don't see why not. People are pretty much the same the world over when it comes to what side of the law you choose to stand on. But I got the distinct impression that any gang affiliations he had wouldn't be Scandinavian in origin. For one thing, Gabriel had told me he hadn't lived in Norway since he was a child.

It seemed more likely, in my wild guesswork, that any criminal connection would involve something like the Russian mob. Especially when I thought about Aleksei. I've seen *Eastern Promises,* and Nikolai Luzhin could kick the ever-loving shit out of one of Tony Soprano's boys any day.

But there was always the possibility I was way off base. One thing all gangs, and Russian gangs in particular, had in common was a fondness for tattoos. Tattoos not only told your life history, they were a declaration of loyalty. Gabriel had none. His skin was perfectly smooth and totally unblemished. No tats, no scars, not even a mole or a freckle. If he was involved in any type of gang, then it was one that required no ostentatious artwork as proof of allegiance, or else he was high enough up the food chain that a tattoo was unnecessary.

Neither thought gave me the warm-fuzzies, and as I reflected on that, another wrinkle came to light. My boyfriend walking on the wrong side of the law was going to put a definite strain on my friendship with Laycee. Especially now that her relationship with Jake was no longer a secret. Suddenly I was very thankful I had kept my silence about being back with Gabriel.

As for myself, I was a lost cause. No matter what truth lay buried in Alaska, nothing was going to take me away from him. Nothing could. I didn't care if he was a half step away from an arrest warrant, I would not leave him. Some unfathomable, irresistible force told me, as sure as the sun was going to rise in the morning, my future was linked with his. And that odd feeling of déjà vu was getting stronger.

Part of me said I should ask Gabriel what it meant, especially as the voice in my head was becoming a royal pain. It wouldn't be so bad if it threw me something different to chew on every now and then, but apparently its entire vocabulary was limited to five words. And I still had no idea what they meant. How could I possibly know who Gabriel was?

Still, there was *something*... if I could only put my finger on it. Perhaps it was all in the wording. Just because you hadn't met someone before didn't necessarily equate to not knowing them.

The weeks that followed were like a honeymoon, with very few nights that Gabriel and I were not together. I did suffer some anxiety wondering how I was going to pull off spending Thanksgiving with Laycee and her family. Canceling due to a sudden, unexpected illness was not an option. If I was too sick to come to them, they would simply load up the car and bring Turkey Day to me.

I'd come to the conclusion that perhaps my best bet was to simply show up with Gabriel in tow. Laycee's mom would welcome him with open arms, tickled pink that I finally had a man of my own. And I knew an extra mouth to feed at Thanksgiving was never a problem. But Laycee would be hurt, and trying to come up with a believable excuse for my silence was going to be difficult. And then there was Jake to consider. Would experience give him some sort of cop ESP that would just *tell* him Gabriel and he were on opposite sides of the law? I was saved when Gabriel informed me he had to go out of town for most of the day. A long-standing appointment that couldn't be changed. It was quite shameful how relieved I felt being able to keep "us" a secret for a little longer.

Thanksgiving Day with Laycee and her family went off without a hitch, but it became even better when I rolled over in the middle of the night into Gabriel's arms. Of course, the argument could be made that our relationship was based on sex, but it wasn't. Not entirely. While it was true we did spend a lot of time exchanging bodily fluids in the most imaginative ways, we still did *other* things.

We went to the late-night Saturday movies, stopping for coffee afterward at the diner where the waitress still flirted shamelessly with Gabriel, only now I didn't mind so much. We also went to dinner at least once a week at the Hungarian restaurant, where the lovely Anasztaizia was forever gracious. And sometimes we just went on long midnight drives or sat in the living room or outside on the porch swing and talked.

A world traveler, Gabriel had either visited almost every country in the world or known someone who had. He could tell stories about places I'd only read about or seen on the National Geographic channel, and his attention to detail was phenomenal. He observed using all of his senses. When he described a marketplace he had visited somewhere in the Middle East, I could almost smell the aromatic spices and fragrant, heady perfumes, while listening to merchants barter in a language I didn't understand. In my mind's eye I could see the bright plumage of caged songbirds competing to be heard over the panicked bleating of goats and the disdainful braying that only camels produce. And don't even get me started on the different foods he had tasted.

All I had to share was my childhood and the devastating effect of my mother's leaving. I was certain there wasn't a day that went by that my father didn't hold himself responsible for her desertion, and I had no doubt she was the last thing on his mind as he lay dying in the twisted wreckage of his car.

But I also made sure Gabriel knew how much my father had loved me, never failing to tell me so every day of my life, even when I made it difficult for him. Like most teenagers I struggled with adolescence, trying to find my place in the world even if it meant rebelling against the things he stood for. I was glad he'd been able to see me come through that period of my life none the worse for wear. I'd always be grateful for the values he had instilled in me before a random spin on the Life Lottery took him away.

Hearing the catch in my voice as I talked about my father, Gabriel took my hands and kissed the inside of each wrist. I remembered him doing the same thing the night he left me, and, both then and now, it felt very intimate.

"Why do you do that?" I asked.

"You don't like it?"

"No—I mean yes, I like it just fine." He looked up at me, his eyes so dark I thought for a moment his pupils had expanded, swallowing up the irises. "It's just no one has ever kissed me on my wrists before. Is it something you do in Norway?"

He smiled, a brilliant, dazzling effect that lightened his eyes and left me breathless. Still holding my hands, Gabriel rubbed his thumbs across the pale blue veins below the skin.

"I don't know if it's Norwegian in origin," he said, "but it's a custom I learned long ago. Pressing my lips to your pulse point is a sign of affection."

"I see."

My throat felt dry, and as with most answers Gabriel gave me, I felt there was a whole lot more I wasn't being told. I don't think he was being deliberately evasive; he was waiting to see if I would ask for further clarification, but I didn't. Instead I turned the conversation toward his own childhood. I was disappointed when he became reticent, and he asked my forgiveness.

"It was a long time ago, and something I'd rather forget," he said, as he twisted his mouth into an uncharacteristically severe line.

I didn't want to poke my nose in where it wasn't wanted, but I was concerned. "It can't *all* have been bad," I told him. "You must have a least one happy memory from your childhood."

He shook his head, the blond mane catching the light, reflecting it back into his face and casting shadows in the hollows of his cheeks. "No, unlike you, the few memories I do have of my past are not pleasant ones."

I pulled my hands out of his grasp and used them to sweep the hair out of his eyes and back over his shoulder. "I'm sorry. I won't ask again," I promised.

His smile was not so dazzling, but it was heartfelt. "As I said, it was a very long time ago."

I laughed. "I doubt it—you're not *that* old!"

"You'd be surprised," he murmured, and something in his voice told me the subject was no longer open for discussion.

My thoughts about Gabriel's involvement in a gang suddenly did not seem quite so farfetched. A common thread that drew many to such a way of life was the need to belong somewhere. If Gabriel had suffered a traumatic childhood, I could see how the allure of a gang would be appealing. The offer of a new "family" to replace one that had been lost or abandoned would be comforting. Humans in general are not solitary creatures. I wanted to explore this further, to see if my theory was anywhere near correct, but intuition told me we had a long way to go before either of us would be comfortable handling such a revelation.

It was definitely time to lighten the mood. At the risk of my own humiliation, I brought out my baby book. Gabriel was, by turns, enchanted and fascinated. He pored over every memory in the form of snapshots tucked behind the cellophane-covered pages: a newborn cocooned inside a blanket, taking my first steps while wearing a most determined expression, the Christmas when my fascination with wrapping paper was all-consuming. And then—it was almost embarrassing—kindergarten through graduation, my life arranged and kept in chronological order for the world to see.

Sitting with my baby shoes balanced on one knee and brushing a finger over my senior class picture, Gabriel listened as I told him how trashed Laycee and I had gotten at the prom party we went to.

"It was the only time I saw my dad lose his temper," I recalled solemnly. "I mean *really* lose it."

He could barely keep the grin off his face. "Now that does surprise me."

I slapped him lightly on the arm. "Yeah, the cops had to bring us home . . ." My voice trailed off as the memory surfaced with a clarity that was picture perfect.

I could remember holding on to the porch handrail for dear life and trying not to fall over as I waved sympathetically at Laycee, who peered at me through the back window of Jake's cruiser. He was only a deputy at the time, but I suddenly wondered just when the attraction between the two of them had first sparked. Could it possibly have begun that night, slowly simmering all these years? It was certainly worth the asking, and I slotted the question away until I'd see her again.

"You never wanted to go to college?" Gabriel asked, bringing me back to the present.

I shook my head. "Not really, although I'm sure I would have if my dad hadn't died. I lost interest in a lot of things after that."

"It's not too late. You have a good brain."

I thanked him for the compliment. "But Gabriel, just think, if I *had* gone to college, I might be shacked up right now with some guy who has a PhD."

Closing the photo album, he put it, along with my baby shoes, on the end table before pulling me into his arms.

"But, Rowan, you already are." He pressed my palm against the front of his jeans. "Feels like a PHD to me."

CHAPTER 25

It was two weeks before Christmas, a Friday, and the last day off I was going to be able to get from the bookstore until after the holidays. Laycee and I were in the bigger of the two malls Greenley Heights boasted, and I was helping her choose a suitable Christmas gift for Jake. It was also an opportunity to surreptitiously look for something for Gabriel.

Buying him a gift was daunting. The last man I'd gone Christmas shopping for was my dad, and he would have been happy with a gift certificate to Pro Bass Outfitters. Actually, he would have preferred that because he could have bought something for himself that he really wanted. Sometimes I wonder just how many useless gifts he held on to because he didn't want to hurt my feelings by exchanging them.

But Gabriel was definitely not a Pro Bass type of guy.

I toyed with the idea of getting him a shirt in something other than the basic black he always wore. Not that he didn't always look fabulous, but I wanted to indulge myself and see if he looked just as gorgeous in, say, cerulean or crimson or caramel. Or hot pink, the new power color. Checking the inside label one night while he was taking a shower, I'd found out his shirts came from somewhere called Turnbull and Asser. I'd never heard of the company and had to look it up online. I was dismayed to discover Gabriel had his shirts made for him in London, England. Getting a Van Heusen from JC Penney wasn't going to cut it.

I thought about cologne, but he didn't use it. The amazing way he smelled was natural. He had pretty much every CD I'd ever mentioned, and judging from what he had brought to the house for us to watch, his movie collection was just as extensive. That left books, but giving him a book as a gift struck me as being somewhat impersonal and not very imaginative, considering where I worked. My choices were diminishing minute by frustrating minute.

Laycee's idea of a gift for Jake consisted of buying lingerie to wear for him. She knew exactly what her man wanted Santa to bring this year, and I dutifully gave her my honest opinion as to what was tastefully erotic and what was downright trashy. Naturally, trashy won hands down every time. I considered stealing her idea, but that would require some sort of explanation on my part, because she would never believe I was buying lingerie for the hope chest I didn't have or "just in case."

I could have easily used the shopping moment to tell her that Gabriel and I were an item, but I didn't. I rationalized my silence by telling myself that when I could fill in at least half of the Alaskan wasteland, I would be in a better position to know exactly what I could and couldn't tell her. Because she was going to have questions—was she ever!—and no matter how noble my intentions, if Laycee sensed I was holding back info, she would ask Jake to do a background check. And I definitely didn't want her finding out things that would be better coming from me.

We left Victoria's Secret (I bought an overpriced lip gloss) and headed for the toy store. As I watched her peruse Jake's kids' wish lists, I realized toy shopping at Christmas was not for the faint of heart. It was an undertaking you carried out because of necessity or love. Both applied to Laycee; neither applied to me. I bailed, but promised a Starbucks stop before heading home. She began to fuss—until I mentioned that I needed to check on her Christmas gift. It was amazing how quickly she did an about-face, wearing an expression that was only mildly avaricious, as she left me.

For Laycee's Christmas gift I had chosen a double-link bracelet along with a letter L charm. It was a good choice because it would mean Christmas and birthdays were covered for at least the next decade. I would just have to make certain I coordinated my choices with Jake. Waiting in the jewelry store for my purchase to be gift-wrapped, I perused the men's section.

The only jewelry I had ever seen Gabriel wear was a watch. I thought I had a gift option when he told me he didn't always wear a Rolex. But it turned out that was his everyday watch. For special occasions, he wore a Patek Philippe. It took me a couple of tries on the Internet to find this one, but that's because I didn't know what kind of a word "Patek" was or how to spell it. I don't know why I bothered.

I looked over the display cases, not really expecting to find anything, when I saw exactly what I wanted. It was a ring. A circle of polished mahogany sandwiched between two matching bands of roped platinum. Discreet and unassuming, it was perfect for Gabriel. I asked the salesgirl for a closer look, and she got it out of the case for me. It slipped over my thumb with plenty of room to spare, so I figured it should fit at least one of Gabriel's fingers. It was expensive but what the heck—it was Christmas! If I didn't use my credit card every now and then, the damn thing would be canceled. I was very pleased with myself as I headed for Starbucks.

I had just found a vacant table when Laycee arrived, and from the frazzled look on her face, the toy shopping experience had not gone so well. She made an uncomplimentary comment about idiot parents and bratty offspring as she sat down.

"Jake is definitely coming with me next time!" she declared grumpily.

I smiled indulgently and pushed one of the foamy coffees across the table to her. She took a sip, wiped the froth from the tip of her nose, and gave me a piercing stare.

"What are you looking so pleased about?" she asked.

I felt my grin getting wider as I shook my head. "I've never seen you so happy," I told her. "I think being with Jake is very good for you."

She smiled, melting like a marshmallow in hot chocolate at the mention of his name. "Yeah, I think so, too."

"And I think he's really going to enjoy that little black and red number you got for him."

"He'd better," she giggled, her face lighting up. "Considering how much it cost, and the fact that I only expect to have it on for thirty seconds, tops."

"Why is it," I pondered, "the skimpier the fabric, the higher the price tag?"

She shook her head, her ponytail swinging. "You got me there, Ro."

We sipped our coffees and indulged in a favorite pastime, people watching. We agreed that in general there were a lot more Scrooges out and about than Tiny Tims.

I was in the middle of an observation about a fortysomething woman dressed like a seventeen-year-old—"Mutton dressed as lamb," Laycee informed me—when her attention was grabbed by something behind me.

"There's a blonde heading your way," she said in a low voice, her eyes impossibly wide.

I felt my stomach lurch and hoped it wasn't Gabriel. Not that I wouldn't be thrilled to see him, but I wasn't prepared for him and Laycee to be in the same hemisphere, let alone the same coffee shop.

"Another admirer?" I said, attempting to play it off.

I could see she didn't remember what I was talking about, and then her carefully penciled eyebrows pulled together as the memory came back. She shook her head.

"Nuh-uh, this is a woman," she murmured, "and she's headed right for you."

Relieved, but also puzzled, I turned my head and saw Anasztaizia making her way toward us. Looking as beautiful as ever, she paid no attention to the heads she was turning. I was certain she took away the breath of every man in the place, even wearing jeans and a turtleneck.

"Rowan, dahlink!" She held out her arms as she approached, leaving me no alternative but to get to my feet for a hug. "I thought that was you!"

She kissed me on both cheeks, and I returned the compliment, asking her to join us. It would have been very rude not to, and I wouldn't have hurt her feelings for anything. The guy at the next table looked like he'd just won the lottery when Anasztaizia asked if she might use the empty chair.

"Anasztaizia, please let me introduce you to my friend, Laycee," I said once she was settled and we were both sitting down.

Laycee looked a little doubtful, as if she thought the beautiful Magyar was going to kiss her as well, but Anasztaizia held out her hand instead. Obviously you had to work your way up to get a peck on the cheek.

"How are you and what are you doing here?" I asked.

"Checking out the competition." Lifting her cardboard cup, she laughed. It sounded like the chime of tiny bells.

Laycee looked nonplussed.

"Anasztaizia's family owns a restaurant, and they make the best coffee I've ever tasted," I explained.

"Is that so?"

I wasn't fooled by Laycee's sweet smile. It told me I was in trouble and so going to get it on the ride home.

"You are too kind to say so." Anasztaizia put her hand on my arm. "So, are you Christmas shopping for Gabriel?"

Laycee's eyes snapped from the Hungarian to me, drilling me right in the middle of my forehead. I thought for a minute she was going to go all *Exorcist* and fully expected her head to begin swiveling around. But I'll give her credit; except for a slight twitch as the muscle in her jaw clicked into hyper-drive, she gave no outward appearance that anything was amiss.

Denial was pointless, and besides, I had the sudden inspiration that Anasztaizia's opinion was definitely worth having. Guiltily I retrieved the small plastic bag from my purse and pulled out the black ring box, passing it across to Anasztaizia at the same moment Laycee was overcome by a coughing fit. We both looked across the table in alarm, but Laycee gamely waved her hand, indicating she was okay. I reached around and patted her on the back.

"Oh, Rowan, dahlink," Anasztaizia cooed, sounding very Zsa Zsa Gabor. "It's beautiful, and I'm sure Gabriel will love it, but then he would love anything you gave him, no?"

"May I?" Laycee asked.

Her eyes were still a little watery, but the bright spots of color on her cheeks were quickly fading. She took the small box from Anasz-

208 • *Carla Susan Smith*

taizia's outstretched hand, and admired the ring before closing the lid and returning it to me.

"Rowan, I must go," Anasztaizia said, getting to her feet, "but I am so happy to run into you like this. If you have no plans, you must come to dinner on Christmas Eve. We are having traditional Hungarian celebration, and I would love for you and Gabriel to share it with us."

She didn't seem to expect an answer right then, which was a good thing because I honestly hadn't thought that far ahead. "Thank you, I'll make sure to tell him."

We hugged, kissed each other on the cheek, and said our good-byes. I watched as the lovely Magyar weaved her way effortlessly through the throng of holiday shoppers.

"So—" Laycee put her elbow on the table and cupped her chin in her hand as her mouth formed a wicked line. "As much as I'm dying to know all about that, *dahlink*," she pointed a finger after Anasz-taizia, "I really want to know just how long you've been back with Eye Candy, and why am I only just hearing about it now?"

In a way, I had some idea of what she had gone through keeping her relationship with Jake a secret, and it felt like a weight had been lifted now that I was going to be able to tell her. Although I must con-fess I kind of fudged things.

For a start, I made it sound as if Gabriel and I had seen each other only a couple of times, and Anasztaizia's enthusiasm was because she had known Gabriel a lot longer than I had. I told Laycee that he had sought me out, which was true. I told her he was filled with remorse for how he had left me before, which was also true. I told her we were seeing each other on my terms only, which was a complete fabrica-tion.

My reason for keeping the relationship a secret was because I didn't want her to worry needlessly that I might get hurt again, which was kinda sorta true. And besides, I added, I wasn't even certain whatever this was between us had much of a future. People have been struck by lightning for lesser lies.

"I'm just taking it one day at a time," I said glibly.

"Uh-huh. Well, One Day is getting a very nice Christmas gift, and it is a very classy ring, by the way," she added generously.

I sighed gratefully when she stood up, thinking how well she'd taken the news.

"Oh, don't think I'm done with you," Laycee said, bending to retrieve her shopping bags from under the table. "I just want to savor all the juicy bits without the benefit of eavesdroppers!"

It was a long ride back home, and as I suspected, Laycee went all poison ivy on me. I don't know whether it was dumb luck or intuitiveness on her part, but she didn't ask me any questions about Gabriel's occupation. Telling her I suspected my boyfriend was involved with something like the Russian mob wouldn't have scored either of us any brownie points. Laycee had been involved in my life long enough to know when I was holding something back. But she was also smart enough to know when to push and when not to. Sensing there were areas that were off limits for the time being, she kept her own counsel, and I loved her even more for that.

"So, just how gorgeous is he naked?" she asked, making the turn onto the county road that would take us home. "And if you tell me you don't know, I swear to God I'm gonna pull over, drag your sorry ass out of the car, and find a stick to beat you with!"

I stared at her, blushing furiously, and got the most awful case of the stammers.

"Wow!" Laycee exclaimed, taking her eyes off the road long enough to witness my discomposure. "He looks that good? I knew it! And the sex is pretty spectacular too, right?"

I did a brief imitation of a guppy out of water, and then nodded and grinned. I don't think I ever actually told Laycee that I was still a virgin at twenty-five. I suppose she assumed that over the years at least one of the guys who'd tried to get in my pants had been successful. Reaching for my hand, she squeezed my fingers.

"I'm not going to pretend my feelings aren't hurt because you didn't tell me about this, and I won't say I understand all your reasons, but I am pleased that you have someone in your life who makes you happy." Her fingers tightened around mine again. "He does make you happy, doesn't he?"

Taking sex out of the equation, mainly because that belonged in a category all by itself, I mulled over the question. Did Gabriel make me happy? Yes he did, and surprisingly, it wasn't because of huge romantic gestures that swept me off my feet. It was the little things—simple, thoughtful moments. Like making sure the coffeepot was set to brew five minutes before my alarm went off, or leaving a glass full of flowers on the kitchen table, or putting a sticky note declaring how much he was already missing me on the bathroom mirror.

"Yes." I nodded reassuringly. "He makes me very happy."

Admitting to myself the euphoria Gabriel brought to my life was one thing; telling him how he affected me was another. But laying it all out for a third party? Whoa! It didn't get any more real than that. Now there was no going back. Our secret was out, and it felt good. It felt right. Laycee peppered the rest of our ride home with salacious, racy comments about Gabriel's expertise between the sheets and bits of unsolicited advice. I spent most of the ride home in tears because I was laughing so much.

It was dark by the time we got back to the apartment complex where she and Jake now lived and where I'd parked the POS earlier that day. I passed on the invitation to supper, grateful to be truthful about the reason why. Gabriel rarely let more than two days pass without seeing me, and it had been that long already. It was the start of the weekend, and I was fairly confident I'd have company this evening. Jake, overhearing my excuse, looked at Laycee with a puzzled frown.

"Don't worry, Jake," I told him with an easy grin, "Laycee will explain everything. It's a girl thing."

I was still grinning at the confused look on his face as she walked me to my car.

"By the way, I forgot to tell you, but we're going to be out of town the rest of the weekend," she said, her face glowing.

"Oh yeah, why's that?"

"Jake's taking me up to the mountains. He wants to give me an early Christmas gift."

I smiled at her, easily infected by her romantic enthusiasm. "Good job we went shopping today." I had a feeling she wasn't the only one who would be getting a head start on the jolly fat guy with the reindeer express. I kissed her cheek and hugged her. "Well, you guys have a good time, and be careful driving. I think they've had snow up north."

"We will," she promised, waving as I drove off.

My heart began doing its own little tango as I pulled into my driveway and saw Gabriel's new Hummer. I had been as overwhelmed by this vehicle as I had by the Fairlane and the Ferrari.

"What can I say? I like cars," Gabriel had said with an unabashed boys-and-their-toys grin.

"So what do you call this one?" I asked. "Henrietta?"

"Actually it's Heloise," he murmured sheepishly.

"I should have guessed."

"Will you let me buy you one?" he asked, boosting me up into the passenger seat while his hand lingered possessively on my rear end. "I promise you can keep the POS."

"Absolutely not!" I stared down at him in mock outrage, which lost most of its effectiveness when I realized there wasn't much of a *down* to my stare. I assumed he was joking. In my world, guys didn't buy their girlfriends cars. That only happened in the movies.

"Why not?" He seemed genuinely puzzled by my refusal.

"Far too many complications."

My answer made him sigh dramatically, roll his eyes, and mutter under his breath. Whatever he was thinking, he wisely kept it to himself.

Pulling alongside the behemoth, I realized my mistake. It wasn't Gabriel's vehicle, after all. His was all black with only the basic chrome accessory work, whereas this one twinkled like a Christmas tree. And just to confirm it was a different vehicle, there was a broad silver stripe running down the side and the windows were heavily tinted. Definitely not Gabriel's, unless he'd traded up for a newer model.

Turning off the engine, I stayed where I was for a few moments. By now Gabriel would have almost wrenched off my driver's-side door in an effort to get to me, but nothing in my front yard moved. My visitor was a mystery.

Getting out of the POS, I gave the Hummer a final glance before hitching my purse up onto my shoulder. A prickle along the nape of my neck and the edgy sensation poking me in the ribs warned me that something was amiss. "Well, you sure as hell ain't gonna find out what it is standing here," I muttered as I pushed my anxiety down. I started forward, completely unprepared for the near heart attack that was waiting to spring itself on me.

CHAPTER 26

"Hello, Little One. Surprised to see me?"

The accent was unmistakable, and I forced my major blood-pumping organ back into my chest as I watched her come around the Hummer's front grille. I noticed she was dressed pretty much as she had been the first time we'd met, the same thigh-high boots and tiny skirt, but today a midriff-baring top and a long, black trench coat had replaced the zippered jacket. Her long hair was piled on top of her head, held in place by what looked like a pair of chopsticks, producing an effect that could only be described as stylish disarray. I felt certain Laycee would have appreciated the effort required to produce such a fashionable statement. She was the last person I was expecting to see, and my anxiety level kicked up a notch as she waited for me to speak.

"Hello, Katja," I said.

My voice was amazingly normal, and she beamed at me, delighted that I remembered her name. I don't think there was anyone she met who would ever forget it. Or her. The kohl-rimmed, violet eyes raked over me, and the gorgeous, red-stained lips parted in a smile.

"Where are the others?" I asked, glancing behind her.

She pouted. "Tonight I come alone. Aleksei is doing"—she waved a hand, long red nails slicing through the air—"whatever it is he does when he's not doing me—"

I raised my eyebrows, wondering if my understanding of *doing me* was the same as hers. I decided it couldn't be because she didn't even pause as she continued "—and Oscar . . . is no longer with us."

Oscar? The guy in the World War Two bomber jacket had been called Oscar? That was a bit of a letdown. Even with his midwestern accent, I had been hoping for something a little more Hollywood. Chase or Tyler at the very least.

"So, what brings you to my neighborhood?" I asked, leaning against the hood of the POS. "Slumming?"

She walked toward me, the long trench coat flapping open and showing flashes of skin visible between the tops of her boots and the bottom of her skirt.

"We need to have a talk, Little One. Female to female."

This wasn't good. When another girl tells you that you need to have a *talk*, girl to girl, woman to woman, or even female to female, I can guarantee the conversation is going to be about a man. The only man who linked Katja and me was Gabriel, and I sure as hell wasn't going to discuss anything about him with her.

"Sorry, Katja, but now really isn't a good time. I'm expecting company." I turned and began walking toward the house. My gut was telling me it wouldn't be a Hallmark moment if she were still here when Gabriel showed up. "Give my best to Aleksei when you see him," I called out with a wave over my shoulder.

I don't know how she moved so quickly in those boots she was wearing. One second she was behind me; the next, she was on the top step of my front porch, looking down at me and blocking my progress.

"No, Little One, I think we will very much have a talk. Right now." Her tone was both imperious and icy.

I took a step back—startled, to say the least. "How did you . . . ?"

I looked behind me, and when I turned back, it was to find she had moved again and was now standing right in front of me. I blinked and realized she was attempting to seduce me with her beautiful violet eyes. Only this time there was no mesmerizing pull, no hypnotic effect, and I had absolutely no desire to find out what her cranberry-stained lips tasted like.

"Really, Katja, is that the best you can do?" I asked, insulted. "You tried that before and it didn't work then, so I wouldn't hold out much hope now."

I was bluffing, but she didn't necessarily know that. Besides, how could she be so blatant about pulling the same move twice in a row? Didn't I at least rate a token show of subtlety?

A frown pulled her perfectly arched eyebrows together, making her look, I'm pleased to say, a little perturbed. "Don't fool yourself, Little One. I almost had you in the palm of my hand last time, but now I think something about you has changed."

I caught a flash of long, painted nails out the corner of my eye as she grabbed the collar of my jacket and almost yanked me off my feet. Leaning forward, she sniffed my neck, reminding me of a dog. I suppose I should've been grateful she wasn't trying to sniff my ass. If I'd felt insulted before, it was nothing to what I was feeling now. I jerked myself free of her hand.

"Well, well . . . I see you have been keeping Gabriel busy." She flashed me a suggestive smile. "But of course, I knew that already."

Liar. She hadn't known, not for sure. That's what all the sniffing was about, confirming her suspicions. Somehow she could smell him on me.

"My name, in case you've forgotten, is Rowan." I spoke with only the barest hint of sarcasm. The patronizing way she was referring to me was getting old real fast, and the smile on her face said she knew exactly how much it irked me. She just didn't care. Katja would continue to call me exactly what she wanted—and my feelings be damned.

"You know you have no future with him, don't you?" Pushing open her long coat, she rested one perfectly manicured hand on her hip. I noticed that her nail polish matched her lipstick. "You are like the others, something to amuse him like cat with mouse. Then he will tire of you and move on."

"Oh?" I wondered why Gabriel's love life was of any interest to her, but you didn't need to be a rocket scientist to come up with that answer.

"Trust me, Little One, I have seen it happen many times before. It always ends badly . . . for the female."

I had to give her credit for the remorseful look on her face. She was one hell of an actress. "And you care about this . . . why?"

"I like you"—*oh, the hell you do!*—"and I don't want to see you get hurt."

"I appreciate your concern, Katja, but you needn't worry. I'm a big girl and can take care of myself."

"You think so?" She turned and climbed the steps back up the porch so she could look down on me again. "I wonder."

Looking thoughtful, she began tapping her long nails against the railing. I was going to get a crick in my neck if I continued looking up at her, and the nail drumming was already beginning to irritate me. Climbing the stairs, I leaned against the opposite rail.

"What do you really want, Katja?"

"I told you, Little One, I like you. You are different from the others."

"Others?" I crossed my arms and waited. Was this the best she could pull from her bag of tricks? Fling Gabriel's previous girlfriends at me? If she thought I was so insecure I was going to be distraught about other women he'd slept with, she was grossly underestimating me. It might have been true back in the summer, when we'd first met, but not now.

"I have known Gabriel a long time." The expression on her face could easily pass for sympathy. "He has had many women, and it is always the same. First there is excitement and curiosity, but too quickly it turns to boredom. I am sorry to tell you that it will not last. It never does."

"Is that so?"

"Yes, it is so. His attention wanders and he is easily distracted by the promise of a new experience."

"How long does it take before he gets bored?"

The cranberry lips pulled into a tight line. I don't think I was reacting in quite the way she had imagined. She didn't answer me.

"I see." A sense of quiet satisfaction rolled through me. "I've already lasted longer than the others, haven't I?"

She glared at me, her violet eyes turning a deep, dazzling amethyst, before regaining her composure and gifting me with what I imagined was her most beguiling smile. "Is true, I have never known him to be as . . . enamored."

"So what's the problem, Katja, jealous?"

She'd have to be a complete idiot to think I was buying her concerned girlfriend routine, and Katja didn't strike me as stupid. What's that saying about hell having no fury like a woman scorned? Yeah, well, it doesn't hold a candle to one woman poaching on another's territory. It seemed that the glamorous cover model wasn't happy about my bedding Gabriel, and I could only imagine why. Clearly she had come to warn me off. Only I wasn't about to roll over simply because she said so.

"Are you upset that it's my bed he's chosen and not yours?" I asked.

She threw back her head, laughing at the suggestion. "Please, Rowan, you think I have envy in my heart because of you?" Holding out her arms, Katja twirled, making the bottom of the trench coat flare out like a prom gown. "Take a good look at me, Little One." Amazed that I would dare put myself in the same stratosphere, she shook her head sadly. For a minute, I too was startled by my own audacity. What was I thinking?

I might not feel insecure about any past conquest of Gabriel's, but Katja scared the hell out of me. Not because she was a past conquest—intuition told me she wasn't—but she definitely wanted to be a current one. Self-doubt threatened to smother me, but then I remembered one life-affirming fact. The gorgeous Goth Queen still had to put her thong on one leg at a time.

She stopped pirouetting and came toward me, her fingernails scraping lightly as she caught my chin. "I am your friend, Little One. I don't want to see you to get hurt."

I jerked my head away. "Bullshit!"

She raised a quizzical eyebrow. "You think I am being untruthful?"

"I think you're full of it!" I snorted. "You couldn't care less if I get hurt." I gave her a hard stare of my own as a warning beacon lit up inside my head. This woman was many things, but my friend wasn't one of them. "Your only concern here is Gabriel. You want him for yourself, only I'm in the way."

She returned to her post on the opposite railing, her hands disappearing back inside the coat as she pushed it open. The skin she exposed looked unnaturally white against her dark clothing, and I wondered if she felt cold. I know I did.

"If I wanted Gabriel for myself, as you say, you would not be able to stop me from taking him." Her mouth twisted into a sly smile. "Besides, how do you know I haven't already had him?"

Because you wouldn't be here if you had.

"If you're so confident you can take him from me, then do it already, and stop wasting my time talking about it." You really can't argue with that type of logic. "Or did you already try? Is that what happened? Did he turn you down?" I wasn't above letting her know I could be just as hurtful as she, if pushed far enough. "Perhaps you overestimate what you have to offer." I made a gesture with my hand, measuring her from head to toe.

I doubted anyone had ever cast aspersions on her packaging before, and if looks could kill, I'd be pushing up daisies. I sighed. Our "little talk" was putting a damper on what had actually been a really good day.

"You have no future with him." She said again, her tone flat and expressionless.

"And I suppose you have?"

Her eyes narrowed. "He and I are alike. I would make for him the better choice."

As much as I hated to agree with her, I was forced to admit there was more than a grain of truth in her words. She and Gabriel were alike, or at least seemed to be on the surface, but perhaps that was reason enough for him not to want her. It was a possibility I could tell Katja had never considered, and probably never would.

"That may be," I said, "but it doesn't change the fact that it's my bed he keeps coming back to."

"If you knew what was good for you, you would walk away from him."

Shit! She just wasn't going to give up. A pit bull had nothing on her. I could feel the edges of my temper start to fray. "Oh, I'm pretty sure I know exactly what's good for me, and trust me, Katja, I'm not about to walk away from it."

She shook her head and blew out a long breath between her red lips.

"It is true; you are different from the others. You give him something he has never had before," she admitted grudgingly, "but can you keep him? Take a good look, Little One." She waved her hand as if she could conjure up an image of Gabriel with a snap of her fingers. "See him as he is. His clothes, his cars, and the secrets he keeps." She nodded her head at the look I flashed her. "Oh yes, I know he is keeping secrets from you Perhaps you are the one overestimating what you have to offer." Her mouth curved slyly upward. "He has not told you the truth about himself, has he?"

I stared at her, saying nothing. Just how much did this dazzling woman in front of me actually know? How much was guess work? And just how close was her tie to my lover?

"Gabriel has told me all I need to know," I heard myself say, but my voice wasn't as strong or confident as it should have been. "And I trust him."

"Then why are you so fearful when he leaves you?"

Was I really that easy to read?

I couldn't help it. Uncertainty *was* my domain, not Gabriel's, and Katja had nailed me dead to rights. Every time I said good-bye to Gabriel, watching him drive off to the life I knew nothing about, a small, insecure part of me would surface. A part that was still standing outside Rosie's, wondering why he wanted to be with me.

Even if I could look as flawlessly polished as Katja, complete with the killer wardrobe, my insecurity would still linger. However, she didn't need to know that, and I refused to let her see just how badly she'd rattled me.

"You know, you're absolutely right, I can't compete with you." Suspicion flared in her eyes. "You look like a million dollars, and I would imagine ninety percent of the male population would kill for the chance to be with you, and not just those looking for makeup tips."

Hoping to break the tension, I was trying for a smile, but no luck. Katja simply continued to look down her nose at me, a member of some imperious European aristocracy wearing a face that gave away nothing. I sighed and wondered if I was flogging a dead horse.

"What did you expect to gain by coming here? I mean, this is all very juvenile, don't you think? Haven't you got enough respect for Gabriel to let him make up his own mind about who he wants to be with?"

Nothing like getting to the heart of the matter.

"What has Gabriel told you," Katja asked, "about what he does when he's not with you? Do you know where he goes? Who it is he sees?"

"Why do you assume he's keeping anything from me?"

"Because I can see it in your face." She laughed. "If you want to survive, you must learn to hide your feelings, Little One."

Well, that answered the easy-to-read question. I decided to come clean. Katja was right. I don't hide my feelings well, but I'm not sure that's always a bad thing, although it does explain why Laycee refuses to play poker with me. Well, that plus the fact I can never remember if a full house or a flush is the higher hand.

And then something else wriggled itself inside my brain. What if there was an entirely different reason for Katja's visit? A reason that had nothing to do with romantic rivalry? What if Katja only wanted me to think that as a way of throwing me off balance? What other reason could possibly bring the Goth Queen to my doorstep?

Oh, yeah, there was another possibility. When you spent your time doing *this and that,* the number of possibilities was endless. And none of them were particularly good.

"Okay," I said firmly, "if it makes you feel better, he hasn't told me anything. I have no idea what he does or where he goes when he leaves me, so whatever secrets you're worried about me spilling— don't be. I can't tell what I don't know."

"He has told you *nothing*? Nothing at all?" She sounded incredulous, and I could see her trying to decide whether I was being truthful.

As I'd already questioned her honesty, it was ridiculous to think she'd not do the same with me. We were two women discussing a man we both had a vested interest in, so it was natural to be suspicious of each other.

"But you have thought about it, yes?" Katja continued. "You lie in your bed when he is gone and you wonder why he does not stay. You think perhaps he does not care for you as much as he says, yes?"

How could she possibly know Gabriel didn't stay all night, unless she was the reason he left? The expression on my face must have told her she was getting warm because I saw her mouth change into a sneer. "Why do you suppose that is?"

"It's to keep me safe," I mumbled.

"Keep you safe?" Disbelief dripped from her lips. "Do you *really* believe that?"

Yes . . . no . . . maybe

Katja shook her head and made clucking noises with her tongue. "I thought you were different from the others, smarter, but I think I make mistake." The slyness returned, only this time it wasn't in her smile but in her eyes. "Why do you need to be kept safe, Little One? You work in bookstore"—*how did she know that?*—"are you important person perhaps?" Her voice dropped to a whisper next to my ear. I hadn't even realized she had closed the distance between us. "Why would Gabriel tell you such a thing?"

I turned my head slowly and found myself staring into her eyes. The night sky was reflected inside two rings of deep amethyst, each shimmering with a multitude of stars. She was part of Gabriel's Alaskan wasteland, staking a claim deep inside its borders, just like the soldier Aleksei and the guy with the midwestern twang.

Clearing my throat, I returned her gaze, and decided I was tired of playing a game whose rules I didn't know. And no one, apparently, was going to tell me.

"Gabriel didn't say anything, but it doesn't take a very big stretch of the imagination to work out what you all are." I was astonished that my voice didn't falter once.

Katja looked startled. "And what is that?"

"Well, the accents are a dead giveaway, along with your clothes and the cars, and as I don't actually see any of you holding down a nine-to-five job, I can only assume whatever it is you're involved in is probably illegal. If I had to guess, I'd say you were part of the Russian mob or something."

Fuck! Had I actually said that? Out loud?

Katja nearly blinded me with the flash of her white teeth in her photo-shoot-perfect smile. She laughed a beer-tavern, rip-roaring belly laugh that I figured old Mrs. Wilcox, my closest neighbor, could probably hear. It was disconcerting to say the least. "You think . . . you think . . ." she gasped, "we are . . . *gangsters?*"

Okay . . . maybe not. Sorry. My mistake. And then, just like that, as if someone had flipped a switch, she became deadly serious.

"Stupid girl—you have no idea what you're involved in."

It was on the tip of my tongue to ask her why she didn't just go ahead and enlighten me because it seemed obvious she wanted to. I have no idea what stopped me from actually saying it, but I didn't. Instead, I asked another question, "Katja, are you sure this is just about me and Gabriel? Is that why you dislike me?"

I got the frosty duchess look again, full force. "I care nothing for you."

That wasn't what she'd said a few minutes ago. Talk about fickle. "Then why are you here?"

"Because this infatuation he has with you, it has gone on for too long!" She spat the words out scornfully. "Every time he is with you—he risks us all."

"But . . . how?" From her reaction just moments ago, it was obvious she thought my notion they were all part of some imported Slavic gang was ludicrous. So what else could there be? "Are you drug dealers? Is that it?"

I watched as she rolled her eyes and muttered to herself in what I presumed was her native tongue. In an odd way I could totally understand her wanting to protect herself and her accomplices.

"I can't tell anybody anything about you because I don't *know* anything," I protested. "I haven't got a clue who you are or what you do. Gabriel has kept your secrets." I didn't think it was prudent to mention that he had promised to tell me everything. All I had to do was ask.

For a few moments there was only silence as Katja mulled over my words. I began to shiver. The thin jacket I was wearing was more decorative than practical, and not meant as a shield against rapidly falling temperatures.

"Yes, it would seem he has." She spoke disdainfully, and I couldn't understand why she wasn't pleased, or relieved, by my confession. I had the weirdest feeling, however, that whatever the reason behind this unexpected visit, I had somehow given her the answer she'd been looking for.

"Gabriel won't be coming to see you tonight."

"How do you know that?" I could have kicked myself for taking the bait.

"Because he's otherwise occupied." She focused her stare on me, and I could see something I didn't like. "Do you want to know what he is doing right now, while he's not with you?"

It was taunting, and it was cruel. I hated her for it, but I also knew she was watching my face, waiting to see the effect her words had on me. Laycee would have been very proud. For the first time in my life, I actually achieved a workable poker face.

"Not particularly." My heart was hammering wildly inside my chest, and for the briefest moment, from the way her head tilted slightly, I though Katja could hear it. Nausea churned ominously in the pit of my stomach as her mouth twisted in a malicious smile.

"Oh yes you do—you want to know so much it's chewing up your insides!"

"Oh, why don't you just go fuck yourself!" I exploded, infuriated by her spitefulness. With my keys in my hand, I pushed past her, needing to get inside the safety of my own four walls. But her hand snaked out, and like bands of steel, her fingers wrapped around my forearm. I was amazed that this pencil-thin girl, who looked as if she would have a hard time staying upright in a stiff breeze, had a grip of iron.

"You may not be so eager to have him back in your bed once you know the truth."

"Don't think for a minute you have any idea what I will or will not do," I spat back with some venom of my own.

Her face twisted into something ugly, and a light flashed behind her eyes, revealing an incomprehensible rage that was gone in an instant. Her features settled back into glossy magazine perfection. "If Gabriel won't tell you, then perhaps you should learn for yourself why you can never have him," she hissed poisonously.

With her fingers still around my forearm, she jerked me off the porch, dragging me toward the Hummer. Flinging open the passenger-side door, Katja dared me to get inside. "It's time you understood why a future with him is impossible," she barked.

I thought about resisting but had the craziest notion that if I did, this slender wisp of a girl would simply pick me up and throw me inside. I climbed in and watched as she came around and vaulted herself into the driver's seat with ease. Looking across the spacious cab, she started the engine, her face perfectly smooth and calm despite the malice in her voice.

"This game he is playing with you has gone on too long already, and now it needs to be ended," she said grimly.

I shivered, only this time it wasn't because I was cold.

CHAPTER 27

Katja had absolutely no respect for speed. Hurtling along the road, she kept her eyes glued to the windshield, staring straight ahead and giving me a taste of what a NASCAR ride-along most likely felt like. I was confident, however, that I'd be a lot less anxious if Tony Stewart were in the driver's seat. I kept a death grip on the seat belt across my chest, and I was pretty sure my other hand would leave an imprint on the door handle.

And her constant muttering wasn't helping the situation either. I was tempted to tell her if she insisted on keeping up a running commentary, then at least have the courtesy to speak English. While I might not be able to grasp the more subtle nuances of her one-sided conversation, I could tell she was furious. And it was strange how "fuck" seems to be a universal curse word.

Staring out the window, I tried to get my bearings so I'd have some idea what direction we were going, but the tint on the glass was too dark. All I could see was my own reflection staring back at me, my face as pale as my abductor's. I was numb. I had no idea what was happening or what to expect, but the feeling that it was going to be bad was strong. In an effort to beat down the rising sense of doom, I clung to the slim hope that Gabriel wouldn't blame me for creating this particular set of circumstances. He cared about me a great deal.

He wasn't yet at the point where he could say the L word, but I thought he was getting pretty close. As if offering its support, my internal torch flared up, and I tingled cautiously.

We turned off the main highway onto a private road, driving over a cattle guard as we did so. I recognized the noise and feel of it. Our way wasn't as smooth as before, forcing Katja to come down from the more or less one hundred miles per hour she'd been averaging to a speed better suited for the uneven terrain. I guess the Hummer wasn't as invincible as I had thought.

Unfortunately the slower speed did little to help me guess our location. Judging from all the trees illuminated by the headlights, we were driving through a forest. I bounced around in my seat, worried that either fear or the jostling was going to make me throw up. I wasn't sure which prospect terrified me more—actually vomiting in my seat or asking Katja to stop so I could upchuck out the window. Thankfully I didn't have to do either because just then the tires gripped asphalt, making the ride smooth out once more.

Ten minutes later Katja brought the vehicle to a stop with an unnecessarily loud squeal of rubber as she applied the brakes. She jumped out and had my door open before my shaking fingers had unsnapped the seat belt. Grabbing my arm, she hauled me unceremoniously out of the Hummer, marching me across a circular driveway like some POW in a bad war movie. Glancing over my shoulder, I saw a half dozen or so cars parked in a long line. They all looked expensive and luxurious, and one in particular caught my attention. The odds of there being two powder-blue Fairlanes in this part of the state struck me as pretty astronomical. A rough jerk on my arm propelled me forward, so I gave my attention to what was in front of me.

"House" wasn't really the appropriate word to describe the architectural nightmare we were headed for. It was an over-the-top monstrosity that was three turrets shy of a real castle. Something the Wicked-Queen-slash-Stepmother from any fairy tale would be at home in.

Every window I could see was ablaze with light. Craning my neck, I looked upward and saw—good Lord—gargoyles! Real, honest to goodness medieval sentinels that snarled down at me, warning me to think twice about crossing the threshold they guarded. Like I had any say in the matter. Perhaps this qualified as a castle, after all, but who in their right mind would live in a place like this? I prayed it wasn't Gabriel's ancestral seat.

Katja pulled me up a set of wide concrete steps to a pair of doors with a bad case of Tower of London envy. Fifteen feet tall, they were covered with iron studs that stood out about six inches. I decided I must have missed the moat and drawbridge on the way in. A pair of enormous black iron rings, positioned at head height where each door met, had me thinking Katja might need my help to push. Amazingly, the doors swung open with barely a whisper, revealing an entrance hall dominated by the most incredible fountain.

Resting on a pedestal was a huge, black marble basin from whose depths rose a three-headed dragon spouting water from each open mouth. And if that wasn't enough to make my eyes fall out of my head, then the banquet room Katja steered me toward definitely was. And yes, I do mean banquet room, as in dining on a grand scale, medieval-style.

Colorful heraldic banners hung from the cathedral ceiling, and the walls were covered with richly detailed tapestries that looked a mile long. The room boasted a fireplace I estimated to be at least ten feet high and twenty wide. I could only imagine the sheer spectacle a roaring blaze would produce.

A huge table ran down the center of the room, with high-backed chairs lining each side. It probably sat fifty people, with plenty of elbow room, and the heraldic theme continued with a coat-of-arms design on each place setting. Personally I didn't care much for the china and silverware, the brightly colored pattern was far too busy for my taste, but the table decorations were very impressive. Enormous pedestal vases, overflowing with snowy Christmas roses and bright green holly, ran down the center of the table, interspersed with elaborate wrought-iron candelabras set with scarlet candles. I felt as if I was in some bizarre time warp. It was glorious and took my breath away.

"Looks like you're expecting company," I said to the black leather trench coat in front of me.

Katja dismissed my comment with a rude grunting noise, dragging me over to the stone staircase against one wall. As I tried to make sure I didn't trip up the stairs, I felt a prickle at the nape of my neck. A prickle that told me I was being watched. Immediately I thought of Gabriel and wondered if his uncanny senses had alerted him to my presence inside these walls. I was surprised our arrival hadn't brought someone to greet us. I would have expected something in the way of staff, but apparently not.

At the top of the staircase, Katja hesitated. The way before us branched off into three separate hallways and she seemed to be in a quandary over which one to choose. Taking advantage of the momentary respite, I caught my breath. It sounded loud and ragged in my ears.

Staring at my abductor's profile, I watched her lips purse and her eyes close. She swiveled her head, first to the left, then the right, and paused as if she was listening to something. Whatever she could hear was beyond my range. Or perhaps she didn't hear anything at all and that was what seemed to disconcert her. I was about to offer my own choice on which direction we should take—retreating the way we had come struck me as a good option—when a figure stepped out of the shadows, scaring the bejesus out of me and making me shriek.

He was in his mid-fifties, if I had to guess, and though he could easily match Gabriel for height, he was definitely nowhere near as muscular. The heaviest thing this guy probably lifted on any given day was a cup of Earl Grey tea or a glass of sherry—both, no doubt, with his pinkie extended. But despite the lack of any showy muscle, there was a strength flowing from him. It made me think that under-estimating him would be a serious mistake.

Couldn't fault him for his wardrobe, though. He was dressed in a dark gray pinstripe suit, his shirt the pale lavender of wisteria blossoms that matched the handkerchief in his breast pocket. Both would have looked effeminate on most other men, but he carried it off with panache.

Jet-black hair, similar to Katja's, was combed straight back from his forehead, revealing the most amazing widow's peak, the kind of thing I'd only seen in old, late-night horror movies on TV. In fact, that's exactly what he reminded me of, a debonair matinee idol lifted straight from a black-and-while celluloid strip.

"Good evening, Katja."

Her name rolled off his tongue; his speech was smooth and cultured, with a casual intimacy and a similar accent to my abductor's. I was starting to wonder if being with Gabriel meant I was destined never to meet anyone born and raised in the U.S. again, and then I remembered Oscar, with his wonderful Kansas accent.

The man stepped forward and grasped Katja lightly by the shoulders, kissing her chastely on the forehead before taking a step back and turning his eyes on me. Tilting his chin, he inhaled deeply. I watched his nostrils flare and his eyes widen. He stared at me with such penetrating intensity, I had to look down and remind myself I still had my clothes on.

"Well, well, well . . . who have we here?"

His voice rippled with an edge that I found unsettling. I had enough on my plate already, with no space left to deal with the attentions of a fifties-style Lothario. Katja tried pushing me behind her but didn't have much success, mainly because I wasn't exactly being cooperative. If her intent was to hide me, it seemed pretty ridiculous, as I'd already been seen.

As she tightened her grip on my arm, I yelped in protest. Any more pressure would result in a broken bone or, at the very least, compromise my circulation. The matinee idol snapped out a few words that I didn't understand, but Katja let go of me. I rubbed the area above my elbow gratefully.

He held his hand out to me, palm up. I glanced at Katja, but she remained focused on him and didn't look at me. A quick movement of fingers told me to come forward. Seeing no other option, I tentatively placed my hand in his open palm and allowed myself to be maneuvered out from behind the black leather coat. I heard a soft hiss following my movement. Katja's face may have been an emotional blank screen, but I could feel the anger rolling off her in waves. It was pretty obvious she hadn't wanted this person, whoever he was, to see me, much less take a decided interest in me.

Dropping my hand, the matinee idol made a slow circle around me. I held my breath as Katja, feigning boredom, leaned against the wall and examined her nails. There were no tapestries here, I noticed, just deep red flocked wallpaper with a design that reminded me of ugly bowls of fruit. Katja appeared to have a bunch of grapes hanging from one earlobe.

"Katja?" The man turned his head in her direction, waiting for an answer. I tried to remember what the question was. Oh yeah, who was I?

"Rowan," she answered with a dismissive wave of her hand before curling her fingers and attending to her cuticles.

He smiled, showing me a mouthful of pearly whites. "Ah, so you are Rowan."

I nodded. He sounded as if he'd been expecting me, which was completely ludicrous, of course. The smile he wore grew broader, crinkling the corners of his eyes and deepening the brackets at either side of his mouth, but all it did was increase my uneasiness. Something was very off about him.

"Charming," he murmured, "absolutely charming."

I remembered Aleksei saying the same thing about me, and I wondered if it meant something different to them.

"You think so?" Katja pushed herself away from the wall and came up behind him, looking positively irritated. "I fail to see the attraction."

"Of course you don't, you can't . . . you're female." Raising an eyebrow, he continued looking me up and down. "Rowan was not designed to inflame your senses."

Inflame your senses? Was this guy for real?

Apparently Katja did not share the sentiment, and behind his back she opened her mouth and made a gagging motion with her finger. I snorted back a giggle. It was the last thing I expected her to do. The man looked sharply over his shoulder.

"Does she inflame yours?" she asked sweetly, her hands disappearing inside the trench coat.

He shook his head. "Of course not, but I do find something intriguing about her." His nostrils flared again. "Designated for one specific purpose, but linked only to one specific male."

I felt better. Whatever I had that intrigued the Lothario, it was purely academic. He walked slowly around me again. I'd never been given the once-over like this before, and part of me said I ought to protest at such demeaning behavior. Being talked about in the third person was especially galling, but for some odd reason I really didn't feel degraded. The matinee idol was making me feel as if I was giving him the most extraordinary gift, just by letting him look at me.

"May I?" He held both hands out in front of him, palms up. His fingers curled, and I noticed his nails were neatly manicured. And long. I've never seen a man his age with long nails before. Actually I've never seen a man with such long nails, period.

I had no idea what he wanted, but I nodded, then almost took a step back as he moved toward me and the long nails flashed past my neck. He caught a handful of my hair and twisted it around so it was piled on top of my head, exposing my neck.

"There, much better."

Katja decided she'd had enough and stamped her foot angrily. "My God—would you stop this foolishness!"

The man sighed loudly and ignored her, which elevated him a step or two in my estimation. I stared at him and concluded he and Katja had to be related because they both had the same black hair and violet eyes. Only his sparkled a little darker. He let go of my hair, watching as it tumbled around my shoulders.

"I'm sorry," I said, deciding it was time to join the conversation. "I don't think I caught your name."

I held out my hand for him to shake. The way he looked at it reminded me of how Katja had reacted when I'd done the same thing with her the first time we met. Oh yeah, these two were definitely cut from the same cloth; however, Lothario recovered a lot quicker than she had. Taking my outstretched hand in both of his, he raised my knuckles to his mouth and pressed his lips against my skin.

"My apologies, Rowan," he said, straightening up. "I am Vladimir." Of course he was. With his widow's peak, accent, and those clothes, what else could his name have been? "Did Gabriel send you to fetch Rowan?" he asked Katja, all the while keeping his eyes on me.

The skin on the back of my hand where he'd kissed me was beginning to tingle. It reminded me of the pins and needles sensation that happens when your hand or foot falls asleep. It was more annoying than painful, and not wanting to attract any undue attention, I ignored it. I needed to stay sharp because a sudden tension had formed between Vladimir and Katja.

"I thought I'd surprise him," Katja said, in response to his question.

I stared at her, noting the whisper of hesitation that colored her words. She wasn't as sure of herself as she would have either of us believe. Seeing my interest, Katja switched to her own language. I have no idea what she said to Vladimir, but it seemed to me she was giving him her version of events. Not being able to contradict what she said was annoying, especially as her scornful expression and contemptuous tone told me it was all rude and disparaging.

Thankfully, Vladimir interrupted her in mid-flow, cutting her off with a sharp wave of his hand. I wasn't sure if the sound I heard as she snapped her mouth shut was her jaw popping or her teeth clacking. Either way it was loud. She stared at me, a feral look gleaming in her amethyst eyes. I swallowed and took a step back, pulling my hand free of Vladimir's hold.

"Katja, have you thought about what you are doing?" Apparently Vladimir didn't have a problem with me knowing what was being said. "If Gabriel has not requested Rowan's presence, your actions may be construed as . . . intrusive."

Katja snorted derisively, and his expression changed. He gave her a look of resignation, one that made me think he was mentally separating himself from whatever course of action she was determined to follow. I didn't take it as a good sign.

"Don't you think she should know the truth?" As if she were doing me a favor, Katja leaned back against the wall and folded her arms. "He has told her nothing, and she believes they have a future together."

She said nothing else, but I could tell from Vladimir's face that he was able to fill in the blanks. I wished I could.

"Be careful, Katja; what you are contemplating will have consequences." His voice was solemn and grave. "Consequences I suspect you have not fully realized."

Oh, shit! This was so not what I needed to hear.

Katja switched back to her own language, and from the cadence, her expression, and the occasional "fuck you" she threw in, I figured she was cursing both of us. I wished to hell I knew what it was I should already know.

Reaching out, Vladimir caught a lock of my hair in his hand, running it between his fingers. He seemed to be admiring the burnished copper color in the light. "If you insist on being so reckless," he said, quietly addressing Katja, while keeping his eyes firmly fixed on my hair, "I will not offer you my protection."

She looked momentarily startled and then quickly regained her composure, her mouth forming a scornful line. It was obvious Vladimir was not going to dissuade her from her purpose. I felt a skein of fear unraveling in the pit of my stomach.

Letting go of my hair, he continued, "Have you thought what will happen if Gabriel's reaction is not what you expect it to be?" His voice was soft, reasonable, and scared me to death. "An error in judgment on your part, Katja, may bring with it more than Gabriel's displeasure. His censure may prove . . . difficult to bear."

Katja snapped out something sharp and grabbed my arm again, jerking me to her side. Whatever she said made Vladimir chuckle, but with no humor that I could detect. He gave me an old-fashioned bow. "The pleasure was all mine, Rowan, and I look forward to meeting you again . . . perhaps."

CHAPTER 28

"Was that your father?" I asked once we rounded a corner and Vladimir was no longer in sight.

"In a manner of speaking." The reply was brusque, punctuated by another rude snorting sound. I definitely wasn't feeling the love.

Katja had lengthened her stride, so I was forced to almost run in order to keep up. If I fell, I doubted she would even notice, and the effort I was expending was beginning to take its toll.

Being dragged down yet another long corridor, past several doors, and up another staircase forced me to acknowledge that I was totally lost. There was no way I was going to be able to find my way out of here without a GPS, and maybe not even then. It occurred to me that perhaps this was her plan all along. Instead of confronting Gabriel, Katja was going to drop my arm at any moment and sprint away, thus dooming me to wander along endless hallways looking for a way out. She was hoping that by the time I did, Gabriel would have forgotten all about me.

At this point, I didn't much care because my calf muscles were cramping. I've never understood the point of power walking, except that it's sadistic. Walking is meant to be pleasurable, and I'm a definite meanderer. I was forced to stop at one point so that I could catch my breath, and Katja made her annoyance plain. Bitch.

I would have given a kidney for a chair to collapse onto, but the hallway was devoid of furniture, so I planted my butt against the ugly wallpaper and bent over. Hands on my knees, I sucked in air as my calves screamed and my thighs trembled. Somewhere to my left a door opened, and I turned my head to see whose curiosity we had aroused now. Maybe Vladimir had told someone else we were here, and they had come to see for themselves. It would be great if they also had a glass of water.

"Katja? What are you—"

The question was cut off by a sharp intake of breath, followed by an explosion, once again in a foreign language, but ending with a *have you lost your fucking mind?* I understood that all too clearly. The tone was incensed and got my attention.

He wasn't wearing his greatcoat, but the buzzed haircut and camouflage pants tucked into military-style boots were reminder enough. And even if they weren't, there was no mistaking the wicked scar on his face.

"Hello, Aleksei . . . 'sup?" I wearily lifted the hand I'd been bracing on one knee and gave him a tired wave. It had been quite a journey from the front door.

He stared at me, his eyes open in horrified disbelief, which wasn't exactly the reaction I'd been hoping for. At our only meeting he'd been pleasant and polite—even, I thought, a little flirtatious—and I was grateful to see him again, hoping I might have found an ally. Or at least someone willing to run interference with Katja and maybe show me the way out. His immediate response to my presence, however, indicated that someone was in deep shit.

Stepping past me, he grabbed Katja by her upper arms, lifted her bodily off the floor, and shook her. It made me think of a pit bull on steroids. The chopsticks finally came loose and her hair fell free of its artificial disorder, but she didn't seem that upset by the manhandling she was receiving. In fact, she gave all the appearance of enjoying the rough physical contact.

"She doesn't know!" she hissed when Aleksei was done with the dog and rat routine and she was once more standing on her own two feet. Her eyes took on a hard gleam. "She thinks we are *gangsters*."

"It doesn't matter what she thinks," Aleksei growled, loosening his hold and stepping back. "It is not your concern."

"Not even when Gabriel risks us all every time he is with her?"

She looked at the Russian soldier, then at me, and then back at him. I saw her take a deep, calming breath, and when she began speaking again her voice was softer, more persuasive. She put her hand on his thick, muscular forearm. "Aleksei, you know every night he is with her, he puts us at risk. One wrong word spoken at the wrong time—"

"This I already know!" The big guy folded his arms across his chest but refused to meet her gaze. He seemed fascinated by the pattern in the carpet instead.

"You are closer to him than any of us," Katja soothed softly. "Can't you make him see how foolish it is to keep her?"

What was I—a golden retriever?

"You don't understand—" Aleksei began.

"What? That she intrigues him?" The roll of Katja's violet eyes illustrated all too well her opinion regarding that suggestion. "I will admit he has kept her far longer than any of the others," she acknowledged grudgingly, "but you must make him see reason." Placing her hands on either side of his face, she tilted his head up so he was forced to look at her. "She needs to be gone, Aleksei. Surely you can see that?"

"Uh, guys, you do realize I can hear every word you're saying, right?"

With my breathing now pretty much back to normal, I straightened up. Aleksei had the decency to look embarrassed, but Katja's response was simply to shrug her shoulders and switch to her own language. I wondered how long it would take me to find the way out by myself. Surely if I just kept heading down, then eventually I would have to come to an outside door. I might even run into the smooth Vladimir, who surely knew the way out.

Katja tossed her long mane of glossy black hair over one shoulder and began gesturing with her hands. The words might have been beyond my comprehension, but I could tell the Goth Queen was starting to get pissed. It seemed Aleksei wasn't being quite as agreeable as she wanted. I began edging my way along the wall, wanting to get as big a head start as possible before I bolted.

I froze when Katja shrieked.

The sound was so sharp and piercing, I was surprised the light fixtures didn't shatter. I whipped my head around to see she was once more in Aleksei's grip, only this time she didn't seem to be enjoying it. The way she was twisting and throwing herself against him, struggling to get free, I fully expected her shoulder to pop out of joint at any moment. But she was no match for his size and strength. She stopped fighting and started shrieking again. It took me a moment or two to realize she was cussing him out in English.

"Stop it, Katja!" The big guy snapped his arm with enough force to make her head jolt back. "You're behaving like a child."

Yep, a six-year-old throwing one hell of a temper tantrum. I waited for him to start with the dog and rat imitation again, but he didn't. I think he decided to see how long it was going to take before Katja realized the futility of her efforts.

"What is this obsession he has," she wailed, "and why her? She is weak! If he wanted someone, then I would be the better choice—you know I would!"

Oh Christ! Not this again!

Something in Aleksei's face changed. It reminded me of the expression the state trooper wore when he stood in my kitchen. The bearer of terrible, awful news.

"He will never choose you, Katja," he said, softening his voice as if that would make his words easier to hear. "This is not the first time he has found Rowan. You don't know what she is to him."

I watched the fight go out of the exotic beauty, watched her go completely still. Her only movement was to tilt her head far enough to one side to clear the hair from her face. Aleksei's statement had the same effect as a hose of cold water aimed at a couple of snarling dogs. Taking a deep breath, Katja gave her complete and undivided attention to the big Russian.

And so did I.

"What do you mean?" she asked in a voice that was filled with both disbelief and suspicion. "Why will he never choose me?"

Aleksei sighed, and let go of her hands. "Gabriel is bound to Rowan in a way that cannot be broken, at least not by you."

"But . . ." She floundered, searching for an answer to a problem she didn't fully comprehend.

"Katja, if you are thinking that you can make Gabriel give Rowan up, I will tell you now, he will not do it. And if he cannot have Rowan, for *any* reason, he will take no other."

I gasped at the familiar phrasing and saw Katja stumble back until she hit the wall. If I hadn't been so astounded by Aleksei's words, I might have felt sorry for her.

The big guy, apparently remembering I was still there, gave me a look that said he had broken some sacred trust. For a moment I thought he might ask for my forgiveness, but I guess the look on my face told him I was on a quick day trip to Clueless Land with no idea what he was talking about. If he didn't pick up on this, Katja certainly did.

"I think you have been drinking too much vodka," she said, snapping her spine back into place and giving Aleksei a scornful poke in the chest with her finger. "You are speaking more stupid than normal."

I could see her calculating *something,* and I knew the minute everything slotted into place for her. Pushing the long curtain of hair back from her face, she moved toward me but found her way blocked by Aleksei's arm.

"Gabriel has been waiting a long time for Rowan," he told her, "and this time he will not give her up."

"Did you ever think, Aleksei, that perhaps Gabriel will not be the one to do the giving up?"

Glancing in my direction, the big guy gave me another look that I didn't understand, which actually was okay because my powers of comprehension had fallen right off the grid. His massive chest moved as he sighed and scrubbed a hand over his face. Like Katja, I realized something had fallen into place for him also.

"There's something you don't know," he said solemnly.

It was good to know I wasn't the only one. Was someone finally going to start making sense? After all, I was involved in all of this, quite intimately as it happened.

"What?" Katja's voice reverted back to the anxious six-year-old whose promised treat was in danger of being taken away. "What is it you think I don't know?"

C'mon, Aleksei, cough it up, I want to know as well.

The Russian rubbed his hand over his bristled head before suddenly pointing a finger in my direction. "Rowan is his *Promise*."

Get outta here! No shit—really? I'm his *what?*

The intake of breath from Katja was so loud it sounded like a whistle. And then she began to laugh, a low chuckle that quickly climbed in volume and pitch before exploding in hysteria. I jumped at the sound of Aleksei's hand slapping her, the resonance bouncing off the ugly wallpaper.

"I don't believe you!" Katja exclaimed. Her eyes glittered wildly as she held her hand to her cheek. It didn't cover the big guy's imprint.

"Is the truth," he hissed back. "Gabriel told me that night at the movie theater." Aleksei didn't apologize for striking her, but he did look somewhat ill at ease, telling me he was more than a little uncomfortable disclosing whatever it was that had been discussed. "Now do you understand why he won't let her go—why he cannot?"

I sure as hell didn't, but that didn't matter because Katja did. And judging from the shocked look on her face, it wasn't something she was about to accept.

"No, no, no!" she sputtered angrily. "No one believes a *Promise* to be real—"

"Gabriel does," Aleksei interrupted firmly, cutting off whatever else Katja might be thinking of saying.

I watched both of them as my passport got stamped and I crossed over from Clueless Land into the Continent of the Totally Lost. What were they talking about? I was a *Promise?* What did that mean? The only definition I knew of a promise said it was a pledge, an oath, or a solemn agreement. But how could a person be a promise? I tried telling myself it was all a ridiculous misunderstanding due to semantics, but I had the sinking feeling there was another meaning I was missing completely. A meaning that had implications I knew nothing about.

I desperately wanted to ask Aleksei what the fuck was going on, but he had his hands full with Katja again, only this time she wasn't being aggressive. She looked very much like someone who was about to have a face-to-face meeting with the carpet. Clutching his muscular arm, she stared into his face, searching for something. A denial would be my guess.

"I don't believe you," she muttered, glaring at me, "and even if you speak the truth, I refuse to believe Gabriel would have chosen someone like *her.*"

Loathing spilled out of her cranberry-stained lips, the depth of her antipathy reaching a level that unnerved me. Katja's visit to my house tonight had revealed her feelings for Gabriel. Her reaction now was a testament to the strength of those feelings, and a warning of how dangerous she was because of them.

Murmuring her name soothingly, Aleksei put his arm around her shoulders and patted her back. Katja dropped her head and gave what sounded like a strangled sob, her hair cascading about her like a mantle, hiding her face. Things had taken a definite turn for the significantly weird. I was also fed up with both of them talking about me as if I wasn't standing less than ten feet away.

I gave up the idea of running down the hall. I doubted I could have outrun Katja anyway, and I knew for sure I wouldn't be able to escape Aleksei. Suddenly jerking herself out of the Russian's hold, Katja stared at him. The amethyst eyes continued to glitter, but now it was with something wild and dangerous.

"Prove it," she said, staring hard into his face. "If she's his *Promise,* then she will be marked."

The big guy began mumbling in frustration. Irritated and angry all at once, he narrowed his eyes and looked at me in such a way that I began assessing my chances of making a break for it. They weren't good. I had absolutely no idea what was going on inside the Russian's head, had no idea what was going on outside of it for that matter, but I wanted to let him know I wasn't going down without a fight. I didn't care how big he was.

Unfortunately, like everything that had taken place so far, I was three steps behind everyone else.

"Rowan—" He stood before me, and I looked up at the ruined face, noting he had made a deliberate effort to calm himself. "I must ask for your forgiveness."

Only he didn't wait to get it. Before I could take another breath, he spun me around, pulling me out of my jacket, and throwing it on the floor. Yanking up the back of my shirt, he tugged at the waistband of my jeans, exposing my lower back.

And my tattoo. The one Gabriel had said was meaningless.

I flailed pathetically against the sold block of granite that doubled as the big guy's arm, stopping only when I heard him utter, "She carries his name."

Setting me back upright, Aleksei apologized while trying to straighten my clothes. Angrily I slapped his hand away, but not before seeing the look of admiration he tried to hide as I did so. Guess he was impressed by my show of temper.

Katja, however, seemed completely devastated. Whatever had been on her mind when she had first shown up tonight, whatever she'd thought she needed to tell me about Gabriel had just been airmailed out the window. By some permanent artwork inked on my back.

"Do you think that is just coincidence?" Aleksei asked.

"Okay," I said, tugging on the bottom of my shirt. "I've had just about enough of this bullshit." I fixed both of them with a hard stare. "What do you mean I carry his name? Whose name?"

The sound of female laughter filled the hallway again. Not quite as hysterical this time, but it was walking a knife edge.

"She doesn't even know that!" Katja spat out in disgust, looking at Aleksei. "And you want me to believe she's his *Promise?*"

Folding his arms across his chest, Aleksei ignored Katja and addressed me. "The tattoo you have on your back is a name," he told me gravely, "and it is Gabriel's."

"Get the fuck out of here!" I so wasn't buying that one.

"You don't believe me?"

"Of course, I don't. It's just a meaningless design."

"No, it isn't," the big guy said firmly. "The symbols on your skin are a language, one that only a handful of living creatures know. It is the Old Tongue, and what is written on your back is the word *Gabriel.*"

"What do you mean . . . Old Tongue?"

"The language of the Fallen." Aleksei placed his hand over his heart in a gesture of reverence.

I could feel my temper rising. Would these people never stop speaking in riddles? What the fuck was Aleksei talking about? Who had fallen? Suspicion suddenly blazed a path in my brain. "Would Gabriel recognize this language, if he saw it?" I demanded.

"Of course," Aleksei answered, looking slightly perplexed. "It is his true voice, it always has been."

I could hear Katja's laughter edging a little further up the hysteria scale, and it began to grate on my nerves. The enormity of the big guy's words hit me. If I believed what I was hearing to be true, then Gabriel had lied to me. My legs suddenly felt weird, as if my muscles were collapsing, and my stomach rolled in a way that was definitely nauseating.

A hundred voices began to shout inside my head all at once, demanding answers to questions I didn't even know how to ask. I braced myself against the wall with one hand and wrapped the other around my waist as I leaned forward.

Deep breaths . . . inhale through the nose . . . exhale through the mouth . . . inhale . . . exhale . . . deep breaths.

Aleksei stood between Katja and me, as solid as a giant sequoia, trying to decide what the next course of action should be. My being here was turning out to be a disaster in the making, and I wasn't the only one who thought so. But the big guy had the advantage. He knew the reason why. I did not. He turned his attention back to Katja.

"You must take Rowan back to her home," he said in a low, urgent voice, "before Gabriel senses her presence."

The dark curtain of hair swung as she stared at him. I didn't know if she was going to agree with his suggestion or not, but I wasn't about to let her off the hook that easily. I rounded on him as my temper got the better of me.

"Wait a minute—she has the nerve to come to my house in all her Goth Queen glamour"—I stabbed an angry finger over his shoulder—"and tell me I'm not good enough for Gabriel, and then, as if that isn't enough, when I refuse to back off, she kidnaps me and brings me here!" I spread my arms expansively. "And I haven't got a friggin' clue where the fuck I am, but now you think she should just take me back home? And do what? Play nice and pretend this never happened?" I made a sound of complete disgust and put my hands on my hips while Aleksei looked dismayed. "I don't know what the hell's going on, or what you guys are up to, but I can tell you I'm not going anywhere until I get some answers!"

Anger is an intense emotion. It can either propel you to great acts of courage or ones of complete stupidity. The jury still hadn't reached a decision in my case.

"Rowan, now is not the time," Aleksei implored. "Please just allow Katja to—"

"Shut the fuck up, Aleksei!" I couldn't believe he was pleading with me. "This is between your girl there and me."

Katja was staring at me, her eyes wide with disbelief at my outburst; her lids began to shutter, and that beautiful pouting mouth set itself in a grim line. Refusing to back down, I dared her to take me on.

"I want you to explain just what the fuck is going on, and you can begin by telling me what it is about Gabriel that I don't know!"

Aleksei took a step toward me, holding out a placating hand. "Rowan—"

"I already told you to back off!" I snapped, so pissed off, I forgot how big and menacing he actually was. I focused my attention completely on the beautiful girl next to him. "What was so important, Katja, that you felt compelled to abduct me and drag me here? What did I need to see that would make me think twice about, how did you put it, inviting Gabriel back into my bed?"

I could see Aleksei from the corner of my eye. If he'd looked horrified before, it was nothing compared to how he looked now. Clutching his forehead with one massive hand, he began shaking his head back and forth and moaning under his breath. Katja remained silent.

"Cat got your tongue?" I goaded.

That worked. Her head snapped up and her eyes glowed like hot coals. I never saw her move. One minute she was standing next to Aleksei, and the next she barreled herself into my midriff, and I was flying down the hallway slung over her shoulder.

"No, Katja! No!" Aleksei shouted behind us.

But he was already too late. She was definitely much stronger than I'd realized because carrying my weight over her shoulder didn't slow her down at all. Coming to a stop, she dumped me on the floor in an undignified heap and dropped to her haunches, squeezing my jaw painfully between her fingers.

"So you are Gabriel's *Promise,* are you?" I could hear humiliation behind the anger in each word as it fell from her perfect mouth. "Well, Little One, better find out exactly what it is you've been promised to."

And grabbing my arm, she pulled open the door before us, and flung me inside.

CHAPTER 29

I landed on my back on thick white carpet, bouncing my head and feeling the air whoosh out of my lungs. Disoriented, I lay still, trying to catch my breath. Movement in my peripheral vision made me turn my head to one side, and I frowned. The wall was moving. The fluidity of motion suggested it was liquid. I was staring at a wall of water.

I felt my eyebrows pull together. A wall of water seemed a little excessive to have inside a room, no matter how eccentric or rich you were. It took a few more moments of focused observation before one of my other senses kicked in, telling me this must be a strange type of water because it was falling without a single splash, gurgle, or drip.

I blinked and refocused, and sighed with relief. It wasn't water after all. What I was looking at was a panel of silky blue material that was moving by some unknown means. Rippling like a waterfall.

Only then I did hear something. A noise that made the hair at the nape of my neck stand up. It sounded part animal, part something I prayed to God I would never meet, not even in my nightmares. Fear got me to my hands and knees, scrambling back against the wall to conceal myself in the shadows. My flight-or-fight response kicked in, its thumb punching my flight button for all it was worth. But the door Katja had thrown me through was no longer open. Closed, it blended seamlessly with the wall, and I had no idea how to locate it. My bounce across the floor had really bamboozled me.

Crouching on the floor, I pressed my back against the wall and wrapped my arms tightly about my knees. I took a number of deep breaths, not opening my eyes until I'd managed to suppress the wave of panic that was threatening to consume me. Hysteria wasn't going to help me find my way out. Able to breathe a little more steadily, I cautiously looked around.

The room was enormous. It probably had as much square footage as the entire ground floor of my house, and it was bathed in candle-light. Not from fancy wall sconces or massive candelabras hanging from the ceiling. The huge pillars of red wax that stood on the floor were bigger than any candles I'd ever seen. I estimated each one to be at least five feet tall and thicker than my thigh. I couldn't see how many there were in total, but they seemed to ring the perimeter of the room, flickering and shimmering as their multiple flames danced. It took only a moment for my eyes to adjust to the illumination. And then I wished they never had.

The room contained a single piece of furniture. A bed. A four-poster eyesore better suited to a Roman orgy than a modern home. Unable to help myself, I found my eyes drawn to the bedpost closest to me. Twining figures elaborately carved from dark, shiny wood were engaged in various acts of copulation. Bathed by the flickering candlelight, the figures appeared to be writhing sensuously, giving themselves over to complete abandon. Heat flushed my face and I assumed the other three posts were carved in similar fashion.

I shifted my gaze to the bed itself. I had a strange feeling of relief when I saw the linens were black and not the red of my fantasies. I have nothing against black satin sheets; they can be just as erotic as red, but I don't think these were actually sheets. It looked more like yards and yards of the glossy material were draped across the mattress, twisting around the limbs of the occupants, with the excess pooling in a black spill on the thick white carpet.

I put my hand over my mouth to stifle any inadvertent sound I might make, because you didn't need a college degree to figure out what was going on. The urgent slide of fabric, accompanied by soft moans and excited inhalations, were descriptive enough. I was grateful, however, that the two lovers were so deeply engrossed in each other that they hadn't realized they had gained an audience of one. I wanted to look away. Truly I did. But some awful voyeuristic inclination took hold of me, making that impossible.

The woman was on her back, her long hair a splash of pale moonlight spread out across the dark fabric beneath her. Her hands were over her head, her wrists held easily by her lover, immobilizing her arms. She raised her legs, wrapping them around his waist, cradling him against her sex, and I noticed, in a purely feminine observation, that her finger and toenails were both painted vivid scarlet. I doubted her lover had detected such a detail. His attention was completely engrossed by the voluptuous swell of her breasts, which were bared for his admiration.

Arching her back, the woman undulated and rolled her more than generous assets across the smooth surface of his chest. From the way she was lying, I could see her face. With closed eyes and a glow of anticipation highlighting her delicate bone structure, she was the embodiment of pure ecstasy.

She pushed her hips up against him, and I saw her mouth turn into a moue of frustration as his superior strength kept her firmly in place. It seemed to me she was upset by his resistance. Putting his lips to her ear, her lover murmured softly. In response she gave a moan of ecstasy, and I watched as her skin flushed pink and her tongue danced across the curve of his collarbone.

My embarrassment changed into something else as my internal flame soared, fanning out to brand my chest while licking its way across the inside of my skin. I knew that it was wrong to keep watching, and that shame would consume me later, but I couldn't look away if my life depended on it. There was something fundamentally mesmerizing about the couple on the bed.

The man lowered his head, his lips against the white column of her throat, and he was pulling her skin into his mouth, sucking slowly. Something about his movements seemed odd, almost as if they were forced, and it made me turn my attention to him. The woman was unknown to me, so it was obvious Katja meant for me to see the man. I felt the breath catch in my throat, because only one person I knew had hair that particular shade of white.

Everything stopped. It was as if I had come across a terrible multicar accident, and even though I didn't want to look at the mangled bodies, I couldn't stop myself from doing just that. Knowing every shattered bone, every open wound, would stay with me for the rest of my life, I still could not look away. And with this mind-set, I stared at the man on the bed.

Because of the angle at which he had positioned himself, his face was concealed from me, but there was no mistaking the power in his upper body. A power that was disturbingly familiar. I watched the muscles bunch and flex in his arms and shoulders as they supported his weight. And then he moved. Sitting up, he gathered the woman to him, twisting his upper torso so I could see his broad back. The hand that I had clamped over my mouth tightened, and then released.

Katja had made a mistake!

This man before me now was admittedly similar enough in build and coloring to make my heart trip over itself, but he wasn't Gabriel.

Katja had screwed up big-time.

How could she have made such a fundamental error? The only thing I could think was that for some strange reason she must have assumed I hadn't actually seen Gabriel totally naked or that I would be so distraught I would accept this imposter in his place.

As if!

Gabriel's body was completely unblemished, and this guy was not only tattooed, he was viciously scarred. Damaged, puckered skin made two angry lines that curved down each shoulder blade, as if someone had taken a knife and cut something out of his back. Only what, I couldn't begin to imagine. I found the scarring strange . . . and troubling.

The tattoos were something else altogether. Running down the length of his spine, they began somewhere up in his hair and disappeared below the black, silky fabric wrapped around his waist. The design was large and complex, each individual symbol linked to both the one above and the one below. It was a moment or two before I realized that what I was looking at were markings similar to the symbols I had inked in the small of my back. Aleksei had said I had Gabriel's name tattooed on my back in the Old Tongue. Was that what I was looking at here? More words in a language I didn't know?

Before I had time to ponder this further, the couple on the bed moved. The woman was now also sitting up. Wanting to face him, she pouted when he swiveled her around, pulling her so her back was flush against his chest. I held my breath. If she moved her head just a little more to the right, she would be able to see me.

Christ Almighty! I had no idea when I'd gotten to my feet, but not only was I now standing, I'd also taken several steps closer to the bed.

One powerful arm went around the woman's waist, keeping her in place, while the other swept her hair free from the left side of her neck. Something glinted as she lifted her arms, making her heavy breasts ride higher on her rib cage. Both of her nipples were pierced with small silver rings that flashed in the ambient light. She stretched, reaching over her head and behind her for her lover. I wasn't that surprised to see that her belly button was also pierced.

Repositioning her arms back in her lap, the man put his lips against her ear, whispering. I saw her eyelids flutter as she surrendered herself to him completely, becoming liquid within his embrace. My own arousal manifested itself in an explosion of wetness inside my panties.

Leaning forward, the man buried his face in the curve of her neck, his hair fanning across her shoulder and falling like a silken scarf over her skin. Strong fingers cupped her chin, tilting her head over until her ear was pressed against her shoulder. Stretched taut, I could see the thick vein running beneath the surface of her throat.

Putting his mouth against it, he began sucking the flesh erotically, making the woman respond with a moan of lustful greed. She didn't care what he was doing; she just didn't want him to stop.

I was soaked. Drenched in my own need, I could feel perspiration trickling between my shoulder blades. My breasts felt full and achy, my nipples hard, and my internal flame a hair's breadth away from total conflagration as desire spiked through me.

I knew that if I were to slip my hand inside my jeans and touch myself I would climax immediately. Any Peeping Tom inhibitions that I might have felt had long since vanished. I should have been mortified by my reaction, but I wasn't.

I thought I knew what was coming next, but I couldn't have been more wrong.

Pulling his head back, the man opened his mouth wide. I blinked and stared . . . and blinked again, unsure of what I was seeing. Horrified disbelief overtook me as I watched two long canines drop from among his upper teeth. Brilliant white and razor sharp, they glistened, and just when the realization hit me that what I was seeing was real . . . he struck.

Puncturing the soft skin of her throat, his teeth found the life-sustaining artery, and I watched, aghast, as a fountain of blood erupted from her neck like a crimson gusher, splattering over her pale skin.

Screaming, she tried to reach for her neck in an effort to stanch the wound with her hands, but she was locked in place by the strong arm clamped across her upper body. Blood poured out of her at an alarming rate, a direct response to the frantic pumping of her heart. In a pure moment of complete disassociation, I suddenly knew what the phrase *arterial spray* meant.

She struggled against her lover, legs kicking frantically as her fight-or-flight instinct took over. It was useless, and she was unable to break free of his embrace. Staring at him, I saw his expression was one of clinical curiosity as he watched her blood flow down her neck and chest, and over the arm that was securing her. Dark and glossy, it pooled like an oil slick on the satin sheet.

My impending orgasm came to an immediate screeching halt as my brain frantically tried to interpret the information being relayed by my eyes. Tried and failed. The breath that I didn't know I'd been holding suddenly escaped in a gasp loud enough to make the woman on the bed turn her head and lock her eyes with mine.

Unable to reach out with her hands, she opened her mouth. I'm sure her brain told her she was screaming as loud as she possibly could, but all that issued was a soft, wet gurgle, followed by a trickle of blood that bubbled over her lower lip and ran down her chin.

Falling to my knees, my stomach contracted violently, expelling its contents. The sour burn of bile coated the back of my throat as I kept heaving, caring nothing about the mucus and half-digested particles of food that splattered in my hair. Tears streamed down my face, and I felt like my gut had been shoved up against my backbone. I lifted a hand to wipe my mouth, and it shook violently, as if I had some terrible affliction.

"Rowan?"

The silken voice, edged with sexual overtones, that had seduced me the first time I'd heard it was unmistakable. The world as I knew it imploded. Unless Gabriel had a twin, one who could match the exact timbre of his voice, Katja had made no mistake. The bitch's arrow had found its mark.

Some sort of weird noise jumped out of my mouth. It was the word "no" jammed in a repetitive loop. I got to my feet, stumbling in my haste to get away from him, needing to get out of this damned room. Turning, I crashed into the wall.

"Rowan!"

There was no liquid silk this time. Instead, his voice was a whiplash that forced me to stay on my feet as I ran my hands over the smooth panels of silk. I almost cried when I found the door, my fingers curling around the handle as he spoke again. This time I froze.

"Rowan . . . what are you doing here?"

I pressed my forehead against the paneling, willing my hand to tighten its grip on the smooth lever and pull the door open. If I could do that, then I would always be able to tell myself it wasn't him, convince myself it was someone else after all. Someone who just bore an uncanny resemblance to Gabriel, but was not really him. That's what I should have done.

So why didn't I? My brain was on my side, telling me desperately that this was a mistake. It wasn't Gabriel I had seen on the bed, his body pressed tightly against that woman's as he butchered her. It was a trick of those huge floor candles. Someone who wore his face, had his voice, who even—a familiar scent replaced the stench of my own vomit—smelled like him. But it couldn't be him. *Please, dear God, don't let it be him.*

And even as I prayed in my head that I was mistaken, I knew it was not a lie.

He called my name again as he did when I was asleep. Able to reach me inside my dreams, he would pull me back to semi-wakefulness and slide himself inside me.

I couldn't answer him. My larynx contracted and refused to function. All that came out of my throat was a guttural moan, a wild, painful sound, like that of an animal with a paw caught in the cruel teeth of a steel trap. I was slipping beyond reason.

"Rowan..."

The huskiness was threaded with sorrow. I should have pulled open the fucking door and run! Barreled my way into the hall and kept heading down it until I found a way out of this mausoleum that fronted as a house. Then I could have spent the rest of my life coming up with some rationalization for what I had seen, all the while denying it was him.

But I didn't open the door. Instead I turned around and stared at Gabriel.

Standing no more than an arm's length away, I was strangely thankful to see he was wearing loose-fitting black silk pants, which meant there was a possibility he hadn't been having sex with the woman on the bed. No matter what it looked like. What was wrong with me? That should have been the least of my worries.

I've just watched my boyfriend commit murder, but on the plus side, I'm pretty sure he is still faithful to me.

Caught by the glow of one of the huge floor candles, his body smoldered, a sheen of sweat making it glisten in the light. He was the embodiment of male physical perfection, a statue created by one of the Italian masters and brought to life. Except I'd made a mistake. His skin wasn't unblemished. Golden illumination revealed the outline of my mouth just below his clavicle—the scar I'd given him when he'd taken my virginity. Seeing it dashed to pieces any doubt about his identity.

Forcing my eyes away from him, I looked over at the bed. With the last of her waning strength, the woman was trying desperately to crawl toward me. It was difficult to know if she was begging for help or trying to warn me. I watched the blood from her wound slow as her blood pressure dropped, and in the space of a few beats from her dying heart it became not even a trickle. A soft hiss of air escaped her lips, carried on a wave of pale pink froth. She stopped moving and fell forward. I was grateful her hair hid her face.

I was in a room with a dead woman and ... something else.

I felt Gabriel move closer to me, and I turned to look at him. His mouth appeared stained, as if he had gorged himself on some forbidden, succulent fruit. Sweet juice, overflowing his mouth, colored his lips and chin and chest. Only I knew it wasn't true. He held out his hand to me and parted his lips, letting my name fall in a rush of regret. The light caught the pointed tips of fangs that had not yet fully retracted, and I knew *this* was what Katja had wanted me to see.

And the voice in my head piped up, the familiar singsong words now expanding their litany.

You know who I am . . . you know what I am . . . you have always known . . .

Silently I screamed back my denial.

Yes, you know this to be true . . . you were there to bear witness to what I became . . . to what I am now . . .

No! Impossible! Not this . . . never this.

Say it . . . say what you know to be true . . . admit what I am . . .

I don't know what you are!

Yes, you do . . . I am Fallen . . . I am Gabriel . . . I am vampire . . .

I don't fucking think so!

The voice in my head began to scream, but as I took a shuddering gasp of breath, I realized the screaming wasn't in my head. Now my fingers obeyed me, gripping the door handle and yanking it open to reveal Katja leaning against the opposite wall, a look of supreme satisfaction on her face. The desire to slap her was strong, but I couldn't contradict instinct. My brain was too busy telling my legs to keep moving as I ran from the nightmare standing behind me.

CHAPTER 30

The hallway seemed at least a mile long. As my legs drove me forward, I risked looking over my shoulder—and ran full tilt into Aleksei, who seemed to materialize out of thin air. I suppose I should have been grateful that he caught me before I bounced off him and really hurt myself, but feelings of gratitude weren't at the top of my list right now. In one of those odd, surreal moments, I realized this was the second time I'd bounced off a vampire—and yes, I had no doubt that's exactly what Aleksei was. As was Katja, the debonair Vladimir, and, I suppose, the wholesome-looking guy with the Kansas accent.

Spinning me around, Aleksei locked his arm across my upper body, holding me to him. The position was so eerily similar to what I'd just witnessed, I shuddered, but if the big guy noticed my reaction, he chose to ignore it. Instead he kept his gaze fixed on the open doorway at the far end of the hallway.

It's funny how the mind will behave when faced with a situation that's just too whacked-out for normal reasoning. It will still record the events as they are presented, but somehow it processes everything that is relayed to it by the senses through an alternate channel of comprehension. This is usually because what is being observed is breaking every fundamental rule of trust and belief. All that you believe to be normal and safe has been torn to shreds. The dark improbability you always suspected existed, but never wanted to acknowledge as fact, has risen to claim a part of your soul, staining you forever.

Behaving this way is, I suspect, a coping mechanism for the brain. At least that's what I told myself my own was doing. It was the multicar wreck happening all over again. I saw everything and felt nothing. Emotionally, I was frozen.

Aleksei motioned with his head, and I followed his gaze, both of us watching Gabriel approach. He was still wearing the loose-fitting black pants, but I noticed he had wiped the blood from his mouth and chest.

I watched him coming closer, I'm ashamed to say I still thought he was the most perfect male on the planet, even if the fury I could feel rolling ahead of him was also reflected in his face—brows pulled tightly together, eyes narrow slits, the mouth that I always found so quick to smile now refashioned in a harsh line that slashed his face.

It took no time at all for him to cover the length of the long hallway, and I felt the fingers that held me flex slightly as Aleksei tensed. I took this as a sign that even the big guy was wary of Gabriel in his fury.

My eyes locked onto Gabriel as he came to a stop a few feet from me. Returning my gaze, he slowly pulled back his lips, giving me the confirmation I needed that I wasn't losing my mind. Fangs dropped from between his upper teeth, white, glistening, and very long. I wondered how it was I had never known they were there, and I began to shake like a sapling in a hurricane, praying Aleksei didn't suddenly let go, because I didn't think my legs would support me.

Shifting his gaze over my head, Gabriel nailed Aleksei with a look that could have stripped flesh from bone. The big guy stood his ground and said nothing, but I suspect the look that passed between them was far more meaningful than any spoken words could be.

I didn't realize Katja had been invited to join our happy little trio until Gabriel turned and spoke to her. "You I will deal with later," he snarled in a voice unlike anything I had heard before. Viciously cold and violently ruthless, it formed a hard ball in the pit of my stomach.

"Why?" she snarled back, her own voice just as callous. "What does she have that you would put—*a human*—before me?"

I had to hand it to Katja, if she was going down, it would be spitting and fighting all the way. Incredibly stupid, but the girl—vampire—had some balls taking on Gabriel. I guess she figured she had nothing left to lose. Having already screwed up royally, her best chance was to brawl her way out of the situation.

A blur of movement made me suck in a breath, and the next thing I knew, Katja was halfway up the wall, with Gabriel's hand at her throat. She struggled, punching ineffectually at his arm, and I saw fear—real fear—in her eyes.

"Rowan is my *Promise*," he growled in a voice I didn't think would register as human. "She is bound to me in ways you cannot begin to understand. She is all that I desire, everything I need, and all that you can never be."

I began to shake; only I couldn't say if my reaction was from horror or delight at this public declaration. But I wasn't the only one affected. Katja was also trembling, but in her case it was easy to tell why. Screaming like a banshee, she redoubled her efforts to free herself from Gabriel's hold. Lashing out with both hands and feet, she punched and kicked and twisted her body into a wild frenzy. Her hair whipped around her as she snapped and snarled. I gasped aloud as her fangs dropped and she tried to strike Gabriel's hand, unsuccessfully. The hold around her neck tightened, temporarily cutting off her air supply.

"Enough!" Gabriel boomed.

His voice was a warning, and Aleksei smoothly moved to one side, taking me with him, as Katja flew past us. With what appeared to be no more effort than a mere flick of his wrist, Gabriel hurled her down the hall. Katja hit the far wall, crashing face-first to the floor.

It's a horrible thing to admit, but I felt absolutely no pity for her. She had brought this on herself. I suspected she'd known all along what Gabriel's reaction would be but had seriously underestimated the depth of his rage. I don't think she ever considered it might turn back on her. A serious miscalculation, and one that Vladimir had warned her of.

Slowly she struggled to her feet, her left arm hanging at an unnatural angle and her right knee already ballooning to twice its normal size. Her eyes blazed with a cold fury, one aimed solely at me. With a cry of what could have been pain, she turned and scrambled away as if her life depended on it. I wasn't so sure it didn't. Neither Gabriel nor Aleksei made a move to stop her.

"Tell me you didn't know," Gabriel growled, fixing his gaze on my newly acquired bodyguard.

I couldn't see the expression on Aleksei's face, but I could feel the tension drain out of him.

I watched Gabriel visibly relax, and he apologized. "I'm sorry, Aleksei. Of course Katja would not have confided in you . . . not about this."

"Not about anything that involved Rowan," the big guy rumbled quietly above my head.

For the next few moments, the only sound I could hear was my own breathing. My heart rate was beginning to slow, making it a little easier to suck in air.

"Rowan?" Gabriel held out his hand to me, his voice returning to the silky whisper I loved. It swept away the fear inside me and allowed an all too familiar quiver to take its place. I hated myself for responding to him so easily.

Aleksei loosened his hold on me, and thankfully, my knees locked into place and kept me standing. I was lost, completely and utterly defeated. The big Russian, who I was certain liked me a little, would not protect me. He couldn't. Smarter than Katja, he was not about to cross Gabriel and certainly not for me. His loyalty would never be brought into question. Pushing off from him, I managed a wavering step forward. My knees held.

"Rowan?"

Gabriel's hand was still outstretched as he waited for me to place my fingers in his palm so he could pull me to him and fold his arms around me. And I wanted him to—dear God, how I wanted him to!

It took all I had to refuse him.

Smoothing a hand over my hair, I tugged on the bottom of my shirt, pulling it down where it was rucked up. I turned my back on him deliberately, focusing on Aleksei, who had moved so he was now blocking my way past him.

"If you don't mind, Aleksei, I would really like to go home." My voice was a pale shade of hysteria, and I didn't know if I was breaking vampire protocol by addressing him directly in front of Gabriel.

I didn't much care.

A part of me knew I should be grateful for his presence. If he hadn't followed Katja, then I would be alone with Gabriel right now, and who could say what would happen. But all I could focus on was the fact that he was standing between me and the other end of the hall. His eyes flickered over my head, engaged in silent communication with Gabriel.

"Come, I will take you home," Aleksei said with a curt nod.

That hadn't been my intention. Right now I needed to put a whole lot of distance between myself and Gabriel—and anyone associated with this house.

"If you could just get me to a phone, I can call a cab," I said stiffly.

Squaring my shoulders, I managed to take another half-dozen steps before my body decided its next stop was a ride on the Oblivion Express. My knees, which had been doing a fabulous job, gave way.

It wasn't Aleksei but Gabriel who caught me before I hit the ground. Holding me in his arms, he cradled me against him; as I came to a little, I realized I was pushing a clenched fist against his hard chest. Ignoring my effort, Gabriel simply pulled me closer, knowing that in his arms was exactly where I wanted to be.

Involuntarily I turned my face into his neck, breathing in his scent as I felt the warmth of his skin beneath my hands. My body surged at the contact, betraying me again. How could I be so weak? How could I still hunger for him, be willing to give myself to him, when I knew what he was, had witnessed it with my own eyes?

Vampire!

Had Katja been correct in prophesying that I would think twice about inviting him into my bed once I knew the truth? I told myself he was a monster, the foulest and most reprehensible of predators. The very worst of nightmares come to life, and I was nothing but prey. But that was my head talking. My heart didn't care.

As if sensing my emotional uncertainty, Gabriel pressed his lips against my forehead, igniting an electrifying pulse that swept through me, destroying the last of my token resistance. I ached for him— sweet Jesus, how I ached for him!

And he knew it.

As he brushed his lips over mine, I felt the velvet softness of his mouth caressing me while a voice spoke in my head.

You are a Vampire's Promise ... given by word ... accepted by deed ... bound by ritual to keep safe that which has been surrendered ...

Surrendered? What had been surrendered—and by whom?

I wanted answers, but my brain decided it needed more time to deal with this unexpected ripple in my reality. A ripple it could deal with far more efficiently without my conscious help. Before I realized what was happening, my ticket had been punched and I was rolling out the station heading for La-La Land.

Oh good. Perhaps the answers were waiting for me there.

To be continued ...

CHAPTER 1

There are some people who will tell you that if you fall in a dream it's a bad thing. I'm not talking about a fall because you've twisted your knee or turned your ankle. I mean taking a dive off a high-rise building, or stepping into an open elevator shaft on the twenty-fifth floor. The kind of descent that pretty much guarantees if you do reach the bottom, you're not going to walk away. Hell, you're not even going to get up. And when you step over that ledge you're filled with absolute terror, because there's no way you can change the outcome.

And these people, whoever they are, will tell you that if you actually do reach the bottom in your dream, then in the waking world, you're dead.

Really? How the fuck would anyone know?

I've had a few nightmares where I've fallen, and it's a truly horrible sensation. I always wake up just as I'm going into free fall, with my stomach now behind my rib cage and my heart in my throat. I feel helpless and panicky all at the same time, and my limbs tremble as I try to catch my breath. But I've never reached bottom.

At least not yet.

I can't say for sure that I was dreaming about falling, but I woke in the grip of the same kind of anxiety. Soaked in perspiration, my heart was pounding so hard I had to have internal bruising. Tendrils of hair stuck to my neck and cheek, and the hand I held against my mouth was shaking so hard I almost slapped myself. But at least I wasn't dead.

I wasn't alone either.

Sitting bolt upright in my bed, I took in a wild gasp of air, and stared at the wicker chair in the corner. Whatever I thought I saw was now gone, leaving behind an empty seat. The only immediate threat to my safety would be getting my foot tangled in the bed covers spilling on the floor.

I shook my head, which, given the sudden pounding behind my eyes, was a bad idea. Lying back down, I put an arm over my eyes. This had to be the worst hangover ever, easily a hundred times more awful than the one following the puke-fest my best friend Laycee put me through when I turned twenty-one. That particular episode had been bad enough to serve as a dire warning on the pitfalls of drinking tequila, especially when there was a worm in the bottle. Apparently I hadn't heeded my own advice. So much for good intentions. I'd gotten so drunk, I couldn't even remember drinking!

My tongue felt thick and fuzzy, and the nasty taste in my mouth said there was a good possibility I might have licked the living room carpet at some point. I swallowed, a tentative action that had my throat screaming and seemed to confirm the carpet-licking theory. Whatever I'd done, it was way worse than anything that had happened the night I celebrated my legal status.

Raising my arm, I opened my eyes a fraction and focused on the square of pale light dancing across the ceiling. It stretched almost to the far wall, which meant the sun was heading for the horizon, and I'd been asleep for most of the day. Of course that might not be so long, depending on when I'd actually made it to bed.

In an effort to minimize the sloshing of my brain against the inside of my skull, I checked the clock on the bedside table. The bright red display read 5:05, and the small dot in the upper corner said it was definitely p.m. Yep, I'd slept all day, which only partially explained why I felt like shit. The rest of the blame was going squarely on the shoulders of Jose Cuervo and whoever he'd brought with him.

Dear God, please don't let me have done anything embarrassing, but if I did, don't let it be posted on Facebook.

The haze fogging my brain started to lift, and in its wake I was bombarded with a series of weird, fragmented images. Any hope of being allowed to recall the events of the last twenty-four hours in a manageable dose was blown right out the water. Taking a page from the sink-or-swim school of accountability, I got shoved in the deep end as everything came rushing back. Ignoring the pain in my head, I bolted for the bathroom.

Somewhere between crossing the threshold of my bedroom and falling to my knees before the porcelain goddess, my cerebral cortex exploded into a B-horror movie nightmare. Kind of like *Twilight* on steroids, but without the generous budget or teenage cast. As I bent over the toilet, it took a little while for my brain to remember I'd already expelled the contents of my stomach several hours before. If I continued to dry-heave, I was going to rupture something.

Slowly I got to my feet and gripped the edge of the bathroom sink with both hands. The face looking back at me in the mirror almost had me falling down again.

Jesus H. Christ—was that me?

I'd aged ten years overnight. Forget about getting wasted on wormy tequila; I looked like I needed a hospital bed. And a machine that gave a reassuring beep so I would know I was still alive. My face was drained of all color. Even my sun-kissed freckles looked washed out. Dark circles ringed my eyes, and there was something white and crusty caked in the corner of my mouth.

The woman in the mirror stared back at me with accusing eyes. *How could you not have known?* she demanded in a shrill voice.

I wasn't ill, and I most definitely was not hung over. It was much worse than that. Panic now threaded through me. Like a wisp of smoke that turns into a flame that becomes a fire, it threatened to run out of control. I took a step back, hitting my heel on the base of the bathtub. A shower seemed like a good idea. Pulling back the curtain, I stepped into the tub and used both hands to turn the faucet on. With my face upturned, I let the water wash over me, sluicing away my panic. A numbness took its place, and leaning my forehead against the fiberglass wall, I gave my aching body over to the shower's pulsating spray. It wasn't until I tasted salt on my lips that I realized I was crying. I didn't fight it. Instead I shut down what remained of my rational thought process and let the tears flow. God knows I was over-due for a sob fest.

I have no idea how long I remained standing in the bathtub. I wasn't consciously aware that the water temperature had changed from warm to freezing until the sound of my chattering teeth forced common sense to prevail. I was pretty sure that, in all the years of its existence, this was the first time the hot water tank had ever been emptied. Wearily, I turned the faucet off and stepped out of the tub.

I was naked. I didn't remember taking off my underwear, but ob-viously I had because my bra and panties lay in a wet pile in the bot-tom of the tub. Just as well, really, because my fingers were now so cold I doubt I could have managed the intricacies involved in un-hooking a bra. I wrapped a towel around me, tucking the end between my breasts. Dealing with my hair was going to take more effort than I currently possessed, so I simply ignored it. If I couldn't comb the tangles out later, then I'd cut them out. Satisfied with my problem-solving skills, I shambled back to my bedroom.

I was in shock. I knew this because my body's physical response was eerily reminiscent of my reaction on hearing my dad had died. The state trooper who'd been with me at the time had told me I was in shock. I had all the symptoms typical of a traumatized condition. Chills, erratic breathing, clammy skin. Who was I to argue with a state trooper?

My core temperature, already lowered by the cold shower, fell a little further, and I began to shake as if I was having a seizure. Curl-ing up in a ball, I hugged my knees to my chest, and waited for the spasms to pass.

My boyfriend is a vampire.

Oh . . . fuck . . .

Carla Smith—Biography

Carla owes her love of literature to her mother, who, after catching her pre-teen daughter reading by flashlight beneath the bed covers, calmly replaced the romance book she had "borrowed" with one that was far less risqué and much more appropriate. Carla was encouraged to include different genres in her reading tastes, and romance—paranormal romance, in particular—has always been her first love.

Born and raised in England, she now makes her home in South Carolina, where she lives with her wonderfully supportive husband, awesome son, and a canine critique group (if tails aren't wagging, then the story isn't working). When not writing, she can usually be found in the kitchen trying out any recipe that calls for rhubarb, working on her latest tapestry project, or playing catch-up with her reading list.

www.ingramcontent.com/pod-product-compliance
Lightning Source LLC
Chambersburg PA
CBHW020741250626
47155CB00003B/861

* 9 7 8 1 6 0 1 8 3 2 9 0 0 *